Faire Game

by

Lori Francis

Faire Game

Cover Art by *Kristian Norris*

The Wild Rose Press, Inc.
PO Box 708
Adams Basin, NY 14410-0708
Visit us at www.thewildrosepress.com

Publishing History
First Fantasy Rose Edition, 2016
Print ISBN 978-1-5092-
Digital ISBN 978-1-5092-

Published in the United States of America

Disgrace and treason.

Khyryn had heard those words before.

The cut across his torso burned with memory. Khyryn watched as Richard's free hand found Wynne and pulled her in front of him. To the audience, she was a shield. But Khyryn recognized the hatred smouldering in Richard's glare and knew the truth. Elleran's truth.

"...much more dangerous than you know..."

He knows. He remembers.

Wynne—Lady Rowena—struggled against the hand that gripped her beneath the jaw, pulling her to her toes as the leather-gloved fingers bruised the white flesh of her throat.

Khyryn avoided looking into her eyes and steadied his own breathing, readying himself.

A curse sputtered from Wynne's mouth as her hand clawed at the leather gauntlet. Richard drew the flat side of his blade across her abdomen, menacingly— silencing her. He spoke with a voice low, and sedate. "Even if your face were different, Khyryn, I would remember you. Tell me, do I look as I did the last time you claimed my life? One should not easily forget a brother, Khyryn."

Dedication

This story is dedicated to the two heroic men in my life:
My father,
who always encouraged me to read and to write,
and to do both with wild abandon;
and my husband
who has always proclaimed me
to be his happily ever after.
As he is mine.

Chapter One

Britain, 55 B.C.

Suspicion clouded the old woman's eyes as she aimed a piercing glance through the veil of smoke and steam that rose from her cooking fire.

"Weakness," her puckered mouth proclaimed. "You, druid, are weak."

"I seek your gifts," he said.

Short, stubby fingers, caked black with spring's earthen offerings plucked at the dried stems that dangled from the ceiling of the hut. Her eyes narrowed momentarily, intent on him, then relaxed to their natural wary stare. He did not doubt her power. But in this instant, she made him doubt his own. Not weakness. Duty. Loyalty. These brought him to the hag's threshold.

And a need to purge his soul.

Elleran. Villagers whispered her name whenever great wisdom and skill conspired to do magic. And trembled in silence when evil crept from the marshland hut.

Such sorcery had brought him this day's journey to brave the bog and find her hut of mud and reeds. So powerful was she, he dared not call her by name now. But she had called him druid, despite aged eyes that no longer witnessed the mortal world.

The fire waned, its low, blue light lapping at the ruby embers.

Fire sprites. Dancing to lure me to doze. Dark magic and light magic wrestle in her presence.

Reluctantly, Khyryn tore his gaze from the elfin movement of the flame and sought the freedom of darkness as he moved toward the doorway. "I wish to purge another from my thoughts."

"A woman?"

He filled his lungs with the acrid, moist air, to clear his thoughts.

Elleran chortled. "Or is it a man who haunts your soul, druid?"

Both. If Gwynndolwyn were not Uddryd's wife, would he not claim her as his own? But a brother's fealty made that impossible.

Khyryn was druid.

Uddryd was king.

"I wish to rid my memory of a woman."

"A lover?"

He winced, and turned again in her direction. How intimately the word fluttered from the crone's lips. Like a moth drawn to the flame she tended.

Passion flared momentarily in his mind and in his groin at the thought of Gwynndolwyn's body beneath his, her flesh meeting his. Of their bodies joined in a rhythm that would steal each gasp for breath.

"A woman who would be a queen someday," he replied.

A childlike smile graced Elleran's face at his answer. Her eyes twinkled as she stared across the fire. She nodded, as if he had answered a riddle, then set her hands once more to foraging through the dried stems.

Thyme, thistle, milkweed, borage, foxglove. These he knew. There were as many, however, he did not recognize. With each leaf or stem she crumbled into the pot, the sorceress whispered words not meant for his ears. Her voice drifted from her body like fog, gathering thickly over the mixture, folding her commands into the concoction as she stirred.

A pungent odor filled the hut, absorbing what little air he did breathe. The old woman leaned over the vessel, inhaled deeply, and spit into the mixture. She stirred it once more then poured the mixture into a bowl.

"Drink," she ordered.

Khyryn did as she commanded, gagging on the putrid thickness of the potion. Even as he held his lips to the bowl, he could feel the room swell. He swallowed and the turf walls and thatch inhaled expectantly, as if breathing in his very soul.

He closed his eyes to shun Elleran's spirits. He knew well the power of such malevolent airs.

Pitch-wood burned his throat, his stomach, and his bowels. *Demon.*

She had poisoned him.

"Now, you have a great gift."

He doubled over in pain heaving to rid itself of the serpent that coiled inside his body from her potion.

In a rage, he dared to call her by name. "Elleran!"

"These sightless eyes see much more than the passion you flee, druid."

The old woman wobbled to his side and found his hair, pulling him upright with the strength of a mighty warrior. Her mouth found his ear as her hatred slithered into his consciousness. "You and your kind will be the end of us all. Let that rest on your shoulders, druid."

Spasms tore through his muscles, dragging him to the floor again, as the aged sorceress stood over him, invoking spirits to aid her wrath.

"I do not—"

"Weakness of flesh. Weakness of soul. Weakness of heart. But the spirits will have their revenge. If only upon one of you."

He collapsed to his side and looked up at her. Grey wisps bounced about, like snakes trying to escape confinement.

"What have we done to make you visit such hatred upon us, Elleran?"

"It is your failure that enrages the spirits. Druids lay down their weapons in blood-drenched defeat and surrender our land to the invaders! Choke on words to praise them. Accept their ways. In time, all will worship their god and smite the ancient ones."

"Madness overtakes you—"

Elleran bent and plucked from his belt the bronze and silver bands he brought to pay her. "No madness. Keen is my vision of the future. Yours. And mine."

Khyryn's body relaxed against the cold ground, as the potion moved through his body, paralyzing his limbs. *Poison.*

"No poison, druid. Only awareness do you drink this night." She grabbed his hair again and breathed into his face. "Fortune's wheel turns again and does make fools of kings who barter with the empire. Close your eyes, druid, and you will see the fate of your queen."

At her words, Khyryn's eyelids grew heavy.

Footfalls. Movement. Warriors. Overhead, an eagle flapped its wings. In the village, fire danced upon

4

the roofs as invaders ambushed those who slept in the predawn—unaware.

Red. All red. The moon paling in the morning sky. The invaders' cloaks. The flames. The blood. Dripping from their spears and swords as they struck down the few who resisted them.

Red. Dawn blazed crimson as the sun broke the horizon.

A feral cry shattered the chaos. A woman's cry. Screaming. Screaming for help. Screaming for Uddryd. Screaming for Khyryn. Screaming in pain. Screaming for salvation.

Then...screaming no more.

Drenched with sweat, and fear, Khyryn's muscles began to tremble as the vision faded.

"You see, druid? They come. The red men. You and yours will let them. And they will wipe us out. But that is no matter to you, now. Your queen is dead."

"Why do you show me this? I am only one. I can change nothing alone."

"You misunderstand, druid. There is nothing to change. It is done. All *magi*—druid, sorceress, wyce— have known for many seasons this day would come. Now...you will remember it forever."

Nausea welled deep inside Khyryn.

"My gift to you, druid."

"Her life will not meet with yours in this time.
Nor any other by the power of rhyme times nine.
Nor will she know of you in another life.
'Twill cause you only strife.
But you will remember her.
Your heart filled with allure.
Remember this day, with the red dawn comes a death to

5

the ancient ways.
Always, Always, Always.
Eligor and Astaroth make this so.
As I will, so be it."

"Her life will not meet with yours in this time. Nor will she know of you in another. But you will remember her. Always. And you will remember this day that with the red dawn comes a death to the ancient ways."

Chapter Two

Wales, August, 2009

"You are a fool, child." The old woman clucked her reproach from across the table as she stroked a withered finger across the tender flesh. "You do not believe my words, and yet you seek my counsel each morning."

Wynne bent her head to examine the grooves the fortune teller fingered gingerly. She had never paid much attention to the lines of her palm before. Silly nonsense. Once the gates opened, a crowd would pay good money to hear the Tarot reader speak their lovers' names, or foretell windfalls yet to come.

Caution whispered Wynne's name. She clasped the old woman's hand in her own, as an amused sigh drifted between them. "You entertain me, Elleran. A stolen few minutes with you puts me into character before the gates open and I deal with the barons, bards, and ale guzzling tourists."

"Words of a cynic."

Wynne straightened. "Words of a realist. By tomorrow's sunset, you and the others will go off to find another faire. The locals who file through those gates will stash their costumes away in their attics for another year. And I go back to bury myself in my books once again."

With the prize, if I'm lucky.

Elleran's sightless eyes creased in reflex like a cat caught suddenly in the sunlight. She looked like the puckered dolls carved from dried apples—skin blotched from age, wrinkled from sun and wind.

The distant bellow of a horn startled them both.

"Damn," Wynne said. The moment shattered. "I'm late. Richard is looking—"

"—to seduce you."

"In his dreams," she called over her shoulder as she hiked up her skirts and raced toward the front gate. Maybe she should seduce him.

Careful, Wynne. Find the stone.

Tree roots and blisters thwarted her as she sped toward the oak plank doors that separated the faire folk from the throng pressing to pass through the portal to bygone days.

Medieval faires had been her passion, once. Still were, really. This one, however, was special. She had waited twelve years for this opportunity. Twelve years to take back what Richard Uddryd had stolen from her uncle. What he had stolen from her.

British crowds smoldered with the centuries' cynicism of their own history. Rowdy revelers and sore feet aside, Wynne needed this game of make-believe to pay off. Otherwise she had just wasted three months she couldn't afford to lose.

She ascended the wooden steps of the gatehouse and swallowed a giant breath of air before sauntering onto the stage.

"Prithee, good Uncle," she shouted. "Do we not owe this man a token of our thanks? After all, he did save the life of your only nephew, as he rescued my brother from the sea."

Wynne turned to cast a smile at the actor whose visage revealed him as the villain for this day's show. Art imitating life.

Damn.

Richard's scowl deepened and conveyed his fury. He knew she had not been in the courtyard when the horn sounded. His glare, and all it implied, made her heart pound harder than her sprint across the grounds had. Not seducing anyone here.

Ogre.

Only two more days. Two days to find *it*. Or to find out why he had stolen it. Two days to put up with his leers.

The hair prickled on the back of her neck. What had he said?

She lowered her eyes to the crowd below. "Nay, my lord. I beseech your generosity," she recited. "If you would offer no more than your words, allow me to offer my gratitude in your stead."

She untied the ribbon from her neck and dangled the bauble before the young actor who played the brave hero. Tall and lithe, with dark eyes that glittered with excitement, the hero stared mischievously at her. He clasped the proffered token and her hand, then pulled her to him and planted a deep kiss on her lips, to the delight of the audience. And to the surprise of everyone else.

"Thief," roared the baron. "Guards. Seize him!"

Before Richard's words dissipated, costumed guards littered the stage. The young hero cleverly avoided capture, and leapt into the crowd, thus incorporating the throng in this performance before abandoning his fellow actors.

Wynne smiled at Richard's fury.

"By this day's end, I will have him split from gullet to groin." The baron turned his attention once again to the anxious crowd. "Gentle folk, I invite you herewith to join our revelry this day. Let the gates open to admit such friends, that we might celebrate the safe return of my—sole heir."

A chorus of cheers sounded as the gates swung open. Wynne stepped quickly toward the stairs, intent on evading reprimand. Two steps down, however, Richard caught her by the arm.

"Collect your things. You are fired."

Through clenched teeth she whispered, "Like hell, I am. I hit my mark on cue. You still have today and tomorrow to worry about. Imagine how your plot line would work if the hero had no one to save at the end of the day."

"I can get any girl here to do your part. Probably better."

"I doubt you could find anyone to portray my intense disdain for your baronial bullying."

Laughter erupted as he forcefully placed a hand to her back and eased her down to the ground in front of him. Wynne held no illusions about Richard Uddryd. He liked this role. When the original actor had quit two weeks ago, Richard took over as the baron. Unfortunately, the part fit the director all too well. Rather like a second skin.

She didn't like Richard. She certainly didn't trust him. But he had what she sought. He had the stone.

His breath grazed her ear, hot as a dragon's. "Ah, such passion as you disguise with that barbed tongue makes me wish our roles were real. Just think of the power and penitence I could wield were I a true custodian of such a shrew."

Wynne gingerly tried to free her arm from his grip. "No doubt the nunneries would be filled with frightened virgins, seeking refuge from your lecherous nature."

Two days left. One, if she mortally wounded him here and now. *Find the stone first, Wynne.*

"Accept my terms, and I shall forgive you."

Her temper flared despite a sickening feeling at the intimation in his voice, and she spun on him. "Forgive what? I made my cue. I played my part. I wowed the crowd. You are clearly the bad guy. And you didn't even have to break a sweat."

Not the way to gain his trust, or get inside his office...

Elleran was right about one thing. Richard tried, repeatedly, to seduce her. To the point of harassment.

"Terms" could get me closer to the stone.

Wynne swallowed the barb that lingered on her tongue and flashed a coquettish smile at her employer, a smile that evaporated immediately as she met the darkness in his gaze.

Hollow. Wicked. Sadistic.

A shiver pricked her spine. She tried again to extricate herself from his hold. He pressed his other hand against the small of her back and lowered his voice to a whisper, low and guttural. "Consider this, my dear. I can take you to a place I guarantee you've never been."

****

"Did you taste her lips, druid?"

Khyryn slumped against the gnarled wood of the

oak. From this vantage point, he could see the gatehouse and most of the grounds. "Aye."

"Did she know you when your mouth met hers?"

Hunger churned inside his stomach as he settled himself on the ground and pulled the apple from the pouch at his belt. "What do you suppose, Elleran?"

Three good bites devoured the small fruit, and he hurled the core into the jousting field. His arm ached from having slept on the cold ground again, without a fire's warmth. At least the swordplay this day would be only for show. Mortals did not fight to the death here.

Khyryn glanced at the old woman. Perched on her chair as if it were a throne, she waited patiently for the people to find her.

"Why don't you kill someone today, druid. That would surely get her attention. Then, perhaps she would remember."

"Is that an invitation?" If Elleran's death could serve any purpose, he would have killed her already.

The old woman *tsked*.

"Boredom overtakes you to make mischief, Elleran. Keep to your cards and magic."

"Bah! Card tricks are for non-believers. Even *she* does not believe my words." Elleran chuckled to herself. "She will soon enough. She comes to me each morning."

"Aye? And what do you tell her?"

"The same as I always speak. Truth."

"And what is your truth today, sorceress?"

Elleran hissed. That his words had struck her made him smile. His temper was foul this morning, and he did not welcome her goading.

"I told your Gwynndolwyn she holds her past and

her future in her palm. Her hand bears your mark."

His body hardened at the words. "My mark?"

"The lines etched upon her flesh meet to form the letter K. Is that not your mark, druid?"

Khyryn's muscles tightened. "I am no druid, here, Elleran."

"Once druid, always druid."

The jingle of coins drew Elleran's attention as two young girls stepped into her booth.

Little had changed in two thousand years.

Khyryn knew only too well that for a trinket of gold or silver, Elleran would let them fondle the Tarot as she told the truths she saw. Or at least what she dared speak of it.

A tingling sensation crept up his spine as the warm breath found his ear.

Gwynndolwyn.

"Well, that was a bit of brilliance, Khyryn. I thought Richard would spontaneously combust. If I had made it to the stage before the horn sounded, were you planning to warn me?"

Khyryn stretched an arm up high and raked his hand over the scaly bark of the tree to regain self-control. Her mouth, so close to his now, taunted his patience—and his nerve.

Grant me strength and will.

"If I had warned you, my action would not have earned the same effect. Your cheek grew crimson at my boldness before the crowd. And with that, I won their approval."

He hefted himself to stand. Deftly, he seized the hand that offered him the necklace on stage and brought it to his lips in an all too formal display of affection.

"And yours?"

Wynne tugged her hand free and smirked. "For as long as we are paired in our parts, you have my loyalty. By tomorrow, though, I shall be nothing more than a memory to you."

Khyryn shivered at her words. Had the witch spoken the secret to her this morning? "I would have you remember me as I remember you. Always."

"Khyryn, I've seen how the ladies fawn over your Sir William. Those dark circles under your eyes this morning tell me all I need to know about you. The hair, the wicked accent, and those leather breeks...the last thing you want for is company. I am not naïve."

Her mouth tempted his desire. Against his own will, his groin hardened at her closeness. "Then I should be pitied for my pursuit."

Wynne rolled her eyes at him and moved to leave. "I'll see you at the chess match at noon. Should I expect any other surprises?"

If only you knew.

"And deprive the crowd of your shocked reaction? Nay, gentle lady. Go forth and play your part. I shall save my thoughts for another time."

"Ooh, mysterious banter. No wonder women flock to follow you," she teased as she turned a quickened step toward the storyteller's corner.

Khyryn watched her saunter through the crowd. Oblivious as she had ever been to the men whose stares lingered when she passed.

And I will have you, Gwynndolwyn.

The tightness in his breeks conspired with the tightness in his chest. Not even two full days remained. She would not remember. She never did. Luckily, thus far, only Elleran had recognized him.

Uncertainty nagged at him. The blade he'd been given seared his flesh through the fabric of his clothes.

"Beware, druid."

Frustration and exhaustion fueled his ire. "Do not call me druid, Elleran, or I shall mete your suggestion for killing this day."

The old woman cackled. "Your anger is misguided."

"As is your counsel. Why do you goad me?"

"I would keep it from you but for my desire to see you gone from this time."

"No more so than I. I shall be gone soon enough."

"The one she calls Richard—"

Khyryn bristled. "You mean Uddryd?"

"He will cause you trouble," she warned.

"And what news is that?"

"Ahh. That he would seduce the girl holds no surprise. He is much more dangerous than you or your queen would know."

I know.

Khyryn left the witch to her schemes. Memory gave him reason to seek solitude.

He had no desire for murder, or vengeance, this day. That fact made this quest so much more dangerous. Before tomorrow's dusk, Khyryn must return to Aberswythe.

He would not return alone.

****

The sun drenched morning yielded to grey clouds that heralded rain. Khyryn played knight to Wynne's queen in the human chess game.

Richard positioned himself as bishop to the

opposing king. Strange. Thus far, he had refrained playing the game board during the match, leaving the troupe to perform the combat, even as he propelled the plot from the sidelines.

The game began. Audience and actors engaged in mirthful exchanges as pawns were sacrificed on each side. Playful parry and gainful gambit stole each actor from the chalked green until only a handful of players remained.

"King's bishop to king's rook four," the king called. "We challenge your queen. Baron, take arms."

Richard—the Baron—bowed, mockingly, to Wynne. Two pawns protected his assault. Should she move to take the bishop, she would sacrifice herself, leaving her king unprotected.

"Queen's knight blocks," replied the court jester who controlled the white team in this game.

Khyryn moved into the square that separated Wynne from Richard, and slid his sword from its scabbard. He bowed to the white king, then to the queen whom he defended, and poised himself for battle.

For the win of the bishop over the knight's placement in this game, Khyryn knew the drill to lose. Twice parry, lunge and thrust, feint to the bishop's kick, then fall in defeat. No need to exaggerate the scene today. Rain threatened.

A kick slammed against Khyryn's ribs sending him flying backward, as Richard's blade slashed through linen. And flesh.

Khyryn's lungs sucked savagely for the air Richard's blow had knocked out of him. He dipped his hand beneath the rift in the cloth. Blood beaded the wound. Touch stung, and a hiss escaped his lips.

His blade is honed.

Richard's eyes flared wildly as he lunged again. Khyryn rolled away and leapt up to ready an assault.

The crowd gasped. Excitement faded to hushed whispers among the other actors as the two departed the script.

Metal whistled as it sliced through the air. Blade to blade, boot to boot. Khyryn met each move Richard imposed.

"Your liberties disgrace me, Sir William," Richard said.

"I assure you, I took no liberties to dishonor you. I merely claimed the prize offered me by the Lady Rowena. Surely you do not seek to disgrace her here, before this assemblage."

The checkered field dissolved into a crowd of wary onlookers, transfixed by confrontation, as Richard Uddryd and Khyryn—bishop and knight—stalked each other with barb and blade.

Richard's eyes narrowed, and a smile slithered across his lips. "Let us say I seek a measure of satisfaction for *her* disgrace. And for your treason."

Disgrace and treason. Khyryn had heard those words before.

The cut across his torso burned with memory. Khyryn watched as Richard's free hand found Wynne and pulled her in front of him. To the audience, she was a shield. But Khyryn recognized the hatred smouldering in Richard's glare and knew the truth. Elleran's truth.

"...much more dangerous than you know..."

He knows. He remembers.

Wynne—Lady Rowena—struggled against the hand that gripped her beneath the jaw, pulling her to her toes as the leather-gloved fingers bruised the white flesh of her throat.

Khyryn avoided looking into her eyes and steadied his own breathing, readying himself.

A curse sputtered from Wynne's mouth as her hand clawed at the leather gauntlet. Richard drew the flat side of his blade across her abdomen, menacingly—silencing her. He spoke with a voice low, and sedate. "Even if your face were different, Khyryn, I would remember you. Tell me, do I look as I did the last time you claimed my life? One should not easily forget a brother, Khyryn."

Khyryn swallowed hard against the memory of murder. "Or a king, Uddryd."

Thunder crashed and lightning streaked as metal seared flesh and bone, releasing the feral howl.

Chapter Three

Britain, 55B.C.

Black clouds hung in the sky.

Not red.

Even as he grasped at hope, Khyryn knew the vision had been real. Nausea argued with his resolve. Smoke and death's scent filled the air, and his chest ached with guilt. And fear.

Khyryn fell to the soft, cold earth and sucked in the smell of the dew-drenched grass.

Must keep going.

Only a short distance separated him from the village. Just over the ridge, he would know the truth. Only the trees and rocks isolated him from that dark sky, and all it proclaimed.

From the depths of the cave a voice whispered, "You have returned."

Hollowness echoed, not from the walls, but from the words. "I wondered."

Khyryn turned. A shadow moved toward him, transforming—rock to flesh—as the form climbed from the earthen hole into the greyness of morning.

"Uddryd—"

"They are dead, Khyryn."

"The village?"

"—Red men."

"The invaders?"

"They called themselves 'Roman'. Before the dawn, they descended and razed the village."

"Where are the others?"

Uddryd's brow slackened, and his eyes widened. "Of what others do you speak? The few who managed to escape fled into the forest. I am alone."

Alone. The weight of Uddryd's words settled upon Khyryn, heavy as the rock he sank to.

It is true then. He did not dare to meet Uddryd's stare.

"Gwynndolwyn?"

Her name hung between them like a tether— binding king and druid to one another more than the blood they shared.

Uddryd slumped against the stone. "They were five to our two. In the darkness, we only heard the pounding of their step as they entered the camp. We moved to stop them, but—too late. They ploughed the village as one turns a field, casting us aside like stones."

"Uddryd—we must search for survivors. We must help the injured."

"A fine effort for one who conveniently escaped the marauders."

Khyryn's nape tingled at the accusation. He met his brother's gaze.

"Uddryd, I did not know—"

"And yet, you were not here. How is it during Samhain, you would abandon your people?"

"I sought wise counsel—"

"And did your wise counsel absolve you of your guilt?"

"Uddryd—I did not know—"

"The druid knows nothing? Where were you as the dawn blazed upon us—bringing down the scourge of this red death? Where was my druid's keen sight, Khyryn, when the marauders swept through and slaughtered my people like animals?"

"Druids were not to blame for this."

Uddryd's face contorted with rage. "Did your keen sight and counsel foretell the danger of this day? Is that why you fled?"

Khyryn swallowed hard against the words wanting to be spoken. Sage to the king, he could not share this truth with his own brother and ruler.

"Well, brother, Samhain is sufficed this day. The earth sleeps. Drenched warmly in the lifeblood of those who would celebrate that sleep."

"Madness makes you speak so."

"Uddryd—"

Uddryd's stare turned vacant, and a gnarled smile crossed his lips. "I sought shelter in my brother's keep. But found no sympathy for the injuries and terror I endured."

Khyryn grasped Uddryd's shoulders fiercely and shook him as if to purge the anger from him. "Gwynndolwyn, Uddryd. Where is she?"

The scorched brow creased as the memory wafted in the trees, surrounding them both.

"She cried out for mercy—your queen—her voice shrill with fear and loathing. Her screams would surely haunt your dreams had you heard her pleas."

A mournful wail sang through the branches and leaves as the wind gusted suddenly at Uddryd's words. Khyryn's hands began to tremble and the skies roiled with thunder. Tears fell from the heavens. Torrential weeping.

Khyryn moved without will, and clambered over the ridge toward the nest of burned huts. Black tendrils smoldered still, even as the heavy rain pummeled the scorched earth. New mud caked his feet with each step.

Hapless forms lay strewn as casually as where they had fallen—infant and elder alike. Near one hut a woman's body sprawled in a pool of blood, a lifeless babe still clutched to her breast.

There. Between the two smaller huts that stood sentinel, rose the straw and mud of Uddryd's house. Strange. No ember smoldered. Thatch still draped the roof protectively. Silence barricaded the doorway as he bowed his head and entered.

Inside, winter's chill, and death saturated the air. No movement within. No wind. No hearth fire. No sound.

Shadow cloaked the fireless hut, taunting Khyryn with false hope. He waited for his eyes to adjust to the lightless chamber, silently seeking that which he prayed he would not find.

In the corner. Atop a pallet of furs.

Gwynndolwyn.

Khyryn knelt beside her. Her body sprawled upon the bed, limbs askew. Even in silhouette she glimmered white. Shimmering. Ethereal.

Lifeless.

Fury and pain raked his body as he pulled her into his arms and cradled her against his chest and allowed a muffled sob to spill from him. Icy flesh singed his lips as he kissed her cheek, her hair, and then relaxed his embrace.

As he moved to lift her body, his hand found a

viscous puddle. His fingers trailed the sodden fur and cloth to its source.

Impaled by the blade Khyryn had hewn for her as a wedding gift!

Gently, he tugged the iron from flesh and fabric, grateful no light shone to bear the fateful color of her death.

****

Ty Ddewi, Cymru, 1016 A.D.

Persistence. The mark of memory. And old friends.

"Some wounds never heal, eh?"

The old druid's words spilled out, breaking the memory. The flames leapt high in the hearth. Khyryn turned to face his mentor, and friend.

"By what magic do you know my thoughts so easily, Aberswythe?"

"Ah. Your thoughts are easily displayed on your face, Khyryn. Each time you sink into memory, the flame turns dark and soars high in the hearth."

"More than a thousand years have passed, and still that day clings to me like no other."

"As to us all. Memory is why I am here. Come. Pour your guest wine. We have much to speak of."

The old man dropped the bag slung over his shoulder, then collapsed into a chair near Khyryn's. The tattered and muddied robes betrayed a long journey.

Khyryn poured honeyed wine into two cups and offered one to Aberswythe. Long, fierce fingers grabbed the drink greedily as the old druid brought the cup close to his nose and breathed the scent of a summer's hive.

"What concerns you enough to travel so far?"

Aberswythe tilted his head back and consumed the

wine with one smooth motion. The cup rattled against the wooden table as he settled the vessel and turned his gaze to his host.

"A thousand years? And still the memory never wanes?"

Khyryn's shoulders tensed. "Aberswythe, you do not come to speak of ancient days. What brings you from the comfort of your village, across the marshes to stand at my door? It is not my wine that entices you. You say we have much to speak of? Speak."

"Your brother."

A chill trickled down his spine at Aberwythe's words. "I have no brother. It is one consolation of this particular lifetime. I am without the binding ties of family."

"I speak of Uddryd."

"Do not. I will not hear his name."

"I must. And you must hear my words."

Khyryn's fists clenched. His body tensed as if the utterance of the name might conjure the spirit. "Uddryd is long dead. It is done—"

"Do not be foolish, Khyryn. Elleran's magic cursed you with memory. Do you believe you are the only mortal who walks the earth with the knowledge of what came before?"

"So long ago—"

"Did I not know you both as children? Your brother lives."

"It is merely a trick of the mind. That is all."

"Would I not know you both as you are now? I would know him as I first saw him." Aberswythe lowered his head and spoke very slowly. "I have seen him, Khyryn."

Despite the chill of the room, beads of sweat trickled down Khyryn's neck and back. The old man told the truth. Khyryn knew it.

Hatred boiled in him. For the persistence of truth, and the cruelty of fate. Hatred of Elleran, of Uddryd, even of the man who sat across from him for resurrecting the dead.

Khyryn finished his own wine and filled both cups again. "Did you speak to him of me?"

"I did not have to."

Khyryn's head snapped up and he searched his mentor's face. Though his hair had turned silver, the old man's eyes danced brightly with an emerald light. The druid who danced with time still possessed a young heart.

Aberswythe leaned forward and whispered, "He remembers."

Khyryn shook his head in refusal. The druid's words pounded in his brain. The threat clung to the air like tendrils of incense, pungent and haunting. "How?"

"I did not speak to him, mind you. But he recognized me. Beltain had scarcely passed when they rode through the old village. He rode with a band of soldiers, headed toward Londinium."

"Then he knows nothing of me."

"Do not be deceived. If Uddryd knew me, then there is much reason to believe he would know you as well. You were of his own blood."

"But you did not exchange words. You did not tell him of me."

"No. However, there is another concern. I have looked into the stones."

"And what sight have they granted you?"

"They bring me troubling dreams, Khyryn."

"What of your dreams?"

"I have seen her."

Khyryn brought his hand down soundly on the table. "That you have seen one whom you believe is Uddryd is madness enough. To imply *she* is here—"

"Not here, Khyryn."

Khyryn's chest contracted with anger. "Aberswythe, I am indebted to you, but I will not allow you to speak of her. If she were here, I would know. Your vision is a folly. Do not make me part of it."

"I assure you, I would not travel as far as I have in jest. Not on this matter. There is something you must—"

"The monks and the villagers pay me well to keep them safe. I have no desire to leave them."

"Does your life with these people soothe your soul?"

Khyryn leaned across the table and lowered his voice to a growl. "No force can soothe my soul. My life here affords me anonymity. My life here allows me the freedom to come and go as I please. I protect them from raiders, and they pay me and leave me alone. Perhaps, old friend, you should do the same."

"How many lifetimes have you spent alone, Khyryn? I offer you a chance to change it."

"There is nothing that can be changed. The old woman sealed my fate with her magic. With her sight. It is my curse to be alone. I will not have another."

"You cannot change the past, Khyryn. But you might change your future."

He clenched his hands, willing his temper to cool. "I tried once. Remember?"

"The stars divine a great storm of events to come."

He refilled his own cup and downed the drink. "Then Ty Ddewi is a good place to be."

"She will be part of it."

He stared at his friend who played this ruse unfairly. *Part of the storm.* "Where? Where is she, Aberswythe? Where is she that you would taunt me so?"

"You must travel to the cave."

"No."

"Would you refuse this chance to be reunited with her?"

"Would I refuse to be *denied* by the fates to be with her again? To face the torture of her vacant stare?" Khyryn stared into the hearth fire. "Aye. I am resolved to my plight, old friend. Lunacy led me to call upon the wyce that night. Elleran's curse lives on, even a thousand years later. Gwynndolwyn would not know me even if she were here now."

The old druid rose then, gathering to him his bag. "Then resolve yourself, also, to failure and death. For Uddryd lives in this time. He rides with an army. And he remembers much, I fear. And forgives nothing."

Khyryn stayed his seat, deliberately. "Uddryd is no longer my concern. In this lifetime, we have no business with each other. I am at peace."

Aberswythe paused in the doorway of the chamber. "Enjoy it while you may. I have gazed into the stones. A great tempest rages in your future. And in the future of this land. It is a storm even you cannot weather alone."

Chapter Four

Britain, 1016 A.D.

A thousand years.

More than ten hundred years since Elleran and her spirits had cursed him with memory.

Khyryn tugged at the the horse's reins and slowed the gait. He had little doubt Aberswythe would catch up. Eventually.

What foolishness was this?

Khyryn moved uneasily in his saddle. The very thought of Gwynndolwyn made him hard now. He had lain upon the floor last night, after Aberswythe retired to his own chamber. Lain upon the cold floor to try to purge memories of her from his mind. The glistening of her skin as it slaked across his. Her lips and tongue trickling across his chest and down his form until it met his arousal.

Memory persisted, and soon his body writhed in the sweat of lust for her. Lust that consumed his spirit and his will. Before sunrise he had saddled the horses and found Aberswythe. By the time the sun crept up from the horizon, the village of Abergwaun was far behind them.

Hooves pounded the ground behind him. "You ride with fervor, Khyryn. That is good. Better than walking. Still, I must rest. And so must our couriers. The sun has peaked, and soon will begin to fall. Let the horses rest and drink their health in the stream."

Khyryn slid from his saddle and led the giant stallion toward the water as the old druid bade. Little time would be lost for their rest. They must walk through this land where the rocks and stream taunted riders as surely as sprites, intent on crippling both mount and man.

"What has *she* to do with Uddryd?"

"Her connection as of yet, is unclear. But her presence is important. The stones do not tarry with lies. Gwynndolwyn is part of the storm."

"Storm. The same storm that brought Uddryd to you?"

"Yes." The old man paused and turned to relieve himself.

"I did not know immortal druids pissed," Khyryn joked.

"The flowing of water helps me think."

Khyryn laughed at his friend. "So, it is your brain you hold in your hand?"

"For most mortal men that is not far from the truth of it, I have found." Aberswythe adjusted his tunic and resumed walking. "It is good to hear the humor in your voice, Khyryn. I had feared yester eve, that you held no laughter in your heart in this lifetime."

Khyryn sobered. "I hold little else, Aberswythe. I have lived this life alone, thus far."

"It is not the best way."

"It is the only way."

"You caused her no harm, Khyryn."

"I did not hold the blade. But I am as guilty as if I took the life from her myself. How many times, have I sworn to protect her and failed? She never remembers. That she does not remember the love and pleasure we shared is painful. I must be grateful she does not remember the rest of it."

"And if she ever does remember?"

Khyryn ignored the older man's query, choosing instead to lead his horse down the slope to the brook. He drank in the water's coldness himself—and with it a change of topic.

"Tell me about the man you saw. The one you say knew you."

Thwarted from an answer, Aberswythe sighed. "Dark of hair and beard, with the same brow as he had when I first knew him. He calls himself by another name. In this lifetime, he goes by Eadric Streona. It is said he commands many men. That he rules Mercia. Some have whispered he even controls the king."

"Well, that is an advantage for our part, then. Is it not? That he wields no crown or torc himself—"

"Does not prove he does not wield great power. It merely means the weight of rulership does not hold him fast. He has the power without the responsibility. That in itself makes him a much more dangerous adversary."

"What if you are wrong? What if this man is not Uddryd?"

"Then we will both be relieved by the folly of my mind."

"If you are right...how is it he remembers with each new life?"

Aberswythe rested on a large slab of rock jutting up from the mossy earth. "That question I do not yet have an answer for. There are murmurs Cnut will rally soon and the victory will be the Dane's. Perhaps that will put an end to our worries."

"Cnut? Son of Wolfru?"

"The same."

Khyryn's shoulders relaxed a bit. "If it is Cnut this Eadric rides against, then fortune will be with the Norse gods, not the Christians. The Danes do not forfeit what they prize as their own."

"Cnut is clever. He will claim the land and its people. Perhaps, he will even give them their temples for worship. He cares not about their god, only their strength and land."

Khyryn stretched his arms high above his head, as if to touch the clouds above. Elleran had been right, so many years ago when she said the invaders would strike down the old ways.

Pagan and druids surrendered first to the Roman gods, then later to the teachings of Christianity. Now, only a few of the wise ones remained. As each died, so did the deities of old.

As if reading Khyryn's thoughts, Aberswythe said, "I remember when you were a young prince—not more than nine then—given into my care. You learned your lessons well."

Khyryn studied his own reflection in the water. "Perhaps not well enough."

"Why say you so?"

"If I paid heed to your teachings, I should never have gone to Elleran."

"Then neither of us would be here now."

"Precisely so."

"Ah. Do you not see, young one? It is the way of the stars, and the old ways, that we are here. Who else would set things right?"

****

Aberswythe tethered his mount, and Khyryn's. Animals often heard the voices of these woods—whether sprite or ghost. While the foxes paid little heed, horses often bolted at the whispers in the trees. Today, Khyryn understood their wariness.

"You see, Khyryn? Little has changed since you were last here."

The cave stood, unchanged by time. New trees stood where others had bowed to time. However, the rock never faltered.

Aberswythe ignored him, turning his attention instead to gathering sticks and leaves to kindle a fire.

"Ah. Someone has left a hare for our supper," Aberswythe said. "It is good you be well fed for your journey."

"How is it done?"

"Roasted on the fire, of course. How else?"

"Not the game, old man. Gwynndolwyn. Will she come to me?"

Aberswythe smiled. "All in measured time. First, you rest and eat. Go to the water. Fill an urn. When you come back, we will discuss it more."

Khyryn took up the large wooden vessel that lay near the opening to the cave and made his way to the stream. Once there, he stripped and waded into the cold water, grateful for its sobering affect. Though the sun was still high, exhaustion plagued his body and his mind.

He prepared both. Scooping silt from the stream floor, he washed away the sweat and musk of four days' ride as he worked the sand against his limbs. Even now in the warm season, the water's kiss was cold, sending shivers down his spine and thighs as he rinsed. The water cleansed his skin. The rhythm of its flow cleansed his mind. He relaxed.

He stepped from the water and let the sun warm his back. The breeze, in competition lapped at his nipples and curled the hair upon his chest and between his thighs.

Reluctantly, he redressed and gathered the water for Aberswythe. He had not thought to be gone long, but when he reached the cave, he met the aroma of roasting meat, and his stomach growled in anticipation of the meal.

Aberswythe hunched over a tree stump, as he bundled herbs into a cloth. "Tonight, the moon, *Ben-reine ny hoie* will dance in the night sky, swollen with her brightness. She will hear our song and guide you to your beloved."

"I would look into the stones first, as you have done."

The old man tied the bundle with the withered entrails of the hare. "Not before the moon gazes upon us. First we shall feed your body. Then your mind."

Hours later, when they had filled their bellies, Aberswythe brought forth a wooden bowl, dark as the earth with age. "You must fill the bowl with the water while I place the stones."

Khyryn remembered. Only the wise would see the vision of the stones reflected in the water's surface. Had twelve lifetimes made him wise? Or would he be denied what the stones knew, staring into the water, finding nothing more than his own reflection?

Aberswythe placed the stones, three counts of nine in angles so the end of each count touched another, to form a belt of three corners. Into the center, Khyryn set the water vessel.

In a bowl, cast of iron, Aberswythe laid small sticks and dried leaves, then taking coals from the fire, ignited the tinder. This, he placed at one corner of the three sides of stones. To the second, he laid an earthen bowl of new-hewn dirt. The third received another wooden bowl—this one empty. Thus, the table stood complete—fire, earth, and wind without; water within—four essential elements beneath the watchful eyes of the heavens as the stars blinked in the early evening sky.

Aberswythe stood behind the bowl of fire. Khyryn removed his tunic and stood between earth and wind, and peered into the water.

Aberswythe began. "Clear your mind of all you fear, *anruth*, noble stream, and all that would distract you from your purpose. Concentrate on the water, the *uis*. Let the water flow through you."

Khyryn listened to the incantation, drowning out thoughts of lands, and wars, and men's lives. Concentrating on his own reflection as it rippled beneath the veil of the water.

Into the fire, the teacher sprinkled dried hemlock and hare hound root and the flame did cast high, reflecting light upon the water's face.

Gwynndolwyn.

Pale, with hair the color of fire upon the water, her eyes gleamed with laughter. Her visage rose up before him. She stood in a glen with others, all playing at some dance. Men and women, draped in fine cloth and jewels. The scene changed. She stood watching men on horseback, shouting and cheering at their sport. Once again the image faded, and with the ripple of the wind another scene swam to the surface. This time, she gazed at her own hand then turned her attention to one who held it fast.

The same withered claw that once touched his brow, stroked Gwynndolwyn's palm, intimately imparting some secret.

Elleran.

Khyryn's body clenched in hatred and jealousy. His temples throbbed with a heat that burned his brain. His groin ached with a hunger to feed the hatred fueled by the wyce whose curse had damned him and denied him peace. Even stronger, it ached with a desire to stoke his untamed passion for the woman he had denied himself so long ago.

The vision faded to his own reflection once more. Muscle and sinew strained against skin and cloth as he stood staring into the vessel, willing the return of the sight. Sweat drenched his torso and limbs. Corporeal.

"You saw her?"

"Yes," Khyryn replied. "Elleran is with her."

"Her part in this is yet unclear—"

"Her part is that she is responsible for this. If not for her 'vision', for her 'truth', I would not be here."

"Put aside your anger, Khyryn. It is misguided. For what evil Elleran did in cursing you with memory, she did not kill Gwynndolwyn. For all we know, her part in the vision may have been to resolve some misdeed, eh?"

Khyryn lifted his eyes from the billowing depths of the water and searched his mentor's face for some sign of jest. Surely, he could not think Elleran would do good for anyone? She who withered with hatred? She who demanded penance from Khyryn for the Romans' crimes?

The flame danced in Aberswythe's eyes, making him look even more serious.

"You are wrong. Elleran is no aid for good in this."

"Are you willing to risk your first chance in a thousand years just to satisfy your own vengeance?" It is not a warrior's skill. Do not forget your objective."

The fire waned and still Khyryn stood, forbidding his body to move away from the ritual. The moon rose high in the sky, staring at his nakedness, bathing him in her brightness. Aberswythe's words flowed through him. Potent words. Words that soothed his ire.

"She is not here, is she?"

"Not yet."

The druid left the stones. He rested now, near the cooking fire. From beneath his robes, he pulled a long flute with a bowl at the end and gently tucked some leaves into it before he held it to the fire. Smoke rose from the flute, and he inhaled deeply. "To find her, you must walk through time."

Through time. The hair rose on his neck. "How?"

"Before the dawn, a tempest will wake the skies and the moment will be right."

"And when I find her?"

"Ah. That is for you to decide. I can only offer you the words that will open the door. You must learn when they will be best used. Be wary. You know nothing of where you go. Nor they of you. If Elleran's curse still thrives, then Gwynndolwyn will not know you. She may be scared."

"Aberswythe, do you know of this time?"

His eyes twinkled. "I do know something of it."

"Have you been there?"

"Aye."

Khyryn bristled at that confession. "How will I find her?"

"When you emerge into the open lands, travel south, to the mighty fortress built of stone. There you will see people like our own. Do not think yourself one of them, for they are not of our time. But they do make a jest of it, as if to play. They will accept you for how you look. The faire they host is where you will find her."

"If your words send me, how do I to return?"

The old druid motioned to the stones "The stones will travel with you. My words will stay with you. As I recall, you never had difficulty remembering any song I taught you. Let the words wash over you like a stream, carrying you to her. When it is time, you will find the stream again."

Khyryn once again cloaked himself and joined Aberswythe by the fire. "And to bring her with me?"

"That may be more difficult. Her time does not worship the earth. She will not know the way. You will only be able to bring her through when you are coupled. For when you are joined, her heart will beat with yours. Only then will your song protect you both."

A deep, dormant lust flickered low in Khyryn's spine. "And if she resists?"

Aberswythe sucked deeply the last curl of smoke from the flute, holding it deep within his chest, finally releasing his breath. His eyes darkened and turned cold as he met Khyryn's gaze. "You must not come back without her. Do what is necessary to bring her with you. If you cannot succeed, do not return."

Khyryn searched the old man's face. "There is more to this, than the guidance of an old friend."

"Aye. There is more to it."

"What is it?"

"I do not have answers yet for that riddle. But the darkness of this time will remain if you do not return with her."

"Uddryd?"

As if conjured by the speaking of the name, the trees began to sway, and thunder rolled overhead. Dark clouds slithered to hide the moon's witness, and light cracked in the sky, opening the heavens.

Aberswythe plucked the pouch of herbs he had packed earlier and placed it in Khyryn's hands. Then taking a pinch from the bag, he cast it into the fire. "Evil walks the earth with a black heart. And many will suffer before this chaos ends. If we are not met again in this time, may I know you in another?"

Ollamh embraced *anruth*. Teacher and noble stream. Wisdom and seeker.

The trees bowed, frantic for the sound of the encroaching storm. Rain began to fall, misting first then threatening to squelch the fire.

Aberswythe handed Khyryn his sword. "I retrieved it when you went to the stream. It is cleaned for you. You may have need of it, druid. Forget not the magic that dwells within your ancient soul. Step into the stones.

As bade, Khyryn stepped into the center, gently tapping the bowl of water as he did.

Abwerswythe took up his staff, a rod of oak, well carved with tiny bells strung to one end, and thus did he chant—

"Whiter than snow be truth
Sharp as sword, keen sight—
Undo the black curse of long tooth
Hence, justice here be mated
By fire, wind and night.
Give flight
Ailim, beithe, coll,
Give strength of triune to bear
This soul with ceo druid hecta
Ancient stones of weir
Let water cast upon the earth
As man onto the air
Through time, with fate and justice rare,
For truth's desire be sated there.
Whiter than snow be truth,
Sharp as sword, keen sight—
Undo the black curse of long tooth
Ground and heaven swelled.
This Khyryn had known before, ten centuries ago.
Breath of the heavens.
It comes upon him again.
Cast water upon the earth
As man onto the air
So be it there..."

The druid's words rose with the gale, as rain poured forth.

Again, Khyryn heard him sing the song. This time the ancient words broke from his own lips and two voices chanted—

"Whiter than snow be truth,
Sharp as sword, keen sight—"
Ground and heaven swelled. This Khyryn had known
before, ten centuries ago. Breath of the heavens. Now it

came upon him again.
"—Cast upon the earth,
As man onto the air..."

With no poison this time to impede his thoughts, the portal did open. Blue as the center of the flame, and scalding cold, it enveloped him in white cacophonic chaos. Blind and without speech, he held tight the sword as he held tight one thought.

Gwynndolwyn.

Chapter Five

Wales, August, 2009

The scream pierced the air before Wynne realized it had not escaped from her own mouth. Khyryn's blade struck Richard's right elbow, renting a gash severe enough to break his hold on her throat.

The sharp coldness of the blade across her abdomen singed her skin as it drew across the fabric of her gown. In the same instant, the reflection of light glinted as Khyryn's sword sliced through the air, aimed for the arm that had threatened her.

Richard forcefully yanked her to the ground, pulling his sword up in an arc that ended in the clang of metal. Both men charged one another.

The damn idiots will kill themselves—and me.

Not in the script.

She grasped her own throat where the pulse surged beneath the flesh again. With the reassuring throbbing came anger. How dare Richard change the choreography? How dare he endanger the actors?

Anger turned to fury at the discovery that Richard's sword had actually cut through the cloth of her costume.

Completely insane. Both of them.

Wynne got to her feet and shouted, "Stop it! Richard! Khyryn! Stop!"

Neither man heeded her. In fact, from where she stood, both men looked as if they had forgotten where they were all together. Hand to hand, hilt to hilt, the two wrestled, beads of sweat accentuating the fact this was no choreographed fight.

Clouds swarmed as great droplets fell on the crowd, dispersing some as another bolt of lightning struck the ground near the field.

"You're lightning rods. Stop, damn it! You'll be killed!"

If the storm doesn't, I will.

Khyryn slid on the slick grass, catching himself on one knee. The slip cost him—his sword slipped from his grasp as he fell.

Richard pressed his advantage, swinging his blade repeatedly at Khyryn's head.

Shit! He's trying to kill him.

Wynne found her own dagger where it had fallen in the grass.

"Khyryn!"

She tossed the knife toward Khyryn as she lunged at Richard, carefully aiming for his knees. She rolled into the dive. The swiftness of the motion threw him off balance, casting him backward.

As Richard fell, his sword arm swung out, away from his body, exposing his trunk to the blow of Khyryn's blade. First came the smack of the steel against the leather of his vest, followed by the hiss of...

He's been struck.

Time slowed. The rain pounded the earth, beating like an ancient drum. Richard Uddryd fell into the mud, a gaping wound in his torso. The sword flew from his grip, plummeting to the ground in a race to join its master.

His gloved hand reached out and found Wynne's hair as she fought to stand. "Not this time."

He spat the words as though they were poison. Both his grip and his voice weakened and broke as his body contorted in pain.

As mysteriously as it had slowed, time resumed. And with it, pandemonium. The scattered audience and actors who had not run from the lightning filled the air now with shouts and screams.

Wynne wriggled from beneath him, involuntarily shrieking as another hand gripped her beneath her arm and pulled her upright.

"Get away from me," she tried to cry, but her voice faltered, even as her feet found the ground again. "Security! Somebody get an ambulance!"

Even as onlookers stumbled out from the tents and stalls, she could hear the distant shouts followed by an airhorn. The flocking crowd shoved past her, gathering around Richard who lay prone on the ground. Bleeding.

The hand that had pulled her to her feet tightened around her arm and dragged her farther from the scene.

"Stop it! Let go of me!" Wynne swung her arm as hard as she could and landed a blow to his stomach. The force of it halted Khyryn's steps, and he bent over.

Wynne drew her hand back from the drenched cloth of his shirt, intent on landing another blow. Rain washed something red from her fingers. She looked at her captor, then at his shirt.

"You're bleeding." Not a captor, a victim. "He cut you. Damn it, Khyryn. We have to get you to the ambulance, too."

"Nae. It is but a scratch."

"Stop with the 'nays' and acting shit. Come on, they need to see you. Security is on the way. We need to file a report. Damned bastard! What was he thinking? What were *you* thinking to play along with him?" Wynne attempted to turn Khyryn around to head back to the crowd.

Even as she asked the question, the realization of it struck her. Richard Uddryd knew she was trying to steal the stone. Somehow, he'd figured it out and discovered her real purpose. Only, he wrongly pegged Khyryn as an accomplice instead of just another actor.

Resistance stood like a stone wall—a sodden and still bleeding swordsman. He tightened his grip on her arm. "We must go. Now. Come with me."

"The only place we're going is to the paramedics. Come on."

"I will recover without help. We must get to the cave—"

"See? Now, you're just loopy. I can make this right. It is my fault he cut you. Richard is a thief, and I can prove it. Now, let go of my arm or I'll belt you in the stomach again."

Khyryn did not move.

Testosterone. Damn men.

Anger and frustration surged once again. She punched him. Nearly. Khyryn bent as she struck out, causing her fist to hit air as he thrust his shoulder beneath her ribs, winding her and hoisting her over his shoulder in one move.

She gasped, trying desperately to take in great gulps to replace the oxygen that had escaped. Whether from the blow, or from her current posture, her body battled against an overwhelming nausea and dizziness that turned the world upside down. From her tilted position, she could neither see which direction Khyryn ran, nor could she stop him from sprinting with her slung over his shoulder like a sack of potatoes.

When she did find her voice, her protests fell mute against the broad backside of the man who insisted on running away from help. She beat on his thighs and tried to claw through the leather of his costume, achieving little more than exhausting herself further.

The rain slapped at her back and rump as it came down in sheets. Gradually, irritation gave way to fear. He quickened his gait as he ventured away from the crowd. Soon, they would no longer be on the castle property.

I have to get that stone.

The unsettling effect of traveling for several minutes upside down took its toll. Bent in half, numbness soaked her legs as the rain soaked the rest of her and dripped into her ears. Dizziness overwhelmed her, and her strength waned. Vision faded in and out.

The fog rose from the ground, and Khyryn's steps slowed. His body thudded soundly as he dropped to his knees, and the vise around her thighs loosened, landing her on her side in the mud. Shards prickled her flesh as the blood returned to her legs. As sensation returned, so did her anger and her voice.

She struggled to stand. "What kind of idiot are you?"

"I might ask the same of you. It is no fool's thought I had to save you from bein' run through. The madman held a sword to you as he tried to strangle you."

Khyryn's speech was labored, his breath ragged.

His face paled, and he clutched his side.

Wynne moved her hand to her boot. Still there. Tucked inside the leather, against her calf rested her *sgian dhu*. Little protection against a lunatic, but even a small blade was better than nothing.

"Come," he said as he climbed to stand. "It is a walk, yet."

She clambered to her feet, her own legs shaking, and turned toward where the castle should be, somewhere in the fog. "The only direction I am going is back to the faire. And so should you. You're bleeding. I don't know where you think you're going, and I'm not particularly interested in finding out right now. If you pass out on me, I will leave you where you fall." She hesitated. "From the look of you, that could be any step now."

Khyryn's hand lashed around her wrist like a whip, yanking it to him, and completely immobilizing her arm.

Instinctively, Wynne's free arm flew back toward his Adam's apple. Self-defense. Plain and simple.

Lightning quick, his right hand shot out and grabbed her elbow. Now he held both arms. "No."

So quiet, she wondered if he had actually spoken.

Raindrops hissed against the sodden ground, as a fearful silence echoed in her ears.

This time, his breath brushed her ear, as intimate as a lover's kiss. "No."

Panic welled from her stomach to her throat. Another sensation just as dangerous fluttered lower in her body.

"You cannot go back. Yours was the blade that stabbed him. There is nothing to be done to change that fact. Trust I do not seek to harm you. But now we must walk. We must get out of the rain. We must make it to the cave."

Wounded or not, his words were logical. The drenching rain was doing neither of them any good.

He loosened his grip but did not release her. In response, she kept her stance rigid as they walked close together.

****

The gash in Khyryn's side throbbed. For this instant, the pain was good, reminding him of the urgency of his task. And of the scene they'd just fled.

Damn the woman. She could fight better than most men. Why had he not seen the danger before in the other man's eyes? Because Richard kept it cloaked until today. Recognition. Deceit. Revenge. He remembered.

Regardless of the century, murder held dire consequences.

Desperation tugged at Khyryn's conscience. He needed to get her to the cave. Tonight the moon rose full. Aberswythe would be waiting for them.

Lust flared in Khyryn's groin at the thought of taking her through the portal. He pushed her an arm's length from him.

She trembled at his touch. Whether from fury or fear, he could not discern.

She must not fear. Fear would foul the spell.

For the moment, he could do nothing more than walk toward the ruins that had sheltered him for the moon's cycle. A moon's cycle to adapt to the language of her time. To fit in. To find her.

The rain had ceased. The sun broke through the grey sky and warmed the earth as they broke through the line of trees that surrounded the crumbling stones of the crumbling fortress.

"Why are we here?"

Khyryn did not answer but guided her toward a section of the inner wall now covered by thick brush. He lifted the limbs from where they touched the ground. A curtain of ivy covered a narrow, crumbling passageway, which descended below the ground's surface.

"Oh, hell no." Wynne slammed against Khyryn, struggling to escape the dark hole. "No fucking way. Not on your life—"

He held her tight in his arms. "Shh. It's all right. I shall go first."

"Feel free," she shouted. "*I* am not going at all."

"The distance to the cave is more than we can risk. The tunnel shortens the path." Her fear burned his skin. "Trust me."

"Trust you. Trust y*ou*? First you and that idiot thief, Richard, fight like two mad dogs in the middle of the faire. You practically kidnap me, and you expect me to follow you into a dark tomb where no one can find me?"

"I am not what you think." Despite his efforts, Khyryn's patience was quickly dissipating. "I would show you if you would but trust my counsel."

Her eyes glittered dangerously with a fire of the fury that scorched her cheeks. "I hope that damn cut bleeds until you pass out. You can rot in that hole for all I care, you son of a—"

Khyryn spoke calmly, despite her ranting. "If I had not stabbed him, Gwynndolwyn, he would have killed you."

A look of confusion crossed her face. "What did you call me?"

Khyryn sighed. "Gwynndolwyn. It is your name."

She stared at him for several moments, as if pondering some riddle.

For a moment, a look of recognition fluttered across her face. A memory?

At last her stance relaxed. A smile curved her lips.

"You're right. Perhaps, I'm a little shaken up. I wasn't thinking of what would be best for you. You need to get some place where you can rest. If this tunnel is the place, then lead the way,"

He released her and she stepped toward the crumbling stone. She bent to draw back the brush from the dark hole. "Come on, Sir William." She winked at him. "I won't bite. I promise."

Exhaustion racked his body, both from the hike, and from the cut he had endured in the fight.

Khyryn stepped down into the tunnel, regretting he had no torch. He could maneuver the path with some effort. He had done so several times. She had not.

"The path will be slow since we have no light. Give me your han—"

His words sputtered and stopped as the searing pain tore through his skull, freezing his brain.

"D'you think I'm that stupid?"

Khyryn sank to his knees and reached toward the opening. A rock landed on the dark ground beside him. Light and vision faded. Even as his body plunged to meet the stone, he saw Gwynndolwyn turn and flee.

Chapter Six

Scraped, and worn, and only slightly less soggy than she had been half an hour before, Wynne waved to the woman behind the steering wheel. The car accelerated, scattering gravel as it pulled away from the gate. Fortunately, the woman who gave her a lift had believed Wynne's story about a broken-down car.

She ducked through the delivery gate, avoiding the flow of the crowd. The long rain and the morning's excitement had purged the grounds of most of the patrons. A few customers milled around the vendors stalls. The empty jousting field, however, made Wynne feel eerily out of place.

Snaking her way through the yard, Wynne made her way toward the familiar green curtain that marked the fortune-teller's tent. Two women tossed words of thanks and farewell over their shoulders as they departed, laughing conspiratorially as they headed for a cluster of carts displaying ceramic wares and souvenir mugs.

Wynne stepped through the drape and collapsed into the chair opposite the old woman.

"So," Elleran called, "you've returned."

"What happened after the paramedics showed up? Is he all right?"

"Richard? The faire buzzes with word that his guards called the police."

"Good. That idiot went insane and tried to kill Khyrin on the chess field. He nearly strangled me during the show, shouting, 'not this time', like it's part of the show. He's lucky nobody's dead."

"And you are lucky he has not found you. Where is the other?"

"Khyryn? Sleeping off a concussion. He's as crazy as Richard. He gets himself stabbed, tries to kidnap me, drags me off to some cave to hide instead of setting things right here. Is everyone in this damned place criminally insane?"

A crooked smile curved the old woman's lips. "Your Khyryn is wiser than you know."

"Ha!"

"*He* will not be caught."

"Richard is the one who has some questions to answer. The son-of-a-bitch tried to kill me. He's a thief. When I tell the police he stole ancient artifacts—"

"He will tell the police you and the other one conspired to kill him."

"That's a lie."

Elleran gathered three small stones in her hand, palming them distractedly. "Yours was the blade that cut him. Was it not?"

"Yes, but—"

"Richard weaves his words well among the people here. They believe what he says. Here, young one, you are the outsider."

Fear welled inside Wynne's gut, and bile surged into her throat as Khyryn's own words sprang from the old woman's lips. "Elleran, Khyryn dropped his sword. Richard was about to slice him in half. When I tell the police what really happened—

"Richard Uddryd has always been dangerous."

"There were witnesses. A crowd of people saw him."

"That matters not. From them that's telling it, you and Khyryn ran before the guards showed up."

Wynne stood and kicked the chair. "Damn it—"

"Do not let him find you. He will kill you. He remembers."

He remembers? "He told you?" *Twelve years.* He couldn't possibly remember her. Could he? How many times today had her stomach roiled with panic?

"Elleran, what do you know about this? What does Richard remember?"

"Ask your Khyryn. The druid will tell you."

"Khyryn is not mine. And he's not telling anything." Dizziness and nausea washed over her in waves. "I broke his skull with a rock."

Elleran's silence fell between them like a lead weight.

The fortune teller clucked her tongue reproachfully, and a curious grimace tugged at the corner of her mouth. Eyes that stared vacantly at Wynne suddenly brightened, as if for one instant they had glimpsed Wynne in their focus.

"The druid is dead?"

"What druid?"

Any answer Elleran might have given evaporated as voices outside the booth stole Wynne's attention.

"Front gate said they saw her come in," one of the security guards shouted to another. Check the jousting field. I've got the shops and booths."

"Behind the drape," Elleran whispered.

"But he'll see me through the cloth—"

"He will see nothing."

"But—"

"Do as I say. He will not see—," the old woman hissed.

Wynne slid between the diaphanous layers of the curtain just as the security guard stepped onto the wooden floor of the tent.

"Dennis, is it?" Elleran crowed. "Long have I waited for you, this day. Have you come to hear what my Tarot says? Or is it a kiss you've come to steal?"

The fortune teller cackled at Dennis' startled response, as if she could see his face.

He stared directly at the curtain where Wynne stood, yet did not see her. Or if he did, it did not show on his face or in his posture.

"Richard's looking for the girl who plays Lady Rowena," he said. "Has she been in here?"

"I only know what the cards tell me. You long for the lust of an older woman to satisfy your desires."

Wynne watched the guard shy away from the fortune teller. Contempt replaced astonishment on his face. He grunted his disgust at the suggestion in Elleran's voice, then stormed from the tent, barking into his radio as he left.

Wynne emerged from the cloud of cloth and hugged Elleran.

"Elleran, I've never seen Dennis look more confused than just now. Brilliant! He never even glanced to the corner."

Cold as a stone, Elleran's tone cut through the air. "Sit."

Tired, stressed, and speckled from head to toe with mud, Wynne took the seat opposite Elleran's. "All right, Madame Fortune Teller, now what do I do? Go the police on my own and tell them what really happened?"

"Richard will not let you."

"Yeah? Well—"

"You must find the druid."

Anger and frustration burned Wynne's cheeks. "What druid? Who are you talking about? I don't know any druid!"

"He knows you. He remembers the feel of your lips against his. That is why Richard will not let you leave."

A shiver ran down Wynne's spine. "Who is this druid you keep talking about? What does he have to do with Richard?"

As if Wynne's question were some joke, Elleran laughed softly to herself. "There must always be a balance. As in the cards."

"And?"

"I made him watch you die, you know."

The hair prickled on Wynne's neck. "Excuse me?"

"Yet still he found you. He is clever, your druid. You must go back. Pray you did not kill him. Only he can save you. And you, him."

Wynne's skin crawled. "Khyryn? What do you mean, he can save me?"

"He tried before and failed." The old woman tsked. "I once thought him weak. Well, even wyce can be wrong. He is strong, your Khyryn. Strong of spirit and of limb—the druid. Wyce were strong once. Elleran was strong once. Now, I am only clever."

Nonsense poured from the old woman's mouth. Insanity. Rambling. Druids and wyce, whatever that was supposed to be, and Khyryn saving her and—

What if I did kill him?

Panic usurped the uneasiness that enveloped Wynne since she stepped through those damned gates. As insane as it sounded in even in her own head, Wynne needed to know. Had she killed him?

"You are mistress of the druid, more than you ever were queen. Find him and mate with him again."

"I never—"

"Evil stirs here and in another time. I hear the spirits whisper when I sleep. The curse would be soon ended for your part in this game. You must vanquish the evil one before the world changes for darkness ever more."

Each spoken word slashed at Wynne's reason. She should leave and run as far away from this tent and this woman, this faire, these people, as she could.

Forget the stone.

Go back to the solace of her history books, of her research. Back to the boredom of the lecture halls. Away from this madness. Artifact be damned.

The fortune teller wove to and fro, like a giant serpent, taunting, "I can smell his blood on you, Gwynndolwyn—"

Her spine tingled. "How do you know that name?"

"Richard Uddryd smells it, too." Her voice rose. "He knows it well. It enflames his passion. For you. And for his bloodlust."

"Stop it, Elleran." Wynne fidgeted. "Someone will hear you."

The witch's hand shot out like lightning. Withered fingers curled around Wynne's wrist like shriveled roots, tightening against her flesh, smothering the life from her hand as it caressed the pulse that beat there.

Wynne leapt from the chair and tugged hard enough to upturn the table, but Elleran's grip only tightened. The moon meets end of day," she shrieked. She held Wynne's arm as tightly as Khyryn had before.

Wynne thrashed against the old woman's grip as Elleran's rhyme turned to cackling. Upturned furniture and scattered cards escaped the crone's concern as she slammed Wynne against a support beam with the strength of a gladiator. The old blind woman looked directly into her eyes.

Elleran's hips pinned Wynne as one crooked finger slithered down her belly, clawing at her abdomen, and rubbing the stones she had in her palm against Wynne's stomach. As clearly as if she could spy Wynne and see into her soul, Elleran's gaze sparkled with vision.

"He will move inside you with the rage and passion of a thousand years to take you through the stones." She cackled again. "Had I the magic to deceive him yet, I would go in your place to feel his body buck with such desire. Take care, Golden one. A man, even a druid, forgets his wits when a woman, ripe as you are, nears. Beware the dark one. He hunts you also. His lust is poisoned by greed and spite."

Wynne's breath came in gasps. Vile and shuddering gasps, filled with disgust at the old woman's words. The fingers on her left hand had long since numbed, but her right hand broke free of the fortune-teller's grasp, and she raked her nails against the pruned skin that clung to the laughing skull with searing eyes.

With a yowl that turned from menacing to hysterical laughter, Elleran's grip broke. The blind fortune teller retreated.

Bile bubbled in Wynne's throat as she turned to run, fear and shock threatening to erupt. Her spine ached with a jagged pain, low against her hips.

Long arms of green silk wrapped around her, tangling her steps, clinging to her, pulling her back. The wind swirled teasingly about her as Wynne flew from the shadows of the tent.

****

Wynne stayed close to the shadows and shrubbery. Managing to slip in with a tour group through the barbican gate, she sped down the slope, toward the buses.

A radio squawked. "Nothing yet," the security guard replied. "You're sure she was headed this way, then?"

Again the radio squawked.

"We've got the exit covered here. We're at the car park. If she comes this way, we should see her. Dennis is covering the staff entrance."

Damn.

Money well spent. Richard Uddryd had better security than some museums. Even from a distance, she could see one of the guards brandished a stun gun.

Anachronistic. And deadly.

She ducked behind a nearby car, and choked on the string of profanities she longed to spew at the three men who stood quite literally between her and escape.

"He will not let you leave." Elleran's words taunted her as she calculated her chances against three of them…one armed.

Damn it, think. How to get past them to the bus?

If she could get to her flat, she could call the police about Richard. And tell them about Khyryn.

Not a bad plan, except her bus pass and cell phone were both in her street clothes inside the costume shop...surrounded by security.

Khyryn. Left in that hole in the ground. To die.

Guilt conspired with the anger and panic brewing inside her for most of the day. Khyryn was dangerous. A madman. After all, he'd abducted her.

She sank to the gravel beside a car.

No. Richard was the madman. He started this. Khyryn had tried to save her.

She could expose him. She knew he skimmed from the profits the faire made. She had seen the books. And he had been the man at the excavation twelve years ago. He had stolen from the site.

But that wouldn't solve the real mystery of Richard Uddryd, would it?

If only she hadn't seen him steal the artifact. If only she had ignored it. After all, something so small as a rock. A trinket. A souvenir. No doubt Stonehenge had fewer rocks than twenty years or a thousand years ago.

An artifact. A life.

If she had never told her uncle, would she even be here?

At this moment, she greatly preferred reading about nefarious characters to dealing with them. History and literature were significantly safer than real life.

What to do?

Find the druid.

Elleran's voice whispered in her head. What would she do if he were found lying dead at the entrance to the tunnel?

Wynne kept low to the ground, moving between the cars and away from the Richard's men. Down in the town she could talk to the police.

"Damn."

Everything she needed was inside the wardrobe room. Identification. Cellphone. Photos of the sales reports.

She needed her bag.

"*...He will kill you. He remembers.*"

She had to get back inside.

****

The crowd wandered out, escorted by a throng of dancers, musicians, and jugglers. Wynne's head and heart pounded with the rhythm of the bodhran drum.

Like a warrior, poised for battle, she hid in the tree line separating the castle wall from the car park. In her hand, she held a branch she'd found unclaimed by the grounds keepers. The *s'gian dhu* concealed in her boot didn't offer much protection against three guards, but the four-foot long makeshift oak club should wield some power of persuasion. She could slam two at once if need be.

Wynne joined the procession that filtered down the trail, carefully dodging in and out among the revelers to avoid the glances of the attendants who still hovered. A group of rowdy students clung to each other, forming a medieval conga line, dragging joiners through the narrow lanes between the cars.

Salvation. A diversion. One of the drivers got out of his car and threatened one of the students—an all too tall, over enthusiastic boy of about nineteen. Sporting a kilt, and a camouflage jacket, the boy hurled a rock at the driver, in reply.

Thank God for testosterone.

The security guard and one of the parking guards

moved away from the front gate and made their way toward the ruckus. One single remaining guard held his post, but only in posture, as his attention was fully on the two brawlers.

Wynne dropped out of the crowd and scurried, low and fast toward her goal. Bent over, holding the limb, she tripped over the hem of her gown, landing just an arm's length from another man who watched the brawl with ample enthusiasm.

Three sprints around the car brought her within swinging distance of the one remaining obstacle between her and the entrance. She only needed to knock the air out of him, not separate his head from his shoulders. She lifted the club and swung hard—

"Hey!"

—and caught only air as her prey turned. The other guard's shout had succeeded. The man in front of her aimed something dark at her. She swung again, knocking it from his hands, just as a well-swung left hook caught her on the shoulder. She stumbled back, dropping the tree branch as she did.

She ran for the open gate.

And flew sideways as the second guard tackled her. Twice her size, he knocked the air out of her as they landed on the sodden ground.

"Yes, sir." The guard she'd tried and failed-to hit spoke into a radio. "We have her at the entrance."

Static crackled. "Is she alone?"

"Yes sir. Should we call the authorities?"

"No." Richard's voice echoed in evening air. "Bring her to me."

****

Wynne's ribs ached. She could breathe now.

However, her head still spun a bit from being sideswiped by Richard's man.

"Call the police," she insisted. "Call them and let's see who they believe more."

Richard Uddryd nodded, motioned to the door, and the guards exited his office. With his back to her, he closed the door.

She heard the click of the lock.

Richard will not let you leave...

On his desk sat her bag, her phone, her passport. Next to her stuff lay a photocopied enlargement displaying her passport photo and name, as well as a promise of reward for information to her detention for attempted murder.

While his back was still turned, Wynne slid her palm over her phone and concealed it in the long sleeves of her gown.

Richard had exchanged his costume for slacks and a shirt. Beneath the rolled cuff, his right arm hung at his side, wrapped in a stark white bandage. "Do you really want to involve them?"

"Don't you?"

He turned toward her, an evil smirk played across his face. "I don't have to."

One hand. He only had one good hand. And probably a bandaged rib. She could escape. She could get the police.

"Imagine how offended I felt when my own people thought you tried to murder me."

She swallowed and remembered the bruise on her own throat. "Too bad they didn't get to see your performance on the chess field. You know, where you tried to kill me in front of an entire crowd?"

He blinked lazily at her. "Why have you returned?"

She stroked the phone hidden in her hand, and glanced to her belongings strewn across his desk. "I just came back for my stuff."

In three strides, he crossed the space. His good hand swung out and clamped down on her neck, pinning her to the desk.

"Fool. If I had been trying to kill you this afternoon, you wouldn't be standing here now."

Her pulse beat frantically against the thumb that stroked her jugular.

"Where is he?"

"I don't know."

He pressed firmly and bent to whisper in her ear. "You never have been as good at lying as you are at *laying* a man. Where is Khyryn?"

Dead probably. "I don't know where he is. I hit him and ran away."

Laughter bubbled from her captor.

She slipped her hand beneath her skirt and dropped the phone into her boot, and withdrew the blade hidden there. "Look, I don't know what this is about. I don't know what game the two of you are playing at. I just want to leave."

"And where would you go?"

Wynne tried to calm her breathing. "Anywhere. Away. Just let me have—"

"What should I let you have, Wynne Hailey? What is it that brought you back?"

His hand shifted to her hair, and he moved his bandaged arm to reach beneath her body. "How long have you plotted this, Wynne?"

"Plotted what?"

He purred, seductively, "The stone, you bitch."

Shit. "I told you, I don't—"

His tongue slid along her throat. "Hmm. Tastes like fear."

She jabbed the knife into his thigh and yanked as hard as she could. Richard arched in howling pain. He released his hold on her, and she ran for the window.

Please, be open. Be open.

The warped paned-window gave way the moment she jerked the handle and pushed. Richard's shout rang out as she lunged headlong over the sill. She landed in a hedge of bushes.

Wynne scrambled out of the brush, bramble and twigs clawing at her, snagging her hem. She slashed the small blade she still held in her hand against the fabric until she pulled free.

The ruckus behind her crescendoed. "Stop her!"

A door separated the guards from Richard. A wall separated them from her.

She ran. Across the deserted parking lot, through a clump of trees, and down the hill, toward the town. Twilight turned to night. Wynne didn't stop running until her feet hit the cobblestones.

She paused to catch her breath.

Police. I need the police.

She pulled the cell phone from her boot and flipped it open.

Just three buttons and send. All she had to do was tell them, and they'd protect her.

9...9...The luminescent display screen went black.

"Sonofabitch! I don't believe it!" She closed the phone and opened it again. "Just one call."

No display. No power.

In the breeze, she heard the off-key bellow of a siren.

He weaves his words well among the people here...

Her passport still sat on Richard's desk....next to a reward poster for her apprehension.

"Find the druid."

Elleran's words echoed in her head.

"All right, damn it. I get it."

God, please let him still be alive.

Dead man or druid maniac, Khyryn was her best hope.

Chapter Seven

Khyryn's lips met the moistness gratefully, sucking in the earthiness of her scent, and the liquid that teased his tongue.

Her hand caressed his forehead, encouraging him to take as much as he could. He did as she commanded.

Her hands moved across the sinew of his neck and shoulders and down his chest to brush the all too sensitive flesh just beneath his ribs.

"It's puddle water, but it's all I've got."

Khyryn struggled to open one eye despite the hammering pain that fought to keep both closed.

Shadowed against the last vestiges of daylight, Gwynndolwyn knelt over him, pressing a soaked bit of cloth to his mouth. She had returned. His side ached as if he had gouged it on a rock. Pain meant he was not dead. At least not yet. Although, just now, the pounding in his skull gave merit to the idea.

He sucked what he could from the cloth, then let her take it from his lips to brush his brow with the still damp fabric.

"Why?"

She did not look at him, but continued to wipe his head with the cloth. "Why what? Why did I bash in your head?"

Swallowing hurt. "Why did you come back?"

She sighed. "Because it's the right thing to do. Isn't

it? I mean I couldn't just leave you here to die, could I?"

"It is to my fortune you did not. Though at this moment, my head would argue with me on that point."

"Sorry about that. I didn't mean to—"

"Shh. If you had not meant to, I would not have fallen. 'Tis no more than I would have done to one who tried to drag me into a hole against my will."

She did not reply, nor did he press her to answer anything more. When she did speak, fear cracked in her voice. "Elleran sent me back. She said—"

"Be wary of the witch's words."

"She mumbled something about Richard trying to kill me, and you being a druid, and helping me, and, and—"

"Do you believe her?"

Her eyes held questions. "I don't have any idea what to believe. After everything that happened today, I don't give a rat's ass what your hobbies are, or your religion, or whether you think you know me. All I know is that Richard Uddryd has my keys, my identification, and..."

Her lip trembled. She cleared her throat. "I have no way to get home. The police think you and I were trying to kill him. Richard is after me. And you. And this is not the way any of this was supposed to go. I was just going to break in—"

"Break? What is broken?"

"Nothing." She shook her head. "I'm just swirling in chaos."

He laughed. "Now it is you who speaks with a druid's soul."

She moved now to sit so she could see his face

properly. A mix of confusion and curiosity played across her brow. "How so?"

"To be druid is to seek knowledge in the chaos. All knowledge. To unlock the wonder of all the elements—water, earth, the heavens. To praise the mysteries of life, even as one laments human failings. Chaos is ever present."

"So what Elleran said is true? You are a druid?"

A fire burned in his side. And in his memory.

"I used to be."

"Why 'used to be'?"

His voice snagged on memory. "What used to be is another lifetime."

"And you and Elleran know one another from way back?"

His mouth twitched at the question. "Aye."

She sighed and her face relaxed a bit. "A lifetime? It seems that way sometimes, doesn't it? You believe something for so long, it seems for a lifetime. Then it all changes. In an instant. And here I am, in England, pouring over old manuscripts and researching people and places that vanished a thousand years ago. Before I started this...it was just a faded memory. Like you said, 'another lifetime.' How could everything get so messed up in just a few hours?"

She parried his words effortlessly. Yet she spoke of a few hours or days. He spoke of centuries.

She fondled the cloth in her hand. "So, how do you feel?"

"Which part? My head or my side?"

"Both. I tried to wash the wound a bit. You were still unconscious. It doesn't look very deep. I think you're right. Just a scratch. I bet this wasn't in your contract, either. Was it?"

The woman who had hired him to play the part had only been interested in his appearance. He had not read the words. Just made a mark where she pointed on the paper.

Suddenly, aware that he was bare chested and much too close to Gwynndolwyn, his body tensed. "How did you get my shirt open?"

"Any self-respecting lady of renfair worth should carry some form of weapon on her body." As proof, she dangled a knife, smaller than a dagger in front of him. "A *sgian dhu* will fit in the slimmest of boots, *Sir William*. To scale a fish, slit a throat, or protect one on the way home from the faire."

"Do not call me Sir William. My name is Khyryn. Khyryn of Powys."

She smiled at him, robustly. Genuinely. "All right, Khyryn Powys. Tell me how you came to be mixed up in all this. For that matter, how did I come to be mixed up in all this? Richard is an ass, and a thief. But I am not a murderer. And somehow, I doubt you are either."

"Aye? Yet you carry a knife in your boot?"

She started to argue with him then paused. "I would not hurt anyone intentionally, but I'm not stupid. The world is a dangerous place. A weapon can be a good thing. Besides, it goes with the costume."

Khyryn surveyed her attire. The line of the fabric as it hugged her curves. She exposed a knee and leg to him now as she slid the knife back into its hiding place—against the smoothness of her calf.

He had seen many flashes of flesh these past weeks—females barely covered their bodies in this time. None, however, had such an effect on him as did hers.

A ravenous, feral hunger flooded his body. Gwynndolwyn. Returned to him.

Soon the moon would rise, full, and expectant. Here she sat. So close he could smell her, touch her if he reached out.

And reach out he did. Still on his back, with her intimately tucked beside him, he brushed the back of his hand across the softness of her cheek.

Her sharp inhale only fueled his hunger.

Do not scare her.

She grasped his hand and held it tight in her own, as she rubbed her cheek against his skin. "I am sorry about this afternoon—about hitting you and leaving you. I was scared."

"You fought well."

She withdrew her gaze from his. "Elleran said you can get us both out of this mess. She said I should trust you."

For an instant, his conscience battled with his heart. If she knew his solution, or indeed the truth about Elleran, she would most likely strike him on the head again and leave him to die.

He pulled himself into a rather uncomfortable sitting position and pulled his left leg up to conceal his body's own urgent desire. "There is truth in her words. I may be able to help. But...not here."

"I know. Some cave. Look, it's just about dark. I don't have a flashlight or a car."

"There is a flint stone, there in the corner. If you can find something to burn, we can make light."

A sly grin danced on her lips, and she scurried up the steps, returning shortly with an assortment of dried grass and sticks, along with a small branch. The kindling, she set immediately. Pulling her skirt to her knees, she ripped the shift beneath, and wrapped the cloth in spiraling strips down the stick for a hand's length, repeating the process twice more to build a torch.

Having been set the task, Khyryn worked with the flint stone until the grass and twigs began to smolder.

She laughed and clapped her approval. "Good job. You'll have to teach me how to do that, someday. I was a terrible girl scout. Can't camp my way out of a paper bag."

"Girl scout?"

"You know—oh, wait. I don't know what they are over here. A girl scout is a—it's a group that goes out and camps in the woods and teaches girls survival skills. They learn crafts and skills. They learn to survive on their own. Camp-fire girls?"

"Girls who tend fires?"

She stopped then and looked directly at him. Long, and deep, a puzzled smile on her lips. "Yes," she finally answered, as she dipped the torch into the flame.

His head still pounded, matching the drumbeat of his heart, but he managed to guide them through the tunnel, ever closer to the cave.

"You know, I've been all over this area. Nobody mentioned any tunnels. How did you know about it?"

"I grew up here. Originally, a massive hill fort sat on top of it, ringed with timber. But then the Romans came and built roads and great walls. They burned down many of the fortresses of wood, as they claimed Britain for their Empire."

"And they built roads."

"No. Slaves built the roads."

"If it weren't for the Romans—and William the Conqueror—Britain would still be a patchwork quilt, tribe warring against tribe, brother against brother."

Khyryn nearly tripped over his own feet.

For the rest of the trek, he dared not speak to her. When the strips of cloth from her shift burned to the wood, he shed his own torn shirt and wrapped it around the limb. Fuel for a fire.

Finally, on hands and knees, Khyryn crawled through the small fissure in the rock that opened into a cave.

His cave.

Too many years had passed since she had stood here. Too many years since she had come to him, weeping for her love of him. Not his brother. Raging against him for his loyalty to Uddryd, instead of his own desires. She had cast off her garments in supplication as she offered herself to him, before the spirits of the heavens and the earth. Giving him her soul for all time.

Here once more.

No dream. No cruel illusion.

His heart beat quicker, at the thought of her. So did the throbbing in his groin.

He pulled Gwynndolwyn through the small crevice and quickly set about transforming the dwindling torch into a small fire to warm the chilled evening air.

The sun had set. A heady pall settled on the horizon forewarning nightfall.

Aberswythe, old friend, I hope you are right.

****

Wynne's stomach growled appreciatively as she

swallowed the last morsel of meat from the skewer. She had promised to cook for him. Instead, he provided supper for them both.

"It is not faire food," Khyryn said.

"Thank goodness. This is good," she said, revulsion giving way to hunger as he settled what was left of a hare's carcass over the small fire. After all, her uncle had been a hunter. As a child, she must have dined on something like this. Unknowingly.

Weariness and a full stomach numbed her anxiety a bit. Sitting so close to the open fire, her skin sweltered with a heat that made her regret the fact she hadn't nabbed her T-shirt and shorts before she escaped the faire.

Across from the glowing flame, Khyryn sat staring at her. His body, taut and lightly bronzed, glistened with perspiration in the light.

"You're feverish. Do you have any aspirin?"

"What is 'aspirin'?"

"I know you're really into this whole character thing, but you need medical help. And I have a headache. Where is your car?"

"I have no car."

"Then, let's get you to your house."

He glanced up at her. "This is where I live."

Wynne swallowed hard against the lump in her throat.

Homeless.

The word conjured pictures of shabby people sleeping in nests of newspapers in the squalor of metropolitan subways. Not in the pristine solitude of a hermit's cave.

"I worked once with someone who was homeless.

His family had been abandoned by the father. The kid worked to buy food for his brothers and sister. But they couldn't afford a place to live."

"I am not without a home. This is my home."

Wynne lowered her gaze from his and studied the stones that surrounded the fire he had laid. Each had been placed with deliberate care. As if they—and the three bowls displayed within—were his most prized possessions.

The panic from the morning turned to pity. "Um—how long have you lived here?"

Something glimmered in his expression. Amusement? Or annoyance? Whichever her question evoked, he masked his answer with a melancholy smile. "Longer than I thought possible."

"You said you grew up nearby. How did you end up here?"

His expression changed from melancholy to wariness. "What is your earliest memory?"

"What?"

"What is your earliest memory from your childhood?"

Wynne sat, dumbfounded. "I don't know. Why do you ask?"

"I remember being stung by a bee, once. I could barely walk, yet I had managed to catch a bee in my small hand. When I did not set it free, it stung me. I remember the welling sensation of pain and anger, and of floating as I fell to the ground."

Wynne's hand stung, as if she somehow shared his memory. She searched the darkness of her surroundings. In the corner lay a drape of cloth, and a small bag. His bed? Her cheeks flushed at the intimacy of seeing where he slept. Why had she agreed to come here?

"So, what now? How do we get to the police? How do we convince them we weren't trying to kill our insane director? I should be able to contact the embassy. Somebody at the colle—"

Khyryn edged closer to her. "You did not answer my question. What is your earliest memory?"

Wynne fought the urge to reach out and touch him, as he had done when she found him in the tunnel. The effect had nearly undone her. Never had anyone's touch affected her quite like his. Shock did strange things to people.

The kiss he had stolen before the crowd this morning. His breath against her ear. The brush of his hand against her cheek. Each time, her body had reacted dangerously. Sensually. Now, as close as he sat, heat radiated from his flesh, beckoning her to him.

Such a private person. Quiet, strong. Yet he had brought her here to show her his home.

Hot. Too hot. Fire.

She fought against the stifling warmth that filled the air and against the dryness in her throat. Definitely not wise to be here. With him. Alone. Stupid move.

Rising from where she sat, Wynne moved toward the entrance of the cave. She needed to concentrate on something other than her own body. Or his.

"Um…I remember being in my crib as a child, a toddler. There was a fire in the back field. My parents left me by myself while they went to put it out. I didn't know if they were coming back."

"Did they return?"

"Eventually. I remember being so frightened. Of

being abandoned. Terrified of losing them. Even at that age, somehow, I knew what fire meant. I knew what being abandoned felt like. That's strange, isn't it? That I could know, so clearly, what I feared?"

The first evening stars twinkled against the dark blue satin of the sky. The crispness of the air bathed her in coolness, calming her mind. And her body.

Sex appeal. That's all it is. Adrenalin and sex appeal.

Recognition of the obvious didn't help much, however. Her body tensed at the sound of him moving to stand behind her. Her breasts swelled against the fabric of her costume, and her thighs clenched instinctively, sending a spasm of titillation up her spine moments before his hand stroked her arm.

Damned testosterone and estrogen.

She tried to move, but her body refused her brain's command. Instead, she leaned against him, allowing him to wrap one arm around her waist even as the fingers of his other hand played softly against the fabric of her sleeve, sliding down to lock her fingers in his grasp.

A shudder escaped her lips, and Khyryn tightened his hold on her. He moved his hand against her waist in a circular motion, spiraling his caress upward until he found the curve of her breast.

Her nipples hardened against his touch, pressing fervently against his palm. Urgent for more.

Her left hand slid down his hip to his thigh. She stroked her hand against solid muscle hidden beneath the cloth, and he moved against her bottom, pressing his erection to the folds of her gown.

Lunacy.

He groaned and hugged her tighter, both arms now enveloping her. She moved her bottom against him, and rocked her head back against his shoulder as he seductively drew his right hand down her torso, hovering near the part of her that throbbed in tempo with the beat of her heart.

"Gwynndolwyn—"

"Why do you call me that?"

He whispered against her ear, "It is your name."

"But no one knows. How—"

The question shuddered and died on her lips as he slipped one hand inside her gown to cup a breast as the other settled between her thighs still protected by layers of linen. He slaked his tongue against her neck, just below her ear where her pulse was strong, and she gasped as he held her tightly, welcoming her convulsions, moving in tandem with the rhythm of her body's dance.

Their touch, their breath, their desires mingled to blend two into one.

Khyryn's body raged against his reason. Every fiber wanted to consume her, whether she remembered him or not. He fought the ferocious lust that rippled through his muscles. Demanding. Primal.

She clung to him, and his breath became ragged, sucking in the feminine musk of her desire. He cupped her breast, firmly, teasing the nipple to a frenzied hardness as she gyrated against the persistent stroke of his other hand. She broke his hold and turned to face him, lacing her fingers around his neck.

Insanity. Luscious insanity.

Pulling his head to hers, she sought his kiss. He captured her mouth with his, devouring her gasps as she pressed her body close to his. He met her invitation by untethering the ties along the sides of her gown, then finally, tugged the dress from her shoulders to pool at her feet, leaving only the sheerest layer of cloth to protect her skin from his scorching desire.

Instead of fending his advance, she playfully tugged at his breeks, slipping her hand inside the last remnant of his resolve.

Her hand, sliding around his erection grasped him fully and expectantly, nearly caused him to cast them both to the ground like rutting animals.

The incantation. Recite the incantation.

He grasped her bottom firmly and trickled a line of kisses down her throat to distract her. She cried out and arched her back as she wrapped one leg around his hips and moved against him.

Patience. All the patience on earth would not be enough to thwart his hunger for her. For what he had forsaken two thousand years ago.

Far in the distance, the heavens roared with thunder.

"Whiter than snow be truth. Sharp as sword, keen sight—" He whispered the words in the ancient tongue as the fabric of her shift, and of this world, yielded to their bodies' meeting. "Ailim, beithe, coll..."

She writhed at his words, as if possessed by a carnal sprite, ravenous for his touch. He responded to her lust in kind.

"...Through time, with fate and justice rare. For truth's desire be sated there..."

Her back now against the rock wall of the cave, he entered her—impaling her. The heat of her soaked them both as he moved inside her as slowly as he could command his body.

Not yet. His body throbbed its protest. His lust would not be denied the release it sought.

He withdrew from her and lifted her away from the wall. Kicking her gown into the circle of stones, he lowered her before him, careful not to break her stare.

Her hands trailed up the length of his legs. Playful. Inviting. He answered her entreaty eagerly, kneeling to lower her still, until her body lay prone. Pale as the shift he lifted away over her arms—her breasts, her stomach, her hips. His hand strayed to that spot on her flesh where the dagger had once penetrated, and he bent with reverence to kiss the mark.

The star-strewn sky outside now crackled with thunderous applause. Lightning clawed at the sky as the woman beneath him stretched her limbs to envelop him.

Khyryn sank into her, laving her nipples as he moved, in and out, whispering against her white hot flesh, "...through time, with fate and justice rare..."

She sped her movement, and he responded in kind. Two bodies entwined. Joined as one, pulsing in unison, each seeking release from within. Unwilling to release the other. Faster. Deeper.

"As man onto the air..."

He held her beneath him as he repeated the words. Breathlessly, desperately, he thrust deeper with each word. Her own cries of pleasure spurred him on as the heavens exploded with their song.

"For truth's desire be sated here."

Spasms racked their bodies, and the world fell away from the shattering climax. A thousand years, falling in shards all around as he filled her, sating the passion that had imprisoned him for all that time.

Joined. One rhythm. One voice. One moment ripping through the curtain of time… "For truth's desire be sated here—"

...and into oblivion.

They slept.

Chapter Eight

England, 1997

Earth spilled from the edges of the hole as the rain began to pelt heavily against Wynne's back.

"Cover your digs," Uncle Derris called to the students as he leapt from spot to spot, like a squirrel checking on its chestnut troves.

She reluctantly stretched from her crouch and stared at the other volunteers on the site. Orange and blue nylon fluttered all around her as others followed the command.

Another worker gave her a hand up from the burial mound, and she made a beeline for the stack of unclaimed tarps filling the bed of the professor's truck.

Ten steps from the excavation she saw him. A dark man, slightly older than the rest of the students and volunteers, squatted next to where her tools still lay. He extracted a small rock from the earth, and turned it over in his hand.

"Hey!" she called.

He didn't even look up. Stone in hand, the man scaled the three-foot gap and took off across the yard.

Wynne sprinted after him. Whatever he had taken, she wanted it back. She had to catch him. It could be important.

"Upf!" She landed face down in a puddle, sucking

in a mouthful of mud. The pain in her toe, revealed the shovel that thwarted her attempt to follow the thief.

"Wynne! Get that hole covered!" Her uncle's face was nearly as dark as the sky was becoming.

"But Unc—"

"Now!"

Another student grabbed her by the arm and began to lift her to her feet as she grabbed the tarp and concentrated on following his order.

Across the marsh she still could see him. The hardening rain made his escape all the more inconspicuous. Running for cover.

Gone in an instant. A few seconds. That's all it had taken for him to steal the stone from the site.

A sickening pall descended with the mist. Whatever he had lifted, had to be important.

He was no casual tourist.

The young man who'd helped her out of the puddle helped lay the bricks over the edges of the tarp to hold it in place, then scurried away like most of the others.

Only a few scattered workers still stood in the marsh, collecting tools or splaying tarps.

Outrage churned in Wynne's belly, nagging at her.

He hadn't looked back when she'd called. He'd known exactly what he'd been doing.

She shook her head and water flew from the baseball cap that shielded her eyes from the rain. Something glimmered in the dirt where he'd stood.

Not the pilfered stone.

Wynne retrieved it and turned the small object over in her hand. Only an inch and a half long, shaped like a fat stick of gum, the cap retracted to reveal a metal tongue. Like a computer cord. A USB. Unlike anything *she'd ever seen.*

****

Rain pelted the earth outside, drowning out the sounds of morning. Wynne struggled against the dream and broke its hold. She moved against the warmth that held her captive and allowed slumber to drift over her once more. Tendrils of memory and guilt melted as she sank into the oblivion of a dreamless sleep.

The cloak of warmth slithered down her arm and squeezed her breast possessively.

The scream escaped her lips as she bolted upright and scared her more than the groping hand had. Confused, head aching, she searched the predawn darkness for a clue to where she was.

"Hush," Khyryn whispered. He clutched her to him, protectively enveloping her in his embrace as he settled her against the heat of his body once more. "Morning is not arrived yet. Rest while you can."

Khyryn. Holding her. In the cave. She had—they had—

Damn. How in the world? What was I thinking?

The throbbing in her head slowed as her pulse turned from a gallop to a trot. The sensation of spinning assaulted her senses. How had what happened last night, happened?

One minute she and the homeless actor lying beside her were talking about childhood memories, the next they were thrashing about like two sex-starved teenagers on prom night.

And like two sex-starved, stupid teenagers, we just had unprotected sex.

Insanity.

Think, Wynne. Think. Have to get out of here. Get

to the police. Explain about Richard. And Khyryn.

A warning thought. Alarming, even. Khyryn. He had a job. And money. Yet he lived here? With nothing?

Shit.

Did he work for Richard? The sickening likelihood made her head hurt even more. He'd kept her away from Richard for the entire night. And away from the stone.

Oh, and she'd played right along. How stupid. How utterly, frigging unbelievably stupid.

Again she tried to sit up, but he draped a leg over her hips and caressed her abdomen ever so intently, until her breathing slowed, and her frenzy subsided. He moved to straddle her hips, gathering her arms above her head, massaging her sore muscles as well as her sore conscience. The stroke of his fingers against her flesh soothed like a balm.

Reason fought with pleasure."Khyryn, let me up."

"Shhh."

"I want to leave. You lied to me." *And I bought every word.*

She wrestled against his caress, embarrassed by her body's traitorous response to his touch, his breath, his voice.

"Khyryn—"

His mouth grazed hers, cutting off all protests.

Damn him. He stopped her brain from all lucid thought. Every cell of her body tingled from the shocking electricity wherever his flesh met hers. She tensed, and relaxed as he flattened his body to stretch the length of her. Warm and firm, and fervently attentive, as he shifted his weight and parted her thighs with his own.

"You have returned successfully, I see."

Wynne nearly leapt through him at the sound of an unfamiliar voice.

Her scream, followed by a string of profanities that would melt most men's ears, fell deafly on Khyryn's as she thrashed against him.

Khyryn also jolted at the sound, but did not move immediately from her. His hand clamped down on her mouth. She realized if he did move, the interloper would have quite a view indeed.

"Leave us, Aberswythe. Come back later," Khyryn said, gruffly.

Khyryn had called him by name.

He knew the guy. *Sonofabitch*. Damn him. And his friend.

Fear and fury welled inside her, and she bit his hand so fiercely he yelped and pulled away from her, leaving her completely exposed.

And free to escape.

"You son of a bitch! Get away from me," she spat out as she grabbed her shift and pulled it over her head, affording her some modicum of modesty.

"Damn! Where is my—" Before she could finish the question, she spied the *s'gian dhu* and had it in one hand as she lunged for her costume.

"Come near me, and I'll gut you both!"

She continued to shout obscenities at both men as she tugged the gown over her. She had poked her head through the opening and fought to clear her arms as Khyryn grabbed her by the wrist and sent the blade flying across the cave. She'd be damned if she'd let them think for one moment she wouldn't fight them until her last breath.

"No."

No yelling. No menace in his voice. He merely held her wrist and repeated the one word. Calmly.

"No."

Wynne, caught off guard by the simplicity his actions attempted to wrest her hand free. "Let go. Now," she ordered.

He might have strength, but he was also, completely naked—a fact Wynne took advantage of as she drew her knee up hard against his crotch, causing him to release her hand as he doubled over in voiceless pain. "Tell Richard, 'nice try'."

She had nearly cleared the cave entrance when she made contact with the wooden staff. And the ragged man who held it.

"It would be unwise to run off into the forest. Come. Break your fast."

A hermit—long mantle and robe, hair and beard white as snow, and plaited. The man who stood before her blocking her escape looked like a character who had stepped straight from the pages of a fantasy novel into the present day Wales.

His face bore a deep scratch that ran from his cheek down the side of his throat.

His eyes glimmered with recognition. Did he know her?

Wynne didn't care. "Get out of my way," she hissed as she tried to shove him aside.

In reply, he withdrew the staff. And promptly applied it to her calves, knocking her feet out from beneath her, and landing her so hard on the ground, she feared her whole body would split in two.

"It is unwise for you to go into the forest. Fury untethered serves neither the bearer, nor the object of intent."

Wynne gathered herself into a sit and stared up at the figure that loomed over her. What the hell did he just say? Her head still pounded, even as a new sensation prickled her spine.

Something...not right.

The old man, motionless, returned her gaze. At the moan from within the dark hollow of the cave, the hermit cracked a weary smile and nodded. "He is still alive at least."

A blush of triumph warmed her cheeks. "A temporary situation. Especially if he wanders out here," she called loudly over her shoulder.

The hermit turned from her and wandered several feet away to a small campfire, and surrendered his attention to a small pot that sat atop the coals. Having stirred the contents to his satisfaction with a small stick, he wrapped the hem of his robe around his hand and pulled the pot from the heat of the embers.

"You'll burn yourself," Wynne exclaimed.

He did not acknowledge her, but brought the end of the stick to his mouth. "Hmm. Come. Eat."

Without waiting for her reply, he poured some of the thick liquid into a small bowl and held it out for her to take. Wynne reluctantly moved to accept his proffered gift, unsure what to do next.

"You need not fear. It will not harm you. It is not what you are accustomed to, but it is warm, and will fill your belly. Eat."

Wynne stared at the dark, murky glop that thickened even as she watched it cooling in chill of morning. The warmth of the bowl did feel good against her hands. "What is it?"

"Berries. Ground chestnut. And the drippings from the beeswax.

His words momentarily shifted in her brain, and she asked, "Honey?"

"The dew from the bees. Yes. Honey. I sometimes forget the modern words. So long have I called it otherwise."

It did smell sweet like honey. Wynne lifted the bowl to her lips and sipped. Bittersweet. And warm. Not completely unlikable. "Thank you. It's good."

He stripped the leaves from the twig he had used to stir the small pot and handed them to her. "Chew. It will help the journey that pounds still in your head."

"Excuse me?"

"Your head. The willow will make the pounding stop."

"How did you know?"

"The body suffers for the trip through the stones."

"The what?"

"Abwerswythe." Khyryn's voice, a bit hoarse, captured the old man's attention. "I did not tell her."

"Tell me what?" Wynne dropped the leaves and turned her attention to the figure who spoke from behind her.

Khyryn's frame eclipsed the entrance of the hermit hole. He had donned a tunic he wore yesterday. Though it covered his body well enough, his legs were uncovered. He had not dared to pull on the breeks. The dark line of irritation and pain that creased his brow brought a heat to her face again. He stood with his arms stretched over his head, braced against the wall of

stone.

Something inside her chest fluttered at the sight of him, staring at her. She could feel the heat that smoldered inside him, even from where she sat.

"Tell me what?"

The old man stared at him, then at her. "You brought her through the stones—"

"I brought her through without telling her. If she had known—"

She didn't like being ignored. "Tell me what?"

"I could not, Aberswythe. Time would not permit it." He winced as he grabbed his side, reminding Wynne he still had a nasty gash on his side from the day before.

Hell's bells. In the sunlight, neither was as scary as the shadows had made them seem. A hobo and a hermit, and no sense between them. She actually felt pity for them, eating berries and sleeping on the ground. "I'm going to the police station today. And you need a doctor—"

"How could you not tell her, Khyryn?" The hermit frowned. "You coupled."

Neither man seemed to notice her sitting between them reminding them of the urgency of the previous day's events.

"Hey! Tell me what?"

Khyryn made his way to the coals. "Uddryd."

"Uddryd? Where?"

"At the faire. He did not recognize me until two days ago. Then he challenged me."

The old man inhaled sharply. "He challenged you?"

Wynne interrupted, "That's why we have to find a

police station—"

"Aye," continued Khyryn. "His face was different. However, his eyes were the same. The hatred seethes in him still."

"Yet, he knew you? He remembered you?"

"As well as you say he remem—" Khyryn paused. "What happened to your face?"

The old man waved him off. "It is a scratch. Nothing more. And yet, with him at you, and her there, you did not tell her? Warn her?"

Wynne shot to her feet, scooped the bowl up and hurled it into the fire. "Son-of-a-bitch! Tell me what?"

As if she had appeared in a puff of smoke, they both suddenly turned their attention to her, in wonderment at her ire.

The hermit climbed to a stand and sighed heavily. "It is too soon for either of you to go back. It is uncertain whether either of you would survive the journey through the portal."

Wynne turned on her heel and strode back into the cave. She rummaged through the darkness, patting the ground until her hand met the cold metal of the small blade she had dropped earlier.

Let them argue over silly stones, portals. Before they talked themselves out, she would be bound for the nearest highway. The town must be no more than five miles south. Or east?

No matter. Regardless of the direction, sooner or later she would find a town or a phone box.

She pulled on her boots and tied the leather laces around her calves. Not the best choice for a long hike. Especially after the previous day's adventure in the rain. Still, even damp leather would beat walking through the woods or on the gravel roadside barefoot.

Wynne tucked the small knife inside the pocket of her gown and strode through the opening, tossing her gratitude over her shoulder as she sauntered past the two men and down the brush-covered slope.

"Thanks for dinner. And for breakfast. Oh, and for that thing we did last night."

"Where are you going?" two voices rang out in unison.

She didn't even slow her stride. "Back to town. Remember? I have a demented director to deal with. There's a price on my head."

****

Long steps worked to soothe sore muscles as well as her bruised pride. The longer she walked, the harder her steps pounded the earth. Whatever insanity she had given into yesterday, she could certainly shuck today.

The old hermit had been right about one thing. Her head did pound mercilessly, despite the chill of early morning. She wished she had grabbed the water skin. If only her head would stop aching, perhaps her thoughts would clear and she could get her bearings.

Which way to the road?

A twig snapped and she wheeled around nearly jumping out of her own flesh. A few feet away, a brindle colored fox halted its own steps to stare at her in curious appraisal. For nearly a minute the two stood transfixed—not a full five feet between them.

"Hello, beauty," Wynne finally whispered. "It's all right. I won't hurt you. How pretty you are—"

The rest of her words fell silently from her lips as she fell to the ground, a heavy weight toppling her, pounding her kidneys and brain as it landed.

The stench of urine and musk mingled with the rotten hot breath that grazed her ear. "Mind, Witch, this is my hunting ground," came the gruff voice. Two rough hands clawed at her hair and smashed her face into the damp leaves and moist lichen covered dirt. "Nae need of yer kind here. Tell the hermit it is fair warning. Else, next time they'll slit yer throat and string you to bleed out like a boar for the spit. You, Witch will be a sacrifice to yer own heathen gods."

As abruptly as it had felled her, the weight lifted from her back, allowing her lungs to drink gasps of air. She did not even try to follow the sound of retreating footfalls.

When she dared to open her eyes, she found two rust colored orbs staring back at her from the shelter of the lowest growth of vines. As she lay trembling, the small fox stepped delicately from its hiding place. Pawing at the earth near her face, it sniffed her hand, her hair, her clothing, never fully wrenching its gaze from hers. Then, for no reason Wynne could fathom, the creature padded in a circle—thrice—and curled up in the crook of her arm, settling, as if to take its guard of her.

"I hope you've had your shots," she murmured as senselessness overtook her.

Chapter Nine

Uffyngdon, 1016 A.D.

Eadric Streona slipped the toe of his boot beneath the boy's chin and lifted ever so slightly, so that the pressure from his foot lifted the boy's gaze to meet his own. The day not yet born and this snipe had wrested him from a pleasing dream.

His temper flared foul with a desire to flay the skin from the child's bones. However, the boy did possess much information to interest him in these dark hours.

He sneered his disdain at the mud-caked whelp. "Are you certain?"

Tears dampened the boy's lashes. Fear. Such weakness caused the youth to shiver as he nodded his ascent.

"Yes, sire. Cnut could not hold the line against the king. H-he f-fell back with his troops. They say the king gained this campaign against the Danes. A-and...they say King Edmund strengthens his legions with reinforcements from the Cymry in the West."

Nonsense The Danes had secured Cymry long ago. The tribal kings would never risk the wrath of Cnut to support Edmund. And yet—if what the boy said was true...

Aberswythe.

He emptied the contents of his cup before he turned

his attention again to the whimpering rat of a boy before him. He loathed weakness, and this runt reeked of it. Had he pissed himself from fear? The thought amused him, briefly.

He leaned forward until his face was only a hand's length from his informant's. "Did you know in ancient Rome and Greece, the messenger who delivered ominous tidings often met an equally ominous reception? Often his life was forfeit for the news he bore."

The boy swallowed hard and fell back onto his heels as if to scurry to the darkest corner. His eyes darted left and right, seeking escape.

"Of course, if I did that each time I received news not to my liking—well, soon, I would have no one I could trust, would I? Tell me, boy—can I trust you?" He waited a beat for his words to settle in the child's head. "Or should I cut your traitorous tongue from your head and feed it to my hounds?"

Eadric reveled at the panic that paled the face before him. A snap of his fingers brought his two menacing monsters to heel, growling and baring their fangs at the waif, as if waiting for permission to attack.

"Y-you can trust m-m-me. It is the truth, sire. I w-would never lie to y-you."

Eadric sat back in his chair and crossed his legs casually, straightening his tunic, as he watched the last bit of color fade from his informant's face.

Power. That's what he loved. More than money. More than land. He loved the power to make people tremble. Kings seldom held such power.

I ought to know.

Kings and chieftains had to fight for the well-being

of their subjects. Kings had to negotiate truces. Agreements. Treaties. Kings yielded to the advice of the Church. To the demands of their knights.

As alderman and counselor, however, he wielded power over Edmund. And soon, over Cnut. After a thousand years, and so many lifetimes, he had finally gotten it right.

He snapped his fingers twice more, and both dogs relaxed.

"Yes. I think I can trust you. You stink with truth," he snarled. "Leave me. You may take sup in my kitchen for your reward. Then get out."

The boy skittered across the slate on his bottom and heels, not daring to turn his back on the hounds that yawned disinterest as he fled.

After all, Streona reasoned, why be a king, when you can control one? Or more? Regardless of the outcome of the latest battle, he would pledge his loyalty to the victor. To each, he had offered information to aid their strategies. To each, he had offered fealty. From both, he now gleaned the rewards of service.

The best reward? More power.

The thought of the old druid in the southlands haunted him, and he wondered at his own restraint when he recognized the face that he longed to wipe from his nightmares. How amazing a dozen lifetimes could not purge the putridness of Aberswythe from his mind.

I should have killed the old man when I had the chance.

For now, though, there were other matters more important than an old hermit who told stories of ancient kings and consorts.

He rose from his chair and strode toward his bedchamber. Slowly and methodically he undressed as he sought the comfort of a warm bed. Tomorrow he would ride to Edmund. Now, his body wanted sleep. And something more.

The tallow wick burned low allowing him to see only the slightest outline of the form that slept on the pallet bed. He would take glad tidings from his wife to her father on the morrow. Tonight, however, she would satisfy her husband's hungers.

Edith had been a keen acquisition. Marrying her had gifted him position, wealth, and a most intimate adjunct with Edmund. In exchange, he allowed his wife to remain on English soil—near her father.

Tomorrow he would use her to ingratiate himself once more into Edmund's confidence.

Edith was a valuable asset.

The thought of her frail body yielding beneath his, not daring to protest his lusts, enflamed his groin more.

He remembered another wife, not so obedient. Another time.

He dropped onto the pallet deliberately startling her as he fiercely straddled her. Her fear mewed— kittenish—as he found her mouth first, then her sex. Finally her surrender.

Surrender marked her his.

His wife. His concubine. His servant. He could take any woman he wanted within his lands. But Edith, as wife, would give herself to him in duty. She would yield to his will, and no other man's. She knew if she dared to cross him, he would kill her.

And she feared him for that.

Yes. In this lifetime, he had finally gotten it right.

****

Khyryn slithered silently through the brush toward the muffled voices. Four of them. Near the water's edge. He flattened himself against the ground and slowed his breathing so as not to give any clue to his presence.

Swords hung from the belts of two of the men. Not plowmen, these men. Another stood quietly behind them while the fourth paced nervously, back and forth as if waiting for an answer.

"I did, did I? I delivered yer message to the druid." The creature—for it was difficult to label it either male or female—rung its hands gingerly and laughed triumphantly.

"Tell us, Bog," one of the guards asked, "Was there another man with him?"

The creature stopped. Two dark, frightened eyes stared out from beneath a matted tangle of leaf and twig-strewn hair.

Confusion. And fear. The scent of fear hung—rank and musky—in the air.

Khyryn stifled the gag that rose in his throat from the odor that stung his eyes. He had smelled this before. He had cleansed Wynne's body of this stench. Anger roiled in his muscles as he fought the urge to strike.

"An—another man? Another man?" the creature repeated. "No. No other man. Bog see'd no other man."

Khyryn heard the tinny change in its tone as it spoke. Bog lied. The eyes fluttered, darting from one guard to the other. Even if the creature had not seen him, Khyryn suspected it had seen Wynne. And used her to deliver the message.

"No other man, eh?" the other guard questioned.

"Well, then, Eadric's coin is well spent. The blood on your hands speaks for your loyalty to our master."

A coin bounced on the ground at the creature's feet. In one swift movement, the dirty paw seized the shiny disc and the creature leapt away from the two darkly clad men, yelping as if injured.

He is the one. He attacked Wynne.

The first guard drew his sword swiftly from his belt and sliced the air to a whistle as he brought the blade to the creature's head.

The creature trembled and cringed, trying to avoid the edge of sharpened blade. For the first time, Khyryn could see that a human held this figure. Hunched and pockmarked, one could not mistake the shuddering figure as a man's.

Beneath the tattered cloak, he wore nothing more than the hair upon his chest and a cloth draped protectively across his hips, barely concealing his manhood.

Now, there was more fresh blood than the dried, caked remnants the hunched man had no doubt wiped from Wynne's face as he had beaten her. A small trickle of fresh crimson fluid poured from the man's ear, down his jaw, across his shoulder.

"An', Bog," asked the bearer of the sword, "If you do see anyone else, what are you to do?"

"Findin' you, will I be," the man creature stammered. "By Bog's oath, I am to find you that tells him, I am."

"It's not yer oath we'll be takin' for our trophy if you cross us. Is it, Loth?"

For the first time, the figure nearest the water's edge shuffled his feet nervously. Khyryn shifted his weight slightly to get a better look at the scrawny figure that stood, glassy eyed, sniffling, and nodding to the guards. *No more than a boy, that one.*

The second guard stepped toward their captive and placed a boot soundly on the man's fur wrapped foot. "The boy knows, don' he? We take what is owed to us in flesh. One way or another."

Both men laughed as the second guard slapped his hand to Bog's crotch, squeezed hard, and twisted. A tiny mewl escaped as the tortured man doubled over.

The first guard withdrew his sword and restored it neatly beneath his belt. "Tha's all right. Bog'll do wa's right by Eadric. Right, Bog?"

Both men turned away then, and calling the young boy, Loth, to follow, they strode away from the stream's edge.

Eadric.

Khyryn considered the name. What did this Eadric want with Aberswythe? Moreover, which other man did they seek?

I am the one they seek. Why?

A low groan fluttered from the mass of filth and hair and rags that crouched at the water's edge. Bog.

Swift and low to the ground, like a badger, Khyryn lunged from his spot in the bushes and tackled the man, slamming his fist into the wretched creature's face. When the one they called Bog cried out, Khyryn clamped a hand over the man's nose and mouth, pressing his other hand over the man's throat.

"Do not cry out again, lest the others return and I give you to them," Khyryn growled. "Do you understand my words?"

Bog swallowed thickly beneath Khyryn's grip, and

nodded.

Khyryn rolled Bog onto his stomach, found the place between his shoulder blades, and promptly slid his knee to the spot that would cause Bog to stop breathing should he shift his full weight onto the informant's back.

"Quietly, Bog. Tell me about the men who left just now. Tell me what message they had for Aberswythe. Tell me about the woman you attacked."

A shiver rattled beneath him as Bog trembled and tried to move his head to speak.

"Nof'rig," came a muffled reply.

Khyryn shifted slightly, increasing his weight between the man's shoulders.

Bog squealed—much like a swine—and turned his head to the side. "Noffing. I did noffing wrong. Get off!"

Vile words mingled with vile odor as Bog began to thrash his arms, clawing at the ground and cursing until Khyryn sat fully on him.

"What sound is that?" Khyryn teased. "Perhaps it is your friends returning."

As if he had speared the man, Bog fell still and silent listening for any sound of approaching footsteps.

"They hunt Bogs and boys for game, do they not? You had best speak quickly, if you wish to escape their strength, and sense of sport."

"Protect me from 'em. Vipers they be. Serpents. By yer leave. Help me. I shall tell of it. All of it."

"Nae. Speak it first."

"I do. I do. It's 'em that wants Aberswythe to leave. No' me. Only I was t' take 'em's message so's 'em what wants it would stay hidden from his view."

The tremor of fear ricocheted through his boot.

"Why?"

"I dunno, does I? I did my part's all. Din I?"

"But you did not give the message to the druid. You gave it instead to the woman. Why?"

"I seen her at the fire that morn wi' the druid, din' I? Then, she gone off an' I can follow her easy enough. Tha's all. Sides, the druid has a stick and magic. I be no good as a frog, or snake, me. But the witch tells him, and her with no stick."

Khyryn moved to stand, carefully placing his boot on the man's back to ensure he did not scurry away. "Keep telling."

Bog wheezed beneath the weight. "An' I climbed the treed and swooped down. I know the druid walks the woods, and finds her he will. An' she would steal my food if she found my berries an' my fish. Thievin' witch."

Khyryn moved his foot to Bog's neck and pressed. "She is no witch."

Bog sputtered, "She be druid?"

"It is nae concern to you. What of the one they called Eadric?"

"I see him once."

"Where?"

"He rode through two, maybe three moons ago. He tries to steal my fish."

"Why?"

"They be fine fish. A morsel for—"

"No. Why did he ride through? Where did he go?"

"In the village I hear 'em. Streona they call him. Say he is brother by wife to Edmund."

"King Edmund? The king's brother-in-law?"

"Aye. Wicked he is. Them that crosses him wish for an easy death."

"And where will I find him? Is he near?"

"Nae—he speaks to Edmund. And Edmund listens, they say. They call him *Auld-ar-man*. Killed the king's other man, they say. Blinded his sons, so they canna smite him. He has hisself a grand house. I know naught o' tha'. I has only what I catches in this forest."

Two or three moons past. The man had recognized Aberswythe, or so the druid had thought. Uddryd?

"Take me to them."

"Them? The villagers?"

Impatience rankled Khyryn. "Nae. To the ones that paid you."

"Paid me?" Bog fidgeted where he lay, moving close to his body as if searching for something. "What pay do I know?"

"One gold coin will not save you from the misfortune of my wrath or my blade, Bog. Dead men have little need of coin. Aye. Dead men wear coins on their eyes, not in pockets." More to himself than to Khyryn, Bog giggled.

Khyryn released Bog then and waited as patiently as he could as the man clambered to his knees. Searching for, and finding the lost coin, Bog finally stood, as straight and tall as his crooked body allowed. His shoulders came only to Khyryn's chest.

Bog chortled again, seemingly unaware that anyone still waited. He turned and began to scurry toward the jagged tree line.

"Come," he called to Khyryn. "Come. I shows you 'em what seeks you."

Khyryn followed Bog as he streaked into the brush.

For someone so bent and twisted, Bog moved as quickly as any animal of the forest. Khyryn stayed at his heels, however, not letting his lead to Eadric's men disappear up a tree or escape into the green and brown hues of the earth that so matched the hermit's cloak.

I could track him by scent. Khryryn's nose burned from the acrid odor that hung in the air. Luckily, the breeze touching their faces meant they were downwind of their prey.

By comparison to Bog's scurried steps, Eadric's men moved with the slowness infected by power, having barely reached the wood's edge by the time Khyryn heard their footfall.

Bog crouched low to the earth, weaving back and forth, prowling. Khyryn kept hidden as well, waiting for an opportunity to pounce.

Two against three.

One of the soldiers stopped. "I need t' piss. Go on. I'll catch up."

Khyryn silently motioned to Bog, and the man climbed a nearby tree. With the inhuman agility of a squirrel, he scaled the trunk to perch amid the thicker first limbs.

With a nod of encouragement, Khyryn set off through the bushes to follow the other two. Bog, an unlikely ally, would no doubt enjoy the opportunity to seek a bit of revenge on the one.

In between the branches, Khyryn could see the young boy, his exhaustion marked by the ruts his feet made in the path as he dragged each step. The guard paid little attention to the boy other than to cajole him into quickening his pace. When the boy did not, he drew his sword and deliberately tripped the child, causing him to fall flat on his face. The guard hefted the sword flat side through the air toward the boy's backside.

Khyryn vaulted to action.

He leapt from the undergrowth headlong into the man, sending him flying face forward into a tree. By the time the man's face hit the bark, Khyryn had pulled out his own blade, two hands in length, and rammed the point beneath the man's shoulder blades.

"Tell your master, the lives of old men and boys are not fodder for sport."

The man yowled in pain and tried to grab the sword pinning him. Khyryn kneed him at the base of his spine, effectively ramming the man's cock fiercely against the tree trunk. Immediately the man's hands stopped their flailing and sought to rescue the endangered body part.

"Take care," Khyryn warned, "Else I reap what you have stolen from your victims from your flesh. Heed my warning. There is only one way I claim a man's flesh. I flay it from his bones."

"Wh-who are you?"

"To you, I am conscience. To your master, I am memory. Deliver my message."

Khyryn withdrew the blade so quickly from the man's shoulder the flesh hissed. Before the guard could turn fully around, Khyryn had retreated silently into the trees.

Chapter Ten

Wynne woke to the darkness of night. The breeze brushed her forearm, and she moved to sit up, tugging the blanket around her as she searched.

Back in the cave. Instead of Khyryn, however, she found a lump of fur at her side. When she touched it, it did not stir, but sighed deeply in its slumber.

Pain. Strange words. Someone in the woods. She'd been attacked.

Aberswythe's voice floated through the darkness. "Khyryn wanders. He cannot be still while you sleep. He fears your death."

"My death? Wait. How did I get here? How long have I been asleep?"

"Two days since we found you. Your body has been through much. We could not know if you would weather the crossing. Had you not been joined—"

"Two days? He kept me here two days? Why didn't he just take me to a hospital? Or at least go somewhere and call for help?

"Hospital? I know nothing of this word."

Irritation scratched her patience. "You and Khyryn are a piece of work, both of you. You put on this hermit act and lure unsuspecting people up here, not to mention that stink bomb of a psychopath in the woods who attacked me. I have nothing to give you. I have no money. I'm just—Two days? It's been nearly three days since the faire?" *Since I abandoned good sense for this hole in the wall?*

Even as she spoke the words, terror began to tingle her spine. Three days gone from her apartment. Three days held captive by these—"What do you plan to do with me?"

There. She said it.

Aberswythe did not move, or even quirk an eyebrow at her inquiry. He merely stared at her, blankly.

"The answer is not divined. Mayhap it is you who will show us your purpose here."

"My purpose? The only thing I plan to reveal is my backside when I crawl through that slit in the wall again. I'll take my chances with the long dark tunnel and that lunatic Richard over you crazies out here in the woods."

"You cannot leave."

"Yeah, well you and druid-boy keep telling yourselves that. Where are my clothes?"

The old man rose from where he sat, stepped through the outer entrance of the cave, and returned momentarily with the shift Wynne had been wearing under her costume. He handed her the garment and resettled himself on the floor of the cave.

"Whatever you believe of Khyryn or the world you left behind, you must put aside. It will not help you here."

"Are you threatening me?"

"There is no threat. Only truth to my words. Your world does not exist here."

"My world is about six miles on the other side of this cave," Wynne said as she dragged the shift over her body, and cast off the blanket. "And as soon as I get there, I assure you I will do everything in my power to forget your little coven, here."

"Where do you think you are, Gwynndolwyn?"

"Damn every last one of you. Why do you insist on calling me that?"

"What would you have us call you? Is Gwynndolwyn not your name?"

Wynne let an exasperated huff escape her lips. "Yes. Once and for all. That's what's on my birth certificate. I have no idea how you, or Khyryn, or that fortune teller found out. But I wish you would stop—"

"Fortune teller?"

"Elleran. She called me by my given name, too. Look, Wynne is what I go by. It's worked for the past twenty-eight years, and it can continue to work—"

"Twenty-eight years is nothing, my dear. Try a thousand plus a three hundred more."

"Fourteen hundred years of what?"

"That is how many years I have walked this world. My name is Aberswythe. And I have known you for nearly as long."

Lunacy. Sheer madness.

"Of course," he continued, "you are nearly as ageless. Except that you have been reborn tenfold. And without memory."

Again that tinge of fear streaked up her spine. "What?"

"What year do you believe this to be?"

"It's 2009."

"Not here."

"What do you mean, 'not here'?"

"The Christians celebrate this as the *ado domenai*

1016. Their leader has been dead for a millenium."

Wynne's ears obviously had misunderstood the old man. Or he really did suffer from dementia.

"Strange is it not? That a land forged from stone and leaf, built by the might of the stars and heavens, yields to the words of a man crucified by the same people who sanctify him?"

All the while he spoke Wynne watched his eyes. He searched hers as if waiting for a response. To what?

She wished she had a weapon. And where were her boots? "What does any of this have to do with me?"

"You were once one of us." The deep somber voice that answered heralded Khyryn's return. He stepped into the glow the small fire cast against the darkness of night.

His hair and clothes were soaked—they clung to his body, a bit too revealingly for her comfort.

Suddenly, she remembered how she had gotten back here. "You! You threw me into the river. I could have died from hypothermia. I could have drowned—"

"Dunking you in the stream brought you back to us," explained Aberswythe. "When we found you, badly beaten about the head, you would not wake or respond in any way. I told Khyryn to take you into the stream. And it is he who brought you back from your dance with the spirit realm."

"Spirit realm, my ass. Where is my knife?"

Khyryn pulled the *s'gian dhu* from his belt and handed it to her. "I used it to cut the gown from your body."

"I'll just bet you did."

"I have clothes for you."

"Of course you do. You keep extras on hand for all

the girls you kidnap, right?"

Khyryn shot her a look of pure innocence. "Kid nap? What does a gown have to do with baby goats?"

"Okay, if you don't like kidnap, how about abduct, steal, hold captive, incarcerate, imprison—"

Aberswythe waved his hand. "You are no prisoner here, Gwynndolwyn. We need your help."

"Aberswythe, she is right. She is captive. I will not let her leave here alone."

Desperation chimed in her ears at his words. She had to escape from this hellhole and these lunatic hippies. She leapt up, slashing at him with the very blade he had entrusted to her again.

Her equilibrium faltered and she missed his chest. Instead, the blade scraped his forearm as he jumped out of her path.

"There is much in the forest that could harm her," he spat as she fell to the ground. "Including her own stubbornness."

He delicately placed a foot across her wrist and bent to slide the knife from her grip. "It is fortunate you did not fall on the blade and cut yourself."

"You cannot keep me here forever." Even as the words escaped her lips, she shivered at her own disbelief. The truth was, if these men lived like this, unheeded by local police, they could keep her here for a very long time.

Or they could just kill her and leave her to rot in the woods. "Someone will find me."

Khyryn grabbed her forcefully and yanked her to her feet. "And if they do?"

For the first time since this nightmare began, his face reflected a fury—a rage—that terrified her.

"Have you any thoughts on what they will do to a lone woman, traveling through these lands without escort? I know what a warrior does. I know what it is to enjoy the spoils of a victory. Your foolishness and pride will not defend you out there on your own. It did not defend you against the one who beat you and left you to die two days ago. It did not defend you from Uddryd or from his guards. It does not even defend you from me."

Nothing protected her from this tirade. Embarrassment heated her cheeks. "I am not a child you can intimidate."

"A child would be wise enough to be scared." He stood over her, unrelenting. His fury crashed in waves over her.

His grip tightened on her wrist. "I know the lust that writhes in the belly of men when they glimpse the curve of your breast, your hip, your mouth."

As if holding her pained him, he released her. To Aberswythe he said, "As long as she is here, she *is* captive."

His voice did not soften as he moved into the shadows. "Captive you are safe."

****

Silence was more deafening than chastisement.

Surely hours, not minutes had passed. The fire had waned. Wynne sat near the wall, petting the fox, which had claimed her as its own. It lay curled at her ankle.

Khyryn shuffled in the dark, and sat upon the cold earthen floor.

Aberswythe broke the spell. "She is safe. She is alive."

"She might have died. She may still."

"You must still your rage. It was not her fault. Nor

is it yours."

"Then whose?"

A slight frown edged the old man's brow. "If blame lies with anyone, it rests with me. I knew him as a child. I knew his strength. And his weakness."

"As you knew mine," Khyryn countered.

"You were ever a better student than he. Ours was never his destiny."

A hiss sounded and all three turned toward the pallet where Wynne had slept. Awakened from her nap, the brindle fox sat crouched on the blanket hissing at Khyryn.

Aberswythe whispered, "The vixen protects her mistress. Beware, Khyryn, lest our fox friend snaps at your ankle as Gwynndolwyn has nipped your arm, and leaves you to lick your own wounds."

At his admonition, Gwynndolwyn gently stroked her furry protector. "Truly a better judge of character than I am." She opened a hand to let the vixen sniff, and then gently scratched beneath its chin.

Khyryn watched her from the darkness. Once more, she sat at the mercy of the two men.

"Such has always been your talent, Gwynndolwyn," the old man said. "To soothe and know the heart of those that walk on four legs. As in ancient times, so is it in the future, and in the present."

Aberswythe's smiled faded. "Uddryd never studied to become druid. Never understood our ways. He was king. At least until the red men claimed the village."

"Who are the red men?" Gwynndolwyn's voice seemed smaller than it ever had.

Khyryn did not move from where he sat. "Romans. The same Romans you claimed built this country into an empire also claimed your life over one thousand years ago."

"And you would know this from—?"

Khyryn's voice had lost its rage. He could not meet her gaze, but stared into the last glowing embers and remembered what she never would. "I saw it."

"You mean like Elleran sees things?"

He shook his head, then realized she couldn't see him. "I do not share Elleran's sight. I did watch in a vision, though, as the soldiers marched toward the village. I could not reach you in time to save you. I could not save anyone."

Wynne shook herself and hugged the vixen to her chest as though the bundle of fur were a talisman from any spell his words might cast.

"You bear the mark upon your flesh still." Khyryn continued. "I saw it the night we passed through the stones."

"The night we—?"

"On your stomach, the scar still rests to remind you of that night."

Wynne's fingers drifted across her waist. "It's just a birthmark."

"The dagger made by my hand and given to you in celebration made that mark. I found you impaled on that blade, abandoned in a pool of your own blood."

"It is a birthmark. Nothing more."

"Because I sought to save myself from the agony of my own desire, I cost you your life."

Wynne's stomach churned at his confession. He actually believed his own words. Wynne's grandmother had once said a chill which makes the hair stand on end was someone standing on her grave. Based on the cold that enveloped her now, dancing was a better description.

A searing pain gnawed at her birthmark, as if responding to his words.

Wynne sighed, exasperated. She had read of people who got caught up in fantasy games, and let it consume their lives. But two in one spot?

"None of this makes any sense. Look at me. I am flesh and blood. Not dead. There are no Roman soldiers pounding down the doors, waiting to carry me off, and I have no wounds—"

"There is still Uddryd," Aberswythe said. "He remembers also. He will not let you leave."

Wynne's head began to spin again. How many times since Saturday had she heard those same words spoken by different people?

Elleran. Khyryn. Richard. And now, Aberswythe.

Each spoke the others' words. Each called her by her given name. A name that only existed on her passport and birth certificate. A name no one had used since her parents' death.

Exhaustion fought against her reason. Why had no one come looking for her?

"Why are you doing this? Why are you making up lies?" Again a pain wrenched her gut, nearly doubling her over.

"There are no lies here," Aberswythe said calmly. "Only the sadness of truth this night. Khyryn's gift was one of celebration and nuptial. He meant to leave the village and so leave you to the life you were destined for."

"And what life is that?"

"See Aberswythe, she does not remember. She will

not. Nor will she be of use to you in any of this."

A great bitterness in Khyryn's words echoed in the darkness of the cave. "You were Uddryd's wife. And his queen.

Chapter Eleven

By morning, summer had yielded to autumn. Frost bit at the grass. Similarly, what little patience she had left gave way to temper. Though her ribs still ached, her head had finally cleared a bit.

"Why?" Wynne demanded. "Why did you bring me back here?"

"Because it is necessary," Khyryn replied.

Admittedly, the thought of running off into the woods on her own again no longer appealed to her as it had a week ago.

"Well, I am not going anywhere with you. Or with your mentor. Let Richard find me. Let him take me to the police. At least they have heat and showers in the local jails. Not to mention coffee."

"There will be no *gaol*. He will kill you."

The sight of Khyryn saddling the horses that had mysteriously appeared outside the cave when she awoke caused Wynne more alarm than anything else. These were not the regular horses she had seen at the faire.

"You and the hermit are a little too into your roles, you know that? Horses? Absolutely-not-going-to-happen."

Shimmering, with a coat the color of cinnamon, the stallion stood at least sixteen hands high. Sixteen of Khyryn's hands. Or more. A Clydesdale. Where would he get a Clydesdale horse here in the middle of nowhere? And how did he manage to hide it?

The second horse stood nearly as tall—dappled grey and white—with a silken mane. Just like Aberswythe.

No one watching.

Wynne ran into the cave, straight to the sliver in the back wall. She crawled through the crevice and the daylight behind her faded to shadow. Stealthily, she padded along the passage. No more than six miles back to the castle. An easy walk on a brisk day.

Truth be told, she almost believed Khyryn and Aberswythe. Several days with no jets overhead. No engines sounded from any direction. And the gown she now wore had been hand sewn. No machine stitches.

Where was the air force? Several times each week, pilots on maneuvers flew this region. Sometimes low and visible, other times invisibly high, heralded only by the roar of their speed far above the clouds. Now, silence blanketed the skies.

She slammed into the wall and landed flat on the cold floor.

A dark panic seeped into her brain as she tried to fathom her error. This had to be the tunnel. No other passages branched off. She pressed her hand against the wall. Rock and dirt.

How could an underground passage just disappear?

Impossible. Tunnels don't just disappear.

It didn't disappear.

It doesn't exist.

She stayed where she had fallen, shaking until her teeth chattered. Her frustration soaked her lashes until the tears trickled down her cheeks.

No, no, no. It must exist.

Silence. As it had for the past three days, silence roared, cacophonous, around her. Where were the fighter jets? Where was the distant sound of traffic?

Footfall sounded on the earthen floor. Wynne sat up, waiting for him to speak. No light pierced the blackness of the tunnel, yet he found her crumpled on the ground and—wrapping his arms around her—pulled her to her feet.

No words. No reproach. Khyryn quietly led her back through the crevice, out of the cave, and to the waiting, massive warhorse that pawed anxiously at the ground.

She sank, utterly dumbfounded, onto a weathered tree stump. What bothered her more? The fact she had not taken him seriously? Or the possibility he had told her the truth?

Khyryn mounted the animal, then pulled her from a tree stump onto the back of the horse to sit behind him. Vertigo overtook her, and she wrapped her hands around the muscular waist swathed in wool. Her fear of falling battled with another, darker thought.

Somehow, Wynne had fallen through a crevice in time and now sat, firmly planted in the eleventh century.

****

Blood splattered as the guard fell away from Eadric's fisted blow. The man's head met the solid oak table with a loud crack as he landed on the slate floor.

Eadric turned his attention to the second guard who hovered in the doorway. "You. Come."

Reluctantly, the man shuffled toward the table. In warning, the first guard groaned in pain.

Eadric paced, stalkingly, around the second man. Even in the dim morning light, bruises marked the man's throat. "Tell me, how did you come to have such marks on your flesh?"

The wary man glanced at his friend on the floor and cleared his throat. "Sir, there was a man—"

"Yes. Bog. I hear he dealt with the old man."

"No. Yes. He did. There was another man."

Eadric watched the muscles contract in the guard's throat as the words spilled from his lips.

Another man. Heat roiled in his neck, spiraling into his brain, scorching his memory. Igniting his temper.

He wrapped his fingers around the man's throat, his fingers carefully meeting the bruises left by some other hand. "Another man? Gareth said nothing of another man."

"We kept walkin' when Gareth stopped to piss. He never saw the man."

"So, you let Loth escape?"

"He ran when the man attacked us—"

Eadric squeezed gently, eliciting a hiss of pain from the man he held in his grip. "Tell me, Marcus, what did this other man look like?"

Marcus's lips quivered, yet the man dared not move against the alderman's hold. "I, uh—I did not see 'is face."

"You did not see his face?" Eadric tightened his hold and lowered his voice to a feral whisper. "Are you certain a whore did not leave these marks upon your skin? Mayhap a whore stole the boy, the same way she stole your ballochs."

"No, sire. I swear. I speak the truth. There another man. He said I should say—"

"Tell me what?"

"Memory. He told me to say you would know 'im as memory."

Eadric loosened his grip ever so slightly. "Did he?"

"Aye. He said to tell you that—"

"What?"

"He said auld men and boys are no sport."

"Are they not? What of grown men, Marcus? What sport do they offer?" He tightened his hold once more.

Marcus wriggled against his master's grasp. "I dunno—"

"Marcus. Such a noble name. Do you know that your name traveled here with the Romans who invaded this land more than a thousand years ago?

The soldier swallowed hard.

"I thought not. Marcus Aurelius. Emperor of Rome. A king of sorts. A weak king. He believed man to be a creature of compassion—the universe benevolent. Do you share his philosophy as well as his name, Marcus? Are you forgiving?"

Gareth, who had remained at Eadric's feet, now scurried under the table. Vermin. Whining like a dog licking his wounds.

"Gareth—you are alive, after all. Come out from your hole and show Marcus how benevolent I can be."

Gareth crawled from beneath the oak-planked table, stammering as he stood. "We'll find him, sire. We'll find Loth, we will. An' Bog, too."

"Silence, Gareth." Eadric lessened his hold on Marcus and eyed the other man.

"Gareth, hand me your dagger."

"Sire?"

Eadric held out his hand. "Give me your dagger.

Surely, you are not so much an oaf you do not carry it on your person. Are you such an oaf, Gareth?"

Gareth lowered his eyes, his head bobbing like a subservient hound as he pulled the dagger from the sheath that hung from his belt. The blade and the hand holding it trembled as the guard obeyed Eadric's command.

Eadric turned the dagger over, inspecting the roughly forged metal. Nicks and dirt marred the sheen. Apparently, Gareth took no better care of his weapons than he did his own person.

"Gareth, your dagger is as dull as your wit. How do you manage to eat?"

"I—it cuts well enough, sire. I will show you—"

"No need, Gareth."

Eadric closed his hand around the hilt of the knife and slashed through the air, ripping the battered blade across Marcus's throat, so swiftly, the guard could not raise his hand in defense. Neither cry, nor shriek left his lips—only a garbled mewl as his hands found Eadric's robes.

Blood spewed across Eadric's tunic. As the life force flowed from the man who delivered Khyryn's message, Marcus' eyes wide with terror glazed quickly.

Eadric wiped the blade on Marcus's sleeve. "I never cared for Romans. They so often bear bad tidings."

Marcus crumpled to the floor in a puddle, as Gareth cowered nearby.

"Gareth, take him away and clean up this mess. And do sharpen that blade."

As the blood flowed from Marcus, so did Eadric's ire dissipate. Replaced, by memory.

Gwynndolwyn had lain on the grass atop her own tunic. Shimmeringly pale, her breasts taut. Her nipples hard as pearls resting on an open oyster shell. A gift from the heavens, this glimpse of the woman who would share his life, lead his people, give him heirs.

Hidden among the reeds, he had reveled in the thought of her yielding to his touch. He watched her as she lounged in the sun's heat, rivulets of water lapping at her curves as her hands played gently across her own flesh.

Three dusks would bring her to his bed as his wife. Three dawns would see his desire sated—his queen ripe and filled with his seed.

The thicket of berries trembled as the intruder broke through the branches, breaking the downy soft moss with his steps as he broke her slumber. The swathed figure knelt beside her nakedness and stretched his limbs to match her length, brushing her hair from her brow as he spoke.

In a moment that stilted time, the future fell away from him as Khyryn's hushed voice asked, "Do you hunger?"

"Only for you," she had replied. "Khyryn."

The thorn of jealousy pierced Eadric at the recollection of the betrayal. Of the treachery.

****

The vice grip around Khyryn's waist slackened. The heat of her breath against his back warmed him. She slumbered. He laid one hand across both of hers, delicately holding her wrist so she would not slip from behind him as they rode.

Once more, Khyryn knew the warmth of her flesh against his, the sound of her voice in his ear, the taste of her tears on his lips. It did not matter that she could not remember the past. He held her now. Alive. In his arms.

Two horses fell to into step with one another. "Your mind wanders like the one who sleeps against you," Aberswythe said. "It is one thing for her to be here. It is another thing indeed to have her be with you. Is it not?"

"That she is here, now, and safe, is all I care about."

"But the heavens may have other plans for your queen."

Khyryn bristled. "It is by the heavens she is here. I brought her. I will protect her."

"Beware your greed, Khyryn, and that your humility is not tainted by your own desires.

"My own desires? Do not preach to me, old man. I have lived quietly this life. I seldom make war with any man. I do not covet what I do not have."

"What of Gwynndolwyn? You do not covet her?"

The wood fell quiet around them for several minutes as they continued their journey. Finally, Khyryn answered his mentor. "I accepted my fate long before this lifetime. You are responsible for her being here—torn from her own time."

"Your own desire sent you through the stones. And your lust brought you both back."

"It was my own lust that cast the curse and killed her in the first place."

"No, Khyryn. The responsibility for Gwynndolwyn's death is not yours. Neither are you to blame for Elleran's rage at the heavens. You will not fail Gwynndolwyn once her task is revealed."

The leaves rustled a murmur of consent as a chill

wind assaulted the riders. Khyryn's muscles knotted in response, not to the breeze, but to Aberswythe's admonition. "What have you seen?"

The old man shook his head as a sad smile tugged at his mouth. "The heavens do not confide in me all things. I know not what is to come. The raven perches low in the oak ahead. Look and tell me what *you* see."

Khyryn turned his gaze to the clump of oaks just ahead of their path, to the right. One branch bent low enough to brush a rider's head. There, perched in wait, sat a great ebony bird. A sentinel.

Foreboding consumed Khyryn, and he tightened his grip on Gwynndolwyn until she moaned and stirred against him.

The raven vaunted his wings, which glistened onyx in daylight, and then craned his head sideways to meet Khyryn's stare, nodding, as if in recognition.

Ravens were portent of change. Of conflict. Of death.

Khyryn tugged the reins and slowed the horse's gait. Aberswythe did the same. Khyryn caught his friend's attention and motioned for him to ready his sword. He nudged his passenger awake and whispered, "You must wake and hold tight again. Do you hear?"

Gwynndolwyn's sharp intake of air confirmed she had indeed heard. A small gasp escaped her as she sat fully upright, fumbling to place a distance between her body and his. He tapped her hand and said again, in a low, reassuring voice, "Hold on tight. I must grip rein and sword."

Her hands tightened on his waist again. "What is it? What's happening?"

"Mayhap no more than a bird eyeing the road for

bugs and acorns. The wind shifts, and so shall we."

The raven recoiled and ruffled his feathers as they drew closer. Talons firmly planted, the beast moved toward the end of the limb. Closer to them.

The nape of Khyryn's neck tingled, and he unsheathed his sword. Aberswythe sat ready to flank and protect Gwynndolwyn.

A gust of wind. Movement in the thicket of the trees. The raven sprang from his perch and swooped down toward them, wings spread two arm's lengths as the jet harbinger of doom flew directly at the stallion. The horse snorted and reared its head in warning as the bird swept shadow overhead.

A crunching of rock and leaves to their right swung Khyryn around, slicing air with drawn blade as he met the sound.

Matted, and rife with the stink of his own body, the familiar form of Bog clambered toward them, scurrying from the brush.

"Bog finds 'im! See. I knows the way of ravens. An' men. See?"

Khyryn pulled up his sword in time not to separate the man's head from his body. That's when he saw the second figure, still hidden behind the tree trunk.

Khyryn pointed the sword at the shadowed form. "Show yourself."

The small creature danced where it stood, one foot ready to follow his command, the other turned to flee.

"Come, I said. Bog, why do you follow us?"

"Finds you, an' the druid, I does. I knowed you would go North, I did. I says so. The raven knows an' follows. So, I follows the bird." Bog bounced around where he stood as if dodging some imaginary winged predator. "Bad bird. Ravens know much. Tell nuffin'. See—" he called over his shoulder, "I tells you we finds 'em what can protect us."

Slowly, silently, the figure in the trees moved from the cloak of shadows and leaves. Sunlight caught the pale streaks of hair atop the youth's head.

The boy, Loth.

Sheepishly, the child moved toward the path. His glance darted about, nervously searching for any sign of danger.

Gwynndolwyn's screech of recognition offered little warning to Bog or to Khyryn as she slid from the safety of the horse's back to the ground and charged at the ragged man.

"You! You're the one who hit me. You stinking son-of-a—"

Khyryn reached down and grabbed her arm, but could do little to stop the boot that met its target when it clipped Bog's chin, knocking the heap of hair and rags to the ground.

"Let go of me. He's the one. He attacked me."

Khyryn had her nearly off the ground by one arm, now. Still she spat and hissed like a trapped animal.

"Stay yer words, woman."

Bog threw a handful of dirt at her. "Witch! Druid's witch!"

Khyryn yanked her away from her victim. "Silence! Both of you stop."

"Witch kills Bog. All of us, I says. The raven knowed where t' find her, it did. Ravens know death. Witch kills—"

"Like you tried to kill me? And nearly succeeded. Mangy animal! You smell like you're already dead!"

As if to fulfill Bog's prophecy, she broke free of Khyryn's grasp and bolted again at the hunch-backed man. This time, Khyryn slid from his saddle—sword still in hand—to stand between the two hissing badgers.

"Stay yerselves, before I thrash both of you."

Gwynndolwyn's face reddened with anger. "You wouldn't dare, and if you did—"

Khyryn lowered the tip of the blade to the safety of the ground. "Then we would be wasting daylight." A wicked thought crossed his mind. "If I did use the blade, the first thing cut would be yer gown. We could see which falls first, your modesty or your temper."

She jumped back from him, two dots of crimson blooming on her already flushed face, and pointed an accusing finger at Bog. "But that man—"

"I saves you. I does. I doesn't tell 'em. Does I, Druid son? I doesn't tell his soldiers I see you. Or the witch. An' I hit the one what pisses in the woods. Don' I, druid son?"

Behind him, a chuckle escaped Aberswythe, who watched from his mount with something more than mild amusement, Khyryn noticed.

Druid son. Son of Aberswythe. Well, the old druid had raised him, to some degree.

The boy crouched as if to disappear by sheer will. Khyryn looked first at Bog, then at the boy.

"Bog, why is he with you?"

Bog shrugged.

"I ran away," the boy replied.

Relief flickered in Khyryn. "And found a kindred spirit in Bog—the two of you, outcasts?"

Snot trickled down the boy's upper lip as he glanced first at Khyryn, then at Aberswythe. In need of food. And sleep. The red circles and dark bruises that marked his face a few days ago had barely faded.

Gwynndolwyn turned away. "God, he smells *worse* than bog water. How can you—"

Bog wagged a finger at her. "Likes the swamps, Bog does. Witches don' like water, do they? Water melts witches. Heaven water melts witches. Witches melt when the heaven water comes."

Gwynndolwyn leapt at the bundle of rags. "Why you—"

Khyryn broke her charge for the second time. "Bog, I told you she is no witch. Explain why you follow us."

"We go with you, now, that you protect us, druid son. We help."

Gwynndolwyn snorted. "Protect you? From what—besides me—is he going to protect you? Nothing would get close enough to touch you, the way you smell."

"Aye, witch. Smart I is that I stink. Animals don' eat Bog that way. But Eadric's men. They are not creatures of the forest. His men—evil. As he is. Druids and witches know this evil? Aye?"

As if conjured by Bog's words, a cold wind howled through the trees, threateningly.

Loth clasped his thinly-clad arms to his chest, shivering in the gust as he stared expectantly at the three riders.

"Sire—" said the boy. "What Bog says is true. Master Eadric is evil. I know."

Nausea welled in Khyryn's stomach. "Tell me, Loth. What do you know?"

"He commits treason against the king."

Khyryn exchanged a knowing glance with Aberswythe. "What treason does he seek to commit, Loth?"

Loth shuffled from one foot to the other, ready to run.

Khyryn crouched as if to coax a wary animal. "Loth. You've naught to fear from anyone here." He looked over his shoulder at Gwynndolwyn, who had retreated to the horse, then he spoke to the boy again. "You heard my words to Bog. Gwynndolwyn is no witch. You have my word. Now—tell me what treason Eadric plots."

"Murder. Like before."

"What do you mean, 'like before'?"

"When he killed Lord Uddryd. That's how he became alderman to the king. And Uddryd's sons. He burned out their eyes and tongues, so they could not name him."

Loth's words poured over Khyryn like the water in winter. He remembered in that instant the evil of an ancient king.

And his soul shivered.

Chapter Twelve

If ever a troll existed, Wynne thought, the stinking man must be one.

Bog emerged from darkness, his scent cloaked barely by the scent of the campfire and the direction of the wind. Clinging to the ground—like a badger—he scurried toward Khyryn. He hovered near his tall 'Druid son', ever watchful, as if expecting Wynne to exact her revenge at any moment.

Good.

Bog sniffed the air. "Something comes."

The hair bristled on Wynne's neck.

"Aye, yer witch feels it, too. 'Tis bad. I smells it."

"Bog—" began Khyryn.

"Aye, I knows. She's nae witch. An' Bog is nae a troll."

Wynne nearly leapt from her own skin. "What did you say?"

"Bog is too small," he said, a wily smile spreading across his crooked mouth and glistening in his wary eyes. "Bog moves like the mist. Quiet. Trolls isnae quiet. Or clever. Bog isnae a—"

"Bog—what comes? Did you see it?"

A self-reproaching laugh tickled the creature. "Bog doesna'see. Tha's druid-magic. Bog smells 'em."

Khyryn slowly straightened and moved to stand. "Who?"

"The red one."

The shock on Khyryn's face nearly knocked Wynne flat. Whatever the troll might have said, Khyryn clearly had not expected this.

Bog hissed and grinned at her, knowingly.

"Do you mean *red men*?" Khyryn asked.

"Nae. The man with flamed hair who rides upon the great red dragon across the sea. Cain's knot."

Wynne's patience waned. "Khyryn, he's talking nonsense—"

A twig snapped, somewhere in the darkness.

In the echo of the twig's break, Khyryn unsheathed his dagger. "Shh!"

His hand clapped around her neck and pushed her to the cold earth.

Bog scurried into the shadows, taking with him any peace.

Snap.

Wynne gasped and tried to melt into the ground as Khyryn wielded to meet the interloper.

Two eyes glimmered in the shine of the camp's fire. As low as Wynne lay, the eyes moved forward, out of the darkness, followed by ears, body, and brush of the fox.

"Look," she cried, too relieved to see the small four-footed creature instead of the two-footed variety. "He must have followed us all day. He must be exhausted."

"She," Khyryn bristled. He stood a moment longer listening, searching. "Your fox is a vixen."

Wynne couldn't repress the giggle that bubbled forth—in relief and amusement as she reached out and scooped the ball of fur into her arms. "Vixen!"

A tongue met her chin in greeting. Then the small black nose tilted upward to Khyryn in salutation.

"See? It's nothing more than a small animal. And a friendly one at that. No monsters. No 'Cain's knot'—whatever that is."

Khyryn, however, did not relax his posture, or his brow. Whatever Bog warned of, Khyryn feared, as well.

****

Britain, 55 B.C.

The evening's revelry left her limbs heavy and ready for sleep as she sank into the pallet, exhausted.

Gently, she removed the garland from her hair and loosened the braid, until her hair fell—freely—down her back. She remembered Khyryn's touch upon her skin, his breath on her hair, and her stomach tightened.

She was Uddryd's wife. And queen.

The flap of the hut swayed.

As if conjured by her thoughts, Uddryd stood in the entrance, staring at her.

As calmly as she dared, she called him to her. "Husband."

"King," he replied, coldly.

"What is it?"

"I am no husband to your bed. Yet. Am I?"

Again, her stomach roiled and heat brushed her face. "The fires have burned low. Your village sleeps. Should we not join their slumber?"

"A king must be ever watchful to protect his kine."

The hair on her neck prickled. "Cannot Khyryn keep his brother's village on this your wedding night?"

Uddryd advanced. The heat radiated from his body, the smell of wine on his breath. "My brother leaves me to my own pleasures and deeds this day."

Gwynndolwyn stood perfectly motionless before Uddryd. His hand roved across her shoulder and down her chest, cupping her breast possessively, before moving over her belly to hover just above her thighs.

"What fortune do you bring me, Gwynndolwyn? Do you bring me a vessel filled with nectar that I alone shall taste? Do you bring me your fealty? Your allegiance?"

Too swift for her response, he seized her around the waist, fisting her hair in his hand, and arched her into submission.

His free hand tugged at the fabric of her gown as he moved his groin against her thigh.

Panic shot through her veins. Her hands slashed at his face, clawing and thrashing as she tried to escape.

"Does a king's lust not warm your heart, wife? Scream, then. Scream for your lover. Call him to you, that he may witness the spoils of marriage. Did you not notice his absence in our nuptial feast?"

A scream escaped her lips, muffled as he bent his head over her mouth to quiet her protests.

Wynne's arm thrust about the pallet, looking for—for—

Where was it?

Uddryd's anger and lust conspired to lift her from where she stood and toss her on to the pallet. He forced a knee between her thighs as he fumbled with his tunic.

"No! Uddryd! Not like this!"

She struggled to move away, groping all the time for the dagger. It had to be here.

"Whore." From beneath his tunic, Uddryd produced the small, slim blade that Khyryn had given her. "Is this what you seek?"

A wedding gift.

Wynne froze. Uddryd's hand glided up her body, pressing the knife to her gown, threateningly, as he moved over her. The point flicked her throat, and she swallowed involuntarily.

"Is this the point you would sheath with your own sex? My brother's blade?"

Fear—cold and damp—slithered in beads down her neck. "It is but a gift. A token. In celebration of our marriage."

"I am not witless. I have seen you together. You have taken him unto you. My queen. My wife."

She shuddered.

Quickly he entered her, claiming his right as husband. She tried not to wretch as he slammed against her, each thrust a roar filled with rage, filled with lust, filled with spite.

Then spent, he laughed at her.

"Ah, wife. You do meet a husband's need well. I shall give you back your blade. It is a suitable reminder of our union."

Without warning, he hefted the dagger high and swung down against her abdomen.

Pain. Laughter. Cold. Darkness.

****

Wynne gasped for air as she tore herself awake, escaping the torment of the nightmare. Still cloaked beneath the thin blanket, her limbs trembled—both from the cold night air and from the horrific dream.

More than just a dream.

A memory?

Wynne inched closer to Khyryn, resenting every rock, every root that raked her body. She stared at the bramble that hovered above, concealing them. A den of vines and twigs.

Her hand traced the line just below her navel that had tormented her through adolescence. The jagged red mark resembled a scar more than a birthmark.

She thought back to her first night in the cave near the faire. To the stones. To the intoxication of Khyryn's lovemaking. To that overwhelming sense of falling. No—rather of the earth falling away—as they sank deeper into each other. The incantation.

The scar on her abdomen tingled.

The photo in the paper had led her here. She'd tracked Richard Uddryd for two months, found him at the faire, and had gotten hired. All for a rock.

Well, that backfired, hadn't it?

All for an artifact that had haunted her for more than a decade. For a theft that had plagued her uncle's career.

An archaeological dig that had discovered the funeral ship of an ancient Briton king.

Volunteers had been plentiful in the beginning. They always were. Students and local enthusiasts flocked to the site. Everyone wanted to join in the dig. Everyone wanted to experience the history, and a hope for treasure. Among the bronze and silver treasures, lay the small soapstone with a rune carving—a rock that could have been overlooked by someone other than a professional. Until it disappeared.

But it hadn't been overlooked. Its absence had nearly brought the excavation to a halt. Following the preliminary investigation, anyone without security clearance had been dismissed.

Years after her uncle's suicide, Wynne still woke

in the middle of the night drenched in guilt.

A trust broken cost her Uncle Derris his life.

Wynne knew who took it. When she saw the new director of the faire in the papers, smiling arrogantly, she knew he was a thief. She only needed to find the stone to prove it.

But in tonight's dream, Richard Uddryd had not fondled a stone. He'd held a knife.

What if what Khyryn and Aberswythe and Elleran spoke the truth? What if Richard did want her dead?

The mark on her abdomen tingled again. Harder. Burning. If Wynne had stepped through a hole in time, had Richard Uddryd done the same?

Alive. In another century.

All for a damned stone.

****

Khyryn snapped awake in the darkness. His hand seized the dagger laced to his thigh. Beside him, Gwynndolwyn's breathing came slow and deep. But the hair prickling his arms and the odd silence made his own heart pound with awareness.

No night sounds.

Someone watched. Someone listened.

Khyryn gently moved to his side and drew his knee across Gwynndolwyn's legs to keep her still as his hand cupped her mouth. Her body tensed against his. "Shh," he whispered against her ear. "Someone is here. Do not move."

Quietly obeying his words, he saw her eyelashes flutter open releasing a look of panic as she strained to hear the interloper.

He removed his hand from her lips and motioned for her to stay still, hidden beneath the cover of bramble. He rolled from the warmth of his spot beside her, blade drawn.

Beneath the cover of brush, the frost of predawn stung Khyryn's hands. No scent of smoke lingered from the fire. No birds heralded daybreak. Aberswythe and Loth were nowhere to be seen.

From the opposite side of the cold timbers, something hidden by the trees scuffed the ground.

Khyryn picked up a rock and tossed it to the left of the grove. Something rustled through the trees, toward the noise. Khyryn charged toward the same spot, tripping and falling face down into the dirt with a resounding thud.

"I tells ye Cain's knot comes."

Khyryn turned his head toward the voice. Bog crouched against the ground, hovering, ready to pounce. Or flee.

"Many feet I sees. Fierce monsters. Long hair and bloody talons."

Khyryn heard the scuffing sound again, followed by a muffled whinny. "Monsters seldom ride horses, Bog."

Khyryn climbed to stand and moved toward the sounds.

The shrill whir of steel halted Khyryn's steps, as half a dozen figures stepped from the trees, blades drawn and pointed toward him.

Their hair—longer than his own—hung below their shoulders, tied in braids on either side of their heads, or tethered at their napes. Fur-lined leather boots hugged their feet and legs and leather gauntlets wrapped their forearms.

In the shadows of early morning, a whisper echoed

in the grove, "Hold!"

The warriors stayed their steps, even as they searched the trees for the source of the mysterious command.

A second time the raspy hollowness ricocheted through the limbs, warning the men, "Hold!"

This time, two of the men visibly trembled as the ghostly cantor stepped into the dawning gray to join its voice.

Aberswythe.

The old druid, raised a hand in greeting, and nodded to the man who stood directly behind Khyryn. The man motioned to his companions, and all lowered their swords to their sides, conspicuously choosing not to sheath them.

Khyryn slowly turned to look at the man who controlled this band. As tall as he, himself, but older. Hair of burnished copper topped a scarred and grimy brow. Steely blue eyes stared him up and down, measuring a man who stood with only a dagger to protect himself.

Bog's words trickled through Khyryn's mind.

The red one. Cain's knot.

Cnut.

King of the northern lands.

Aberswythe cracked the silence, "Your Highness."

Cnut's eyes flickered to gaze beyond Khyryn's shoulder. "Are you priest or pilgrim?"

"We are travelers on a simple quest for truth," replied the druid.

Cnut cocked an eyebrow, inquisitively. "Two. Alone. Father and son?"

"And Bog and Loth," cried the oaf, still crouched

as he skulked from the trees. Quietly, the young boy slithered down from the covering of a nearby tree, eyes wide with fear, and awe.

Amusement chortled from the circle of Cnut's men, spiraling heavenward into a raucous roar of laughter at the sight of the troupe of travelers. An old priest, a madman, a boy, and Khyryn. Aberswythe ignored the laughter. "We travel in search of—"

"—the boy's family," interrupted Khyryn. "Loth has been separated from his people. We would see them reunited."

"What would take a whelp so young from his village? And for such an escort?"

What could they say? Cnut's question betrayed his suspicion. Royalty or clergy would travel with an armed escort. Not orphaned boys.

Loth had turned a paler shade of white than normal. Indeed, with Cnut and his men staring at the child, Khyryn feared the boy might die of fright where he stood.

"My father is an ironsmith. He travels from village to village for work." The words escaped, leaving Loth's lips and chin trembling. "A band of soldiers set upon us—"

"Soldiers? Where?"

"Nearly two winters hence."

Cnut's shoulders relaxed a bit. "That is a long time. How do you know your family is not dead?"

Loth's eyes widened at Cnut's question. His silence answered for him. For all the boy knew, his family might very well be dead.

Khyryn's gut twisted. *Dead by my brother's hand.*

A movement at Cnut's feet interrupted his inquiry

as a small fox scurried between the man's legs, sniffing at his boots, hissing.

The vixen.

Cnut raised his sword and aimed at the furry attacker.

"No!" The scream punctuated Gwynndowlyn's assault as she flew from the brush and lunged, seizing the creature, and placed herself between animal and man. "Don't you dare! She's mine!"

The sword descended, slicing through the hem of Gwynndolwyn's gown. It grazed her boot as it plunged into the ground, eliciting a feral yowl from the woman that eclipsed the animal's cry.

"Damn you!" she yelled. "Son-of-a-bitch! You could've killed us both—"

Khyryn swooped down to where she lay, one hand clutching the fox, the other beating against the Viking king's leg, and ripped the fabric free of the sword's grip and pulled her into the center of the circle.

She continued to kick and bellow curses at Cnut until Khyryn pressed his hand once again to her lips and said loudly, "Quiet! He spared your life. Do not challenge him to do otherwise."

She mumbled against his hand, which he held firmly against her mouth. Her eyes blazed her fury, and she tightened her hold on the vixen. Aberswythe knelt and inspected her leg where the blade had sheared the boot.

Cnut withdrew his sword from the dirt and took a step backward. Khyryn opened his mouth to speak, but the look on Cnut's face sent a chill through him, and he stayed his words.

The Dane's eyes were as wide as an owl's. Fear

and awe lit his expression. He shifted his gaze to Aberswythe. "You are Sage."

Aberswythe made no answer, but pulled some moss from a pouch on his belt and packed it between the leather and skin on Gwynndolwyn's leg.

Cnut continued, "She is the Golden One?"

Still no response.

"Sage. Answer me. Is she the Golden One? The one prophesied to guide us?"

Her wound tended, the old druid stood and calmly sighed as he returned Cnut's attention. "She is Gwynndolwyn. That she would lead you is not for me to say. The Heavens guide her. She answers only to destiny."

A satisfied smile settled on Cnut's face. "Your Gwynndolwyn has met her destiny this day."

Chapter Thirteen

Winchester, 1016

Eadric relaxed his shoulders and curled his mouth into a smile as he ascended the narrow wooden steps to Edmund's chambers. The sun's glare splashed across the room, blinding him momentarily as he crossed the threshold.

"Streona." Edmund's voice betrayed nothing about his mood this morning.

Eadric bowed, cautiously. "My king." As he stood, his vision adjusted to the brightness of the room.

Edmund sat in a tall, thick chair—a scowl of a man this day—his hands gripping the armrests tensely. Expectantly. "What of it? Have we pushed that Danish bastard back into the Woadlands?"

"That 'Danish bastard' controls the lands that extend south of the wall. Cnut chooses not to run so quickly from our troops, my Liege. It seems he believes his failed reign of the North entitles him to maintain the same terms for rule that you held with his father, Sweyn."

"Hmph. And how do your own lands fare? Does Cnut attempt to claim you as an ally?"

Eadric bristled at the thought. He had given up his lands once before—a century ago—placating the invasion force and striking a treaty. All to his own forfeit.

Another mistake I will not repeat. He removed his gloves. "My lands remain in my sovereign control. I am very protective of my possessions."

"Especially your ships?"

The words stood as solidly between them as a wall.

Forty ships sacrificed to Cnut. That's what his lands had cost him. Eadric had paid it willingly. And had just as willingly convinced Edmund to pay the Dane geld to prevent the sacking of Londinium.

"You rule England, do you not? Tend the shepherd and take his sheep. Isn't that the rule your father lived by? Pay the Dane geld, and kill the Dane?" Eadric accepted the cup offered to him by the servant and sipped the contents.

Bitter. Too quickly drawn from the draught, the wine had not aged. The aftertaste matched the conversation. "Tell me, your highness—do you share your father's philosophy?"

The king grunted his disapproval. "Your lands are yours at my pleasure. Do not forget I can take them back. A king's pleasure can change. As can an alderman's allegiance."

"You doubt my loyalty? My spies and agents infiltrate Cnut's camps as we mull wine and words. My soldiers collect your taxes and bring supplies to your troops. As alderman to you and your father before you, I protect you from dealing with the vulgar peasants, including those whose veins run cold with Viking blood—those your father chose to spare as the children of his new England."

He spat the last words like the vile concoction that passed for wine in this court. At least the Romans had kept decent wine. He lowered his voice to a whisper and smirked at Edmund. "And I keep your hands clean and free of blood as a loyal subject should. Do I not?"

Edmund's sharp intake of air assured Eadric his words hit their mark. Edmund's father had been only too willing to commend his trust and his dirty work to his aldermen.

The king rose from his seat and walked to the rail overlooking the courtyard below. Ironside they called him on the battlefield. Indeed. Astride a horse with a sword in his hand, the king maneuvered well enough. But he had no stomach for murder. Only for what it yielded.

"He has moved west." Edmund's words spilled into the baily below, his back to Eadric. "What will we do about that?"

West. Cnut's troops had moved like lightning. Viking blood. The Dane did not see the practicality of building alliances. That had proved to be his downfall.

Once his father, died, Edmund had reestablished rule over lost lands.

Whether an alliance or attack, if Cnut moved into the west, he moved toward Cymru. That meant he could circle to the south of Londinium and push Edmund's troops toward the sea.

Eadric fisted his hands beneath his cloak. "Our troops are strong, sire. And well fed. Cnut will not plunder the Saxon lands again. He will not find alliance in the south or west."

"*My* troops, Streona. They are my troops. It is *my* kingdom the Dane seeks."

Eadric's skin flushed at the admonition. "Your father trusted my counsel. I assure you my spies will bring word to benefit us both."

Edmund chuckled and released the railing to turn. As he did, his arm arced and the king slammed his fist into Eadric's cheek. Eadric stumbled backward, his vision blurred by the searing pain in his face. And by his own fury.

"For your sake," the king said, "make sure of it."

****

Khyryn accepted the wineskin Cnut offered and gratefully swallowed the mead.

"It is strong. Drink carefully, Druid son."

Khyryn drank once more before returning the honeyed wine to the man who held the camp's full attention. "Men call me Khyryn."

Cnut's eyes twinkled. "And trolls call you Druid son."

"Trolls?"

"Bog," Gwynndolwyn replied.

Cnut nodded. "His name matches his scent. He is of the bog?"

Khyryn laughed out loud. "Bog is clever but he is no troll."

Cnut looked at Aberswythe, then back at Khyryn. "As you are no druid? Tell me Khyryn Druid son, where did the bees dance to make honey that would give us such mead this night?"

Khyryn took up the wineskin again and drank the heady liquid, tasting and inhaling the spring's bounty as each drop slid down his throat. "Heather flower, barley. Juniper?"

"You speak like a man of the earth."

Khyryn ignored his comment. "These plants grow beyond Antonine's wall."

"The Pict lands," Cnut confirmed.

"Aye. I know them."

Cnut cocked his head in surprise. "You know of the Woad? I am surprised. Many never travel beyond the old Roman wall. You know much for a Saxon."

Khyryn did not reply. Who would believe he had marched with the legions of Roman soldiers when Hadrian ordered the wall built? Or that he had walked through the fields of heather blanketing those Northern hills in the summer? Or that he had rolled the barley between his hands, inhaling the musky, earthy scent of the grain.

Instead of incriminating himself, Khyryn handed the wineskin to Aberswythe, then said, "And what has our band of travelers to offer a king?"

Cnut's eyes narrowed. He stared at Khyryn and Aberswythe for several moments. Then he turned his attention to Gwynndolwyn. "I have come for the Golden One. The one your Bog calls, 'Witch'."

Gwynndolwyn came to life, growling her protest as she forcibly grabbed the wineskin from Aberswythe and downed a good amount of mead, presumably to keep the words from spilling out.

Khyryn smirked but his words were serious. "She is no witch. And she stays with me. She is mine."

"The soothsayers say she will sew together the lands of England for me that I may rule the country as a great king. The soothsayer's words tell what will be."

Gwynndolwyn's anger radiated through the night air.

Aberswythe cleared his throat and motioned for the mead. After he had drunk his fill, he spoke boldly. "The heavens have given us the sight to know her when she arrives. She is possessed of a great will. Yet it is not for any to say her destiny. For that, we consult the elements."

Gwynndolwyn rubbed the sides of her head as she sat slumped against the broad base of the oak tree as she concentrated on the fire. "I don't belong here."

Khyryn shook his head. "The stones tell a different tale."

Aberswythe stood and nodded to Cnut, then to Khyryn and Gwynndolwyn. He claimed a torch from the fire before he departed the circle. By dawn's light, Khyryn knew Aberswythe would return with an answer for Cnut. Hopefully, an answer that all concerned might survive.

Taking a cue from his old friend, Khyryn stood. "We invite you and your men to enjoy the warmth of the fire as we have partaken of your company this night. By your leave, we will return to our rest to await Aberswythe's return."

Cnut nodded his consent and dismissed them.

Khyryn pulled Gwynndolwyn to her feet and guided her toward the brush.

"I don't care about 'stones'," she said as she yanked her arm from his grasp. "That's all rubbish. Nobody looks for answers by looking at rocks in my time."

Khyryn held his own temper and whispered, "Hold your tongue. If you do not, I cannot be responsible."

She reeled so quickly, Khyryn nearly trampled her. "For what, Khyryn? My safety? Gee, well that has gone so well, hasn't it? I'm not safe here. I've been beaten, drowned, dragged through caves, over rocks and hills, all against my wishes, and—"

"The man who sits only a few paces from you could do much worse to you than kill you. He claims half of the land beneath our feet. He wars to hold it all. This night he seeks to claim you as his own talisman to that victory."

"It's nothing more than superstition. Stones and soothsayers. Silly make-believe."

"And yet, here you stand. On ground you once knew well."

Wynne trembled at the simplicity of his words. She couldn't explain how she had ended up here. And she certainly couldn't explain the cave. Most aggravating of all—the calm, matter-of-fact way that Khyryn and Aberswythe treated all of this. As if people popped in and out of centuries all the time.

Elleran.

"Khyryn? Do you remember Elleran? The palm reader at the faire?" She turned to find him stopped, his fingers curled into a fist. The greyness of predawn aged his face suddenly. For a moment, his face gleamed pale. His fingers curled tighter as he halted his steps.

"Khyryn?"

"What of her?"

"She wasn't right, the last time I saw her. She said things. Things that didn't make sense. If what you said is true—is it possible she's in the wrong century, too?" She waited for his answer but he only stared at her. The hair on her arms prickled.

"Khyryn? What's wrong? What is it?"

"Be wary of her. Always. She is dangerous."

"How?"

His chest rose and fell as he sighed deeply.

"This all began with her. She cast the curse. She is

the reason we are both here now."

****

Eadric Streona's feet had not met the earth when his voice thundered through the yard, "Find me Cnut!"

Hens flew in frenzy as he dismounted and crossed the threshold of his own motte and entered the main hall looking for his wife.

"Edith—"

Silence met his call.

"Edith!"

Damn. The only presence in the keep was a cat. Lounging in the corner, the rat catcher bolted when Eadric's voice echoed through the timbers of the house.

In the central hearth a fire burned. Someone had tended the house recently. New logs burned. Had she seen him approach and sensed his fury?

Edith, daughter of Aaethelred, sister of Edmund knew of the darkness of court as well as the scourge of rage.

For the first time that day a genuine smile tugged at the corners of his mouth. To make most women weep took nothing more than a hand in the dark silencing babe's breath.

But to make a king's daughter—nae, a king's sister, cower—made great his wrath.

His cock hardened at the thought.

She is hiding.

Edith, no doubt, watched from the woods, waiting for night to fall and for his temper to sop mead to softening. Her fear reminded him of that moment he had gloried in so many lifetimes ago.

Gwynndowlyn.

Rape.

Vengence.

Murder.

Edmund's insults pricked Eadric's thoughts. The memory of the fist blow burned against the stubble of his cheek. Both stoked Eadric's fury, enflaming his lust for vengeance.

As it had a thousand years ago.

Of the moment of his epiphany.

Loyalty means nothing. Fear wields power. Power commands fear.

Everything else is fleeting.

Chapter Fourteen

Aberswythe returned to the camp early in the day, concern etched on his brow. Wynne sensed him before his lanky form broke through the brush where she and Khyryn secluded themselves. Nearby, Cnut and his men sprawled, snoring. She hoped they could not wield a broadsword well enough in their sleep to decapitate anyone.

"Khyryn." The whisper so faint it whistled like the fluttering of a bird's feathers. Wynne doubted she had even heard it until Khyryn stirred beside her.

"Aberswythe? What is it?"

"Come. Both of you."

They emerged from the warmth of the foliage and followed the wisp through the trees toward the sound of water. A stream. By the time they caught up to him, Aberswythe had planted himself on a large rock near the water.

"How do you do that?" Wynne asked.

Aberswythe smiled at her. "Do what?"

"Glide through the air, over roots and leaves, past trees, as if they weren't even there. It's absolutely annoying."

To emphasize the point, she tripped over a bit of root protruding above the ground. A slew of profanities and curses flew from her lips. Frustration vented, she scowled at both men, only to see them smirking in

149

amazement at her. Or amusement. Either way, she did not appreciate their expressions.

"It is the old way," he explained. "As we move, one with nature, we become one with that which surrounds us, and gives us comfort and safe haven. Thus it yields to our touch as a lover would."

The heat rose in Wynne's cheeks. If she had thought him a wizard before, her suspicions hardened as the druid's words wove a web of seduction and intimacy.

Khyryn cleared his throat. Wynne bowed her head slightly, embarrassed by her own reactions. From the corner of her eye, she spied Khyryn, squatting awkwardly. He, too, had been seized by the music of the elder's words.

Did he miss it? Did he miss the magic? The knowing? The oneness with nature?

Khyryn did not look at her, but kept his attention on Aberswythe. "You have seen something?"

The druid nodded. "Cnut would use her to defeat Eadric."

"To do what?" she asked.

"The stars foretell you will conquer this slayer of princes. You and you alone will deliver Eadric to Cnut."

Khyryn shook his head. "No. I will not let her."

"Your insistence is of no consequence, Khyryn. This is what will be. Whether she does so willingly, or against her will and yours, she will bring the two together. Cnut will succeed in conquering the Saxons. One banner will claim these lands, at least for a time."

Events of the last few days, and the gang gathered near them, drove home the truth of the situation. How had she gotten into this situation?

"Tell me about Elleran. Elleran. What does she have to do with this?"

Aberswythe sat silently, frowning at her. Then at Khyryn. So, there was something more.

Wynne promptly plopped herself down in the damp grass. "I am not going anywhere until I have the whole story, gentlemen. Face it. I've been so patient, I should be sainted. As I see it, I have nothing to lose by sitting right here until I hear it all. If your magic eight ball is right, it doesn't matter what my next move is. Eventually, I will be in the right place at the right time. But I sure as hell am not doing anything until I know it all. And the brooding prince-of-pout here won't tell me anything. So, Merlin, start talking."

An all too audible sigh wooshed from both men's lungs.

Good.

"Do you remember nothing, child?"

The question caught her off guard. "What am I supposed to remember?" A dream wasn't necessarily a memory. Was it?

"Aberswythe, do not—"

"Khyryn, the more she knows, the better prepared she will be for what, or whom, she may yet encounter."

"Yes, Khyryn, I shall need to be prepared." Though her words mocked, a faint fluttering in her stomach echoed the old man's trepidation.

"Gwynndolwyn. That is the name your people gave to you."

"Yes. My parents named me Gwynndolwyn. It's an old name. I never use it."

"Nae, child. Listen to my words. Your village gave

you that name more than half a century before the Romans built towns here. You were Celt. Ancient royalty. And to another royal house you were promised."

"An arranged marriage?"

"Aye. In those days, Briton still stood virile against all—Earth, Heavens, and Man understood each other. We watchers read the sky and listened to the trees and streams. Creatures, long since vanished, used to dance with us in the night and whisper secrets in our ears. Sometimes their words were folly meant to fool us for their amusement. Sometimes, their words gave warning, portent of ill, that we could save ourselves.

"The druids were magicians, then? Fortune tellers, like Elleran?"

"We were never magicians," Khyryn interrupted. "We were magi. Men of letters and of wisdom. More wisdom than many in this time possess."

Aberswythe waved him off. "There is something to be said of ancient ways. And yet, even our ancient ways did not warn us of the coming of the Romans."

"Keep talking."

Khyryn took up the tale. "You were betrothed to my brother, Uddryd. Had been since childhood. Just as I had been entrusted to Aberswythe's teaching, you were trained to be queen."

"And?"

Khyryn shifted his body to face Aberswythe rather than her. His voice strained and cracked, "And from the time you took your first steps in our village, your duty and your desire did not agree."

"How so?"

He did not answer.

"Khyryn? Aberswythe? Out with it."

The old man rested a hand on Khyryn's shoulder. "Uddryd sought counsel as any good ruler should. So Khyryn's counsel brought him into the village. You two were brought together more than once. You both battled with duty and desire."

A love triangle? "And Uddryd knew of this—"

"Nae. He knew nothing. Born to a role you did not seek, you sought consolation. We found comfort in each other's company. And soon in each other's embrace. Thus, one brother's fealty turned traitorous."

"So we were lovers?" Again, her cheeks warmed. "How does Elleran fit into this story?"

Aberswythe answered. "Elleran's wisdom and powers with dark spirits were well known then. She had gifts greater than any of her kind."

"Her kind?"

Khyryn shrugged. "Wyce. She could seduce the spirits, make them do her bidding." He still did not look to Wynne, but turned toward her. "Blind of eye, yet her sight was keen. She could see much. And she did."

"Elleran foresaw the coming of the Romans," the old man explained. "Her spirits told her of their great might. They spoke to her of the legions that would follow. Of how they would drive us from our villages, how they would drive us from our ways. In that, her vision was keen. As the Romans turned their backs on their own gods and knelt before the sermoners of Christ, so did they command those they enslaved to do the same.

"In her panic for the future she saw, Elleran sought vengeance. Anyway she could. One moment of anger cursed us all."

Both men sat silent. As if they could not speak the words.

Khyryn's hands fisted. That and the frown masking his face hinted at the tension building within his body. Apparently, neither man had told her yet the worst of it.

"Well?" Her patience waned. "What happened?"

Khyryn's voice rasped when he answered, "Instead of granting me my wish to rid myself of my desire for you, Elleran poisoned me and brought the vision upon me. She showed me the slaughter. I saw with mine own eyes the thunderous hoard of red men, wrapped in leather and metal, shielded from our weapons. I saw the fires burn as they razed the village. I saw the coming of death and the subjugation at the hands of the Romans."

"And in that moment when I could do nothing to escape Elleran's madness, she spoke the curse that lingers to your time. She blessed you with no memory of me, and cursed me forever, that I would never forget a single moment in your presence. For all time. Every life."

"Every life? You mean like reincarnation?"

"Aye."

"You mean...wait. Say it precisely. Just what do you mean?"

"You died that morning when the Romans burned the village. However, in the dozens of lifetimes I have known since that day, we have met. Often. As I am cursed to know you and to remember each meeting, you are cursed to know nothing of me. All too often, Uddryd is poised between us."

"But he is not your brother in these subsequent lifetimes?"

"It matters not. He remembers."

A bitter taste stung her mouth. Memory. The dream. "Do you know what he does remember?"

He remembers how I failed to warn him of the raid. How I had left the village on the eve of your wedding."

"And this Eadric is the same man we know as Richard Uddryd from the faire?"

"Aye."

Like the last few pieces of a jigsaw puzzle, Wynne's brain shifted the final pieces, and she started making her own connections.

"Then he must have known about Elleran, too. I mean if she is as notorious as the two of you say, he must have known who she was. And who she is. He must know who I am. And if he knew you and everyone else, then why—"

"I did not know if he would recognize me in your time. Some do not. I hoped he would be without the memories in your time. I had to get to you."

"Hold on. What do you mean by some do not?"

"Many of those who walk the grounds at your faire have fallen out of time. There are faces I meet who have passed into a new life, having left their memories behind them. Many, however, seek the comfort of that which is familiar to them. Though they do not remember prior lives, these folk find lives that are comfortable to them. Do you not see that?"

Wynne mulled this new fact for a moment. "In other words, not all the people at the faire are actors?" Well, that certainly explained a lot about Elleran. "She knew who you were and why you had come. Didn't she?"

Aberswythe broke his silence. "So did Uddryd."

Something nagged at her. "Aberswythe? How is it

possible I can understand and communicate with you and Khyryn? It isn't logical. I'm from another time. A time so different from yours that my language should not be like yours. I'm talking about the difference between the English languages as it has changed and evolved over, well over a thousand years, right? And between the old English, and the Celtic based languages, Angles, Saxons, Welsh—"

"Your mind hears with an ancient's soul, my child."

Tingling in her chest. And at the nape of her neck. "With what?"

"We were a people of language. Of spoken histories. We carried our ancestors' memories here," the old man said, tapping his chest. "We gave our pasts to our children through the spoken words. And they listened with the souls of their grandchildren yet to come. You are an ancient one, Gwynndolwyn."

Again the tingling. Ancient soul. "Khyryn...how did your Gwynndolwyn die?"

He hesitated. "In the Roman raid. I found you still clutching the dagger I had given to you as a wedding gift. That same blade was used to kill you...on your wedding night.—"

Khyryn's voice faltered. Wynne saw his throat constrict as he swallowed hard against the memory that burned in his soul.

"He blamed me for not being at his side to warn him and fight with him. We have fought over that night ever since. I killed him once."

Again, the bitter taste of fear stung her tongue. Copper. Like blood. Khyryn spoke the truth. Uddryd— or Richard—did remember. He had forgotten nothing in a millenium. His memory had surged in his pulse when he'd seized her by the throat on the field that day. Jealousy had flowed from the blade he ran over the spot he had once carved on that wedding night.

Images began to swirl in her brain. The insanity of everything she had heard and seen since the day on the chess field began to fall into place, like players on the board.

Richard remembered everything. Perfectly. Not just that day at the archaeological site, but every moment he had ever spent in her presence.

Dream and memory danced hand in hand. The same magic that brought Aberswythe the certainty of her future, brought her the certainty of her past.

Wynne's dreams were more than sleep's illusions.

Some part of her remembered. Everything.

Even her own murder.

Chapter Fifteen

Wind twirled in the branches of the evergreen trees as the group plodded through the muddy soil of the road. Some fine road the Romans built. A thousand years old. Yet Wynne knew she had ridden across every bump, every rock, every broken stone the Roman Empire laid as they conquered this island country—sitting astride a horse, with no shock absorbers.

Of course, they had spent the better part of the day galloping at a fiendish pace, as if the earth were on fire beneath them. Loth rode behind Aberswythe. Bog had refused to ride a horse. When he tired and lagged behind, two of Cnut's men had tossed him onto a supply cart. Disgruntled, muttering curses, he nevertheless stayed where they put him. She couldn't blame him. Cnut's men looked almost as ill-kempt as Bog. They didn't, however, smell quite as bad.

Now that they had stopped, Wynne concentrated on the course of the day's events wondering if she might spontaneously combust.

Khyryn and Aberswythe had barely finished telling her about Uddryd and Elleran when Cnut emerged from the tree line, hiked up his tunic and relieved himself into the stream. Without as much as a nod, he then bent to the rushing water, scooped a clear handful of water from upstream and splashed his face and hair before turning his attention to his audience.

He raised his hand in greeting as he moved toward them. In the light of morning, Wynne could see him clearly. Tall. Nearly as tall as Khyryn, his face weathered from wind rather than age. His hair, streaks of russet and blond, hung in braids on either side of his face. A great warrior's mantle.

Younger than she would have expected. Despite his tanned complexion, no grey hair lined his brow or arms. Strange. She had always assumed he came to power as a middle-aged man. But the great Cnut had obviously seen no more years pass than Khyryn.

In this lifetime, at least.

Cnut. History revered him as 'great'. But only she knew that. Here, he represented just another marauder to Britain's shores.

He stroked the short growth of beard that covered his jaw. "Druid. The sun brings us a fair day and you have returned. What do your stars and stones show you?"

Aberswythe stood to meet the Dane. "You ride today to the lands north of Londinium. But your band is small. You do not ride to fight?"

"We fight wherever Saxons make war with us. My father ruled these lands. Now I rule them. Our golden witch ensures it. Is that not so?"

Wynne flinched involuntarily at Cnut's words. Temper flared inside her. She opened her mouth expecting a slew of curses to bubble forth, yet no words sounded.

Aberswythe tilted his head gently, never glancing her way. Only her own breath escaped her mouth. She waited for an answer as anxiously as did the red-haired Viking prince who stood appraising his new talisman.

The elder did not commit to answer for either of them. "What of Edmund?"

"Edmund would take what is mine. He seeks to break a pact sealed by our fathers. To dishonor them both."

"Honor seldom endures, one generation to another. Like the Dane geld, honor oft demands payment," Aberswythe observed.

"We ride to victory," Cnut said. "You will ride with my men."

Khyryn pulled himself to his full height and faced the Dane. Though his face stayed as still as stone, heat radiated from his body. Silently proclaiming her his own property, Khyryn wrapped his arm around her waist and pulled her to him, then placed his hip protectively in front of her, strategically positioning himself between her and Cnut.

She wasn't sure what unspoken words had passed between the two men, but soundless meaning ricocheted between them, and from every surface. Like elk during rutting season.

Yep. Testosterone poisoning, all around.

His fingers flexed against the fabric of her gown as he responded to Aberswythe's observation. "If not of flesh, of soul." Khyryn would honor her with his protection.

Beneath his tunic, Khyryn's muscles tightened as he held her fast, his grip fierce. The cadence of his pulse drummed against her, like the pounding of the bodhrain.

And her heart had responded in rhythm.

Now, a full day's ride later, a band of Viking warriors, and the motley crew of misfits crossed a thick woodland border. Storm clouds bruised the northern sky. Portent of things to come?

Wynne wrapped the leather reins around her hand and slowed her horse's pace. Cnut had gifted her the animal proclaiming his Seer deserved to ride like a warrior.

Golden witch, Cnut called her. *Witch*, Bog had proclaimed her repeatedly.

As if the heavens had waved a wand and granted her vision, Wynne understood. A grin tickled her mouth as the truth of her situation dawned on her. They were right. They were all right. Especially Aberswythe.

Is that why he did not press an argument when Cnut insisted they ride together? He had simply put himself between Khyryn and the Dane, and proclaimed her an oracle. As her guardian, the old druid forbade any man to obtrude with her meditations, or with her advice.

The giggle inside her grew to a chortle, then to a bellowing laugh. The echo of her own laughter made her laugh even harder as she realized just how right Bog had been. How right they had all been.

By their standards, she was exactly what they thought her. Witch. Oracle. Prophet. Seer. A wise woman.

Wynne knew the future. Or rather...she knew the past that was to come. Years spent thumbing through texts, studying history had gifted her with a sight no one else here held.

Gwynndolwyn's past might be a mystery to her. But Cnut's future was not.

****

Streona sat taller in his saddle as the rider

approached. "How long?"

Gareth nodded, but did not raise his eyes. "The scouts say another day's ride will bring them this way, sire."

"How many?"

"No fewer than fifteen. Danes."

"So...Cnut comes to us. How fortunate for everyone." Eadric smiled. "Gareth?"

"Yes, sire?"

"Make sure Cnut and his band receive the hospitality of our escort. After such a long ride, they will want for food and bed. Assure him that the House of Strigul will offer him succor."

Gareth tugged the reins with no more than a stilted bow, bucked his horse to retreat. An action Eadric admiringly acknowledged. If the imbecile learned nothing more from Marcus's death, he now knew never to turn his back on any man. Especially one who held power over him.

Eadric reached into his pouch and curled his hand around the cool hard smoothness of the stone. He stroked the rock with the gentleness of a favorite lover. More rare than any jewel. More dangerous than any weapon. Elleran's stone had brought him so very close to complete, absolute power.

Once the lands were united, he would rule mightily. No longer did he seek to rule merely peasants and merchants. Now, he would rule kings. Ironside or Cnut—it made little difference. Both men had much to offer England. And Eadric.

Imagine. The lands. The warriors. The Dane geld.

Eadric turned to home. More than a dozen buildings stood within the outer protective wall. The tallest building stood in the center, flanked on each side by smaller buildings.

He plodded quietly into the courtyard, slipped from his saddle, and made his way to the building where his wife chose to spend her days, weaving.

The wooden slats slapped against the rail, cloaking the sound of his boots on the rushes as he crossed the threshold. Edith slid the wood against the yarn, thus tightening the weave of the thread beneath her fingertips, and then slipped the spindle of yarn in and out until she had traversed the woof threads. Having done so three times, she reached up to the wooden slats and again pulled them tight, massaging wood and yarn to mold it beneath her touch.

Eadric stood behind her. Her shoulders tensed, but she offered no smile or greeting to her husband.

Eadric pulled the leather glove from his hand and traced his forefinger across the nape of her neck and down her collar until he found what he sought.

She faltered in her weaving, but did not stop her work, allowing him his privilege to fondle his wife, but never surrendering her attention to him.

"Your hands are quite talented, wife. They fondle the yarn with such delicate caress as to make a mortal man quite jealous of sheep's wool."

The muscles beneath her jaw constricted in a swallow, and he slid his hand lower to the ribbon of her gown. His groin grew hard at the thought of her fingers pressing and tugging against his flesh. "Tell me, wife, where do you hide these nights? It is long since I have found you in your bed."

Her voice fluttered, husky and breathless. "I—there is a fever among the children. Sleep eludes me. I have been tending the babes so their mothers who work in the fields might sleep.

Eadric's envy grew, and with it his anger. He dipped his hand beneath the fabric of her gown and firmly squeezed a taut young breast. "And do you tend to their husbands as well?"

A whimper of pain escaped her lips as her nipple hardened against his palm. She wrapped her hand around his wrist as she struggled to loosen his grip.

He plied his other hand to her throat and tilted her head back until she could do nothing other than stare up at him. "Be careful, wife. Your body would confess your own lusts. Is it for the farmers that your body buds so willing?"

"You are my husband and my lord. What my body yields to you is yours and yours alone. I assure you. I only go to help the helpless young ones and their mothers."

This time her quake rippled through his thighs as she sat pinned against his body. He rocked against her, his own fervor swelling. He gave her a moment's reprieve as he paused to strip the glove from his other hand before he ploughed both hands beneath the neckline of her dress and raked her body against his form—from sit to stand. She stumbled over the stool and nearly fell atop him, giving him even greater cause to take her flesh.

He held her tight against his body, as he savagely rubbed himself against her. He released one tit to seize her hem to her waist that he might find a softer, more telltale sign of her affection for him.

This time, no whimper, but a cry as he cupped his hand against her womanhood and held her to him.

"And what of your husband's needs. Would you abandon me to suffer a long night alone, in an empty bed? Lonely and wanting for your caress?"

She tried to push away from him. "You have never had trouble taking company to your bed. It has never been my *caress* that you sought."

Eadric slammed her face down, against the loom, assaulting her soft downy mound with one hand as the other held her face pinned against the wooden slats she had moments ago fingered so superbly.

"Ah, is that jealousy I hear in your hiss, Edith? I shall have to tell your father—oh wait, I can't, can I? He is dead. I shall tell your brother, then, that you prefer your stable boys and swineherd to pleasing your own husband and master."

He hiked up her skirt as he fumbled with his own tunic. With one hand masterfully clamped across her nape, he braced her knees apart and let his cock find the entrance into her the way warring raiders would use a battering ram to fell a defensive wall.

Her attempt to escape his ardor just moved her against his surging girth until he pierced her firmly and began to thrust wildly against her bucking hips.

She cried out in pain and pleasure as he slammed against her buttocks. Again he slid one hand beneath her belly and probed for that bud most dire that would make her convulse and yield to him ultimately. When she came, rubbing against his hand and his cock, speeding her frenzy, and milking his passion from his aching balls, he spent himself inside her, in an explosion of victory until she writhed against him.

After he claimed what was his to take, Eadric bent close to her ear and kissed her with genuine tenderness.

"You have much talent to offer succor to a king or to a king's men. By this hour on the morrow, I shall seek to assuage a Viking's hunger and rage."

She crawled from beneath him, seeking the wall for support. "I am no concubine. I am your wife. A sister to your king."

"All to more reason to see that you are properly attired and prepared. Unless you would rather be stripped of your robes and left to the pleasure of your milkmaids' husbands and the wifeless soldiers who fight for me."

Retching with fury she growled at him. "What vile demon do you serve that you would treat me so? Claim me, kiss me, and threaten me with the same breath?"

Pure, joyful laughter burst from his chest as he stood, straightening his tunic. "That is a conversation for another time. You have other tasks to tend. Entice the Dane's lust as you have thusly mine, and you will please me greatly, wife. Fail me, and there will be hell to pay."

Chapter Sixteen

"I need a bath. A long, hot, bubble-filled bath."

Khyryn shot her a sideways glance. "Did the last dunking not rid you of your demons?"

The troupe of riders had stopped a short distance on the road ahead. The wind had picked up since they last rested their horses.

A twinge of guilt prickled his conscience. He had given no thought to her comfort. Her time offered luxuries this time knew naught of.

She leaned sideways over her horse, gathered her hair in one hand, twisted it into a loose knot, then straightened as she said loudly, "Hot water, please. With soap. And shampoo. And a toothbrush. With toothpaste—"

"Speak to Aberswythe. He gathers plants and roots and is much wiser than most. If you tell him what you need, he will know what to do."

Gwynndolwyn slid from her horse. "I know what to do. Give me those stones you used and start chanting." As her feet met the ground, her gown snagged on the stirrup, revealing a leg nearly as long as his own.

She loosened the neck of her gown, and a bundle of fur appeared from within, dark eyes blinking wearily at the daylight.

Gwynndolwyn pulled the reluctant creature from

her bosom and affectionately nuzzled it before she set it down on the ground.

Khyryn inhaled deeply to cool his thoughts and body. He lowered his voice to a growl. "Mind your gown, lest you find a dozen Danes ruttin' like stags to get at you. With me to stand against them for *your* honor."

At the moment, however, with golden hair tousled, and the day's ride—as well as the linen gown—clinging to her flesh, Khyryn struggled to concentrate on her honor. Not her other, rather visible parts.

"Never fear." Her face grimaced as she fanned one hand in front of her face. "Neither man nor animal would come within an arm's length of me right now. I smell like roadkill."

Khyryn shifted uncomfortably in his saddle. "You know nothing of men."

She tethered her horse to a tree limb and stepped toward the woods.

Khyryn nudged his horse to follow. "Where are you going?"

She turned, hands on her hips and shot him a glance that dared the horse to move one more hoof. "I am going to find a bush or tree that will offer me some privacy. Men may prefer to pee in front of an audience, but women do not—even in this primitive time."

Heat brushed his neck and cheeks. He nodded and reined his horse to a halt. She did not wait for his response, but hiked her skirt and disappeared through the trees.

He had kept her within his sight since the arrival of Cnut and his men. Thus far, no one had questioned his claim as her protector.

In this uncertain time of war, however, he well knew there was no such thing as complete protection.

A scuffle behind him stole Khyryn's attention. In the middle of the road stood Loth, kicking and swinging his arms as several of Cnut's men tried to calm him. Khyryn dismounted and strode to the center of the fray, pushing one man out of his way, then shoving the others away from the boy. He cuffed Loth by the nape and thrust the boy's head down to his ankles to stop his flailing.

"Loth—what is it? What has happened?"

With his head pinned, Loth could neither swing, nor kick at his assailant. "Let me go. I won't go back—"

"Not until you calm yourself enough to speak sensibly. Tell me—"

Khryryn felt the earth tilt beneath him as Loth's hands encircled his ankle. The boy fell backward using all his weight to throw Khyryn off balance. It worked. Khyryn let go of the boy too late and the two tumbled to the ground, the younger scrambling over him like a treed animal scurrying to escape a hound.

One soft boot sank into Khyryn's shoulder as the boy moved to sprint away from the throng. Khyryn gripped the ankle and twisted hard enough to turn the leg as well.

"Owww!" The yowl of pain rendered the boy motionless long enough for two of Cnut's men to grab the youth by his arms and drag him once again to his feet.

Bog leaped from the cart where he rode. "Loth! Bog's 'ere, Loth. Comes t' Bog, boy." The screeching creature clambered across the ground, pushing aside onlookers as he strained to break the wall of Viking soldiers that separated him from the hysterical youth.

Khyryn stepped into the middle of the group again to block Bog's approach. "Bog, step away. Loth is safe. No harm awaits him."

"Lies, Master Khyryn." Spittle flew from the boy's mouth with his accusations. "They lie, Bog. I know where we are."

Khyryn clasped his hands over Loth's shoulders. The child trembled so furiously that Khyryn's own arms shook from the contact.

"Loth, look at me. What is the lie? What is this place? What do you fear?"

Someone tugged on Khyryn's shirt. Bog's voice crackled in a soft whisper. "Druid son. Let Bog. Loth talks t' Bog. 's right, eh, Loth? Bog be Loth's friend. Druid son be Bog's friend. Bog helps both. Let Bog."

Panic and fury flickered in the boy's eyes as he glared past the two of them. Khyryn did not need to turn to know that Cnut and Aberswythe had joined them.

He released his grasp on Loth's shoulders, nodded to Cnut's soldiers to do the same, and let Bog pull Loth through the center of the crowd to the supply cart.

"What's going on?" Gwynndolwyn called as she emerged from the trees. "What's wrong?"

The group of gathered men splintered and fell away as she advanced. Khyryn rolled his shoulders and stretched his arms high above his head, nearly puffing his chest and like a cock preening in the yard, warning other males to stay away.

Hot breath grazed his neck. Gwynndolwyn's horse nudged him from behind. He raised his hand and stroked the velvety softness of the mare's jaw.

Loth turned at the sound of her voice. As if she were a beacon, he pried himself away from Bog and flew to her side, nearly tumbling her in the process. Gwynndolwyn wrapped her free arm around the waif and hugged him, then cast Khyryn a questioning glance.

A hysterical child and a raid of Danes.

"Please. Bog says you are a witch. Make them stop."

Khyryn edged nearer and squatted so he was shoulder to shoulder with the boy. Loth clung to her like a babe.

Gwynndolwyn sank to her knees and held the boy. She shook her head and her eyes widened, as she silently queried Khyryn again. When she spoke, her voice was as soft as a feather. "Loth, tell me why you would have me stop them? I cannot help you until I know."

Khyryn moved not, but made sure that he stayed by her side in case Loth began thrashing about again.

Yet the boy only trembled more.

"Loth? Can you answer me?"

He nodded against her shoulder.

The breeze picked up, blowing the leaves to billow and clap against one another, reminding Khyryn of the crowds at the chess match.

"I know this place. We approach his lands."

Gwynndolwyn's brow furrowed. "Whose lands, Loth?"

In response to the boy's whispered confidence, crows cawed tauntingly in the far off branches as the limbs continued their ovation. Thunder rumbled from behind the trees, urging the cacophony.

Cnut cleared his throat and spoke in his native tongue to his soldiers. The men quickly averted their curious stares, and turned their attention to their own horses' needs.

Bog crouched close to Khyryn, bobbing up and down, anxiously.

Gwynndolwyn implored the boy once more. "Whose, Loth?"

"The king's alderman. Eadric Streona." Loth pulled away and pointed eastward. "Just beyond that hill. He waits for Cnut. He means to kill us," he said, turning to look at Khyryn. "Once he knows you're coming, he will kill you, too."

Aberswythe made no move—standing as still and silent as the pillars of the Great Circle. Khyryn could smell the earth. Memory persisted, propelling his mind to a previous time…*East Anglia, 628 A.D.*

Pitch and smoke on the field of war filled his nostrils. Metal clanged all around him and the shrill screams of horses mixed with the angry cries of men meeting death as the battle waged on.

A shadow fell across his path and Khyryn wheeled to find the great grey stallion bearing down upon him. Above the monster of horseflesh sat the one he had hoped not to see that fateful day of war. Uddryd.

He sneered down upon Khyryn. "As ever, on the wrong side, eh, brother?"

Khyryn, cursed to remember old lives, exhaled slowly. The man he had once called brother, spoke with memory as well. "This war serves none, save you."

"In this lifetime, I rule my own fate."

"You seek to destroy all that is peace. You have dismembered the Bretons and Saxons. You build your

kingdom on the dead bodies of those you claim as comrade.

"I claim the right that history stole from me. I claim the infamy that I was due before you and the whore denied me."

Khyryn's fingers numbed as his grip tightened around his sword's hilt. "Your memory falters. I sacrificed my own soul for you. "

"Ill and putrid thoughts do I ever hold for you and for her—"

"She died at the hands of a common enemy. You cannot find treason in that."

"Do you think me so stupid that I did not know of your treachery, Khyryn? Of your treason?

Khyryn's knees weakened at Uddryd's words.

"I bore you no false loyalty."

"I did spy my bride at the water's edge that day—so many lifetimes ago—glistening and wet. She basked in the sun, naked and Circean, even as I waited for our betrothal. Yet, I found my faithful priest, my brother no less, at her side, hearing her confessions of desire. And like a serpent did she writhe beneath me on our wedding night. Loyalty to whom? Her liege and husband? Or her lover?"

Khyryn collapsed to kneeling, disbelief girding his limbs like ropes. "For you, I sought Elleran's aid to strike Gwynndolwyn from my mind and heart. That is why I left."

"Ah, but that did not happen did it, Khyryn?"

Mesmerized by his brother's vicious recollection, he shook his head.

"A useful crone, Elleran," Uddryd sneered. "Her celestial spirits did convince her there must be 'a

balance'. Instead of casting her curse on you alone, she gave me a gift of eternity. That you would remember what you lost is a small pleasure. That I recall five hundred years since, the moment I sliced Gwynndolwyn's womanhood with my cock as sharply as I slit her belly with your blade, brother, stirs my bloodlust, and gorges my hatred. For that I would thank you."

Nausea swept over him and his body retched to purge the memories of that visit from his being. The confession burned like molten lead on Khyryn's soul. *"The hand that killed Gwynndolwyn...yours?"*

"Like slitting a snake in two—"

"Not the Romans?"

"Even as I wiped her blood from my hands, Roman steps did cadence on the turf, announcing their approach. Hail, Caesar."

Not the Romans.

Gwynndolwyn had died by the hand of her own husband, bound by marriage and by duty.

Khyryn sank the broadsword deeply into the soft soil and dragged himself to his full height to meet his brother's gaze.

"And now, Khyryn, I shall mete my vengeance on you. Die, brother."

In that instant, the earth fell away from the ancient druid's sword.

Khyryn brought his sword up swiftly to gouge the flesh of a man who, in youth, had fought beside him...not against him.

Blood spilled from the hole in Uddryd's side. His eyes opened wide as did his mouth. No words, but droplets of red poured from his lips as his hands

174

loosened their grip and he fell from his mount.

Uddryd lay on his back in the mud, his eyes staring Heavenward.

A life for a life…

Time tilted and memory returned to dust. Loth's tear-stained face floated into view once more—a face that had seen the truly murderous nature of the madman who made foul play for pleasure and profit.

Khyryn claimed to be conscience and memory when he rescued this child from the ravages and brutality of Eadric's henchman. Perhaps the true curse of memory was his own conscience as its companion.

He cuffed the boy's nape again, gently tugging the child to him, embracing the boy as he might a son. Or brother.

"If it is murder he is about, then we must surprise our host with our arrival."

Chapter Seventeen

"Ride!" At Cnut's command, the hooves of a dozen horses bludgeoned the ground, headed away from the direction of the sun.

Wynne climbed back onto her mount, then held her arms out for Khyryn to hand the vixen to her. The fox, all fluff and growl, wound around in her arms, settled across her lap, and licked at her hand as she tugged the reins and nudged her own horse forward.

Heading into the enemy's lair.

She had calmed Loth enough to coax him to the cart. Her resentment of Bog thinned as she watched him guard the boy as his own. Like a mother bird, nervous, and ever watchful.

A shudder rippled through her.

Fear.

Here, riding a horse in 1016. In the past. In history...and no one will ever know.

The silence that lingered between Aberswythe and Khyryn prickled her conscience. Although neither man had voiced it, their hesitance lingered in the air.

Did they also fear this meeting?

She tried to look over her shoulder. Khyryn rode too far behind for her to read the expression on his face. Aberswythe wore his cloak. His face remained hidden.

The dream echoed in her head. So did the story Abwerswythe and Khyryn told.

Everyone said Gwynndolwyn had been Uddryd's wife. That she had been killed when the Romans invaded.

And yet, she hadn't. Someone needed to know the truth of it. She knew Gwynndolwyn had not died by a Roman's hand.

She ran her fingers over the fabric that concealed a nearly diagonal birthmark on her abdomen. Birthmark or death mark?

Her muscles replied by seizing and cramping into a tight knot, just below the mark. Her breasts ached in sympathy.

Great.

If precedent followed her through the stones, then hormones should give her the mood to maim and dismember within the next few days. Her period.

Her mind slithered over random thoughts of Cnut's reign, trying to pry any pebble of historical reference she could use.

Thunder rumbled in the distance, cajoling the riders, taunting them to take cover. Twilight descended, and the scent of rain wafted on the breeze.

Rain. No rain had fallen for days. Wynne's sinuses welcomed the teasing scent of rain, as if it were a rare and delicate perfume. Clean and pure. No dust. No musk. No stench of sweat and horses. Only water— filtered and cleansed by the air.

Water falling back to the ground to nurture the earth. The wind rolled faster, carrying with it the promise of a storm and the band rode faster. In the far distance, Wynne could see a basin of water—a lake, and a cluster of trees and bushes. Halfway between her and the water rode a force of Danes, and a slightly worn supply cart sporting a boy and a troll. That is where they would make camp.

Wynne looked around for Aberswythe and Khyryn. No sign of either. She could hear the rain approaching, a legion out of step with itself, thrumming drops pummeling the ground to a cadence of nature's creation. She reined her horse, and slipped once more from the saddle. The vixen jumped from its perch and stretched reluctantly, ears folded back in protest to the rain, or the end of a comfortable ride, or both.

Wynne ran her hand over the horse's neck. The horse stamped at the ground nervously, yet Wynne did not yield. She guided both animals to a scraggly bush where she tethered the mare. Then, like a child, she lifted her head to the clouds and let the drops fall upon her face, turning around, dancing as the rain poured over her, dampening her clothes, her hair, her senses. Drenching her in the pristine water as it fell from the Heavens.

She had once heard that water washed away all the bad energy of the day. She had had enough bad energy to last a lifetime.

She thought of the last storm she'd seen. That day had ended with a trip through time. Perhaps this rain would send her back.

She opened her mouth and drank as the rain came harder now, beating the earth beneath her boots. Rivulets streamed from her hair. Wynne bent and pulled the boots from her feet, then loosened the ties of her kirtle and pulled it over her head.

She sought refuge from this insanity.

If Bog were right, she would melt in heaven's water.

Cold and stinging against her hands and face, the water drenched her gown, sodden with dirt, with dust, with sweat. Faster she twirled, spinning in the rain, until she fell into the grass, arms outstretched to receive the water from above.

Is this how Ophelia felt before she drowned?

A cleansing of body and spirit. A sacrament. Each drop that met the earth serenaded her with its beauty. Splashes pounded her eyelids. She giggled as droplets trickled into her ears, between her thighs, even sinking through the fabric to her navel.

Glorious and never-ending.

She lay prostrate, vulnerable to the ecstasy of the storm. She prayed to melt away in the rain. This all started with a storm, hadn't it? She prayed for this horrible joke to end. She prayed to wake up in the middle of the twenty-first century.

No bubble bath, no shampoo, just a shower from on high.

Wash it all away. Or let me drown.

Her muscles began to cramp from the cold, and she struggled not to move. Her teeth rattled, protesting her skin's chill until she could bear no more the tingling caress. Soaked through to the marrow, she rolled into a ball and forced herself from her trance.

The rain was more real than anything else here. Tangible on her tongue and flesh.

Both vixen and horse huddled close to the brush that offered no substantial protection. Both animals stared at her with eyes wide and ears bent in disapproval.

"Stop it both of you. It's rain. You won't melt. I didn't. Besides, you should be used to this," she chided.

This final observation earned her a snort from one and a growl from the other.

She gathered her kirtle and boots, scooped the fox into her arms, then wrapped the reins around her free hand and began to walk toward the lake in the distance. A knoll to her left served as a pedestal for the giant warhorse that offered seat to the quiet, proud young druid who had brought her here.

He sat astride his horse, watching her dance in the rain. Even now, as her waltz with nature ended, he watched her. Protecting her. A sentinel for the Golden one?

Not this time.

She spied him from the corner of her eye as she splashed along in the rain. Even the damp cloak of the rain could not hide the dark, brooding expression etched on his brow.

Wynne quickened her steps as she passed him. Kind as he might be, Khyryn still possessed the body and mind of an eleventh century mortal man, whose gaze clung to her like the drenched linen to her flesh...and nearly as chillingly.

She owed him no explanations or apologies.

The wagon perched on the edge of the small lake. The few remaining barrels, as well as Bog and Loth, had been removed from the cart, which stood on its end near a tall oak tree. The warriors' shields hovered above, strung on the tree limbs. Branches and swords interlocked to form a roof extending on either side from the wagon's yoke. Blankets provided a modicum of cover as rain continued to pelt the Danes.

Beneath the edge of the wagon's protection, sat a large clay bowl. Within, glimmered a small fire.

Aberswythe joined Wynne and gathered the reins from her grasp as she stalked toward the camp.

"The vessel keeps the fire alive and sheltered from the wind's breath. That way we might have light and warmth this night."

Wynne's teeth chattered uncontrollably. The shower she had so welcomed half an hour before, tormented her tired muscles now that the sun waned.

"You, young one, have need of that fire's warmth—eh?"

Wynne could only nod at Aberswythe.

Instead of guiding her to the fire, he led her to his horse, and then pulled her to the other side, hidden from the Danes. "The water washes away more than the day's ride. Undress."

Wynne whirled around. "What?"

Aberswythe neither replied to Wynne, nor looked to her as he fiddled with the horse. Finally, content with the condition of his animal, he removed a length of wool from its back and unfolded the fabric, turning around to reveal the drape to Wynne.

"Undress," he repeated.

"I can't. Cnut's men—"

"The Danes fear you. Do you not see? Cnut has instructed them you are to be left alone. They will not risk the wrath of the Heavens, or their leader. Now undress, lest you die of the rain's wrath."

"Or mine."

Wynne flinched at the irritation in Khyryn's voice. "What are you all ruffed up about?"

"A witch they call you, and so you may be. A temptress of nature. You are fortunate no one sought to seize you in your frenzy."

Khyryn tugged the kirtle and boots from her hand, gruffly. She opened her mouth to snap at him. Instead, she let out a yelp as he grabbed the neck of her gown and pulled the cloth straight down her body to her ankles. As quickly as the cry escaped her lips, his hand cupped her mouth and pulled her back against him. "Shh. You, Golden One, are consort to the gods for these men. Show no fear."

Comfort did not reach the timber of his voice, which trembled with fury at her foolishness.

Before she could protest, Aberswythe draped the wool against her body wrapping her in the warmth it still held from the horse's back. She stood stunned and mute as both men layered her in the thickly woven cloth. Aberswythe wrapped a length of leather around her chest, above her breasts, to keep the wool in place and protect her modesty, then gathered the end of the fabric over her shoulders, much like a toga, and secured it with the brooch from his own cloak.

Once satisfied, Aberswythe patted her shoulder and nudged her toward the circle. "Go, sit by the fire. If the rain stops soon, your gown will dry by morning."

Wynne hesitated.

Darkness cloaked the ground now, but not the old druid's face. "That Cnut seeks your counsel is fortuitous for all. Whether your words yield succor or treachery to his cause I cannot affect." His eyes twinkled and he smiled. "Fear no man at the fire, Golden One. Khyryn of Powys and your guard will keep you safe."

"My guard? I don't have a—"

A noise overhead snatched Wynne's attention. She looked up into the branches. Something shifted slightly.

Bog.

Another movement on the ground. The ragamuffin child shifted in his spot near the trunk of the tree.

Loth.

The high-pitched chitter told Wynne the vixen had settled on the boy's lap.

Her guard.

Khyryn cupped her elbow not so gently, and pulled her toward the fire and the throng. Aberswythe had been right. She did feel warmer having shed the cold wet gown.

Draped in a dry cloth, her hair and skin clean from the rain, Wynne felt every bit the goddess. Her cheeks flushed as they broke the ring of huddled Danes. Khyryn moved her to a spot near Cnut, and plopped her down in front of the fire. Claiming a bit of the ground next to her, Khyryn crossed his legs to sit and pulled his tunic from his body.

Cnut grunted and motioned to one of his men who offered her a drinking horn. Khyryn reached out and took the horn from the man, nodded slightly to Wynne, then sipped the liquid. Having satisfied his own thirst— or curiosity—he surrendered the horn to her.

Cnut laughed out loud. "Our Golden One is wise to drink only what we would let pass unto our lips."

Wynne sipped the water slowly. The whole scene reminded her of the stories she had read as a child. Khyryn had shown Cnut and his men that they could trust him, by baring himself to them. He had shown them he returned their trust by drinking the water first, then offering it to her.

Find the druid, she had.

"Tell me, Golden One, what secrets did the

Heavens whisper to you this afternoon when you danced with the wind and rain? Did the wind speak the victor of this land?

Victor of this land. Wynne tried to remember what she had studied about Cnut. Son of Sweyne Forkbeard. Ruled England? When? Married? Died?

"Well?"

Wynne handed the horn back to Khyryn. She turned to look into Cnut's eyes.

Months on a war campaign had bronzed his skin. Tiny creases around the Dane's eyes told the story of a young man who in the past year had questioned his own claim to England. A man much older for the battles fought who still questioned.

A sliver of history classes long passed pressed against her memory.

1016 A.D.

"Edmund's rule will end before this year is finished."

The aged eyes of the warrior king narrowed to slits. Cnut's men fell silent. Only the sound of her own breathing reached her ears in that moment.

"What of his successor?"

She stretched her arms toward the flame, letting the heat slither up the length of her arms and neck to restore her strength. She stood, and with a deep breath, found her character and addressed her audience to give them the show they sought.

She glanced at the men who sat, listening, watching. Then, she focused her attention on Cnut's question. "The man who would be king of Angles and Saxons."

****

Streona did not bother to look at the sentry who spoke. "A woman?" He dipped the quill in the ink and continued to draw the delicate lines of the letters on the vellum.

The young man closed the door behind him and took a step closer to the table.

"Aye, sire. She has at least two guards."

Streona clutched the pen tighter. "A consort, perhaps?"

"Mayhap. She has taken seat with the Danish king and shares wine with him."

"Describe her. Is she fair of face? Or stooped and grizzled like an ogre?"

"She is nearly as tall as some of the men, with golden hair. She rides her own mount.

"The king's whore?" Whores among soldiers were not uncommon.

The man shook his head. "If so, then Cnut treats his concubines better than most men treat their wives."

"Most men do not fancy their wives. It is a wise man who keeps a woman of desire close to his side, else she find another man's bed to her liking."

He set down the quill and took up his cup, eyeing the sentry.

This information nagged at him. "If this woman travels with Cnut, then she is something special to him. I would hear more about this mysterious woman. Send a party to escort them."

"They are within a day's ride. By midday, tomorrow, they will be arrived."

Did Cnut ride to Mercia without legion in hopes of conferring with him? Privately? How fortunate.

"That makes her all the more important. Tell my

wife to ready a place for Cnut's woman."

"Aye, sire."

"And ready your men. One can never tell with damned Viking stock."

The sentry paused, expectantly. Questioningly. Waiting for Streona to explain.

"One can never tell with the Danes, which side they are on."

Chapter Eighteen

Morning broke with ominous clouds splintering the sky. Khyryn sat quite still at the water's edge, watching the reflection of the rainmakers overhead. Occasionally a drop would crash the water's surface, warning of its power.

"You are weary, Khyryn Druid son?"

Khyryn glanced up to find Cnut standing a few paces away.

"Aye. I am weary."

The Dane sat down next to Khyryn. "It is our lifeblood, yours and mine. This." He motioned over his shoulder to the camp. You give your fealty to the Seer and the Priest. I give myself to war."

"I have fought many battles in my time."

"That gives us immortality, eh? Holding a man's life in our hands—throwing our own life to the will of the gods? Sadly, it leaves us with dark dreams."

Khyryn glanced sideways at Cnut. "Dreams that torture a king's sleep?"

"I have not slept well since my father's death. His spectre haunts my slumber."

"What fears does a Viking have of ghosts? You serve his memory by fighting for his legacy."

"I am weary, like you. I no longer seek to make war on those who have surrendered their will to so many kings. What was my father's should be mine. I was not here to forge my brand on the crown my father wore, and thus gave yield to Ironsides, and his father before him."

"Why do you speak so plainly to me?"

Cnut sighed. He held the silence several moments before he spoke. "I would have your Seer."

Khyryn closed his eyes to shut out the reflection of the clouds. "She goes with no one, save those of her choosing. I am sworn to protect her."

"And would you die to that end?"

Khyryn understood the king's question. How easy it would be for the Dane to nod to his men, inciting them to murder the small nomadic band. Four or more to each one, with only Aberswythe and himself to fight the marauders. "It is the way of honor."

"So much bloodshed. Vikings should kill warriors on the battlefield. Not druids in dens of slumber. It offends the gods."

"Then I am saved this morning from dying. And you are saved from bad dreams."

A laugh rumbled within the Dane. Cnut nodded his head. "You have much wisdom and mirth. The Golden One is fortunate to have you at her side."

Khyryn did not answer Cnut.

"A Seer and a Sage. What a fine pair the two of you make. And a Sorcerer completes your circle. That my men fear you when they fear no other in this land says much about your abilities. Khyryn of Powys, you and the Golden One, and the one you call Aberswythe all weave great magic."

Cnut's conversation had changed course.

So easily snared by the hunter am I. Khyryn realized too late that his own silence was tantamount to surrender.

"I am neither sage, nor priest. I will fight you if it is necessary to protect the woman. Or the others."

"Why would I fight you when you are so valuable as an ally? A king needs allies. Especially in a time of war. If I take your Seer, I must kill you, or leave you to fight me on the battlefield. I know the look in your eyes, Druid son, when you speak of defending her. You would seek to kill me. The fight would be good, but wasted. And you would turn to a king you hold little loyalty for. Am I right?"

Cnut's reasoning impressed Khyryn. The Warrior prince knew men's minds and souls, as well as the swing of their swords. "Do you know the one the boy spoke of yesterday?"

"Eadric Streona? He is Alderman to Ironsides."

"It is whispered that he speaks for the king. And that he kills for the king. From the look of your waif, yesterday, there might be much to fear from this man."

Khyryn shook his head. "In truth, I know not what befell Loth's family. However, the boy did serve as slave to Streona. And he did escape near death and worse. He will not go back."

"What of your Bog-troll? Can he keep the boy safe from harm?"

"Aye. Bog is clever enough to hide close to Streona's fortress, and to discover what we are about."

"Then I will do the same. I will save six of my men to scout and keep watch for us. More troops follow us by one day."

An eerie dread crept up Khyryn's spine. "What troops?" This is why Cnut did not fear riding into Streona's compound.

"Danes." Cnut winked at Khyryn and spat onto the grass. "Do not think me such a fool that I would travel without an army. I seek to build an alliance with Streona that we may find a peace between two kings."

Revelation and rage flooded Khyryn's brain, his blood, his soul. "Streona is much more dangerous than other men. Loth has good reason to be afraid of him. You should not make alliances with devils to do your bidding."

"It is wiser to share ale with the demon in your sight than to try to accept succor from a stranger. At least one can scent the poison on the demon's hands. War is a Viking's game. But a king recognizes the strength of live subjects over dead soldiers."

"And you would have us help you?"

"Make no mistake, Khyryn of Powys, the Golden One is Seer to Cnut, son of Sweyn Forkbeard, now. That you choose to stay at her side—yourself, a hound from Hades—bodes well for me. You will keep her safe. She will keep me safe. This is a good arrangement."

Khyryn fisted his hands to calm his words. "Stay away from her, save for her counsel. She will not serve you with her body."

The Dane laughed at Khyryn's threat. He stood over Khyryn, hands on his hips in an all too proprietorial pose. "I will find my pleasure elsewhere, Druid son. I would not anger the Heavens by raping their vessel. She stays with you. For now."

Cnut turned and strolled away from the lake's edge as Khyryn pondered the king's words. From a distance, the Dane called out, "Keep close your Golden One. Anyone powerful enough to sway a king would surely be valuable plunder to one who keeps company with demons."

****

The warm wet tongue tickled the skin just beneath her ear, urging Wynne to consciousness. She lay still wrapped in the wool Aberswythe had given her last night; her head and shoulders resting on her own saddle kept her dry. Mostly.

Shielded from the rest of the camp by the horses Wynne could hear movement in the distance.

How long had she been asleep?

The vixen whined, urging her to sit up. When she did, she found herself staring at Khyryn's boots.

"I thought to do that myself, but worried that you would not take it as well from a man, as from a beast."

Wynne scrunched her eyes into a squint and peered up at him. Sunlight flickering through the tree limbs cast him in silhouette.

She reached for her furry companion, tickling the vixen just beneath the chin. She glared up at him, again a retort on her lips, and then remembered the group of men gathered so near. "You're right."

Khyryn knelt and extended his hand toward the fox. The small dark nose sniffed in greeting, then licked his knuckles, welcoming him. "Cnut rides to Streona's fortress."

"Loth told us that much."

"Nae. Loth told us we rode toward Streona's lands. Cnut told me this morning that he is bound for Streona the man."

"Why?"

"He says he is tired of war."

"And so he plans to march into Streona's camp and

surrender?"

"I do not believe that is his thought. I suspect he wishes to negotiate a truce. And he would have King Edmund's alderman deliver the message."

Wynne shook her head. "No."

"Aye. He plans to leave half his men here. As a precaution."

"No. He must not negotiate a truce."

Every science-fiction time travel novel she had ever read screamed, *never do anything that could affect the past,* inside her head. "I—I don't think that will happen."

Khyryn tilted her chin and stared into her eyes for a very long moment, as if searching for some secret within her gaze. "What will happen?"

"I don't know. All I remember from textbooks is that Cnut becomes king."

"Cnut is convinced that you will reveal to him his next move now that you have proclaimed him king. You are an important tool to his future."

Wynne pushed the vixen from her lap and moved to stand. "That is ridiculous. I did my job. I did as he asked. I played my part as 'Seer'. He is on his own. He and his merry band of marauding Vikings can go play war on their own."

"Nae. Not on his own—"

The ground trembled.

Wynne grabbed for her boots and reached inside for the *s'gian dhu* within, then slipped her feet into the leather stockings.

Before she could do anything else, two hands grabbed her around the waist and hoisted her upward, into the tree.

"Stay! Do not come down for anyone, save for me or Aberswythe," Khyryn's voice commanded. "Do you understand?"

From her perch, Wynne looked through the branches to see a dozen men pull rein not more than thirty feet from where she sat. Between the camp and the horsemen stood a line of Viking warriors, swords drawn. Slivers of light bounced off their shields, held high in defiance.

Words were exchanged, and the sound of horse hooves soared again, then dimmed as riders moved away. The sounds of men and horses had long ended when Wynne finally climbed down from the tree. Once her feet hit the ground, she stayed crouched for a several seconds, listening for any sound of any humans.

Gone.

Now what do I do?

Her horse still tethered to the tree flicked its ears at her question and snorted. A bit of luck that they had left behind a couple of horses as well as the supply wagon when they rode away with Streona's men.

Wynne pulled her newly dried clothes from a nearby branch and quickly dressed. She carefully folded the woolen that Khyryn and Aberswythe had dressed her in last night and draped it across her horse's back before she slid the saddle into place. If she hurried, she could follow their path.

She had nearly finished when the thud and grunt halted her every move.

Including her breathing.

"'Em's goin'. We go too. Aye witch?"

Her exhale strummed a significant sigh of disapproval as she turned, trying to calculate how she might be able to get to her knife.

"We stay behind. They doesn't see us. Bog doesn't likes 'em, Streona's men. They beats Bog. Hurts Loth. Loth! 'Em's gone. Safe now, witch and Bog is."

From high above her head, somewhere in the thick branches of the tree she had slept under and hidden in this morning, came the scurry and rustle of leaves, as if a very large squirrel were dashing about from limb to limb. Within just a few seconds, the boy's lanky legs emerged, followed by the rest of his body.

"Do you mean you were both up in this tree the whole time?"

Both boy and Bog nodded at her, then looked up into the branches as if reconfirming the fact to themselves.

Bog, still gazing upward, spoke first. "Water's supposed to burn a witch. Tha's what Church says." Bog stepped closer to her. "No burns on yer skin."

Wynne's jaw dropped. "Because I am not a witch!"

"Sorcerer's magic," blurted Loth, his eyes were wide with respect. "That they did not see us."

Wynne's cheeks warmed. No doubt if the two had been in the tree, they had watched her undress. That's how Bog knew she had no burns on her body. That, and the fact that they had escaped notice by Streona's men had just elevated her from witch to sorceress in the boy's mind.

She smiled at both of them. Let them have the last word. Did it really matter what the two of them believed her to be, as long as they were not afraid of her?

Or at least wary enough to help her.

"Loth, can you show us the way to Streona's

fortress?"

The boy scrunched his brow in hesitation.

She grasped the boy by his shoulders, leaned close to his face, and spoke quietly. "Loth, Khyryn is with Cnut and his men. Do you remember what you said yesterday?"

Huge, darkened eyes gazed back at her.

"What you said could come to pass if we don't follow them. I know Streona frightens you. But if we do not help Khyryn, then Streona may do just as you said. He may try kill them all."

Bog squatted, and bobbed up and down—not unlike a frog. He grabbed a twig and began to scratch at the ground.

Loth tamped the ground, kicking it as if he were angry at the soft earth.

Bog did not look up from his work but spoke. "Loth will take us to find Druid son an' the Red one. But first, we eat."

Still digging in the soil, Bog replaced the twig with his own hands, delving deep into the ground, and retrieving a palm full of turf, and something squiggly. Without another word, he plucked a huge earthworm from the mess, wiped it on his coat and tossed it into his mouth, then reached for another.

"Dear merciful God in heaven! You are insane. You're eating worms?"

Bog stopped in mid chew and stared questioningly at her. "Worms eats Bog when 'im's dead and in the earth. So does Bog eat worms while 'im's alive." He winked at Wynne and swallowed. Then popped another one into his mouth as he held his hand out to her.

Wynne fought hard against the nausea erupting in

her own stomach and shook her head vehemently in protest.

Bog offered the boy the same. Loth reached out and pulled one from the proffered hand. Loth looked at the worm for a moment then dropped it back to the ground.

Bogg continued to chew. "What does witches eat? Bog would know—what feeds a witch? A Seer?"

Wynne grimaced against the image of the troll-like creature that sat eating worms like popcorn. "Aaagh. Anything but worms. Or live stuff. You've seen what I eat. I eat what the others eat...berries, cheese, bread—"

"Fish?"

"What?"

"Fish. Fish comes from water. You like water. You danced in water when it rained. You eat fish?"

"Yes. But not live fish."

Bog crawled toward the wagon where the fire had burned last night and returned with a bowl he handed to Wynne.

She peered at the contents then back at Bog.

Fish. Dried. Smoked. Not live. Not raw. Not worms.

"Fish." Wynne broke off a piece and tasted it. The year 1016 could definitely use some lessons in seasoning food. However, she received the offering gratefully, and shared what she had with Loth.

Bog smiled and nodded at the two. "Bog thinks they will not hear our stomachs growl. We will be clever, then sneak upon the viper's den."

"Viper's den? Streona?"

"Aye. Beast with fangs. Bellywalker."

"Bellywalker? What is that, Bog?"

Bellywalker. Viper. Witch knows. She talks to bellywalker. Bog sees. Bog hears much. Bellywalker eats men's souls. Witch knows."

Bog's ramblings had unraveled into a series of broken blatherings. "I think you've eaten too many worms, Bog. I have never met Streona. I have never talked to him."

"Not you," Loth interrupted.

"Not me?" Wynne stared at Bog, then at the boy. "If he isn't talking about me, then who does he mean?"

"Dark magic. Wind swirls and the trees scream. Bog sees 'im come through the stones. Hears the witch cackle, Bog does. Balance she says."

Balance. Where had she heard that?

"She dances with druids, she dances with vipers. She eats men's souls that they would live an eternity. Bog sees. Bog hears. Bog is clever. Bog does not stay about when the witch is near."

"Who, Bog? Who are you talking about?"

Bog stopped his rant in mid speak. He and Loth exchanged glances.

Loth turned to Wynne—his voice barely more than a whisper. "Her name is Elleran."

Chapter Nineteen

Uffyngdon

The soldier spat blood onto the floor, and lifted his face to meet his master's glare.

Eadric repeated his question, more calmly this time. "Where is the woman?"

The guard of troops he had dispatched to intercept Cnut's troops had returned with the Dane and his soldiers, but without the mysterious woman who had been seen with them less than two days ago.

Eadric Streona sneered at the soldier who knelt in utter subservience to his wrath.

Details.

Long ago, he had learned that details could undo a scheme. Details could undermine a kingdom. Details left untidied could return to bear witness against him. Eadric Streona never left witnesses or untidied details to chance.

Voices outside proclaimed the arrival of his guests.

Time to be charming. Time to win a king's confidence.

He bent very close to the sentry and growled in a voice so low and threatening, beads of sweat spotted the man's brow. "Take a message to your mistress that our guests and I command her presence. Once you have delivered the message, ride out once more and find the woman. If she had her own guard, she is important to Cnut. If she is important to Cnut, then she is important to me. And therefore, that very important woman could save your life. Do you understand me?"

The soldier nodded, stood, and retreated.

Streona breathed deeply and perused the standards that hung in the room. Edith had draped the room generously to receive a visiting potentate. Not nearly as grand as the great Roman halls had been, yet this room did reflect something of grandeur. If he had his way, it would outshine Winchester. Soon enough.

He resumed his seat just as the large gated doors of the keep's main building swung open to admit the party. Even he, who had walked as a king himself, quaked. A tremor shot through his body at the site of Cnut and his band of Viking warriors.

Eadric smiled as seductively as the throng moved toward him.

"Son of Sweyn Forkbeard, I welcome you to my table. Come, feast and rest your troops. It is a brilliant day filled with good fortune that brings you so far from the lands of your father."

Cnut motioned his men to halt as he stepped forward. "Eadric Streona, alderman of Mercia. Your generosity and escort are met with favor." He paused to take a long look at the Hall.

"It seems the fortune is ours. Edmund gives greater largess to his vassals than to his soldiers. That is indeed fortunate."

"Is this your entire party? I would be remiss if I failed to offer succor to any who were not among you this morning when my men greeted you. If such is the case, I assure you we can make amends."

"My band is complete. This is a journey of diplomacy, not of battle. You can see that we do not carry the manpower to offer any offense."

Again a tremor raked Eadric's spine. A cold chill clawing from tail to tongue, causing the hair on his neck to bristle.

A man to be wary of.

Diplomacy.

Did Cnut's words mock him? Or did he see the truth beneath the façade? Had Cnut come to negotiate a truce after all? Or did he have something more lucrative in mind?

The band of men spread apart, reluctantly seeking the warmth of the fire or the comfort of a carpeted bench. Vikings. Barbarians as far as Eadric could see. Beards as long as their braids, some of them. Ragged clothing stained with blood and dirt—badges of war. A few wore cloaks that covered their tunics. One even kept his hood drawn—

A sound drew his attention from the stranger as a woman cleared her throat behind him. Eadric turned to see Edith standing perfectly still just inside the entryway.

Demure, poised. Edith, looked positively royal in a gown of deepest blue wool, trimmed with fur at the collar. She held her arms folded across her waist, a white linen cloth draped over them. A perfect hostess, ready to serve her guests.

Applaudable. Edmund's house had trained this princess well. Best of all, she had taken special care to comb the braid from her hair so that it splayed across her shoulder in rippling brown waves, pouring down to her waist.

Eadric's groin hardened at the sight of his own wife. Had he not needed her to conduct his business, she would find herself kneeling before him, serving his desires instead of Cnut's.

"Ah, Cnut, allow me present the lady of this house. My wife Edith does keep your needs well met this day. Come, wife, join our revelry."

Edith kept her eyes lowered, as she moved across the shadowed floor to join her husband. She did, however, lift her chin to the Viking king.

"Good wife, tend you to Cnut and his men, our guests. See that their hunger is sated and that they want for nothing."

She dipped in courteous greeting, never removing her gaze from Cnut's. Eadric admired the long straight neck holding that chin so high as she met the Dane. More than her regal stance, he appreciated the admiration in the Viking's face as he bowed in response.

"Enjoy all that my house can offer you and your men. When you are rested well and of a mind to talk, we shall engage each other in conversation. Wife, bring these men drink."

As if conjured, two serving women appeared at Edith's side, one with cups, another with mead. Once a goblet had been filled, Edith brought the cup to her lips, poured the wine into her mouth so that Cnut could see her drink the liquid, assuring all present that no poison tainted the cup. She then offered the goblet to the king.

Once Cnut accepted her goblet, the serving women moved about the room, tending to the other men, who received the mead warmly.

Eadric smiled at his wife. "Well shown, good wife.

I shall leave you to your work. The son and daughter of kings should have much in common. Spare not our guest your generosity of spirit."

Already, he could see that mead married well with the thirst of Danes. Cnut's men laughed and cheered the servers with howls of approval each time a new pitcher emptied. Soon, the mead would loosen their tongues as well as their trousers. When it did, he would hear their secrets. And plan his future.

One element still niggled at him. The woman. A woman of enough importance that she had attendants. A woman who rode with the king. A woman who had vanished.

Wherever the woman had disappeared to, he wanted her found. Whatever she meant to Cnut, her absence meant more. Details should never be left to chance.

****

The serving woman tried to refill his cup, but Khyryn placed his hand over the top, earning him a frown from the girl.

Hidden beneath the hood, he had watched the man who had been his brother manipulate the two—Edith and Cnut.

She bore the stance of a princess, straight and tall, proud and prudent in her carriage.

Does she know the man she is married to?

Pehaps no more than Gwynndolwyn had.

Khyryn asked for bread, and enjoyed a round of freshly baked crust when the loaves were brought to the tables. Soft and warm, he had not had such fine fare in many weeks.

Cnut's men enjoyed the offering as well. They

drank profusely, never wavering when offered more. Lady Edith and the other women brought forth trenchers with apples, bread, currants, and broken chunks of cheese. The food, though simple, appeased the group. Tired of camp work, the luxury of being waited on quickly sated to excess Cnut's fine warriors.

Khyryn sat comfortably guarding his goblet, lest another enthusiastic female try to refill it. He listened to the sluggish speech of his companions as they filled their bellies and their eyes.

Cnut remained seated at the head of the table, allowing Lady Edith to cut an apple into small slices and serve it to him. Son and daughter of a king.

Eadric had married well. Edmund's sister, Edith, provided the alderman with more than a wife. She provided a link to the throne. And a tempting diversion for a visiting ruler.

Where nature had failed to touch Edith with beauty, heritage had given her grace. The daughter of Aethelred possessed the posture of a priestess—reverent and commanding. No person in the Hall could be unaware of her presence. At the moment, she seemed intent on capturing every bit of Cnut's attention.

Eadric—Uddryd—had changed very little in this life. He still surrounded himself with the plunder of a king's world. He held power over men, existed in luxury, and cared little for entertaining anyone save himself.

Eadric's conceit had proven lucky for Khyryn. Eadric had not recognized him in the crowd. With a bit more luck, no one would notice his departure.

Streona's men had charged the camp on the

premise of inviting Cnut to the alderman's fortress. An escort of four would have been expected. An army of twenty marshalled the entire camp.

Except for four.

Khyryn had not seen Aberswythe since daybreak. Bog and Loth no doubt heard the riders and stayed hidden where they slept. Neither man, nor boy wanted to be recognized by Streona's men.

As for Gwynndolwyn, she had done as he warned. She had remained silent, hidden within the thick limbs of the tree, wrapped in the brown woolen that served to disguise her. She had food, water, and a knife for protection.

If she stayed put.

Khyryn's thoughts faded as the scene between Cnut and Edith continued to play. She spoke softly to him, plying him with mead. She did not smile beguilingly at him. Rather, she tended him solemnly. When she had refilled his goblet for the third time and saw it touch his lips, she slid her hands to his boots and untied the straps from around his calves, as a servant might do for a master.

She called for a maid who brought forth a large bowl of water. Setting the bowl before the fire, she led Cnut from the table to Streona's chair by the hearth, and bade him sit as she removed his boots and set about washing his legs and feet.

No task for a princess.

Gently, she dipped a cloth into the water and trickled it over his skin, rubbing the shank with the cloth until Cnut's eyes glazed with the pleasure of her touch.

The other men in the Hall had found comfort in the

mead as well as the attention of the house's servants. These Danes cared not how or where their lusts were satisfied.

Khyryn remained in his corner, hood and cowl drawn to hide his face. Though he could not be seen, he could witness much.

And for what played before him, he envied Uddryd—or Eadric's absence. He too would have deserted such a scene. Reminiscent of the Bacchanal celebrations brought upon these lands when the Romans brought their gods. Doubtless, his brother had studied diligently the deals and deceits conferred in such settings.

And now as Alderman, Eadric set the stage himself for such a seduction as would befit or break a king.

Edith finished washing Cnut's legs and feet, then dried them with a towel. Her gaze darted warily around the room, as if searching for some evidence of spies. Finally, content that no one watched her, she rose and extended her hand to Cnut. He accepted her invitation, and she quietly ushered him through a darkened archway.

The structure of the keep and of the fortress walls were purely Roman. Little more than a hill fort, the structures combined stone and wood to create a sound, weatherproof main building with smaller buildings on either side. Wooden walkways, like bridges, connected the outer buildings, with lattice overhead. As they had dismounted, Khyryn had seen the telling remnants of grapevines now drying to mark the season's end. Soon autumn and Samhain would bring the colder rains to wash away the dead leaves and shriveled fruits.

How unusual that one who resented so much about

the Roman occupation had sought to recreate so much of it within these walls.

Beyond the rampart—at the bottom of the hill—lay a marsh to impede invaders. If anyone could make it through the mire and up the steep slope, the tall barricade of the rampart built by tree trunks lashed together and mortared with mud would surely discourage their efforts.

One way in. One way out. Simple hill fort strategy. As ancient as Khyryn himself.

As did Uddryd so many lifetimes ago, Eadric Streona kept careful rein of that which belonged to him, as well as that which he did not yet hold in his grasp.

The voices of the bawdier soldiers swelled and subsided their native tongue slurred in their revelry.

Khyryn downed the last bit of mead and set down the earthen goblet.

So...where does our host hide himself these hours while his guests sate their desires with tainted bait?

More importantly—how can I join him?

****

Wynne bristled at the sound of the name. "What do you know of Elleran?"

Loth's eyes widened as he peered at Wynne. "She—she is wicked. She comes to those who seek the magic of the Darkness."

"Hogwash. That's all nonsense." Despite her own words, Wynne believed there might be something to the boy's assertion.

Particularly after what she had experienced in Elleran's tent at the faire. "Tell me what you've seen and heard. Is she here?"

If Elleran were nearby, Wynne suspected the old

woman could propel her back to the twenty-first century. Stones or no stones.

"Alderman Streona's men brought her to the keep once," the boy said. "Mad and wild she was, that they had dared to drag her from her home, she said. She warned that their ballochs would shrivel, and they would not be able to sleep for the loss of their manhood."

That's her, all right. Wynne suppressed a smile and nodded the body to continue.

"I had fallen asleep in the vestibule between the main Hall and where the servants slept. I heard him accuse her of trying to trick him."

"How?"

"He said she knew the stone. He knew she had taken it and the treasure, and that he would have it back."

"What stone?" Icy recognition clung to her.

"I don't know. Elleran called him a fool. Said she had no need of stones or gold. Her power came from the unseen ones."

"What else did you hear, Loth?"

"She said, 'Only see the here and now—not the future or the past.' Said women see both because they dance with both when they give birth. Said that all time lives in the belly of the woman."

"And?"

"Nothing more. She sat for a time, quiet. She told him if he could not find the stone, the victories he sought would be short lived."

If he could not find the stone...

"Loth, did either of them say anything about what the stone looked like?"

The young boy shook his head.

Wynne knelt in front of Loth and took his hands into hers. "Loth, this is important. Did Elleran ever say anything about me or about Khyryn?"

Surprise. Confusion. "Nae."

Bog, who had been silent during Loth's discourse, now started to bob up and down excitedly. "Witches ken witches. One dark. One light. The blind kens sight. The sight kens right. Kings beware the witch so bright. For she kens who will win the fight."

Again and thrice Bog repeated his song, all the time weaving and bobbing, as if dancing to his own cadence. "The blind kens sight. The sight kens right. Kings beware the witch so bright."

Wynne's head began to reel. Elleran. Here. So close. Helping Eadric Streona. Or as Aberswythe and Khyryn would have her believe—Uddryd.

What if the stone he sought from Elleran was the same one she had seen Richard Uddryd steal from the excavation site? What significance could that have for Eadric Streona? If he held his memories, as Khyryn did, then the stone apparently had little or nothing to do with his ability to recall the past.

Could it have something to do with his ability to control his future?

"Loth, what happened when the alderman and Elleran finished their conversation? Where did Elleran go?"

The boy swallowed hard, and stared at Wynne, not answering.

"Loth?"

"Witches dance around the fire...raise the flames e'er higher," sang Bog.

"Shh, Bog. Now's not the time. Loth, answer me."

"They took her off into the night. He told 'em to put her under a rock, so she could not crawl out."

"Who took her?"

"The alderman's men."

Bog's cadence changed. "Brimstone and ballochs. Good and Evil dance around, and one will soon be in the ground."

The boy's hands trembled as she held him. "Are you a witch? Like Bog says?"

She narrowed her eyes to slits and glared at the troll weaving, trancelike, singing nonsense. *If I were, I'd zap him back to the pond he came from.* "Do you want me to be, Loth?"

"Bog says you have special magic."

Magic...From the root magi...knowledge. Finally something English Language coursework is good for.

Well, this she could play up a bit. "Magic, Loth? Not so strong as you may have seen. But enough to win Cnut's favor."

Loth frowned at her. "But Streona's men took them."

"And what would make Cnut and Khyryn of Powys hide me so Streona's own men would not find me, eh, young one?"

The boy frowned deeper, confusion etched on his brow.

She had nothing to lose. "Loth, I have read the future."

Not a lie.

"Cnut will be king. Edmund Ironsides will fall from power."

Bog stopped his singing.

A blank, wide stare stole over the youth's face as comprehension dawned. "If Cnut is king, then he will protect Master Khyryn."

She shrugged. *Not likely*. Vikings were never known for their goodwill.

"And if Cnut is king," Loth persisted, "then Alderman Streona will not kill Master Khyryn?"

Such innocence reflected in young, wishful eyes. Wynne brushed her hand across the boy's dirt-smeared cheek, and smiled.

She would not whisper promises she could not keep.

And in Loth's single question, she found her own despair. Despite Bog and the boy, Wynne realized she stood abandoned. The only three people who knew how to get her back to her own world were gone. Dead perhaps.

Her hand strayed to the scar over her abdomen. Streona...Uddryd...Richard...Eadric Streona. All one man.

She had to make certain Cnut did not die by Streona's hand. According to Loth, Streona killed without conscience. What would stop him from killing Cnut?

Not what. Who.

Wynne brought her finger to her lips as if sharing a secret with the young boy. "Take me to him."

Chapter Twenty

Uffyngdon

Streona gripped the candle and closed his hand around the tiny flame, extinguishing it. The searing sensation jolted him. Exultation in anticipation of the pain wrought familiarity.

The Romans had taught him to embrace the pleasure of pain. Use of such a skill carefully, and it became a constructive device for torture and persuasion. Fear and pain were great motivators. And of course, in more intimate settings, when one transcended the suffering, sensory pleasure took over. Such small ecstasies had served him well. Both in battle and in bed.

Uddryd learned the lessons well. *Thus, I profit from my memories...from his penury.*

Adrenalin surged through his veins as the heat of the burn radiated from his palm up his arm. Shortly, Edith would bring Cnut to him. The Viking's appetites, once sated, would put him in a better mind to negotiate.

Oh what torture would Edmund suffer to know his sister had lain with Cnut. *And by mine own consent.*

A king and kingdom could be ravaged, plundered, destroyed in many ways.

A tingle rippled through him. Someone had entered the room.

Without turning to favor her with his glance, he

goaded, "So, wife, did our guest prick you with his Viking's horn? Did you give him ample port? Tell me you did drain him of his ferocity so he will accept me as—"

Shock cast him back against the wall. Two arms' length separated him from the brink of hell. Where Edith should have been, stood a figure cloaked in drab wool. Cowl and hood drawn, Eadric bore no doubt as to the face hidden in shadow.

Before the familiar hand rose to pull back the hood and reveal the interloper's identity, Eadric closed his hand and traced the burn mark on his palm.

"Ah, my memory has returned at last."

A smirk marked the druid's mouth. "I am glad to hear my message made its way to your ears safely."

"Your message was delivered. And the messenger discarded." He shook himself and braced himself against the wall, taking in the visage of his once trusted brother.

"You must lose many good people that way."

Now it was his turn to smirk. "Seldom. No reply is necessary when I send a message."

"And yet here I am. And by your generous invitation."

An unexpected surprise. "You ride with Cnut?"

"For the present."

The Dane had gained a dangerous pawn. Eadric paced. Better the cat than the mouse. "That explains the smell. Treason has a distinct foul odor."

"A scent you must be familiar with by now."

"I only reek of prudent judgment."

"You are advisor to Edmund. You are married to his sister."

"And treason is something you do know a bit about, isn't it—dear brother? Perhaps you can impart some revelation about the proper way to—"

"Edith is your wife."

"And as such, she does as I command. She is a commodity. A prize for deeds accomplished. Although I might reward her for her performance today, if Cnut is amenable. If he is not amenable, then perhaps I should have her taken to the stables and scrubbed down with horse shite. That should take away the stench of a Dane. But then how would her brother know her from a stable boy's wench? For that matter, how would I?" Even in the shadows, he could see Khyryn rankle. Such a waste of sentimentality.

"You have learned nothing from your many lifetimes, Uddryd."

"Oh, I have, Khyryn. I have learned to survive. And to thrive among the flies. In this life, I have managed to master the game. Why squander precious time and energy seeking the crown when all I need is my hand on the throne?"

"It is whispered you steal the Dane geld with one hand while you sign Edmund's name with the other."

Eadric roared his approval. "That is the best description I have heard yet. Someone else did say I could crush a landowners' cock in one hand while culling gold from the king's with the other. Hence the name, Streona. Acquisitor."

"And you speak to me of treason?"

"It is your first treason I have to thank for all my earned wisdom dear brother. Have you learned nothing in your own experiences? Oh, wait. I forgot. You swore your allegiance to the whore. Whereas, I make whores swear their allegiance to me."

Silence engulfed the room.

Rage pumped through Khrym's voice as his words built to a crescendo. "Another name could not hide the visage of hate that utters such insults. You are Uddryd, once, and evermore.

"Tell me, Khyryn of Powys, have you forsaken your vow of abstinence in this lifetime. Do you ravish every fair-haired woman who bears resemblance to your fair Gwynndolwyn? Do you steal the brides from their marriage beds to taste the honeyed nectar of their womanhood before their husbands can feast? Or do you merely stroke your…*conscience*… with a chaste palm to seek release for your cursed soul?"

"The curse is yours as well, is it not? You had her blood upon your hands when you sought sanctuary within my cave."

"A wasted sacrifice. If I had known of the impending invasion, I could have offered her to Caesar's troops. A priestess and queen to gorge the carnal appetites of the Romans."

Khyryn's arm swung out and cracked against Eadric's chin, knocking him back a step. He retaliated with a blow of his own, his right hand meeting Khyryn's cheek.Khyryn countered by slamming his left shoulder into his brother's chest, charging like a beast to send him flying to the wall.

Khyryn lost his balance for a split second, and Eadric retrieved a dagger from the table, slicing the space between them, the blade halting against Khyryn's right arm.

Satisfaction glinted on the metal. "Oh, foolish brother, you must learn to control your temper. It will

be the end of you yet. This time, the game is mine."
Tauntingly, he ran his tongue along the dagger's edge,
wiping the blade clean of Khyryn's blood.

Khyryn wrapped his good hand around the cut on
his arm. "How inconvenient for all of us."

"On the contrary. I can honestly say I've never
been more grateful see to you. A chance at the ultimate
revenge. And a king for the taking."

Khyryn smiled. "A worthwhile sacrifice for my
part to see you lose."

"What loss would be mine? I would have your
heart in my hands, a Danish king for ransom, and
Edmund would be at my command once more, grateful
that I rid him of the mess of prolonged war. Win. Win.
Win."

"Not according to Cnut's prophecy." His smile
broadened.

"What?"

Blood trickled through Khyryn's fingers as he
spoke. "Did your spies not tell what has been
prophesied? I find that hard to believe. Why else would
you entertain Cnut? Even send escort for the northern
king?"

A current of caution passed through Eadric like
lightning. "Where is the woman?"

Khyryn took a deep breath. Another shift in the
game. Who?"

"Cnut's concubine. Consort. Whatever she is to
him. Where is she now?"

Khyryn's smile faltered. Blood soaked the sleeve
of his tunic. "I know of no consort."

"My men saw her. If she is no consort, then by
what warrant does she travel with her own guard?"

As the blood seeped from the wound, so did it blanch his face. Eadric did not miss his shiver.

"This woman. She is the soothsayer. Is she not?"

"Perhaps it would be best for you to kill me."

"In time, Khyryn. In time. But this game intrigues me more with each passing shadow of the sun. Who is she? And why was she not with you when my men found your camp?"

"I cannot speak to either query."

"Damn you—"

"I am already damned. Tell me, Uddryd, why would Elleran gift you with this curse as well?"

"Elleran called it 'balance'. I call it justice. Why should you have all the fun? Tell me of Cnut's soothsayer. Of the woman who rides with a king."

"Mayhap it was a spirit your men saw. A spectre that clings to the Norse. They follow ancient gods still. Per chance, they met Elleran."

Eadric's reply came swiftly as the tip of the dagger sliced Khyryn's cheek. The tearing of his flesh hissed like a branding iron. He blocked the return swipe with his good hand and sent the blade flying across the room to land in the blazing hearth.

A voice called from the door. "Sire?"

"Enter!"

A waif of a girl pushed the curtain aside and hovered at the threshold. "Master Streona, your wife awaits you in her chamber."

Eadric watched the dagger smoldering in the fire. "Call the sentry. Tell him I have captured a spy sent to kill us."

The child did not answer, but turned and ran, yelling for the guard as she retreated.

Khyryn wiped his face. "You cannot hold me as prisoner here. I ride with Cnut's men."

"And when they discover one of his men dead, and you with the bloodied dagger on your broken body? Who will defend you?"

Even as he contemplated his escape, Khyryn could hear the guard's footfall in the corridor. "Cnut will know it is not so."

"Cnut will be unable to do anything about it. I assure you Edith is possessed of a rare talent with herbs. If she has done her work well, Cnut has spent himself into a slumber from which he will not waken before the moon is high. Which gives me time to fix my plans. Oh, did Cnut's prophet not see that as well?"

Mirth of evil filled his smile of victory, as a heavy thud cracked the back of Khyryn's skull. The blow splintered his concentration and Khyryn fell into oblivion.

****

Eadric slid his hands across the thick carved oak of his wife's chair, bringing them to rest on her forearms. He breathed deeply the scent of her hair, freshly rinsed and powdered with ground cloves. She shuddered as his breath met her ear. "Did you please the Viking king?"

"I did as you commanded, husband. I served his desire."

She tugged against his clutch, which only served to tighten his hold. "Tell me, wife, how does a Saxon princess pleasure a Dane? Did you ride him as you would an unbroken stallion? Or did he bind you to a table and impale you as a master binds a slave to the mast of his ship?"

Edith gave no answer, save a sharp intake of air,

accompanied by the heaving of her body as she staved off a fit of retching. The barb had stuck.

"Women are so simple and weak. The mere mention of an activity so common to the most basic of creatures evokes such violent horror in them."

"No doubt it is the thought of that most common and vulgar act committed by your very person that so reviles them."

He cupped her jaw to cease her speech and tilted her head back until her eyes met his. "Surely not." He held her head locked against the back of her chair, his left hand gripping her left wrist tightly, until she moved her right hand to claw and entreat him to release the pressure against her throat.

"Did you know, my dear, that in the Roman houses, it was acceptable for husbands and wives to have several lovers? Some slaves were bought purely for recreational purposes."

"I am not a slave," she hissed.

"No. You are a prize worth having. A king's daughter. A woman of noble birth. You are the consummate hostess for a king's most trusted advisor. That is why I entrusted this task to you—the only one with the ability to seduce a nobleman—a royal spawn. See how important you are to me?"

He pressed his fingers into the flesh of her face and bent his head to press his lips against her puckered mouth. "I hope he pleased you as you no doubt pleased him. Most importantly, will he be receptive to my words when we break bread together? If you wish, you may join us. Then we can proclaim of your many talents. You are something he and I share in common."

He released her, letting her wilt where she sat,

gripping the armrests, drinking deep gusts of air into her lungs. He filled a cup with water, drank his fill, then set the near empty cup before her on the table.

"You see, Edith? I thirst for you and you alone. And yet my want goes unfulfilled this day."

"By what evil seed were you born?"

A witch's cunning under a blood red moon. "That is a story for another time. I have many affairs to attend to."

"Do your affairs include the man my maid saw bleeding in your chamber, my lord husband?"

He slowed his retreat. "He is of no concern to you."

"Yet he interests me greatly." Her speech was measured. As if she had rehearsed each word.

"What interest do you have in a thief and murderer?"

"The maid tells me he is a killer."

Details. "A killer is a murderer. Why this parry of words?"

Edith stood and faced him. Her hair hung loosely about her shoulders, still damp. Against the pallor of her skin he beheld his own seal. The imprint of his fingers bruised her flesh. "He is one of Cnut's men. I spied him in the Hall this afternoon."

"What of it?"

"He did not care for our mead, as his companions drank to excess. Mayhap he is as you say, a killer, employed by Cnut to kill you? Alderman and advisor to Edmund, and by my own brother's vow, Cnut's sworn enemy?"

Eadric bristled at her gibe. "Precisely why he must be dealt with quickly."

"Killers and rapists. I think I shall join the supper this night. You are correct. There is much common ground between the two of you. Perhaps I shall forge the bond of your alliance." She sighed and shook her head. "Such a pity, though."

Outside her chamber, voices sounded, shouting.

"What say you?"

"I fear, husband, that in my duties as hostess, I have inadvertently set your plans awry."

Eadric turned on his heel and bounded toward the yelling. He quickened his pace as the frenzy grew in the courtyard. Two grooms and the maid stood in the baily, the stable door opened wide.

A more maddening sight, however, hovered near the fortress gate, which swung wide and unattended save for the slumped figure of the guard Eadric had entrusted to shackle Khyryn.

Far beyond the marsh bridge, the shadow of a figure in motion, moving away as if carried on the wind. More precisely, on a horse.

"You!" he spat at the girl who stood trembling, the drugged cup in her hands. "You set him free." *His life in my hands. Gone. Set free. Bitch.*

Shock dawned on the child's face. "As m' lady set me to. She said to tend his wounds, an'—"

He rounded on the maid. "Traitor!"

"No, sire! Lady Edith bade me—"

The maddening fury drowned out the sound of the girl's cries and pleas. Eadric seized the metal ladle that rested in the water bucket near the stable. Clutching it with the strength of a gladiator, he brought it soundly down upon the shrieking whelp's head. Metal split flesh and bone as she fell, voiceless, into the mud.

The ladle slipped from his fingers and bounced off the lifeless body. Somewhere nearby, someone screamed. Then, all fell silent.

Still. Reverent. Fearful. As it should be.

Even Cnut's men stood, staring in mute acknowledgement. Acquisitor and Alderman of Mercia, Eadric Streona served as judge and executioner within these walls.

He ordered the gates closed, the mess cleaned up, and then he turned his attention to his guests.

"Good warriors, let us return to revelry. Such domestic strife misguides your treaty of friendship. Let tonight bond us, friends and allies."

At his command, the Danes fell into idle whispers, clearing the doorway as they drifted back to their games.

Edith stood in the archway, tall and fierce in her victory. She stared beyond the bloodied remains of her maid, at him.

Anger and admiration warred within him as he noted her stance and her expression.

She had woven this deception as she wove fine cloth upon her loom. While his wife entertained her husband's curiosity, she had set her maid, Hannah to unravel his plan. She had set Khyryn free. She had bested him.

A dangerous detail he had taken for granted.

An arrogant smile played on his wife's lips, one he could not ignore. He was well matched this day in the game. Edith had learned much at the lap of kings.

Chapter Twenty-One

Thorns and scrub scraped Wynne's hands and knees, and she cut her fingers and palms on the sharp edges of the rocks hidden beneath. The tall grasses had secluded her as she and Loth maneuvered through meadow and marsh.

Climbing ever higher up the hill toward the fortress wall, she did not need to wonder why there were no sentries posted on this side of the barbican. "When we do get to the top, how am I supposed to get over that?"

The protective wall had been built of individual logs, mortared and bound together, ended with rough-hewn points where the trees had been chopped.

Loth looked at the spires. "No one climbs over that. There is another way. Underground. It is where they keep the stores in the winter.

"A cellar?"

Loth stared at Wynne blankly. "Seler?"

"Just show me."

"It is beneath the ridge. There is a hole in the earth. The yard wall stands over it, but the ground is hollow."

"A cellar. Perfect. Where does it come out?"

Loth gripped the side of the hill fiercely, digging his fingers deeply into the grass to grab onto the rocks. He frowned at Wynne. "It goes nowhere. It is a hole."

Wynne sighed. "So I can be seen by anybody walking by?"

This time the boy grinned at her. "The alderman's guards did not see you when you were just over their heads. Who would see you beneath their boots?"

"Remind me to explain sarcasm to you when this is finished."

As Loth had indicated, beneath a part of the earthen ridge of the hill, the grass thinned. The earth gave way to a cool, dark, cave-like hole nearly three feet wide, nearly two feet high. Even from her perch, Wynne could see from the sunlight streaming over her shoulder, that there were casks deep in the hole.

"Loth? Who knows about this hole?"

"The guards and the people who work in the kitchens."

"Not the spot where the casks are. Who knows that there is a tunnel that leads out of the fortress?"

"Everyone. Why?"

"Why? Because it isn't much of a secret getaway if everyone knows of its existence."

"But this one is not used anymore. They use it only to store the barrels. And the food they dry after the harvest."

"This one. There are others?

"Of course. Where else would people squat and—"

"Oh, Loth! No. Don't tell me!"

"What?"

"This is a latrine?"

"A what?"

"A place to—a place to relieve yourself?"

"To relieve the bowels. Aye. At least it was once."

"Why not now?"

"None go near it. The alderman's wife, Lady Edith says it is haunted by spirits."

"A haunted latrine? You must be joking."

"Nae, no jest. I heard her say she herself sees the ghosts of those her husband has killed dancing from the hole, climbing from the depths of hell, come back to seek their revenge upon him. Says we shouldna' stand about, in case they see us as servants to the alderman and reap their revenge upon us."

"And yet it is safe enough for the wine and ale that they keep within the walls."

Loth considered this for a very long moment. "Mayhap, spirits are not fond of wine and ale."

Wynne held her breath to keep from laughing out loud. "Loth, I think the Lady Edith is smarter than her husband and his guards credit her."

The boy stared blankly at Wynne for a while, then his eyes widened in realization. "D'ye mean tha' she kens abou' this?"

Wynne winked at him. "I do."

Loth grinned. "Then she is nae wary of spirits 'erself?"

Wynne nodded and mimicked the boy's rural accent. "Aye, lad. She's nae wary of spirits. But she is wary of the alderman. And anyone who reports back to him. She can sneak out, just as you did. And no one dares investigate for fear of ghosts."

A commotion overhead forced them both flat against the hillside. Wynne's muscles burned with fear and effort as she clung tightly onto the hardened ridge, the toes of her boots hanging onto the thin, chalk-like rock that protruded from the grass.

Far above them, from the top of the fortress wall came voices and the sound of commotion. A blur swooshed past them and tumbled down to finally land on the marsh grass at the base of the hill.

Something had fallen. No. Something had been dropped.

Wynne focused on a crumpled heap of rags in the mud.

Grey and willowy, a small arm protruded from the cloth. Lifeless.

Not something. Someone.

Loth's face paled as he looked, first at her, then over his shoulder toward the pile.

A gentle wheeze escaped his small frame.

"Loth. Look at me, Loth."

Suddenly as fragile as a dragonfly, the child turned his eyes from the scene below.

She reached out her right hand and placed it against his cheek. Seconds became minutes as they stayed perfectly still, listening to the sounds of footfall on the opposite side of the wall, only inches from their own heads.

Wynne held his attention, struggling to keep him from looking at the body. And struggling to avert her own gaze. The quiet enveloped them both.

Once certain no one could hear them, she fractured the silence. "Loth, you have done what I asked of you. Go back to Bog. He will keep you safe. You hear me?"

He never severed eye contact with her, but Wynne knew the images he dwelled upon were of his own time imprisoned within the barrier walls—caged like an animal.

In all her years of studying the past, she never understood until this very moment, reading this boy's face, just what it meant to be common. In her world, castle walls possessed the magic and romance of glorious historical stories.

History is written by the victors.

In Loth's world, however, those who lived within and without the protection of the walls paid for their choices. Often with their own lives.

Nobody here cared why Richard Uddryd had stolen a rock from a burial site. Nobody here cared about her studies, or her ambitions, about warm baths, or coffee.

More importantly, nobody in this world cared about the limp, lifeless creature that littered the soft soggy ground below them. Or the effect it had on the boy who stared, glassy-eyed, shock stealing his expression, at the visions of his own, recent past.

"Loth, nod, or tell me you understand. You must go. Now. Do not look at it again. Just keep your eye on the trees near the brook. That's where Bog waits. Go to him."

Loth nodded gently as she planted her feet on the edge of the cleft in the earth. As she had instructed, he did not look back, but moved hurriedly, scurrying down the hillside toward the marsh, his head tilted as if he were scanning the tree line in the distance.

She watched the boy until he was a very small figure moving rapidly, shrinking into the distant shadows, headed toward Bog, while she headed toward the danger that haunted the child's memories. Hoping the hole did not still hold evidence or odor of its former use, she closed her eyes, said a prayer, and slid through the grass concealing the portal.

At least, it provided some respite from the breeze. While the ground itself was cool, no wind burned her cheeks. Her hands and thighs ached from hours of climbing and holding onto rocks. The calves of her legs cramped from exhaustion.

She lay as flat as she dared, allowing her limbs the rest they desired. Her brain, however, would not turn off so easily.

Puzzles and ponderings waltzed through her brain. Her body slowly regained its strength as she waited for the activity outside to subside. Whatever had caused the death and ejection of the body down below, Wynne wanted no part of it.

The tunnel ran into the hill for nearly ten feet before expanding into a four-foot square pit. Wynne tilted one of the casks onto its side, and then she wiggled from the hole into the pit. Perched atop the casks, she could easily see the feet of any passerby. Thanks to the cloth Aberswythe had provided the night before, she stayed blanketed and not so easy to notice.

What of Aberswythe? Khyryn? Cnut?

What if Streona had injured or killed them? How could she get back?

What if Eadric, Richard, and Uddryd really were one man? Could he actually remember, as Khyryn did, his past life as Uddryd? What if he remembered her? What if he injured or killed her?

He already had, hadn't he?

The question is what, if anything, will I remember?

Wynne's hand traced the place on her throat where Richard Uddrich wrapped his hand warned, 'not this time.' A chill rippled through her again and she bundled herself tighter in the wool.

She also remembered the pain. Not of that day at the faire, but of that night long ago, when he stole her life from her body.

****

Khyryn slid from his saddle, slamming to the ground in front of Bog. "What do you mean she is not here? Where is she?" His right arm ached where the blade had slashed hitting muscle, twice slashed by his brother's hand. "I told her to stay in the tree."

"Aye. An' she did so 'til 'twas safe for Bog and Loth to be out. But the witch—"

"She is nae a witch!"

"Aye. A sorceress of great magic. The soldiers did not see her. If no magic hid her, then 'twere a *naiad*."

"Bog, where did she go?"

Bog bounced up and down then rocked from side to side, nervously. His head dropped so that Khyryrn could no longer read his eyes. "Red one's Seer is with Loth."

Khyryn relaxed a bit. "Good. Now, where is he?"

Bog's body stopped in mid sway. "Bog goes now."

Khyryn put a heavy hand on Bog's shoulder. "Bog, tell me where Loth and Gwynndolwyn have gone."

"They go to find Master Khyryn."

A twinge of cold dread bristled the hair on his arms. "At Streona's keep? To Uffyngdon?"

Bog bobbed again. "Aye. Said I should stay and wait, she did."

Panic overtook the dread.

Gwynndolwyn, against his orders had wandered straight into the enemy's den. He had escaped certain death to find that she had marched right toward it. And she had taken the boy, as well.

"Where is Aberswythe?"

Bog's brow creased, and he stood very still. "Druid is gone. Druid was with Khyryn and Red one this morning?"

"No. Aberswythe did not join us."

Bog sniffed at the breeze. "Cnut's men go with Cnut. To sit at the chalk horse."

"Not all of them." Khyryn released the troll. "The rest follow the Dane by a day."

Bog considered Khyryn's declaration. "Hmph. Vikings. Vikings smell like fish they eat."

Khyryn nearly laughed despite the severity of the situation. "Bog, those Vikings will scent you a mile from here. If they do not turn tail and run at the smell, then mayhap they'll think you smell tastier than fish. They may skin and roast you for their dinner."

"Aagh." Bog poked his own arm. "Bog is too tough for Vikings." His eyes flashed and he pointed to Khyryn's arm. "Master Khyryn is tender to the knife. Mayhap Master Khyryn will feed Vikings."

With this, Bog chortled and began to bob up and down again, amused with his own jest. "If Master Khyryn and Bog go toward horse and keep, we lead Vikings where the Red one and the witc—the Seer are."

Khyryn harbored little confidence that Cnut's soldiers would be as welcoming as their leader had been, especially with no "Golden One" to lead them.

He wished Aberswythe were nearby. The old druid wore wisdom like a torc. Close to mind and heart, seldom did he move without a plan of action. Where had his old friend and mentor gone?

Bog's plan, for the moment, served everyone best. No matter what Cnut's warriors brought, Khyryn must stop Gwynndolwyn from walking into Streona's lair. Even if that meant killing Streona himself.

He gripped Bog's arm with his good one, and pulled him toward the horse. "Come, Bog, we shall let your scent ride on the air as you ride on horseflesh."

"Bog don't like horses to ride."

"Bog doesn't have a choice. If Bog hopes to see Loth again, then Bog and Khyryn must go and get—"

A muted cry sounded, and both men flattened to the ground. Someone scurrying at the edge of the woods. Khyryn could hear the unsteady steps as the interloper tripped over limbs and rocks, unwary of the path or strangers.

A rasp of breath brought Bog's head up. "Loth?"

The boy coughed and staggered through the dense growth of branches, half sobbing, half choking for air. Even in the shadowed forest, his face glistened from the trail of tears and snot that covered it.

Khyryn jumped up, nearly casting the boy to the ground in surprise. The resulting scream made Loth wheeze harder, until he collapsed on the ground at Khyryn's feet, weeping and coughing.

"Loth, where is she? Where is Gwynndolwyn?"

The boy shook his head, trying to speak, but could not manage any real phrases, merely pointing and croaking,"

"Lef...m'stress. Sed...run. Bog saves... Master?" Loth's eyes cleared, momentarily, focussing on Khyryn. "Master Khyryn? You are alive?"

Khyryn stooped and gathered the boy into his arms. He rubbed the boy's back, partly to calm his breathing, partly to calm his own fears, which now leapt at his brain like flames from a fire.

Loth. Alone.

The boy wept into Khyryn's shoulder and grabbed at his shirt, clinging like a newborn kitten. "She's idne groud."

Bog pulled the boy from Khyryn's grip. "Wha's da, Loth?"

"I left her in the ground. Said I should nae look a' it. When I saw the body—"

Khyryn cut him off. "What body? Where in the ground?"

"In the hole."

"What hole?" He had no time for games.

"The one where the spirits dance."

He lunged toward the boy, grabbing his elbow and kneeling so that he was at eye level with the child. "Loth, you speak as Bog does. Tell me!"

"She had to save Master Khyryn, before the alderman killed him." The boy sniffed and cleared his throat.

"Where have you left Gwynndolwyn?"

"At the keep. She went there looking for you. Then we saw the body."

Khyryn hesitated. "What body? What did you and Gwynndolwyn see?"

Loth's lower lip trembled and his gaze darted between Khyryn and Bog, uncertain how to answer. "I-I dunno."

"Was it Cnut?"

"Nae. She—"

"The body was a woman's?" Not Cnut, then.

"We couldnae see it. Only the arm stuck out, strange like. D'you ever see a calf birthin' its legs first? 'Twas like that. Covered in blood and stuck out in the air. Only the skin was so pale it looked grey."

Revelation poured over Khyryn, icy and halting. A girl. Sent by her mistress to aid his escape. Streona had killed the waif. Loth had the right of it. The girl was little more than a child. Eleven or twelve perhaps, certainly no older. Certainly not ready for a grave.

Murdered out of spite.

Khyryn had two reasons to return to the fortress at Uffyngdon.

To rescue Gwynndolwyn. And to avenge the death of an angel.

Chapter Twenty-Two

Avebury

Aberswythe plopped down on the craggy stone to rest. For most of the day he had walked, seeking the symbols in his dream to guide him. She had whispered his name, summoning him to save her from her tomb. In the darkness, he followed her call. Blindly.

Cnut and his Norsemen would make their way to Eadric. Aberswythe had little fear of that. Gwynndolwyn spoke not only with the truth of a Seer, but of one who knew things that had already come to pass. One day, her past and her future would collide and she would have to choose which life she preferred…the life with knowledge of the future or memory of the past?

The earth before him bore its history well. The hills had not changed in over a thousand years. Only the kings who claimed dominion over the land had changed.

The wisdom of the aged feared monotony of war. The ancient tribes were dying. Celts, Britons, Romans, Saxons, and Norse. So little passed from one civilization to the next. And so it would be for a time longer.

"Emrys. Emrys ap Aberswythe. Son of the sons of the dragon. Come to me."

Aberswythe hoisted his weary frame from the rock and began to walk again. If he did not find her, eventually her voice would fall silent. Once that happened, the balance would tilt once more.

Balance. Always, balance must be maintained. His ancestors had handed down the stories of how the heavens plummeted into chaos when the scales tipped too far. His ancestors had witnessed it. He did not wish to share their experience.

He could not speak for the one who summoned him, however.

She had always guarded her motives.

Yet now, finally, she called him to her.

In the middle of the night he had left Cnut's camp. Abandoning his own horse and his own sense, he trudged across the hills, heading farther south, away from the objective. Away from Uddryd.

That Khyryn's brother inhabited another corporeal form now did not conceal the evil in the man's veins. Aberswythe would know that scourge regardless of the mask it wore.

Just as a father might recognize his own child, regardless of the clothes.

The sun shone upon his face as he dragged his feet along the path. Blazing bright orange, it shot long curling plumes of pink clouds into the heavens. In turn the clouds cast great shadows upon the ground.

Tired and hot, he trudged along the shadowed course, expecting another word or clue. As he walked, his mind drifted into a daze of daylight dreaming.

Plumes to feather. Feather of bird. House of white owl. Aviary to nunnery. Haven of the faithful.

The circle.

Aberswythe hastened his steps. He could see it on the horizon. He stared at the waning orb in the sky. He could not tarry. If the sun set before he found her, the prophecy would be broken.

He must rescue her.

The damned wyce had allowed them to imprison her beneath the stones.

His robes weighed him down, as much as his memories so oft had in the two thousand years since their shared first breath. Fiendish girl to fiendish woman. She had not changed. Did anyone?

"Emrys. Bratu..."

Sister, all the same.

She had not spoken his name since their parting. She had never called him to her nor uttered an endearment such as 'brother.'

His footfall upon the grass of the circle sent a tremor into the stones.

"Swesre." He whispered the word, casting it onto the wind, waiting for her to guide him. When she did not, he stepped into the circle and cried out, "Swesre!"

Sister. Hear me.

"Emrys?"

Aberswythe let his voice billow into the air. "I am here."

The turf hummed beneath his feet, drumming a gentle rhythm as the sun crept closer to its blanket. A turning of the moon she had been interred. By this moon's rise, the earth would beat with her pulse, claiming her once more, dust to dust.

As it had always been. The mother claimed the daughters and sons with the moon and stars and wind. Eight times a year, her heart would sound the cadence.

Mabon. Harvest before *Samhain. Mug Ruith*—deity of Sun—would dance in the sky with *Ben-reine ny hoie*—the moon, then yield to *Danu*—goddess Earth this night.

Uddryd—Eadric Streona in this life, had done this. Curse him, and his memory! Alderman Eadric Streona paraded his politics on his sleeve, but Uddryd hid the ancient rituals from those who would condemn them. He would defile the soil with the evil of an unhallowed death.

"Druid, I am weak."

He replied with spoken words this time. "I know Wyce. I am here. All will be well."

Aberswythe tamped the ground with his staff and listened to the vibration. Across the circle it faltered. She lay there, beneath the obelisk.

He dropped his staff and sprinted to the stone. Near the base the earth had been piled with smaller stones, to offer support.

Recently moved. The larger stone had been recently moved.

"Swesre!"

"Here, bratu. I am here." Her voice echoed from beneath the rock. *"Is the time arrived?"*

"Nearly."

"Ah. Then I am ended."

"Shhh. Not yet."

Aberswythe loosened the pouch at his belt and retrieved the talisman and runes. Holding the torc in his withered hands, he murmured the words of his ancestors.

The torc, he placed at the base of the obelisk. He took up the runes and warmed them in his hands, then laid them in the gateway of the circle.

He fell to his knees in a feverish pitch and thrashed at the pebbles that had filled the valley around the giant stone.

Gwel...Aurinia...Veleda...Gallicenae—Grac'h...Dryades...

Bandruaid—Aberswythe summoned gods and priests, deity and magi to empower him to shift the towering stone.

To save his sister.

A drummer's cadence pounded in his ears. He roared their names into the Heavens, beneath the tangerine sky. He called to the gods, to the elements, to the spirits for help.

"Dagda, Danu! Do not yet cede day to night!

Yield not thy son or daughter of thine might.

Give strength and grace that to our hands may fold.

Hear our plea to Earth, and Air, and Sky—the heart of two that in thy womb did hold."

The pulse had become a radiant hum, ringing through the stones as the sun slithered into the valley of the sleep.

"*Mug Ruith*! Do not yield to celestial night!"

Aberswythe dug at the earth, frantically, clawing at the mud that had settled with the rains around the stone. Tears, sweat, blood trickled down his brow.

He could hear them coming now. Their vigil would begin as night claimed rule. He had to move the stone before they entered the circle. In the distance he could hear their footfalls. Druid, Veleda, priest and priestess alike.

Romans built altars. Christians built shrines. But the earth holders did not forsake the old ways.

Aberswythe placed the torc around his neck. Flame-hot metal seared the flesh of his hand and of his neck.

"*Bratu*—Brother!" she called to him from deep in the ground, her voice a shriek.

He pressed his shoulder to the stone and did heave the obelisk with the might of Cierne, the giant, "*Swesre*—sister of my blood—give me strength."

A cacophony of silence rent the circle. Time slowed to the breath between two beats of the heart, Mug Ruith, slave of the wheel, paused—the sun hovering still—flames of day lashing high into the purple heavens. Torches burning brightly mirrored the sun god's wrath, proclaiming the day forfeit to goddess moon.

In the gloaming, a mysterious emerald glow radiated from the circle, casting a protective belt around the stones, preventing interlopers from trespassing on the sacred ground.

Danu—goddess of the earth—inhaled deeply, and Aberswythe lowered his head as an ox to plow, hefted the great rock away from the dirt to reveal the contorted, fragile form of the aged wyce, caged by evil's minion.

Shimmering silver and blue, the stone stood, suspended in the air, and from within its hole, water did spring forth, and lift her from her grave and lay her softly upon the grass.

Danu sighed and the elements reshaped themselves. Water drank in the earth, as sun sank into night. The obelisk righted itself, and the stones resumed their song.

Aberswythe dragged the limp body through the

outer circle, across the threshold as the first pilgrim stepped into the ring to celebrate Mabog. Cadence and incantation rushed with the blood to his brain, shifting the world to tilt until he collapsed upon the path, next to the sodden body.

Hands flailed and torso writhed as air flooded into withered lungs. Not a *bheanseidh*, but a babe's first breath shattered the star-filled sky as Aberswythe looked upon the face of his sister.

Two hearts. Two bodies. Two millenia old.

One druid. One wyce.

Balance restored.

The gods had been gracious this day.

The face contorted in fear relaxed and took another breath. Eyes wide open stared at the sparkling sky. Blindly. "Bratu, do you hear my heart's beat?"

Aberswythe reached for her mud-caked hand. "Aye, Elleran. As I hear mine own."

Chapter Twenty-Three

Uffyngdon

Brilliant light erupted from the ring as though a fissure had exploded, erupting, spewing radiant liquid light high into the sapphire sky.

A newborn's cry shattered the light into a thousand stars.

Wynne bolted awake, nearly toppling off her perch.

She had fallen asleep. And so had missed the transition from day to night. She shivered from the evening's cool breeze, and pulled the woolen tighter.

No cries in the night. Not even her own. Only a dream. A dream of—a ritual. That was it. A festival. A celebration. Something about the child's cry annoyed her.

Her head reeled. Her stomach growled in reply. She hadn't eaten since early morning. Even worms were tempting right now.

Aberswythe. He had been in her dream. The druid had been praying. Or singing? She couldn't remember.

But that couldn't be. Aberswythe had come with Khyryn and Cnut.

A dream of the past perhaps. Or bad fish.

Twilight set a purple haze to the courtyard. Standing, she could raise her head above the level of the ground. A few people milled about restlessly. Two young boys busied themselves just inside the stable door, tending the tack and grooming the horses.

On the far side, near an outer building, a woman sat piled in a heap, crying as another covered her with a blanket and offered her something to drink.

Wynne remembered the body at the foot of the hill. Swallowing that memory, she lifted one of the casks from its hold and stacked it on top of the others, to create a ladder. Like a cat scaling a pile of books, she climbed the stack of wine until her hands and feet found terra firma.

Now to find Khyryn, and Cnut, and Aberswythe.

Wynne pulled the woolen cloth up over her head, like a hood, and walked toward the largest of the buildings. Though not at all like the stone castles that decorated the countryside in modern times, Streona's hillfort did meet the definition of a castle. She listened to the hum of activity within the large house—the keep.

She searched the building for some entrance other than the main front access. She preferred to keep her arrival a secret from the owners for as long as possible.

Light burned in some spots where windows, for lack of a better term, had been carved into the structure. The openings were draped with thin pale coverings. Velum? Interesting. She had never considered the design of these earlier fortresses. These were no arrow slits. These openings were only wide enough to admit light. The cloth covering provided privacy and protection from the wind, yet allowed air and light through.

Long reeds lashed together created a thatched roof that extended far beyond the top of walls built of stone and mud and timbers, thereby providing extra buffer.

Mud and stone did not burn like sticks and leather.

Even if the roof caught fire, the sides would stand.

Streona had combined the elements of the Iron-age hill forts with the technology of the current era, and an eye toward the architecture of the future to build a castle.

Architecture of the future…*'can take you to a place I guarantee you've never been…'*

Crap.

That's it. Richard Uddryd *was* Eadric Streona. He took the stone—so he could change the past.

Was that even possible?

She snorted at her own question. How was any of this possible?

Along the side of the great building, a ladder stood, expectantly. Wynne made her way across the courtyard and gently climbed the first rung, lifting her high enough to peek through one of the windows. The covering had been drawn back partially, giving her a one-eyed view of the celebration inside. Even from where she stood, she could smell the oil burning in the torches, the char from hearth fire roasts. The faint scent of piss mixed with the sweet scent of honeyed wine.

Streona entertained his guests well. Raucous laughter mingled with the high-pitched murmurings of women's voices.

Not so different from some of the rowdier house parties, or the after-hours revelry at the faire.

The faire tended to smell better.

A room full of drunken Danes, a bloodthirsty bad guy, a dead body about three hundred feet away, and I'm armed with a paring knife in my boot.

First thing, a weapon. She needed something that

could take out a Viking or a guard, whichever tried to stop her first.

Wynne heard a jangle from the stable and slid back down the ladder. Without pausing, she sprinted across the grounds to slip through the doors.

Warm, humid stable air, wrapped her in the scent of hay and horses. She hadn't realized how pleasant horse manure could smell. Of course, she also hadn't realized just how bad human beings could smell, until lately.

At the end of the stockade, a tiny light glimmered. A puddle light. That's all the stable boys had to see by.

Wynne smiled. She drew the blanket over her head, to hide her face, and gripped the corners in each hand. Then slowly, silently, she moved through the walkway, one step in front of the other so delicately that her movement flowed, as if she floated toward them.

At first they did not see her, engaged as they were in a game. Ever closer she moved, searching all the stalls for any-thing that might help her.

There, on the wall. A long metal rod. And a horseshoe. Excellent.

One boy nudged the other. "Halt! Speak thy name!"

Wynne said nothing, but continued to walk slowly, silently toward the boys.

"Halt!" the other one chimed. "Who—who's there."

Still she did not speak. If what Loth said were true, Edith had so convinced everyone of ghosts that the boys would faint soon from fear.

The younger one tugged on the older one's tunic. "Cai, it floats, like it has nae legs beneath the cloak."

Both boys sat frozen to their spots. Eyes wide and dark, they dared not move as the figure moved ever closer.

Wynne did not lift her head or acknowledge them in any way, but whispered, "Hhhhelp meee…" so softly it disappeared into the darkness. "Hhhhelpmmmmeeeee—" Then holding her mouth so that the sound would be round and full, she inhaled deeply and exhaled making a sound like the wind whistling on a stormy night.

"Hanna, that is—come back to blame us fer naught that we could do to save her from his hand. Run, Marroc! Run! Do no' look at her. If she catches us she will eat our souls. Hurry!"

The two boys tore past her, running so hard, she thought the younger one had left the ground for sure. She turned to see them clearing the doors, and bounding for one of the outer buildings, screaming as they ran.

Boys gone? Good. Screaming? Not good. Screaming meant she had about thirty seconds to find something she could use.

She grabbed the poker and horseshoe from the wall, then pocketed some of the rope and a bridle. Never could tell what could come in handy in an emergency.

Something glimmered on the floor where the boys had been.

Aha. A small spear-like tool to clean the hooves, perhaps, caught the candlelight and winked up at Wynne.

Perfect. She grabbed it and headed for the entrance.

Too late. The two boys and a burly guard already covered half the space between the other buildings and the stable. She couldn't get out without them seeing her. The boys might buy her act again. The guard probably would not.

A snort near her right ear caught her attention, and Wynne found herself nose to nose with a dappled grey resident of the barn. The mare flicked its ears at her, and shook its head, snorting and nodding as it nudged her shoulder.

At the animal's invitation, Wynne stooped and slid through the wooden slats into the stall. She huddled down in the front corner, next to the horse and pulled the blanket over herself, trying to flatten herself as much as possible.

Steps, hurried, and searching.

"Hanna. It had to be. It did no' move like a human. It were a spectre, Uncle," Cai explained.

"Ye both listen t' the cook's tales too much. There's naught here but horses.

The younger one, Marroc, piped up. "But Uncle, it called t'us. Asked for us t'help it."

"It werena' Hanna though, boys. Hanna is gone away from the keep. It were probably the horses pleadin' fer ye t' shovel the shite ou' o' th' stalls. Righ'? G'on the two-o'-ye. There be nae ghoosties in this barn t'nigh'. Look a' yer horses, lads. They would tell ye if the spirits were about. An' they're as calm as if spellbound theirselves. Now, back t'yer posts, or I'll be the one t'chase ye both."

"Uncle—"

"Take care that puddle lamp doesna go out. The moon is high, but ye'll need the candle to keep yer dreams lit. G'night, Cai, Marroc."

Footsteps receded as the uncle made his way back

across the yard, leaving the two frightened and distress boys alone. In the stable. With a ghost.

Wynne's heart skipped a beat. The trick had worked. But their voices still trembled as they muttered to one another in hushed tones, trying to convince themselves that their uncle spoke the truth.

She sat huddled in the stall for a long time, listening to Cai comfort Marroc, who couldn't be more than eight years old. The mare dipped her head low and snatched a piece of hay, snorting a reprimand at Wynne as she did.

Wynne rubbed the horse's front leg, reassuringly and mustered the courage and humility she had left. "I am not a ghost," she said quietly.

Both boys froze.

"Did you hear that, Cai?"

"I am certain he heard me," she called. "Cai, Marroc, I am no spectre. No ghost come to haunt you. I only needed a place to rest for a bit."

Cai stood up. "Ye're a woman? Of flesh and blood?"

"I am."

Boys of Cai's age carried an inimical suspicion. "Why're ye here? In the stables then, an' no' with Lady Edith or the Master?"

Time for a good story. "I am a special guest. A guest of Cnut's.

Marroc chimed in. "But the Dane is a guest in the Master's house. So must ye be a guest, also."

"Sort of. I am a 'special' guest, as I said before."

"Wha' makes ye so, then?" asked Cai. Adolescence made him brave enough to take a couple of steps toward her as she moved through the stall slats and stroked the mare's nose.

Wynne eyed the young Cai. Eleven years old. Perhaps thirteen. His voice had begun to change so his speech no longer trilled with the high-toned pitch that Marroc still had. Not this boy. Through the dirt she could make out, even in the darkness, blemishes and the smallest lump on his throat. He soldiered the full brunt of puberty. And that she could use to her advantage.

She unwrapped her woolen and let it drop to the ground revealing much beneath the thin shift. Before them, she stood, a fair-haired woman, much younger looking for her twenty-eight years. Most women her age would be grandmothers or widows, or both in this time. But she possessed the body of a twenty-first century woman. Ample and toned, and strong from a lifetime of nutritious food.

If her intuition were correct, Cai had never seen anything quite like her.

Careful words, careful actions. "Flesh and blood. Some hail me, 'Golden One'. Others call me 'Seer. Loth calls me 'Sorceress'."

Having captured their attention, and their imagination, Wynne gathered the wool and retied it around her, once more concealing her form.

Cai's eyes were nearly as big and round as the horse apples he shoveled. A flicker of confusion mixed with awe shimmered behind their reflection.

"Loth? Ye ken Loth?"

"I do. Loth and I have shared many secrets."

"Loth is alive?"

"Of course he is. Why would you think otherwise?"

Cai fumbled with the bottom of his tunic, and

turned his glance to the ground.

Marroc's voice sputtered, "He disappeared, thas all. He left wif the Master's guards two moons ago. We never seen 'im agin. Well, I seen him once at the last full moon. It were the nigh' tha' we heard the *bheanseid* screamin'.

"A ghost he was, tha' Loth, risin' up from the pit, like Lady Edith tells us they do. An' I kent he were no' real, cause he would nae have come back if he were alive, no' after the things—"

Cai elbowed the younger one, hard in the ribs. "Shut up, Marroc. Stop yer tongue waggin' like a hound's. Some things ye dunna' speak."

Wynne strained to focus on his hands. Even though his body remained straight and poised, his fingers twitched nervously, betraying a hidden frenzy.

She moved to him and with a finger tucked beneath his chin, lifted his face until she could look directly into his eyes.

Darkness swirled, cold and uninviting. Behind his veiled gaze, she spied the memories that played out in his mind. Torturous hours spent hiding in the stables, covered in muck and hay, waiting for Streona's guards to pass out from drink, before they sated their profane lusts.

Or to find satisfaction elsewhere.

Cai did not fear her. He did not care about her. He cared about ghosts. And other things that disturbed the night.

"I know what fear you bear."

The boy blinked furiously at her, jerking his eyes in one direction, then another, to look anywhere, save at her.

And in that, he had given her the gift she needed. If she knew how Eadric Streona and his men managed to threaten the villagers, then she could figure out how to outwit him.

Wynne cradled his head in her hands and gently pressed her lips to his forehead. By his trembling, he had never been handled so gently. Perhaps never kissed by anyone, save a mother. If he had a mother. "I am here to help, Cai. I will share a secret with you, for the trade of three horses and a message delivered."

Marroc put his hand over one of Wynne's and nodded at his older companion. "I will help, Golden One."

"First, I need to have three horses prepared to ride out of here this evening, if I am to be successful. Keep them readied, but in the stalls so no one suspects."

Cai and Marroc nodded.

"Next, I need to know where Cnut's men are this hour. I am looking for the two who traveled with him this morning who were not dressed as Vikings. They were dressed as priests. Long robes, simple clothes."

"A long robe with a hood?" the younger asked.

"Yes. You've seen them?"

"Only one rode in with the Danes."

Wynne paused. "Only one you say? Well, take me to him, will you?"

Cai scrunched his face in disapproval. "He is nae here, anymore."

"What do you mean, he is not here? He must be. I saw him ride with Cnut this morning. Look, there in that stall, that is his stallion."

Cai looked to the dark warhorse. "Aye, tha' be his horse. But he didna' ride tha' one when he flew from here."

"Flew from here? When?"

Marroc jumped into the story. "This afternoon. Tha's how it happen't."

"How what happened?"

"Mistress Edith had Hannah come tell us to ready a horse, which we did. Then she told the guards that carried him that Lady Edith bade her bind his wounds before they carried him further."

Wounds. Wynne sighed in frustration. "What wounds?"

Marroc had relaxed into an impish eight year old once more. "He had a slash on his cheek and his arm. Hannah had them bring 'im in here and dump him on the stump over there while she tended his wounds. She offered them drink while they waited—Hey, Cai! Hannah never brought us drink!"

"And?"

Cai placed a guiding hand on the little one's shoulder and pushed him to sit. "And the guards drank until they passed out. The wine must have been mulled with heavy herbs to make them pass out so quickly. Once they snored, she jumped up, pulled the nearest horse from its stall, and helped him onto it, barebacked, no saddle or anything. Just the man and the horse."

"Did he escape?"

Marroc could not contain his excitement. "He did. An' tha's when Master yelled and ran into the yard, chasing after 'im. An' when he saw Hanna standin' there with the cloth in her hand, an' his guards on the ground—"

The boy faltered. The great escape turned to nightmarish reality as the young one stared at a spot just beyond the stable doors. Wynne turned and caught sight of the darkened damp spot on the ground, shimmering in the moonlight.

Cai put his hand around Marroc's nape and pulled the younger boy to his chest, as the little one's breathing began to drag with sobs, he swallowed hard against the fresh recall. "He swung and cracked her *heid* wide and sent her thrashing to the ground. I saw the bone shatter, an' bits o' her brain stuck to her hair. An' he just turned and left her there. As if he'd stepped in a pile of shite, 'sall.

A young man too soon, Cai looked Wynne in the eye, and she saw him for the child he longed to be. His face contorted in shame and grief, and tears poured down his cheeks. His body shook violently as he held the younger boy, gripping him as if holding on for his own salvation, until filled with revulsion and sadness, his body convulsed with the pain pent up for too long. He bent in half and vomited.

Wynne pulled both boys to her, cooing to them to sooth their injured souls as they wept. "Shhh. It is done now. It will be all right, soon. I promise. Cry and let her hear you. She is safe now. She is with God. No more pain. No more fear. Shhh."

What else could she offer them?

She knelt beside them and gave them explicit instructions to prepare for her return.

Khyryn gone. Aberswythe missing. A child murdered.

While the universe sacrificed one child unto heaven, across the bailey, the future king of England sat, sipping mead with his men, and making plans.

With the devil, himself.

Chapter Twenty-Four

The fires burned low in the hearth. The raucous crowd waned to snores and muffled laughter of those who still toiled at table games. Apparently, Danes could drink heartily and not tip into their cups. In the dim light, Cnut's eyes glittered warily and his hair framed his face like flames. A fiery king to claim Edmund's throne.

Cnut eyed Eadric across the long dais. "Why would you turn against Edmund to fight alongside me?"

Eadric strummed his fingers, pensively. "I prefer to be on the winning side."

Cnut considered this logic. "What of your loyalty to your brother-in-law. Do you not advise your king, give him sound counsel in his court? After all he is the brother to your wife."

"My wife yields her loyalty to her husband before all others. As to Edmund and my loyalties, the king's petty jealousies have given him short sight. He is a weak ruler."

"Yet all here call him 'Ironsides'."

"Titles, like laurels are merely crowns upon one's head. Some fit soundly, some fall easily to the wayside."

Eadric sipped his wine and smirked at his guest. "Heavens reward those who forge their own fortunes and futures."

The Dane, yet wet upon his nape from his mother's milk, sat before him, proclaiming himself possessor of half of Britain.

Cnut nodded at Eadric and sighed deeply. "I shall be victorious."

"I am sure of it, my, your Highness." And when the warring fields were red with blood, Eadric would wipe his hands of both men.

"It has been prophesied. Edmund will fall. I shall have my father's kingdom and more. The sages sing of it."

Eadric fought to keep in the taunting laugh that threatened his throat and burned his cheeks. "Ah, the Wisdom of the village Fire-readers.

He paused as Cnut's brow straightened into a visible line of disapproval. "You mock the ways of my forefathers?"

"Not at all. I, myself, have oft depended upon the advice of others. I assure you, I do not begrudge you the counsel your soothsayer whispers unto you."

"It is not the soothsayer that foretells my victory. It is the Golden One."

The words played fancifully upon his ears. "Who?"

"The Golden One. The Seer. She rides with us to our destiny."

"She must be the one my men spied in your camp. This 'Golden One' is not your consort, then?"

Cnut laughed gently. "Her body floats upon the air like a cloud upon the morning sky. She is fire and wisdom, bound by nature's mould. If any man could lay her down and know the folds of her maidenhead, I might risk a kingdom for that prize."

"A provocative treasure, to be sure. If she is your

Seer, then she yields to you, her king, does she not?"

Cnut narrowed his gaze. "She yields to no man. Not even those who serve to protect her dare such."

"Perhaps your Seer is a Greek warrior princess, intent on claiming her own spoils of war."

"The Golden One is no warrior. She tames the earth to her will, as she commands the troll, and the Druid son."

Eadric's head snapped up. The hardened shaft between his thighs softened at the words that chilled his veins. "Druid son?"

"Aye. He rode with us this day. Khyryn of Powys. He is one of our band."

"He protects this Golden One?" Where did she hide? How had she eluded his men?

The Dane emptied his flagon. "He and the others."

Eadric leaned forward and stared at his guest. "What others?"

Suspicion dawned on Cnut's face at his question.

"Forgive my curiosity. I do fear that the one you call Khyryn departed our company this afternoon. Our meager offerings did not meet with his favor."

Cnut sat back in his chair and sighed heavily. A sneer tugged at his mouth as his eyes narrowed like an animal about to pounce. "I am no fool, Streona. Your entire house whispers of Druid son's escape, as well as the murder of innocents by your hands. A king does not rule wisely who forges enemies before he is seated upon the throne."

Eadric refilled Cnut's cup. "I wish only to offer my hospitality to your company. If I have neglected any of your party, I am obliged to make my amends."

"We are served well by your house's hospitality.

My men languish in your favor."

"As it should be for a king."

"Tell me, Eadric, Alderman of Mercia, what part does your wife play in this game?"

The bait. "Cnut Sweynson, I am honest in my ignorance of your meaning."

"You have given your wife, openly as a whore for the taking. What price do you put to her services?"

Time for the snare. "As I stated before, my wife's duty is to her husband, and to her king. If she serves you then she has done her duty by me. She is yours for your pleasure while at my tables your men gather. She is well trained at satisfying the urges of a man. And by royal birth, she is your peer.

Cnut snorted. "It is only by her father born, that she is sister to Edmund. He cares only for his own greed and ambition.

"As to mine own ambition—I seek only to serve you with wise counsel, which you already have, it appears."

"One wonders if a clever king can ever ignore wise counsel?"

"I assure your Highness. Never."

****

Avebury

Aberswythe brought the cup to her puckered mouth. This time the wyce sipped.

"Many years have passed between us, Emrys of Aberswythe."

"Our paths have crossed."

"But not our words." She coughed, a brittle rattle in her chest as she lay upon the trunk of the tree where he had placed her.

Hare hound root he shaved and boiled for her now, to soothe her throat, with willow bark for her pain. "What words would you spare for me, sister?"

"Words. Hmphf. Words mean little, now."

"And yet they still manage to summon the elements to our aid as they did last night. Now tell me. By what spell did you find yourself cast beneath the circle stones?"

"No spell. Brute force."

Aberswythe refilled the cup and handed it to her. "No match for such a strong mind as yours."

"Ah, once strong. Of late, too sentimental."

"How say you? Elleran verch Aberswythe gave naught to sentiment. You possess a warrior's heart."

"'Twas no other than Uddryd's soul that did condemn me to that place. 'Put her under a stone'—he told his men—'that no one else will find her.'"

"And what did prompt him this time?"

"I could not answer his question satisfactorily."

"Could not? Or did you choose not to divulge all that you knew?"

Her sightless eyes twinkled. "Eadric is a fool. He uses Uddryd's memories to build an empire that is not his to hold."

"It is the same with all men who seek to rule others."

She sought the druid's hand. "He seeks the rune."

"He does not have it?"

"Nae. He lost it when by Khyryn's hand he did last fall."

"But that happened over—"

She chortled and tried to sit up. Dark grey and purple bruises smudged her face and arms. Never fair of face, the wyce did now retain an owl's visage, the cheeks flattened, eyes wide open, her nose jutting out awkwardly.

"Time means nothing, Aberswythe. You and I know only too well the truth of timelessness.

"That it did pass from his hand four hundred-years ago means little to him that would use it to change his fate. He thought I had stolen it back."

Aberswythe soaked the cloth in the warm water steeped with lavender and hemlock. Gradually, he washed her arms and neck, rinsing away the dirt.

"I smell hemlock, brother."

"Gathered in the early mists of summer. The water strained through its fingers. To numb your pain, 'tis all. It is not potent yet. Lavender to help you sleep."

"Aagh. Herbs I ken well enough. Tell me. What of the young druid?"

"He is the same as ever when you knew him. Honorable to his own ruination."

"And he rides with you?"

"He does. And another."

"Another, eh? A pupil?"

"No pupils do I teach in this new world. The old ways fade evermore with the aging of the earth."

"Not a pupil? Then who?"

"Herself."

A shocked gasp escaped the old woman. "Gwynndolwyn? No. Does she remember?"

"Gratefully, not yet. But her dreams pitch her in a battle with the past. Soon enough her past and future will meet."

"Her future? What have you done?"

"All that I could. I sent Khyryn through the

stones."

"You did not go yourself?"

"I have stepped through the seam of time often."

"But—"

"I am old. Khyryn found her and brought her through safely."

"Did they join?"

"Aye. They did."

"Is the prophecy fulfilled?"

"Not yet, sister. Not yet."

Her craggy hand sought his. "It will be, brother. Harmony will be restored. What you have done is right."

"The sun set the sky ablaze this evening."

"There is much discord. That is why the prophecy is so important. What color is the sky this evening now that *Mahob* is upon us?"

"The darkness has faded to orange. *Mug-Ruith* will rise soon. Then we shall see—blood in the sky, death will sail high over the lands and the sea."

Elleran finished the verse. "If golden, the orb, then the earth will absorb as the Heavens rain tranquility." She relaxed and closed her eyelids. "My body seeks sleep, now, *Bratu*." Years had passed since she had called him brother. "I shall wake when the sun is high. Do not fear."

Aberswythe covered her with his cloak and slipped Away into the predawn darkness. There would be much bloodshed and chaos before his task was finished.

****

Bog and Loth were both silent as they crawled through the high grass surrounding Uffyngdon. Khyryn did not encourage conversation. His brain instead, played over the day's events—the arrival of Eadric's men in the morning, the ride to Streona's fortress at Uffyngdon, his encounter with his brother.

Strange to think of Eadric Streona as such. However, within that body of the most feared man in Edmund's court, beat the heart and soul of Uddryd, ancient chieftain, and king.

A murderer.

Khyryn had not shared that with Gwynndolwyn. He had shared that revelation with no one. Not even with Aberswythe.

He had claimed one life this day. Would that satisfy the bloodlust or would Uddryd's soul seek more killing to quench his thirst for revenge.

Gwynndolwyn sat somewhere within the madman's lair. The moon rose full in the evening sky. Mabon. The second harvest moon. Soon the winds would turn cold and bring the frosts.

They had reached the outer edge of the marsh grass. Khyryn's elbows sank in the soft mud and he shivered from the cold dampness of the earth.

"Bog, stay here with Loth. Loth, tell me where the entrance is."

"On the back side of the fort. Near the northwest corner. Grass covers the hole. Ye'll nae find it in the dark without I show you."

"Stay, boy. You served to guide one this day already. I know the ways of hill forts. I will find the entrance.

"Bog, if Gwynndolwyn and I have not come to you and Loth by morning's light, take the boy back to the lake where first we met. There is a cave in the hills just north. A hermit's cave. You and he will be safe there.

D'you understand my meaning?"

Bog fidgeted, eyes bright beneath the scrub of hair that covered his brow. "Bog and Loth will wait here."

Khyryn bristled at the troll's reluctance. "Do not wait past morning's first light. Streona will send men looking for others. If you are found, he will kill you. Do not let him find you. D'you understand?"

Bog's body stopped its motion as he looked into Khyryn's eyes. "Bog and Loth understand."

Khyryn nodded to the two and turned toward the hill. As he plodded through the soggy ground, a faint whisper of Bog's voice carried on the night air. "God go with you, Druid son."

Khyryn wasted little time scaling the hill. Such fortresses had been his playground as a child. He and Uddryd and the other children of their village would race to the top of the hills, climbing over the bramble to claw to the tops of the steepest hills. The first one to the top would pull pebbles from their shirt and pitch the stones at the others to keep the invaders away.

Khyryn always won, until at the age ten, Aberswythe had pulled him aside and chastised him for spending more energy trying to outrace his brother than on his own studies.

From that day on, Khyryn had made sure that Uddryd found victory when they raced. The sacrifice meant little to Khyryn, and satisfied both Uddryd, and the elder druid.

Moonlight illuminated the hill so that Khyryn easily climbed the rock-strewn knoll. He had to search for the hidden hollow. Once found, he slipped in easily as he made his way toward the pit.

He emerged into the courtyard unseen. The

majority of the people were either inside the keep or passed out in one of the outer buildings.

Despite the torches burning brightly and the sentinel's flame, the main keep had fallen quiet.

Where did he hide Gwynndolwyn? Had she been discovered and dragged to the main keep? Or had Eadric secreted her away in one of the outer buildings?

Most importantly—did she still live?

A life stolen. That is exactly what he had done to her when he ripped her from her world and dragged her through the centuries to stand beside him in this one.

Guilt gnawed him. Not guilt for what he had taken from her. Guilt at the realization that he would do it again to keep her safe from the vengeance of the man who had claimed her as his queen. Guilt that he would do it for more than her safekeeping.

In the millennium since Elleran had cursed him, he had never loved another woman as he had loved Gwynndolwyn. He no longer cared that she had been betrothed to Uddryd, or that he had betrayed his brother. He no longer cared that she had been the queen and priestess of his village.

He cared only that she returned to his side this night. That he might confess his one true sin.

His passion for her.

Everything he had done had been for love of her. He had sacrificed himself for her future, and in doing so had sealed both their fates.

A simple truth nagged at him. If he had not stepped through the stones, and found her at the faire, he would not fear for her life, at this moment.

Near the stables he heard movement. He crept forward, listening for any sound of footsteps other than his own.

Instead of steps, Khyryn heard a familiar voice coming from near the front entrance of the keep's main house.

"Find this Golden One. And bring her to me."

Gwynndolwyn, wherever she might be, had not found Eadric.

"How far shall I ride to find her, sire?"

"Ride *until* you find her. Or until you cannot remember what the punishment will be should you return without her."

Khyryn lay still upon the ground, not daring to move—barely breathing—until Eadric and his henchman retreated.

He must find her before Eadric did.

The beam of light cast upon the ground slithered to darkness as the door closed.

Disable the rider before he departs.

Khyryn slinked toward the stable. As he passed through the door, the rustle of words whispered, then suddenly hushed, lingered in the darkened room.

He stood perfectly still, listening, waiting for his eyes to adjust, motionless until his muscles began to cramp, threatening to make him cry out in pain.

He was not the lone human in the stables. That he could sense. Someone also hovered in the pitch-blackness.

A rustle of hooves upon the straw. Orion stood, black as Jet. The moon's light streaming through a hole in the planking, dancing on the ebony coat.

Khyryn moved deftly toward his horse, when another movement made him stop. Someone crouched in the stall, hand upon Orion, sliding the saddle into place. The horse casually regarded Khyryn, then snorted at the hand that patted his side.

Khyryn charged the figure, tackling it from behind and thrusting it into the hay, then falling on top and pinning the person beneath him. A muffled cry sounded against the stack of alfalfa and pampas.

Khyryn, no friend to horse thieves, grabbed a handful of hair and yanked back roughly, as his knee sank into the thief's back.

"What business have you with another man's horseflesh?"

Breathlessly, a woman's voice replied, "The horse is mine."

Panicked, he grabbed her and rolled her over onto her back.

"Gwynndolwyn, what are you—"

"Let go of me you ass. Damn you. You nearly scared the life out of me, not to mention nearly breaking my ribs and startling the horse. What are you doing here? What if Eadric finds you here? You're supposed to be miles away from here."

"I could ask you the same question. You should still be up a tree, safely waiting."

She writhed against his grip. "Apparently, you mistook me for a cat. Why stay stuck up a tree when I can scale a mountain to save your ass. Cai and Marroc said you—"

"Who are Cai and Marroc?"

"Stable boys. They're the ones who told me that you escaped. That's why—"

Khyryn covered her mouth with his own, savoring the taste of her lips, of her anger, of her protest as he halted her words. He dug his fingers into her arms and raked his hands over her flesh until he found her breasts. He straddled her and cradled her beneath him, melting her frustration.

The soft steps of leather crunched the dirt on the opposite side of the wall.

Soon, the familiar sound of water pouring onto the ground revealed a sentry pissing. Nothing more.

"We can talk once we are safely away from here," he whispered when he had pulled his lips away from hers.

"Khyryn? Eadric killed—"

"I know. Loth told me."

"You found Loth?"

"He is safe with Bog. As you should have been when I made my escape."

"I had to find you. What if Eadric—"

He brushed her lips again. "He would have, if his wife had not helped me."

"He murdered that child. We have to take the others with us."

"What others?"

"Marroc and Cai."

"No."

"There is no 'no' to this. Those boys have unlatched the door and they have a plan to take Orion out into the field. That way we can all escape."

"And what if you are all caught? Even now Eadric sends a man into the night to hunt you down."

"Me? Why me? How can he even—"

"Cnut or one of his men must have said something. I heard Eadric call for your return."

"But no one will be able to return me if I am not lost. Who would think to look right here in Streona's own keep?

Do you think that Eadric would treat them any less severely than he treated the girl who risked her life for me?"

A movement near the door brought Khyryn to his feet, throwing Gwynndolwyn back into the pile of hay.

"Dammit. Stop tossing me about like some rag doll."

"Shh. I heard a noise—" came a whisper from the door.

A shaky voice cracked, "Hello. Are you here?"

Gwynndolwyn shoved Khyryn out of her way. "I'm here, Cai. Is the front gate open?"

"It is," the voice whispered. "I told the guard that one of the horses is frothing and could make the others sick. Said tha' the master would take all our heids if some mangy Viking's horse made his own stock sick. Now all we have t'do is get him t' follow our lead."

Cai had the rein in his hand, ready to lead Orion when Khyryn emerged from the stall sending the boy backward so fast, he fell over his own feet, and landed on his backside.

"It's okay, Cai," Gwynndolwyn called. "This is Khyryn. The one I came to find."

"I thought he—" the boy searched Khyryn's face in the darkness. "Ye're the one Hanna helped?" Confusion and fear quickly transformed in to anger as he stared at the man who had been the cause of Hanna's death. "You! Hannah died for you."

In a flash the boy retreated into the yard and began shouting. "Help! Guards! Intruder!

Damn.

Khyryn yanked Gwynndolwyn up onto Orion and

slapped the stallion's backside harshly to set it to gallop. As the beast tore through the stable, Khyryn could hear the guards responding to the boy's shouts.

Gwynndolwyn flew past the boy, and bounded through the opened entry gate. Her departure captured the guards' attention long enough to allow Khyryn to dash from the stables to one of the outer buildings.

The shallow wooden structure stood dark and quiet against the gathering fray.

Khyryn stepped in, and quickly looked for anything that would offer him concealment.

Ride Gwynndolwyn. Ride and do not turn back.

"Why have you returned?" a woman's voice whispered.

Khyryn reeled in the darkness, trying to find the speaker.

No light within the room, no chance of escape without.

Khyryn stared into the face of a woman caught off guard. A face that wore no mask of comely nobility. No beguiling host. Only a woman, weary of conflict, stricken with grief.

Edith. Eadric's wife. Alone.

He could not speak at first sight of her. Her ghostly thin form and pale gown bore her on the night like a ghost. Mourning.

He understood her solitude. And stood embarrassed by having intruded on her private suffering for the servant who had been faithful to her mistress, and had fallen to the master. And the guilt for those left behind to wallow in her death.

Again she queried, "Why have you returned?" Her voiced rippled like the dropping of a raindrop on a lake, gentle yet unyielding in its intent.

His heart beat furiously, echoing in his head, throbbing in his veins. The arm that Eadric had sliced earlier, stung with each heartbeat.

He flexed his hand and the muscles in his arm echoed pain. "I came back to save another."

"The Dane?"

He leaned against the door, considering which answer might keep her from calling out. "Does Cnut need saving?"

"By morning's light he could be dead."

"By wine and fornication, perhaps?"

An eyebrow raised slightly at his boldness. "You apparently know something of my husband. Cnut will not die by Eadric's hand, directly."

"I know something of your husband's character. Cnut and Edmund gift him with power and leverage. Does he not manipulate even you to his advantage?"

"My husband manipulates all whom he meets. He possesses great power. And great cruelty."

Khyryn heard the words not said. "I am grateful for your aid, though I am sorry for the cost."

She neither moved, nor changed her expression, but her voice harbored a cold edge when she replied. "Your gratitude means less to me than the injury your freedom caused my servant. I did not help you to be kind. My motive was more of a selfish nature."

"No less the cost of your servant is my appreciation for your grief."

"I envy men. They war. They rule. I am thought a whore by my duty to my husband. Yet a man who takes such liberties is more revered by his peers."

She waited for a response, but he offered none. "If

you did not care for our hospitality this day, then why, do you intrude upon our house once more?"

"My obligation rests with Cnut. Not with the House of Mercia. Your generosity did sate my hunger and thirst. My own foolishness sated my curiosity. I desired to know more about your husband's conspiracies."

Despite the darkness of the room, her eyes sparkled with her fury. "Do you believe me weak?"

"Nae, Lady Edith. I know the strength of a queen. Men with ambition have cold hearts for those they keep closest to them."

Now she nodded. "You are wise. For a man."

He relaxed against the doorframe. "I have had much time to ponder the ways of men. And women."

"I heard the call and the sound of a rider. Who did depart this night?"

"Her name is Gwynndolwyn. She serves as Seer to Cnut."

"Ah," she said, her tone a mocking one. "Cnut's Golden One. The prophet that would take a crown from my brother to cast upon the Danish swine."

"Are the Danes worse than any others? The Danes at least recognize a widow's right to retain her property and wealth. Could your brother not promise Eadric's lands to another, stripping you of everything, purely at his royal will?"

Edith stared, smiling at Khyryn. "You surprise me, sir. I am not often surprised."

"You ask why I returned, my lady. I came to save another. She once wore the same courage as you do."

She moved to the window, allowing the breeze to push at her gown, as if she floated. She gazed out at the yard, reverently. "Do you believe in ghosts?"

Khyryn considered her question honestly. "Yes."

"My nights are haunted by the specters of my husband's sins. And by mine own cowardice. I see the apparitions of my father and of Cnut's sire, as well. And now, I will hear the voice of Hanna when I lie in bed at night."

"She will not find fault with you—"

"And yet she will not rest. I will hear her childish laughter in the courtyard, and her cries. Just as I hear the others."

"What others?"

She padded her way to the loom and took her seat. Her fingers played silently upon the threads as she continued to stare toward the yard. "North Umbria's sons. He did blind the boys that they could not identify their father's murderer, nor claim his house. And then, when the landowners did not cower, he killed the boys for spite."

"And their spirits linger here?"

"They come to whisper at our doorways and laugh at our timidity. And they wait for other playmates. Now they have one."

"Lady Edith—"

"Take the stable boys with you. Cai and Marroc. Forcefully, if you must. I will not have their blood stain my dreams further. Stay here until the keep is asleep. The guards will not awaken this night. "

"The boys sounded the alarm. They will fear me."

Edith rose from her loom. "They fear my husband's wrath. Tell them I ordered their departure. Leave the way you entered. Find Cnut's Golden One and depart Mercia with the stable boys. Do this for me and your debt will be repaid."

"What of Cnut?"

"As you said, by my very husband's hand your Vikings sleep safely this night."

****

Wynne gripped Orion's mane as the horse raced into the night. Try as she might she could not slow the animal's speed. *Damn Khyryn.*

Down the slope and across grassland, the animal carried as if bent on taking her as far away from the keep as possible.

Slow down.

Have to go back. Rescue Khyryn. And Cai. And Marroc.

On the heels of these thoughts came one nearly as frantic.

Someone now searched for her. Alive or dead.

She tried to sit up and lost her balance. She dropped from the horse in full gait, landing on her back, the frenzied beating of the horse's hooves thundering into the distance.

She lay there in the grass, looking up into the sky waiting for some dark agent to stumble over her and drag her back.

Quite an interesting day. *Vikings ride off to fight the bad guys. Khyryn gets caught. Escapes. And I end up in the middle of the night, more alone than I started out this morning.*

Warm moist air brushed her hand.

Orion.

Damn, her back and head hurt. She listened for sounds of pursuers.

The horse snorted and nudged her arm.

She rubbed the stallion's nose and cursed against the universe, once more.

God, keep him hidden until I can get to him.

When she tried to sit up, the world fell away and she sank into oblivion.

Chapter Twenty-Five

Drums pounded in Wynne's head as awareness flooded too quickly into her brain and limbs. Her back ached as if she had fallen from a cliff. No. Just a warhorse.

Through the hammering pain, she tried to take inventory of the body parts that had not yet turned on her. Slowly, she wiggled her toes, ankles, knees. She continued up her torso. God, she could barely breathe. Her arms were numb. She tried to move them and found them caught. On what? The saddle?

No. Orion had nuzzled her—

Wakefullness overtook Wynne, and she opened her eyes to blinding darkness. And silence. No sound of hooves, or of vermin in the grass. No wind.

Nothing. Except her own pulse pounding in her head.

She tried again to move her arms, to wiggle her fingers to free herself from whatever she had managed to land in when she fell. She willed them to move and sensed they tried to respond, but could not. She shifted her weight, only to discover she no longer lay flat on the ground, but sat flat against a wall—her arms tethered above her head.

"Damn—no wonder I hurt. What in the—"

Fear, icy and stinging, washed over her. She had ridden out of Streona's fortress in the black of night—

leaving Khyryn behind to face the guards—only to end up back inside. Should she be glad or irritated?

Neither. Scared definitely suited the moment better.

She scuttled to shift her weight evenly on her buttocks, then slid her left foot along the length of the boot on her right foot, seeking the bulge against the calf of her leg. Her *s'gian dhu*. Apparently whoever trussed her hadn't searched her for weapons.

Now, she only had to figure out how to get it out of her boot, and into her hand—the numb hand attached to the numb arm dangling above her throbbing head.

Hours passed. Or minutes. All she knew for sure was that the wall and floor, though inside, were colder than the ground outside. Much colder, which didn't help her headache. Despite discomfort and dread, her body and mind again surrendered to the only comfort exhaustion could give. She slept.

****

Cold. Firm. Threatening. Something glided slowly down her throat, along her collarbone. Slithering gently toward the swell of her left breast.

Wynne gasped and her eyes snapped open.

Hidden within the darkness, his eyes shone brightly as he stared at her. She swallowed thickly as her eyes adjusted to the dimness. To the danger.

Richard Uddryd. Or Eadric Streona.

The stench of male sweat and alcohol made her gasp involuntarily a second time.

Her captor flashed an appreciative grin. "Tell me, *Golden One*—did you foresee this meeting as you have foreseen your new king's victory?"

He drew the point of the knife across her sternum.

"Or is it your memory I have to thank for your presence here, Gwynndolwyn?"

The pressure of the knifepoint thickened with each breath she took. If she moved, the blade might pierce her flesh.

The birthmark on her abdomen burned with memory of him. However, she cautiously kept her mouth closed as she struggled to keep her eyes focused on the man before her.

A gloved hand tugged a handful of hair and forced her head against the wall. His grin curled in to a threatening frown. "What is your name, Seer?"

Wynne's eyes stung at the pain in her scalp, and fought to hold her tongue from spewing the plethora of curses and obscenities at her captor. She knew him to be a murderer at least. But what other atrocities could he claim credit for?

"You already know. I am called 'Golden One'."

"I know what Cnut calls you." He slid the knife slowly down the front of her gown to her navel, drawing small circles with the point of the blade just above where the birthmark lay hidden beneath the cloth. His mouth pressed close to her ear, his breath damp, his voice guttural. "Tell me what Khyryn calls you?"

Her own pulse thundered in her veins, pounding against her chest, even as she tried not to panic. She struggled against the ties that bound her hands above her, and tried to sit taller.

His eyes glittered by the stray moonlight trickling in from the hole high in the wall. She saw he sensed her fear, and she breathed as deeply as she dared to calm her heart.

"You first—" she whispered. Remembering what Bog and Loth had said, she countered, "By what name does Elleran call you?"

His sharp hiss as he gasped at the name told her she had hit her mark. The cold sting of metal against her jugular confirmed it.

He suddenly stood, releasing his hold on her, and used the knife to cut the leather tether overhead.

Wynne's hands fell quite literally upon her head. Prickles of pain flooded her arms like red ants feasting as the blood flow returned. She carefully pulled her legs under and rolled to her knees. The leather still wound around her wrists made it difficult to balance her weight as she tried to stand. If she could just get to her boot—

A walloping thud collided with her stomach, and Wynne found herself sideways on the ground. The blow of the kick winded her, and she opened her mouth to gasp for air as well as yelp in pain and shock.

With a snap of his fingers, someone entered through a flap in the wall, carrying a torch. The room now glowed red and gold, making him look all the more like a demon.The flame glow revealed nothing more than a mud and stone hut—empty except for a stool and the rushes scattered on the floor.

The servant made no move to speak. He did not even acknowledge her presence. He merely stood straight, his legs slightly apart, holding the fiery stick with both hands. Wynne tried to prop herself up on her elbow, but couldn't support her own weight.

Eadric tsked. "You really should remain where you are for the moment. I haven't invited you to move. I would offer Cnut's Golden One hospitality equal to that which I have granted him. You are, after all, very important to your king."

Wynne followed his advice and stayed where she lay, eyes and body closed, drinking in air as deeply as she could. Daring overcame discretion, however. "I have no king."

As the words echoed, Wynne realized their impact. She opened her eyes just in time to see him bend as he grabbed her hair and yanked her to her knees. Her eyes watered at his force and the pain it produced.

He stood over her, glaring down at her where she knelt still weak from the kick and from the exhaustion in her arms.

"You haven't answered my question. I asked you what your guard calls you. Cnut tells me you command a great respect, even fear, from his men. No man dares to touch or harm his great Seer. Even your sentry makes no bold move toward you." Eadric let his free hand trail the outline of one breast. "Pity. Such a waste of ripe flesh. But Khyryn has always been a fool. Now, tell me what name does your beloved Khyryn call you?"

She flinched at his touch. "My name is Wynne."

The hand closed tightly, clenching fabric and flesh until she screamed. "What name does he whisper in the night?"

Her fingers clawed at his wrist trying to break his hold. Her gown began to tear and he pulled viciously as he peeled the layers of cloth away to reveal naked flesh.

Eadric grabbed the leather of his glove between his teeth and tugged, freeing his hand of the casing as he let it fall to the ground. The hand that held her hair gripped the back of her head and pulled her to standing. He slammed her against the wall and firmly planted a boot on her foot, while he forced his knee between her thighs, immobilizing her.

Where had he put his knife? If she could get to that—

Wynn fought bitterly not to wretch at the smell of him, reeking from drink, and lust. Her birthmark ached as his hand cupped her breast, weighing it, pinching the nipple greedily. Never releasing his hold on her hair, he carefully pulled until her head followed, tilting her chin up so he could look into her eyes.

"Ah. Just think what my blade could do with this. With one swift slice, I could remove the whole tit. Or just the nipple. How painful that would be. Or—"

He bent his head to her breast, as he crushed his hips against her belly. Throbbing and eager, he closed his lips over the nipple and bit down hard.

She screamed, and he bit harder, accelerating her frenzy.

Her blood and adrenalin flowed into every part of her body now. Unfortunately, the more she thrashed against him, trying to break his hold, the more inflamed he became. He moaned gratuitously and moved his hips against her, as he slaked his tongue up the length of her throat.

He paused as he reached her lips. "Speak it, witch. Speak the name."

"Gw—Gwynndolwyn. He calls me Gwynndolwyn."

"Gwynndolwyn," he echoed. A laugh churned in his chest, bubbling up like lava. Hot and menacing. "Whore of kings and priests. I thought as much. Gwynndolwyn, do you remember me?"

She closed her eyes and shook her head. Anger and revulsion swelled in her throat. "I-I have never met you."

"Ahh, another lie. You know exactly who I am."

"You are…Eadric Streona, Alderman of Mercia—"

"Indeed I am. But you may call me Uddryd. You remember that name, do you not?"

The words stung as if he had struck her with his fist. Memories of Khyryn, of the village, of a wedding, flooded her mind. Followed by memories of a dream. A wedding night long, long ago. Her murder.

"Tell me, oh Golden One, what is it you foretold the Dane?"

She did not answer. She could not answer without vomiting.

"What future did you speak to him?

"Nothing," she finally spat.

"Cnut tells me you have proclaimed he will be victorious against Edmund."

Silence.

"Did you also foresee I will be at his side when he wins his victory?"

Only as long as he lets you. "For how long?"

His fist slammed against her chin. Her head hit the stone wall and stayed, as if set upon a shelf. Wynne tried to move, to dodge the next blow, but her body wouldn't obey her. Something warm trickled down her neck, and she tried to raise her hand to find the source. "Long enough to claim the spoils of the fight. That is the advantage to being on the winning side."

One hand wriggle free of the leather bands to find his face—still dangerously close to her mouth. She raked her fingers across his cheek. He howled in surprise, loosening his hold as she dug his skin beneath her nails.

A second blow sent her toward the ground. He landed on top of her with all his weight.

A small cry escaped her lips as Eadric straddled her. She looked to the man at the door for help. Eadric's servant still stood as he had a few minutes before, eyeing the events and keen with enthusiasm for the rape he was about to witness. He ignored her cries, instead allowing one hand to stray to his crotch, which he massaged tentatively.

Eadric reached into the cuff of his gloved hand and pulled out the dagger. The sharpened edges winked at her in the torch light. "A thousand years has not changed you, Gwynndolwyn. You still enrage me to passion. I should think you enrage most men to that end."

He turned and motioned to the man holding the torch, ordering him to move closer. "Hold her hands."

The man moved closer, pausing only to thrust the end of the torch into the ground. At Eadric's command, he knelt and grabbed her arms, pulling them taut until her shoulder joints strained. His tongue played across his own lips hungrily as he stared down at her exposed breasts and stomach.

"Malvic is a loyal soul. He has the mind of a child, and the body of a bear. I bought him a whore's favors once. He broke her, poor thing. In his excitement, he crushed her and broke her spine. Amazingly, he never realized what had happened. Once spent, he kept trying to wake her up, shaking her limp body fitfully, like a child with a toy."

Eadric straddled her thighs, twisting the dagger in his hand. "She's tempting is she not, Malvic?"

The man grunted his approval.

Wynne looked up into the starkly blank face of the giant who held her arms extended above her. Her vision blurred and cleared. Eadric's voice echoed as though he spoke from far away.

"There is a wickedness inside such a creature, though, Malvic." He balled his fist against her stomach until he found the scar and she yelped. "An evil that needs to be cut out."

"Such glorious, seductive wickedness, Gwynndolwyn. Do you not realize what you sacrificed that day with Khyryn? You and I could have ruled together. The two of us at a general's table, me enjoying the benefits of a command in Britain instead of groveling as a slave."

He traced the dagger's point across her birthmark. "Do you know what they do to the male slaves in a Roman prison?"

Wynne's vision blurred and white lights blazoned like flashbulbs. Flashbulbs. What would he think of that? Lights that needed no fire. She struggled to shake her head.

"Besides working to build their roads, we entertained the Caesar's soldiers. Sometimes we wrestled one another for their entertainment. Other times we served them in more intimate ways."

A chill slithered over her body. Warm fluid trickled from her scalp and the sweet scent of blood burned in her nostrils.

I'm bleeding. What happens when I am dead? Will I remember next time? Will there be a next time?

Her arms had numbed, and her head grew ever heavy, falling back against the ground between

Malvic's feet. Somewhere a single drummer droned, slowly—thump, thump...thump, thump...the cadence jerked and resumed, thrumming in her ears and in her chest, slowly, distantly. Waning.

Eadric's voice surfaced once more. "That first raid served as a warning. The Romans came back. I played my role well. First as a prisoner and slave. Much later, I mingled as one of them. A slave who buys his freedom is a special citizen indeed."

The drumming had withered to the rhythm of raindrops falling onto leaves.

Her heartbeat. So slow. So faint.

What about...? Her thoughts collapsed, like silk fallen to the floor. *Khyryn—what about Khyryn?*

She should fight. She tried to move, and failed. Her mind drifted even as she lay, prostrate on the dirt floor, the devil and his minion conveying her body toward the river Stix.

What will hell be like? Am I already arrived?

Eadric droned on. "The first time they had burned the village. The next time I encountered the enemy, I had fought alongside others who battled the legions. Those who survived the blade, served as slaves. I had been born to rule, as my father and his father's father— me, a slave to other men.

Gwynndolwyn struggled weakly against him.

"Luckily, Khyryn had confided to me the magic that Elleran placed upon him. He called it a curse. The ability to remember a previous life. I called it a gift. A chance for revenge."

A thin thread of drool dangled from Malvic's lips as he stared down at her.

Eadric traced the point of his blade across the curve

of her breast, up the line of her neck to rest against her jaw.

"I went to the old witch myself and demanded she give me the same magic. Blind troll that she was, Elleran just laughed at me as she took the gold. With the ability to remember who I had been, where I had lived, my enemies, at any given time I might seek my vengeance."

Pinned between the cold ground and his fevered touch, her body trembled between the hope of heaven and the threat of hell.

****

He slid the flat side of the blade along her flesh. Her shudder infused him with the drunken stupor of power.

His. She had once been his.

For all he hated her, she was still a nymph, lush with beauty—alabaster skin, mounds of soft curving flesh to cradle a man, and hair the color of the combs that dripped sweet nectar in the spring. What delicate pleasure to know the poison she used so guilefully would be extinguished.

He would extract a payment in flesh, but let her live. The Dane would have his Seer—alive.

Eadric would have an exquisite measure of justice against Gwynndolwyn. But so very much more against Khyryn, faithful, virtuous protector of Cnut's 'Golden One'.

He waited for her resistance. A plea. A cry for mercy or one last struggle that would send him over the precipice. What sweet cacophony her screams would bring.

Yet only a tiny whimper gurgled from her. She

lifted her head slightly, her eyes dull and unfocused, and she mumbled, "If I die first, I win…" Her mouth slacked as the words died on her tongue, her eyes closed, and her head lolled.

Her whispered words tingled his spine, taking hold of him and yanking him from his revelry.

"Wake up." She would not take this from him. *Not yet*. "Wake up!"

He rose and slapped her hard.

Nothing.

Wake up. Surely, the heavens would not take this moment from him! He had waited too long to reap this revenge on Khyryn. Her protector. Her conspirator.

No response.

He yelled at Malvic, "Wake her damn it. She does me no good asleep. Or dead."

Malvic peered down at the limp body attached to the arms he still held, and then spared a glance of uncertainty at Eadric.

"Fool. Shake her!"

The servant hesitated, fear creeping into his eyes.

He slapped her again.

How could she die and rob him of this? Of this?

Malvic let her arms go and they fell to the ground with a dull thud that reverberated in the hollowness of the room.

Only the sound of the torch flame, flapping like a bat's wing answered.

Streams of sweat trickled down Eadric's scalp, chilling his neck. He stared down at the still body beneath him that shimmered palely in the light. Twice this day he had been cheated.

Whore. Now he would have to deal with the Viking

who proclaimed her a great prophet and let her lead him by his balls.

Damn them all.

He grabbed the torch, and waved it threateningly at the clumsy oaf. "Malvic, get rid of the body. Take her out of the compound without Cnut's men seeing you. Quickly and quietly. Do you understand, Malvic?"

The giant oaf looked down at the lifeless body on the ground. Then at Eadric. As if he were to blame for the broken toy, the childlike creature hung his head in guilt, a silent regret forming on his brow as he did his master's bidding.

Eadric stormed from the hut and back toward the main longhouse of the keep.

The last thing he needed on the eve of committing treason against Edmund, however, was a dead 'Seer', and a hall of drunken Danes weeping for their future.

Chapter Twenty-Six

The bloody stone. The stone that bore its holder through the darkness of the otherworld, defying death and robbing men of their memories. The stone was the portal key. Where is that damned rock?

Is this death, she wondered? How and why had she ended up dead? In the wrong century? Murdered by a man who resembled a souvenir thief?

Death smelled like horseshit.

Remember.

She had been riding and had fallen. Then, even now in death, the nightmare faded. Eadric, his insanity fierce in his brutality. The scent of the blood on her face. The odor of perversity. They drifted through her mind and trailed off like the mist dissipating, leaving behind, only darkness. And a curious smell.

Horseshit.

****

The sun would crack the horizon soon. Khyryn had followed Edith's advice and waited until the keep had fallen silent and dark before he crept from the sanctuary of her weaving hut.

Upon emerging from his hiding place, he found both boys waiting for him, at the command of their mistress. Both eyed him warily, too keen to be dismissed by the man they considered responsible for Eadric's murderous justice against the young girl who was their friend.

True to Edith's word, the sentries had fallen into a dead man's slumber from their thirst for wine. No doubt, her skill at herbs also served her guests this night.

Did Eadric drink from the same cask? Or did he know better than to trust a wife who bore him so much hatred?

The darkened outline of the fortress stared at his backside in mocking silence as he waded through the swamp-like fields, two boys in tow, all three searching the night for a horse and rider.

A movement in the distance drew him further south, and to the west, ever closer to the lake.

The damned horse had lost his rider.

He told the boys to stay, as he moved closer to the stallion, clicking his tongue at the beast to get its attention.

The horse grunted at him, then pawed the ground, defiantly.

Khyryn moved closer, warily. A horse, especially one he had trained, that would not move, was either tethered...or frightened.

Khyryn sank to the ground, and listened for any sound that might reveal the horse's mind. Did Eadric lurk in the darkness?

Damned woman. Could she not stay put?

Only the wind answered his query.

Khyryn crawled through the tall grass as quietly as his body would allow, until he was certain that the horse had not been tethered to trap him. As he rose and once more began to walk toward the stallion, he tripped over something in the field, nearly flying headlong into the soft earth.

There, beneath him, half covered in mud lay the bloodied body of a woman.

A weak sound broke from her as he stared down at Gwynndolwyn's twisted figure. Even in the dark, he could see the trickle of blood covering the left side of her head and neck.

Fallen and trampled, at least she still lived.

Khyryn gently brushed the dirt from her face as he tried to rouse her once more.

Four outlaws and a horse, they had escaped Uffyngdon by way of a dung tunnel, and made their way back to the Dane's camp. They collected their horses, including the grey he had ridden earlier in the day. Aberswythe's horse, still wanting for its rider, allowed the fox to lay across its back as it trudged along.

Unsure as to whether Gwynndolwyn lived or not, he had slung her body across the stallion and collected the boys who trembled at the sight of him and the limp form.

Not until he made his way back to where Loth and Bog hid, did he speak to anyone. He pulled her from the horse's back and laid her down, cradling her head in his lap. That's when he noticed she had lost the woolen fabric she had been wearing when he had sent her flying from the stable.

He trailed his fingers across her cold flesh, waiting for the flutter of a pulse, however slight.

He lowered his face to her lips. Almost imperceptible, but her breath brushed his cheek.

Bog appeared, eyes filled with fright. "She lives?"

"Aye, barely. Have the boys fetch some water and

a blanket. Anything to warm her. Her skin is as cold as the death that courts her."

Without a word, Bog sent the boys to their task then went about stacking wood and bramble.

"No fire, Bog. We cannot risk anyone seeing the light."

"Dawn soon. Day will hide the fire then."

"That may be. For now, we must do what we can without fire."

In response to Khyryn's command, Bog abandoned the bramble stack and turned his attention to Gwynndolwyn's feet. "Lie with her."

Khyryn looked up.

Bog bobbed his head, and repeated, "Lie with her. No fire that the eye can see, but the flesh can feel. Give her yer heat, Druid son. Else, she will die."

Khyryn knew it for truth. Her battered body was blue not only from being trampled, but for being exposed for so long.

Deftly, Khyryn stripped the tunic from his head, even as the boys came running with water and blankets.

He draped one blanket across her thighs, a second one beneath her head. He stripped naked and moved to lie atop her to warm her body. He must warm her before her pulse faded completely.

"Loth, and you," he said to Cai. "Grab her hands and rub. Like you would tend a sore muscle." The boys followed his directive as he followed Bog's. He scooped a handful of water and trickled it across her lips.

Cold. Too cold.

"Spread two blankets on one of the carts and help me move her."

Marroc scurried to the cart, blankets in hand, as Khyryn hoisted her from the ground to follow. He climbed into the cart with her, wrapping his body—heat-soaked from fear—around her frail limbs. He lay down upon the blankets, dragging her body on top of his. Once more he commanded the boys to drape another wool over her upper body and head and a last one to her legs.

"You must rub her hands and feet between your palms. And Marroc, lie on your back on top of her, that she might have your warmth."

He cradled her head in one hand as he warmed her neck with his mouth. Dried sweat and blood stung his lips. Furiously he rubbed the cold flesh that yielded to his touch.

Bog kept the boys working, as Khyryn waited for the iciness to melt.

He could hear her pulse beating against his ear, now, stronger than before. Dark night gave way to silver, then to dawn as he lay beneath her, holding her to him.

He had nearly passed out from exhaustion when a muffled gasp for air rent through her body, sending the boy lying on top of her, rolling to the wooden slats.

Nearly numb from lying in one position for so long, Khyryn rolled to his side, moving her to her back. Still unconscious, her breathing had deepened.

Now, he could see better the damage she had suffered beneath Orion's frantic trampling.

Grotesque black and purple blotches covered her face and body. Her hair was matted stiff, and a thick line of dried blood framed her face. Even her throat was marred by the darkened marks, and scrapes, and...

Cuts. By her ear and jaw. Dried blood dotted the pale skin.

Khyryn peeled the ripped cloth of her shift away from the tortured flesh. He trailed his hand across her stomach. There, near her navel, red oozed, thick where she had been nicked.

Not scratched.

Gwynndolwyn had been cut.

Khyryn moved his hands and gazed along the patterned expanse of her body. Red, blue, purple. The marks were unmistakable. Finger marks bruised her stomach, her face, her wrists.

Hands, not hooves, had marred her body.

Bog nudged Khyryn's shoulder and handed him a bowl of water.

"Water washes 'way blood. And poison."

"Poison?"

"Aye. Rinse the evil from your eyes and mind as you wipe it from her flesh, Druid son."

"What poison, Bog?"

"What ha' dun this day. Poisons all. Child. Man. E'en witch. Like the bellycrawler. Rinse away his poisonous touch else it infects you as well."

Bog dipped the corner of one of the blankets into the water and wiped at Gwynndolwyn's face. "See? Water wipes his sin from her."

Khyryn's anger erupted, guttural and ferocious. He pounded the wagon as rage raked his body. "He tried to kill her. Water will not wash that away. Twice today he has stolen a life. The servant and now Gwynndolwyn."

Bog stared at him. No wavering. No cowering as he most often did. No madman's laughter. Bog held the bowl out to him once more.

"Bog sees no dead witch. And witch that is not dead may be stronger. Drink Druid son, that you will be stronger, too."

****

Wynne's head throbbed each time the mallet slammed the back of her skull. At least that was her brain's interpretation. A mallet slapping against her head, drumming repeatedly as she fought the urge to scream. Instead she groaned her aggravation at her rude awakening.

"You are well enough to feel pain. That's a good sign."

Khyryn's voice echoed through Wynne's head as she returned to consciousness.

She groaned again at the pain in her back. No, in her legs and head. Damn. Pain surged through her limbs and made it nearly impossible for her to open her eyes as her head kept bouncing off the floor.

The bouncing, at least, had some sort of rhythm. Like a heartbeat. No. A horse. No. More like the rhythm of wheels.

She fought to open her eyes, and found spots dancing before her eyes. No. blotches. Light and dark blotches dancing in and out of her vision.

Leaves. And sunlight. Fluttering through the branches, taunting her toward wakefulness.

"Ouch!" The bump packed more power than a mallet applied directly to her back. "Won't this thing ever stop?"

Wynne pried one eye open and peered up at the figure of Khyryn, riding astride Orion. She frowned at both man and horse from where she lay piled on some blankets in the cart. Her grimace had the desired effect.

Khyryn whistled and the cart slowed to a halt.

Above her, Bog's head danced in and out of view.

"Witch wakens. Aye?"

Khyryn reined in beside her. "We had wondered if you would ever wake." She thought she glimpsed relief, and maybe excitement behind the serious eyes that found hers.

Her head and limbs ached as if she had been thrown from a horse.

Thrown from the horse.

She stretched her arms up over her head and a gasp escaped her. What a fall it must have been. A movement by her side brought her hand down, protectively, to be met by the rough tongue that licked at her fingers.

Wynne found the vixen crouched, attentively laving her hand.

She tried to think back to the night before. She couldn't remember anything after she lost her balance and fell sixteen hands to the ground.

"Well, apparently I must have climbed back on that horse and ridden in to save you before you were tortured." She grinned up at him. "Since you're here. And so am I. Did I save all of Britain? As I was supposed to?"

Khyryn exchanged a look with Bog.

"Your horse threw me like I was a sack of flour it didn't want to carry. I hurt all over. He must have trampled me."

In testament, she tried to move to sit up and discovered it nearly impossible to accomplish.

Again, they looked to each other, over her.

She decided not to move. "What?"

Khyryn sighed deeply, his brow creasing as he stared at her. "Do you recall falling from Orion?"

"Of course I do. He bolted from the stall and tore out through the yard. I nearly slipped from the saddle before we made it through the gate. I managed to hang on until I was halfway across the marsh grass."

"What then?"

Khyryn's expression left little doubt he was expecting her to say something else. He nodded at Bog, who climbed off the cart, leaving them alone. Khyryn slid from his mount and nimbly settled himself next to her.

Wynne's brain felt soggy. How tired she was. She didn't know how to answer. "I-I don't know." She tried to sit up once more, this time accepting the support that Khyryn offered.

Upright, her head ached more than it had while the wagon had been moving.

Khyryn put a water skin in her hands. "Here, drink."

Wynne started to push it away, but he insisted, until she drank. The water did help. It also woke her bladder.

"Umm..." She suddenly realized she needed privacy. Quickly. "I need to..."

Khyryn recognized the immediacy in her voice and moved to help her as she scrambled toward the end of the cart. He helped her to her feet, and began to walk with her toward a large rock.

"No, Khyryn. Please, this I can do by myself." Slipping behind the cover of the boulder, she asked, "Where are Bog and Loth?"

"Nearby. With Cai and Marroc."

"You have them? They came with you?"

"Aye. By Lady Edith's leave."

"What? She found you?"

"Aye. Rather I found her. And she found a use for me."

"What use?"

Khyryn paused. "Absolution. For her husband's sins. Eadric sent her to bed Cnut. She bade me take both boys from the keep, lest they follow Hannah's fate."

"Cnut is still alive? The one thing we cannot afford is for Eadric to prevent Cnut from marching against Edmund."

Another silence.

Wynne finished relieving herself and rose to find Khyryn staring at the ground. For the first time, she looked at her own clothes. Little more than a thin bit of wool gathered and tucked around her. Above her chest, the gathered weave had been clasped with a simple metal brooch.

Gwynndolwyn stopped in her tracks and stared at Khyryn, completely stupefied. "Khyryn? What happened to my clothes?"

"You never answered my question."

"How long have I been out? Asleep?"

"Gwynndolwyn, what do you remember after you fell?"

The world began to spin, in slow motion, as it had at the faire the day Richard had seized her. Wynne's legs faltered, and she fell into a sit as Khyryn lunged to catch her.

Remember? She couldn't remember anything other than falling from the horse. Khyryn's expression darkened as she struggled to recall something. Anything.

The weight of her own limbs overpowered her will, and she collapsed into Khyryn's arms.

Wynne heard her own voice echo in her ears. "He who has the stone controls time."

Chapter Twenty-Seven

Elleran sat upright, rocking back and forth. "What color?"

Aberswythe stared at the crimson clouds. "It is pale, yet."

"You lie. Aagh." She tsked at him. "What color? Tell me."

He tucked his herbs back into his pouch and tied it. "The skies are red this morning. I must return to Khyryn."

"Then with you I shall go."

"No, Elleran, You are not well to walk yet."

"I cast the curse. We share the prophecy."

"And so you must live to see it fulfilled. Eadric will be no threat next to Khyryn if he should see you."

"The young druid is wiser than his mentor. Khyryn will harm me not. He knows my power."

"He is still in love with her. He carries with him not only memories. He carries the guilt as well. For that, he harbors great enmity for the one who did pitch her own wrath into the fires of fate."

"Had I not, where would the balance be? Do not forget, it is because of his memory she is here, now. You said she remembers nothing. Not even you?"

"Strong is your tongue for incantations. She looks upon me as one looks upon an old man."

"Ha. You *are* an old man. Come. Our feet must

take us over many such hills this day."

Aberswythe helped her to her feet and placed his staff into her gnarled fist. For one without sight, her steps were as light the child she had once been.

"Do you remember our youth?"

He smiled to himself. "I do. We gave no mercy to our parents."

"Nor to the villagers. What they endured at our folly."

"You played with them until they feared you."

Elleran puffed up. "They did not fear me. They turned their backs on the truth. Lived in ignorance."

"Sometimes ignorance brings solace. The mother does not wish to know her babe will die before it walks. A young woman dares not think about her lover's death upon the field of war."

"Aaagh. Fools."

"Not fools. Creatures of the earth. As you and I are. You played at telling tales no one sought to hear. And when they turned their backs upon you, your vanity turned to spite."

Elleran fell silent. She did not speak again until the sun climbed above the clouds.

"It is wrong to bear a womb, yet never bear fruit."

"It was not your path. You are a great priestess."

"I am blind of spirit as well as sight."

"You are only weary. You have suffered at the hands of the one who seeks to break the balance."

"Uddryd was an idiot."

"No, He merely lusts for power as most men lust for the cradle of a woman's sex."

The old woman snorted. "He thrusts his cock for more than a crown. His hunger is carnal as well as political."

"Hunger unsated. His soul must be purged of the covetous venom it consumed a thousand years ago when he drank from your fires."

"Blame not my potions for his odious blackened heart. He is as he always has been. His brother's twin."

"I taught them both. Gave counsel to their father. I knew them in their youth. Uddryd possessed not so poisonous a spirit as he bears now."

"The wolf and hound pups will play in kind, until the wolf grows fangs and claws. The hound will seek man's hearth. The wolf will hunt man's flock. One prepared to be a priest, the other a prince. Was it not the same with us?"

Elleran's words struck a blow of truth.

Though they had started life together, they also had followed different paths. So had a rift grown between them when he took up a wife and left the village of their youth?

Aberswythe sighed heavily. "I thought us different. I sought to be like the villagers."

Pale withered lips curled into a smile. "I thought you foolish. We were both wrong. You are certain Gwynndolwyn knows not the power she carries within her veins?"

"I am certain."

"Have you spoken to her of her mother?"

Aberswythe's throat tightened. He had not spoken to anyone of Rana since the day she had been taken from him. A great druidess, she had marched with her people against the red men. She had been slaughtered.

As Gwynndolwyn had been sacrificed to unify their families when given in marriage to Uddryd. The firstborn daughter to the firstborn son. Priestess to Prince.

"Gwynndolwyn does not speak of gifts from gods. She believes her knowledge is from the scribes that record histories in tomes. She denounces the druid and wyce ways."

"Ah." Elleran reached her gnarled hand toward Aberswythe and patted his cheek. "It is difficult. The wisdom of the parent and the innocence of the child."

****

By the light of the orange harvest moon, Khyryn and their band had left the camp and began their march north. Toward Edmund. Toward Ashingdon.

Though he still did not understand Gwynndolwyn's murmurings, Khyryn had used a piece of cloth and the charred end of a stick to draw a message for Cnut, calling him to meet Edmund by the next new moon.

Bog, however, had taken the stick from Khyryn and set down the words in Latin as Khyryn spoke them. Strokes of black, as fine as the threads of a spider's web lined the linen cloth that Khyryn had ripped from the tail of Gwynndolwyn's shift.

All the while Bog worked, Khyryn paid attention to how still and fixed the troll's hand and body stayed. No bobbing, as he usually did. He kept his attention on the cloth and on the stick that drew each letter on the page.

When Bog had finished and Khyryn had inspected his scribe, he pulled a strip of leather from around his waist and tied it to the rolled cloth. He bade Bog and the others stay while he rode back to Cnut's camp where he tied the message to the tree to swing where Cnut's men would see when they marched through.

Once they were closer to Londinium, Khyryn

would send a similar letter to Edmund.

For Gwynndolwyn's safety, he would see this finished. For nearly three days she had existed in a fitful sleep. Her body and mind still fought wakefulness, as if sleep brought respite from memory. Blue marks turned to burgundy, then brown as the bruises near her eyes faded.

She is not of this world. She does not belong here.

Reason mocked his desire. He could not protect her. Had never been able to. The same curse that had robbed her of her memory of him, of their past, also served to protect her from that same past.

Soon, past, present, and future would be satisfied. She would return to her own world. To safety. Then, he would kill Eadric.

When the sun was high, they stopped to rest. Khyryn lay on the sun-drenched grass, eyes closed in partial slumber. In the distance he could hear the grousing shouts as Bog tried once and again to teach the boys how to catch fish in their hands. And the giggles of the boys each time the fish escaped their grip.

The wind moved clouds to dance above him, so that the sun no longer warmed him. The breeze lulled him to doze, until his breathing grew heavy.

"I had a dream last night." Her breath and words jolted him from his rest and he reluctantly lifted one eyelid to look at her.

She lay on her stomach, her head propped on her fists, staring at him. She did not smile.

"Tell me. What disturbs you?"

"What does Edmund look like?"

"The king? I know not. I have not seen him."

"But you did see Eadric, right?"

"Aye. You know Streona's face as well."

"Everybody assumes I would recognize him. But I didn't."

"He has the face he has worn for a thousand years. Two thousand even. He is the same as he was and as when you knew him as Richard."

"But I did recognize him at the faire, did I?"

Her stare grew distant. "I dreamt he's going to kill again."

He rolled to his side and stared at her. "Who?"

"Edmund. I think. In the dream, Eadric killed a man and when the man fell, he lost a crown, which Eadric picked up and placed on his own head."

"That is an action of my brother, aye."

"But then he did something else."

"What?"

She hesitated. Khyryn sat up, and pulled her to sit as well so that they were face to face.

Two crimson spots blushed her cheeks. "He...he wiped the blood from the dagger on his fingers and pressed them to my lips and said, 'now it is your turn.' Then he handed the knife to me."

"It is a dream, Wynne, nothing more."

"What did you say?"

"It is a dream. Gone with the daylight."

She pulled away from him. "You called me 'Wynne'."

"Is that not how you call yourself?"

"Of course it is. But you have never called me that. You have always called me by my given name."

"You do not use that name, so I shall not use it."

She shook free from his grasp. "But you have to."

"I do not."

She swung at him, clobbering his head. In retaliation he grabbed her fist. The touch of her pulse throbbing beneath her flesh, pounding against his palm hit him like a hammer against his heart.

Her eyes darkened as she stared up at him. Gone was the blush of indecision. "You used that name to bring me here. It was good enough then." Her lips curled into a wickedly covetous smile, as she traced her free hand along his thigh. Pausing at the bulge beneath his tunic, she whispered, "Say my name. Properly. As you used to. You brought me here. Say it." Her hand slipped beneath his tunic and cupped his balls, squeezing them. "Say it. The right way."

He had no desire to play games. Especially a game as she was tempting him with. He forced her hand away from his groin and tried to ignore the interest that had grown between his legs. "Let me rest. You are still weak. We both will have need of—"

The air exploded from his lungs as she landed upon him, pinning his shoulders with her own hands, leaning over him, a fierce scowl on her face. "Say it."

For a moment he could say nothing. The woman hit him like an ox. Breathlessness ripped through his torso and burned his eyes. Had she been a man, he would—

She lowered her mouth to his ear and delicately bit his earlobe, which immediately sent a message to his groin. "Say it the way you said it in the cave. When you made me a part of this."

The tone of her voice—something not right. Khyryn pushed her away from his face. "To what end? So you might continue this game as Seer? Parading in front of Cnut and Edmund and Eadric?"

Like a twig she snapped. The shrill, sour note of frenzy in her voice raised his hackles. "This game is not mine. It never was. It is yours. You are the one who tore me from the faire. You and Aberswythe."

"I would remind you that my brother had a hand in tha' as well."

Her face pinched in hatred and recognition. "He knew."

"Knew what?"

"Richard must have known. Everything. That's why he took the stone. He remembered everything."

Air squeaked in his lungs as he tried to inhale. "Get off of me—"

"Not until you say it!"

"Why is it so important to you tha' I call you by your given name?"

Her strength transformed in fury. Words dripped from her lips. "Because none of this is real until you make it so. It is all a game. Like the faire. It's all make-believe, fantasy. Nothing is real. Not the death. Not the dreams."

Her hands clenched and pounded at him as she ranted. "Nothing real. Not the fear, the cold. Not that madman, Richard, or Eadric, or whoever he is this week. Not these bruises, or the putrid fear that haunts my sleep!

Khyryn had regained enough sense and breath to fend off her fists, which punched at him, albeit weakly.

"Say it. Say my name. Damn you! Say it!"

He rolled to his side, to slide from beneath her, but she grabbed his hand and slipped it beneath her robe.

She dragged his hand across the flesh of her stomach. "Can you feel that, Khyryn?"

He attempted to yank his hand from her.

She clenched her legs tighter around his ribs, and pressed the hand harder against her skin. "Can you feel the place where the dagger cut? I dream of it. Over and over. Every time I close my eyes I smell the pitch. I taste the blood. I hear my own scream. From a thousand years ago, I can feel it."

"Shhh. Calm yourself."

"I have dreamt of it each time I close my eyes since you brought me here."

With his free hand he tried to break her grip, but she seized the hand and twined her fingers in his.

She drew both hands across her abdomen. "You asked what I remember, Khyryn?"

Khyryn ripped his hand from her grasp and grabbed her arms, rolling her over and flinging her to her back. The world shifted, as if something had torn. He tried to stop the words from spilling out. "Stop it."

"I didn't die at the hands of the fucking Romans, Khyryn! I died by his hand—"

"Gwynn—"

"Your brother raped me on our wedding night. He knew. He saw us. He saw it all. And still he married me. I was sacrificed like a lamb to slaughter. The Romans did not kill me—"

He pressed his hand to her mouth to halt the stream of accusations. "Stop it—"

"Uddryd had already murdered me. He slit me open with the dagger you gave me as a wedding gift. For revenge. Just like he killed Hanna—"

"Gwynndolwyn—"

She gasped, choking on the words that bubbled out of her mouth. "I didn't meet Eadric the other night. I met Uddryd. A new name. A new time. An old, ancient hate. But it was Uddryd. Just as evil as that night a thousand years ago."

"Shhh." He tried to hold her and she pushed him away.

"It's not a dream, Khyryn. None of this is. It was never just a dream. Even Aberswythe could not stop him."

He looked into her eyes and saw...her memory.

Crystalline and wild. Memory curled like smoke behind the sparkle of her eyes. "I remember, Khyryn. I remember what happened after I fell from the horse. You and Bog know! You found me. You both knew! He tried to murder me over and over!"

A scream rose up from deep inside her. A scream he could not stop. A scream she had held pent up since he had brought her through the stones. The sound echoed through her body and the ground beneath, carried on the wind high into the heavens.

A scream she had kept locked away since that night ten-hundred years ago.

Khyryn could do nothing to soften the infernal cry that made them both tremble. He wrapped his arms around her, and she writhed beneath him and clung to him, releasing the pain and anger.

Tears welled in his eyes, blurring his vision as he watched her torment. He bent his head and kissed the mouth that raged against it all, shrieking and ranting.

Khyryn had loved and lusted for her through half a dozen lifetimes, each more torturous than the last. He had searched for her and given up hope. He had lived the life of a celibate man when he could not stand to touch another.

He held her against his chest and rocked her. He wept for not telling her. He wept for bringing her here.

Cursed with the memory. Now, Gwynndolwyn would never forget.

He had wished for death. And revenge. He had wished for her to remember his face and the love they once had shared.

He had never wished for this.

Chapter Twenty-Eight

The fire cast a blanket of warm air upon the night. Bog had found branches and sticks long dried by time as they had walked. Loth, and Cai, and Marroc all tried to best one another, fighting for the privilege to carry each branch Bog gathered.

The torches they had taken from the Danes' wagon would not be missed, but here gave a sense of safety to the night.

Now, soft snores rose from the pile of arms and legs where the boys had collapsed, exhausted.

Bog and the boys had caught enough fish to feed them all.

But Khyryn had no appetite.

They had all witnessed her madness.

At first the boys mistook her shrieks for a game between two lovers. When the cries continued, they turned their backs, looking nervously over their shoulders at Khyryn as he held her tightly.

She had screamed, and cried, and spit, and fought until exhaustion and shock once more silenced her, and dredged her in unconsciousness.

Bog poked at the fire. "She is possessed by demon spirits, yer witch?"

"Of a sort. Aye."

"Where be the druid?"

"Aberswythe will find us when he is ready."

"Mayhap he lies sick or deid?"

"No. I would know."

"How say Druid son?"

Khyryn considered Bog for a long time, watching him bob, nervously as he tended the fire. "Aberswythe and I have been friends for many years. I would sense if he were ill."

"Did Druid son sense the witch's demon?"

"No, Bog. I did not."

"Yer witch is not like others. Water doesn't burn her skin?"

Khyryn picked up one of the sticks gathered earlier and poked at the fire. "No. Water does not burn her skin."

"Mayhap she's nae witch, after all."

"You are correct, Bog. She is no witch."

"Ah. Mayhap, Bog can help."

Khyryn focused on the troll who bobbed in the dancing shadows of the flames. "How?"

"Bog listens. Bog hears. Bog helps. Let Bog help."

"How would you help her, Bog?"

Bog winked at Khyryn and jabbed fresh wood into the fire, mumbling to himself as he moved the coals and made the ash fly into the star-strewn sky.

Ignoring Khyryn's question, he rose and waddled over to where Gwynndolwyn lay, wrapped in Aberswythe's wool. He stood over her, peering down at her for a long time, mumbling all the while to himself. Or to some invisible companion. Khyryn knew not which.

The vixen, curled at her lady's feet lifted its head drowsily and chortled at the bobbing troll, sending him back to the flames.

He took up his seat again and tossed another branch into the fire. When he had satisfied himself that the fire was right, he lifted his gaze to meet Khyryn's and winked. "The morrow be soon enough, fox says. First we rest. Rest now, Druid son. Bog helps."

He pulled his cloak around his frame and settled in like a bird, nesting. He snickered as if he shared a private joke, and nodded. "Bog has secrets, too."

****

A voice called from behind the bolted gate set deeply with the thick stone and wooden edifice.

"Brother Oswig!"

A second shout echoed on the opposite side of the wall, hailing others. Khyryn looked up to see a monk sitting atop the wall, yelling to the people inside. Shortly, the gate swung open and half a dozen men in modest robes milled around the band of weary travelers, ushering them into safety.

Bog danced around the horse that carried the three young boys, lightly patting the animal, and laughing, as a stream of monks filed into the courtyard to greet the familiar face.

One man, slender and tall, broke through the crowd that had formed around Khyryn and the others. Slightly older than Bog, yet nearly as animated, he hugged Bog to him in an embrace meant for a sibling. "Oswig, for truth, I would think mine eyes to play me for an oaf, or that you are a ghost come to trick me, did I not with mine own arms, embrace you."

"Brother Daniel," Bog replied, "Friends I brings. An' horses also. Master Khyryn and his lady, have need of you. Horses need water."

"Long have you been away from us, Oswig. And

now have you returned not only alive, but with a brood in tow. Come, rest your horses and yourselves."

Loth, Cai, and Marroc slid from the grey and took off, having immediately found a litter of boys of their ilk. Khyryn untied the tether at the horn of Aberswythe's saddle and lifted Gwynndolwyn from the horse.

In the clamor at their arrival, she had remained silent, watching the revelry that received them, yet making no move to acknowledge or join the celebration.

Two young men guided the horses toward a tented stable as Khyryn and Gwynndolwyn followed their host and Bog into the large, stone building.

Brother Daniel led them through the towering corridor and into a common room where the scent of clove mixed with the aroma of barley and honey.

"Sit, friends of our brother, and take your rest. Break your fast at our table."

Bog, bobbing up and down giddily, turned to Khyryn. "Bog has friends, aye?"

Khyryn allowed a smile to tug at his mouth. "Aye, Bog. And friends such as any king would envy. It is a fine secret."

Several others milled about the room, tending to the various tasks.

At one end of the room a great hearth fire burned to warm the frost chilled air. Samhain was yet more than a moon away. However the sun no longer warmed the earth with its bright light.

Elsewhere in the room, two smaller flames glowed. In the center of the room, a small pit had been dug from the floor. Within the pit, embers glowed red and gold.

Above their heat the thick-yoked limb of a tree suspended an iron pot. From within the pot, one of the monks filled bowls of steaming liquid, which he quickly offered to Khyryn and the others.

In the corner closest to the great fire, sat an oven in two tiers, molded of clay. Hot coals shoveled into the lower opening warmed the small frame of the cavernous design. Into the top, the monks slid flat discs of bread that swelled to twice their size as the hot air baked them.

"The ale does double the bread by half our work," Daniel said as he broke one of the rounds of bread and offered it to them. "It fills our stomachs with sustenance and the room with heady scent. Do eat your fill, gentle friends of Bog."

Khyryn accepted drink and food both for himself and for Gwynndolwyn. Cloves and young wine mulled with honey and water to make a warming brew.

"We have long missed our brother, Master Khyryn. He is lost to us five years now."

Khyryn caught the telling glance in Daniel's smile.

"Aye. He lived among the people of the forests, until our paths did cross."

Bog interrupted. "Bog did fall upon the droit witch and threatened the old druid. The viper set Bog to die."

Khyryn cut in. "Eadric, Edmund's alderman, set his henchmen to brutalize Bog."

"I finds the Druid son and takes him to the viper's nest. Dun I, Druid son?"

Khyryn nodded.

"Bog is clever, aye. No troll, though. As Master's lady is nae a witch. Witches nae like water. The Seer likes water, yet 'er soul burns to thirst. She is possessed, Daniel. Bog sees the demons that drown hearts in weeping. She drowns."

Daniel listened to his friend's disjointed tales, never interrupting his friend. When Bog had finished his drink and tale, Daniel called another monk and bade him ready a bed for the guests.

"We have a modest dwelling, Master Khyryn, but can offer a private chamber for you and your wife."

Khyryn's chest tightened at the monk's words. Wife. Long had he dreamt of Gwynndolwyn at his side, but never had he uttered the word "wife". Beside him, Gwynndolwyn flinched and her brow furrowed slightly, but she neither spoke, nor acknowledged Daniel.

"My gratitude to you and your brothers. We are bound for Ashingdon and our trip has tired my lady beyond speech. I fear she is too weak to continue the journey. Too many nights has she found her bed upon the ground without a pallet."

"Oswig, you do well to bring your friends to our keeping. Master Khyryn, we are possessed of a well, long since abandoned by the Romans that gives us great comfort. Mayhap the miracle of its waters will restore the rose and health to your lady."

Bog grinned a nearly toothless grin, as proud as if he held a fish in his bare hands.

"See, Druid son? Secrets have I that none but Bog kens."

This time Khyryn did grin back at the bobbing figure. "Aye, Bog. And fine secrets they are."

Movement across the room caught Bog's attention, and he leapt from his seat to scurry to the corner where a grey and white kitten sat, cleaning itself. Like a great dog, Bog crouched next to the animal, watching intently as the young cat preened and washed its face, pausing occasionally to paw at Bog's tattered coat.

"I had not hoped to see Oswig again," Daniel finally whispered. "You have done right by God to bring him back to us."

"I can claim no honor for this doing. It is he who brought us to your door."

"I believe it is your wife that brings him home."

Sadness clouded Daniel's eyes as he looked upon Gwynndolwyn's frail posture. "Brother Oswig once moved amid the world as one of us. Indeed, his youth he spent raising these sturdy walls."

"Bog grew up in the monastery?"

"He did. Brother Oswig's father built our forge. When his mother died, he and his father found solace within our halls."

"Why did he leave?"

"His heart led him away."

"His heart?"

"He took his father's place at our forge. He and his wife—"

"Bog had a wife?"

"Oswig like many young men found his calling to be one of family. He and his wife had two fine sons."

"Had?"

"We live in an age where peace is fleeting. The promise of kind accord from one overlord means nothing when a king is dead. One spring, he and his sons and wife did travel to her family's village. Too soon, though they were set upon by soldiers who beat poor Oswig severely."

"And his family?"

"The boys were taken as prisoners. His wife

killed."

"For what purpose?"

"There are those who do not act by purpose—but for the sport they derive. For the destruction of innocence. Oswig did carry his wife back to this, his home. Too late to save her body, however, for her soul had gone to be with God."

"And Bog?"

"About the head he had suffered wicked blows that nearly killed him as well. He thrashed in painful fits for many nights as he recovered. By midsummer, he departed our sanctuary. No word or farewell. He simply wandered off one day and did not return. We did think he had returned to the site of the attack in his madness. We searched, but to no end. We feared him dead these many seasons."

"And his sons?"

"Never a sign or word of them."

"What of the soldiers?"

"Master Khyryn, you and I know the way of those who are taken by the army. Often children are given to fill the lines of battle, or to serve those who make war. A slave to one faction or another. Whether taken to fight or to serve, or to die as sport makes little difference. Battles are not fought by generals, but by pawns. Women and children are dispensable."

Khyryn caught the telltale grimace that shadowed Daniel's weathered face. "What knows a priest of war?"

Daniel pointed to the sword and to the cowled tunic Khyryn wore. "No less than a warrior would know of priests."

Chapter Twenty-Nine

Tewkesbury, November, 1016

Wynne sank into the warmth as water rose around her, enveloping her, swallowing her with gentle memories. Had it really been nearly a month since their arrival?

How suspiciously she had watched the convoy of individuals that paraded into this room, preparing it for guests. The monk, Daniel, called for a great vat to be brought to the chambers where he led Wynne and Khyryn.

Carved from the trunk of a dark tree, the tub reminded her of a canoe—one long piece of wood with a crater deeply carved. The interior, however, had been lined in bronze, as if the inside of the tree were made of the precious metal, which had been chipped away.

The monks had filled the tub with water, hot from a hearth, causing steam to rise from the log vat like fog. To every three buckets of hot water, the monks added a bucket of water drawn from a well just outside the door.

When filled, the tub offered a pool large enough to accommodate the length of a person. Nearly. Two feet deep by nearly five feet in length, it had welcomed her comfortably, soothing muscles that had suffered too much trauma over the last three weeks.

Each day, Daniel called for the tub to be filled in

the same way. Each day he had blessed the water and departed the room, leaving Khyryn to lift her, fully clothed, into the healing waters.

Today, however, she asked him to leave. She had disrobed, and slipped into the tub with nothing to separate her skin from the metal of the tub.

She scrunched down and filled her hair with the water, letting it wash over her neck and ears, finally holding her breath, and dipping her face beneath the surface as the water seeped into her pores, every cell, nurturing every fiber of her being. With her eyes closed, voices sounded in her head.

"Time draws nigh, Seer."

"Tell them, Golden One."

"The moon grows ripe."

The voices sang to her, lulling her.

"Fate tarries for no one."

Whose voice?

"Two kings will rise—"

"Two bishops flanked."

Two bishops? Why bishops in a war of kings?

"Mad monks dance in the light"

"As the moon swells

"And grows ripe—"

The words swirled around her like the water that covered her, drenching her.

"The moon grows ripe—"

Wynne floated in the water listening to the cacophony of voices singing to her, floating in the water. Healing. Body and soul.

"As do you."

Cold air slapped her face as two hands yanked her up in a vice grip, sending water spewing over the sides of the tub to the floor and ripping her from the warmth.

If coughing and screaming could coincide, she did both, swinging every limb she could move as Khyryn dragged her over the edge of the pool.

"Are you so mad tha' you would give up your own life, rather than share it wi' me, then? An' I did but carry you for a half a moon's wax and wane?

Her feet slammed against the floor as he threw a linen sheet over her, and wrapped her like a mummy in the cloth. While she spewed water, he spewed curses and accusations, until both had cleared their lungs, and sat glaring at one another.

"What is it with you and water? First you nearly killed me by dunking me in a freezing stream, now you try to drown me in two feet of wat—"

"Me? I am nae the one trying to drown herself—"

"I am doing no such thing—"

Khyryn's hands vibrated vigorously rubbing the sheet against her shoulders as his voice vibrated against her head. "Do you not trust tha' if I could take you back, I would? It is nae so easy with two."

She threw her head back and clipped his chin. "Well, you certainly had no trouble getting me here."

His cheeks and neck grew dark red. "Aye? An' to my memory, ye were nae so much opposed to it then, were you?"

Now Wynne felt the heat rise in her own cheeks. "You tricked me."

"I had a knot atop my head, half my blood spilt, an' a ghost standin' o'er me tendin' my wounds."

Wynne curled her tongue around an accent to match his own. "Yet ye kud nae mention tha' I might be draagg-ed a thousan' yeeeeers back in time? An' aboot the crazy mad monk what eats worms from the ground like an early bird in the moornin' sae the viper willna' hear his stomach growl?"

The sound of her own voice rocked Wynne with laughter. Khyryn looked at her as if she had truly lost her mind, before he broke into a fit of laughter that shook his body.

Laughter poured from her chest into her arms and legs and her brain, filling the empty dark holes left by dark memories.

For the first time she could remember since arriving, Wynne's body did not ache from anger, or from riding a horse too long.

"Where is Vixen?"

"She has taken to Bog's kitten like a mother cat."

Wynne felt a pang of jealousy. The little fox had been by her side since she stepped through the stone wall. Well, at least since she had tried to leave the druid's cave.

Khyryn sat back and rested his head against the wall, his body drenched from head to toe. "It is nae an easy task t' take you back to your time. We must be joined, for you do no' speak the words that call the elements together."

"I did once, though. Didn't I?"

The question hung in the air between them like a dagger.

"Aye. You once called the powers of the elements to you, as had your mother before you. And her mother before her."

Wynne scooted closer to Khyryn. "Why didn't you tell me all of it? Why didn't he?"

"The whole story Aberswythe does nae ken. Nor

did I, before Uddryd confessed his triumph. I killed him for it. Once."

"Would you have killed him on the chess field that day?"

"'Twas he who drew first blood."

"If you had stayed that day, would you have finished him?"

Khyryn's face turned pale and somber. "Aye. I would have. To avenge you."

"What of Aberswythe? Does he know? About Gwynndolwyn's—of my—murder?"

"I never told him the truth."

"He had a right to know."

"He buried a wife. And a daughter. Naught could be gained by telling him he had led one to her own death. What could he have done? His memory has lived on in the same body for two thousand years. Immortal he is. As the gods themselves. I could not burden him with that truth. Aberswythe had borne you with your mother into the world. He had a right to bury his dead. Not resurrect them."

"You said you would have killed Richard to avenge me. Is not also that the privilege of a parent?"

"It is."

"Khyryn?"

"Aye?"

"What if my purpose was never meant to affect history? What if the stones did not reveal me to Aberswythe because of Uddryd, or Eadric, or Richard?"

"Then for what purpose?"

"I have seen so much in my dreams. My childhood from my own time, as well as our love from past lives. There is more at stake here than the war between

Edmund and Cnut. What fate has dealt for them is not for us to meddle in."

"What then?"

"We must find Aberswythe."

"Daniel has sent word into several of the villages in all directions. If he is near, he will come."

"I think I have the solution to your curse, Khyryn of Powys."

Dumbfounded—without words or reason upon his face, Khyryn stared at Wynne, waiting for an explanation.

She breathed deeply, and smiled at her druid.

"When challenged by a viper, let staff cast from your domain—that it may seek no sanctuary, nor feast upon your harvest grain."

****

Eadric sat astride his horse, watching the battle litter the field with the bodies of Edmund's soldiers as Cnut's horde surged from the coast.

"This is my brother-in-law's doing." Playing kings against one another had brought him perilously close to the fighting. Even now, Streona's own soldiers were called into the fray, despite his manipulation of the battle lines.

He had promised to give the support of his troops and ships, not surrender their lives.

By their agreement to meet at Ashingdon to discuss a truce, both kings threatened Eadric's livelihood. After all, to serve two kings brought great reward. As long as Mercia was prized by both rulers, he could sell his fealty to the highest bidder. If peace were achieved, however…Cnut as king?

The prospect held some modest gain. After all, the

Dane geld would be collected in the lands Cnut claimed. Already men whispered Cnut sought higher Dane geld from his northern lands even while he sought support from the Bishop of York.

Danish gold does weigh heavy in the purses for the blessing of Christian priests upon his rule."

Edmund's line fell back, and Cnut surged forth to close the gap. From the West, the Cymri tribes gave support to Edmund, bolstering his valiant effort to outfight the Danes.

Eadric pulled back his own troops, defiant of Cnut's army. Support. Not stupidity.

I will not sacrifice my own men for a battle twice won this day.

Once terms of surrender had been met, Eadric would move once more to kings' counsel. For now, he could do no more than lend his support to both Cnut and Edmund—king and countryman.

****

Winchester Castle

November waned. Eadric's purse grew thin from the geld of the people who called Cnut king.

Despite his victory, Cnut had stripped Eadric of much of his holdings in punishment for his departure from Ashingdon. Still, Cnut held a golden apple in his hand, luring him with a promise to restore his lands. Once Edmund had been handled.

Edmund speared the bit of meat upon the trencher and tossed it to the hound that lay at his feet. "What have you to offer that I would seek your counsel, Eadric? Have you lost favor with the Viking, as you have with me? "

"Your sister sends you kind wishes, your Majesty."

"I hear my sister gifts more than wishes these days. Is it by your leave she invites Danish mongrels into her bed?"

Eadric's temper flared.

"The Dane geld must be paid, sire. Whether by coin, or cunning, Cnut cares little."

Edmund found humor in Eadric's words. "Too soon, you will all be ruled by cunning skirts. Then will we see England back in the hands of Britons once more."

Eadric sneered at Edmund. "I think not."

"You who let your wife—my sister—ride horn upon that Viking scum would be the first to fall at her hands or bidding. Do not turn a blind eye to my sister. She is, after all her father's daughter."

"Nae, sire. Your sister is far wiser than her father. Or her brother. She has learned well from your failures. She, like I, prefers to play a victor in this life."

"My sister is the geld due you for services past rendered. She spread her legs wide to pay for your services to my father and to me. And now she shows favor to the one who collects geld from you."

Hatred simmered beneath Eadric's skin.

Edmund called a servant and demanded drink and two goblets. Edmund disliked drinking alone. He always had preferred an audience for most things.

Eadric entertained Edmund's disdain for much of the evening. Once Edmund had tipped his cup, and his head had fallen to a snore, Eadric finished the drink. With great facetious flourish he thanked his host for a congenial meeting.

As he bid his brother-in-law goodnight, Eadric Streona bent to share a secret with his former king.

His hand moved swiftly in its duty as it snapped Edmund's neck in two, killing him.

Immediately. Silently.

The king is dead. Long live the king.

Chapter Thirty

Tewkesbury

Yule solstice had passed, and still Wynne and Khyryn lingered in the monastery. Each day brought hope for word of Aberswythe. Each night brought disappointment. They could not wait forever.

Christ's Mass would be soon. And with it, a new king crowned. Blessed by the Church. Attended by his new alderman.

Eadric Streona. A viper to their sanctuary.

Khyryn spent his days working with Bog in the old forge. Bog, Brother Oswig to the other monks, had settled into a quiet routine, choosing to sit with Wynne's vixen and the kitten when he found a need to be confined indoors. Even during these coldest days, Bog found his peace outside in the company of his brother monks.

To the boys, he had become a beloved uncle. Loth revered only one above Bog, and even Bog revered the one who had saved so many from Eadric Streona.

Khyryn of Powys.

Wynne's heart leapt when the gate bell rang. Long had she waited to greet the man who had once been Gwynndolwyn's father, for that is how she thought of herself now.

She ran to meet Khyryn when it sounded a second,

telling time. He had laid down his tools and moved toward the gate.

The gate admitted not one, but two visitors. Aberswythe. And Elleran.

As Wynne watched, his steps faltered, and his limbs froze at the sight of the fortune teller. The one who had cursed him with memory. The one who had started everything.

Wynne moved to greet the old druid.

"We have expected you for some time," she called across the yard. "We worried at your disappearance."

"Sometimes, when called, we must answer." Though his words were weak, his eyes shimmered brightly.

Wynne wondered at such a calling that would bring him together with Elleran, but she held her own questions.

"Brother Malacai?" Wynne called. "Guide our guests to the common room. Khyryn and I will join them in a moment's time."

"I have dreamt of you," called Elleran.

How should she respond to the woman she knew from another time?

"And I of you, Elleran. I have long heard tales of you."

At this, the old wyce cackled, and took Malacai's arm to be led to rest.

Wynne ran to Khyryn who stood like a statue in the courtyard.

Whether from the forge, or from the shock of seeing Elleran, beads of perspiration glistened on his face.

"You are ashen pale."

"A ghost I saw."

Wynne humpfed. "She is no ghost. And she is on the arm of our druid. Come quickly, before Bog finds out." Wynne heard the lilt in her own voice. Excitement. "Then again, a show between the mad monk and the witch could prove entertaining."

Khyryn's arms had thickened from his work as a smith. Always broad shouldered and taller than most men, he now resembled some of the Danish soldiers who had marched with Cnut, so heavily muscled were his arms.

The sight of him made her giddy. The pallor of his cheek made her move.

She cupped the back of his neck and pulled his head toward hers. "Down you go," she said as she thrust his head down to his knees to redirect the blood flow.

He allowed her to hold him, straining to touch the ground to the count of five, before he grabbed her around the knees and upended her over his shoulder.

"Put me down, Khyryn—right now."

As if she were indeed a queen, he bowed to her command and redeposited her to her feet.

"You know what happened the last time you did that to me."

The color returned to his cheeks, and he smiled down at her. "Aye. I got my wish."

"And more than you could handle that day, too."

Her reference to their departure from the faire, nearly five months ago, sobered his mood and returned his attention to the newly arrived guests.

Malacai had sent word to Daniel who had taken a seat with the two elders, and now engaged them in conversation. When Khyryn and Wynne approached, however, their banter ceased, silence cresting and ebbing like an ocean between them.

When she could stand it no more, Wynne did the only thing she could think of. She crossed to Aberswythe, knelt before him, and placed her hands over his. "Welcome—Father."

The old druid's hands began to tremble as clear eyes clouded grey. Aberswythe looked warily upon her face as if fearful of what he might see.

He glanced to Khyryn, then back to Wynne.

She squeezed his hands. "I remember."

Tears welled in his vibrant eyes. When he spoke, he chose his words carefully. "How have you fared, Golden One, so long a time away from all that is familiar to you?"

"Better, now, for seeing you."

"Then glad we are of it."

Khyryn cleared his throat.

Wynne reached for Khyryn, whose face darkened at the word "we".

"Aberswythe," Khyryn began, "Perhaps, you would speak of why *we* are all met here? Long has Daniel sent messages to the villages inquiring of you."

"Indeed. Brother Daniel tells me my horse is well fed and brushed by Loth and two others each day."

Daniel slapped his knee. "Two of the boys work as stable hands. For truth, they would sleep in the horses' stalls, were I to grant them favor to do so." He stood and excused himself, slyly giving the four an opportunity to speak without an audience.

Elleran's voice strained. "Sit, Khyryn. We are too weary to war with your vengeance just yet. Perhaps when we are sated with sleep and food."

Wynne tugged at his tunic.

"Nae. I think I shall return to my fire."

Aberswythe drummed the floor with the end of his staff. "Sit, Khyryn of Powys. We have great need to speak to both of you."

"Why do you, who were Gwynndolwyn's father, take league with the one who did place this curse upon us? Has she not wrought enough misery in ten hundred lifetimes? Do you come to steal our comfort yet again, Elleran?"

"Do not allow your tongue to make you the fool," growled Aberswythe. "There is more here than you know."

Wynne tugged harder at Khyryn's tunic. This time he did sit. His temper made him look every bit a mad rooster.

Wynne looked from Elleran to Aberswythe, and back again. "I think I may be able to break the curse."

"It is not the curse you need concern yourself with now, Golden One," croaked Elleran. "It is the fulfillment of the prophecy." Elleran leaned toward them. "The prophecy is the reason you are here. You are returned to see the balance reset."

"Elleran, Aberswythe—I think I figured out why I had to come back. I was never meant to be here for Eadric, or Cnut. It's you I'm here for."

"For all," interrupted Elleran.

Khyryn's temper flared. He rose, defiantly, and began to pace. By what power are you called here, Elleran? We have nae call for wyce."

"Khyryn," said Aberswythe, "Elleran is as much a part of both your pasts as you two will be a part of our futures."

"Balance must always exist, eh brother? There is beauty in balance."

Aberswythe's eyes glinted. *"And the two, joined, become one in soul. Two hearts. Two bodies. Two millennia old."*

Wynne joined his chant.

"One Druid. One Wyce.

By Imbolg's light, the goddesses draw near.

Enchantment, ripeness, and wisdom

Dance this quickening.

Maiden, mother, crone.

The moon grows ripe and so will she.

A balance to invoke."

Wynne's heart slowed to a constant drumming in her ears as she reached out for Khyryn's hand as she spoke to the men. "I have much to learn, and you have much to teach me."

"I do no' understand—"

"You and I, druid. Across the centuries, until truth's desire be sated. You and I, Khyryn. We are the prophecy."

Khyryn stared at her as a hound pondering its master's command.

A low-pitched chuckle escaped the elder druid and Aberswythe bade Khyryn sit. "You two will one day bring the change that keeps our balance."

Khyryn still wore a scowl of incomprehension. "Your balance?"

He looked first to Aberswythe, then to Elleran, then to Gwynndolwyn.

Elleran leaned forward and grinned conspiratorially. "Druids can be as blind as those with no sight, eh?"

"We were born by the same mother of the same heartbeat," Aberswythe began. "The spirit of the wyce and druid, cast into one womb, we grew to two hearts in balance."

"The two of you were twins?" asked Gwynndolwyn.

Elleran snorted at the young woman's words. "Are still, in flesh and spirit."

Following Gwynndolwyn's action before, Khyryn voluntarily bent his head to his knees.

"One druid, one wyce, we are the balance. Earth, air, water, fire—spirit both. For nearly two thousand years we have walked among those whose bodies and spirits live only for one lifetime. Soon, our bodies will perish."

Twins. Aberswythe and Elleran. Born of a druid and wyce.

"And yet you, old woman, bound by blood to Gwynndolwyn and Aberswythe, cast the curse that brought so much misery to all who sit here?

The old woman's voice was calm. "It is not I who called for a spell to purge memory. You sought me. And in so doing, cast into motion the wheel of events that have been played out by time."

Gwynndolwyn moved to sit across from her. "Elleran. Tell me about the stone."

Eyes that could not see brightened with clarity as if they gazed her clearly. Khyryn, moved to stand protectively behind her.

She needed to know about the stone. Eadric's talisman.

The old woman's features crumpled a bit, making

her appear once more like a shriveled fruit of apple, shrunken by age. "The stone had to be given. It was the only way to maintain the balance."

"To Khyryn's brother? Why?"

"To the twin. When the spell was cast, Khyryn alone held the memory. To avenge your death would do him no good. Twin souls would be cast again, reborn and bound to find one another, as are those whose souls are mated. Like interwoven circles they are. He could not keep his memory, and Uddryd have none. Lack of memory would make Uddryd a victim of his brother's vengeance."

Gwynndolwyn stared up at him. "You were twins?"

He nodded. "Born of the same mother. Our faces were not the same, nor our desires, but we shared a womb."

"Wait," she interrupted. "Vengeance. Because of my death?"

The old woman nodded.

"You mean because Khyryn would remember, you thought Uddryd needed to remember, too?"

Aberswythe sighed. The old friend looked not to Khyryn, but to the fire, as if the truth blazed before him in the flame. Khyryn's mentor had finally realized the truth of a thousand years' secret. Uddryd had murdered Gwynndolwyn. Not Roman invaders.

"She speaks with truth and wisdom, Khryryn," Aberswythe said. "If you were condemned to remember, so too must he."

Elleran continued. "Uddryd did not come to me for many cycles of the moon. The land had grown red with blood that had soaked the earth. A new generation, begat of Redmen's seed stood knee-high when your brother found me. I knew him by the greed in his voice."

"Why did he seek you?" asked Gwynndolwyn.

"I had seen him in dreams. I knew what he had done, and I knew that you, Khryryn, would eventually discover he owned the treachery that befell your tribe. And that you would never forget, or forgive when in your next life you met your brother's soul. By the whisperings of the wind, I gave him the rune stone so he might remember, as well. Not to save him, but to condemn him. And to save your soul from the hatred that would grow there. The heavens know what he is. He must remember as would you, or justice would be hollow."

Gwynndolwyn reached out and brushed the old woman's hand. "Elleran, did you know me when we met at the faire?"

"A blind woman knows those whose voices haunt her dreams."

"So, you moved through time, like Khyryn did. Did you know Richard was Uddryd?"

"I warned you of his danger."

"Did you know he had stolen that stone from the excavation? Did you know I had followed him to the faire? That I was trying to get the stone back?"

"The spirits tell me only what they wish me to know, child."

"Uddryd—Richard was never part of this prophecy, was he?"

"Like the web a spider weaves, there are many strands. A moth is caught the same as a fly. The web does not distinguish between the two."

Khyryn's breathing tightened. He held his temper in check. Gwynndolwyn shook her head, as if to argue. "So Uddryd really only has to do with our past?"

Elleran tsked, scrunching her nose as though she caught the scent of something rotten. "Past, present, and future ever intertwined in a web that has no end, no beginning. Have you not figured that out?"

"Tell me how we are to fulfill this prophecy of balance."

"You already know, child."

Khyryn braced his hands on Gwynndolwyn's shoulders. "Say it."

The old woman's lips curled into a smile, more gentle and wise than Khyryn had ever seen upon her face. A withered hand reached out and grazed Gwynndolwyn's lap, one finger finding her stomach, as she spoke.

"Twins."

****

Uffyngdon Keep

Eadric moved the candle in a circular motion, swirling the wax to seal his letter. When the chamber door opened, he did not bother to look up. He had been expecting her.

"You murdered him."

Edith's voice trembled. Even without raising his gaze, he knew her body echoed the waver of her voice.

"What madness is it that takes hold of you this day, wife?"

She stormed at him, knocking the candle from his grasp, and landed her hand soundly across his face. "The king is dead! You murdered my brother."

A sting burned on his cheek where she had struck

him. "Your grief consumes you."

"He was your sovereign! He gave you everything. And this is how you show your loyalty?"

Eadric pushed back his chair and stood, deliberately not meeting his wife's stare. Her breathing grew ragged with anger. *Rage can be so useful. So...satisfying.*

He rounded the table and clamped his hand against the nape of her neck, pulling her to him. "He gave me you, didn't he?"

"A lamb to slaughter."

"I earned everything I hold as my own. I served your brother well."

"You serve only yourself," she spat.

His body tingled at her words. Odd how truth could sometimes bring him to hardness, raising his desire to devour it.

Edith fought against him, trying to break his grip. He always preferred her this way. Passion over passive. She would have made a fine queen. Pity.

"I, too, have lost a king, my dear. I mourn your brother. He was my brother-in-law as well as my liege. I gave him service. He gave me his blessing. I gave him his crown." He smiled down at her.

The last words stopped her instantly.

Her eyes narrowed as she tried to grasp his meaning. "His crown?"

Eadric delicately kissed her quivering mouth. "My loyalty to your brother knew no limits. Upon his wish, I gave him his opportunity to take the throne. One might say I *expedited* his ascension. And in return, he gave me a princess to warm my bed. You see, our loyalty was two-fold."

Ever stoic, ever proud, the woman he held against him stopped struggling in his arms. Her warrior rage melted as his confession began to hold. "You? You killed my father?"

"At your brother's wish. You see, Edith? I was your brother's most ardent supporter. What would I gain from his death?"

Her breath caught in her throat. For an instant, regret tugged at him for her loss. She had so loved her family.

He would miss Edmund. After all, he had profited greatly by the king's favor and generosity.

Now, however, he would serve a new king. No more playing one side against another. A new puppet. How cleverly he had played his game.

So much more lucrative than sitting the throne, myself.

Edith's voice vibrated, low and guttural. "What evil did God rain down upon us to deliver such a serpent to live among his people?"

Eadric had to chuckle at her naive perspective. If only she knew. What horror would he find in her eyes?

"Centuries ago, there lived a king who took to bed a wife. She would have been his queen. Instead of loyalty and love, however, she sowed treason." Memory rolled off his tongue. "She took her king's brother as her lover, forgetting that her fealty lay with her husband."

Edith's body grew taut, once more.

He closed his eyes to draw upon the memory. "Evil so sown had to be purged else it would have taken root and ruined all that surrounded it. Thus, the king killed his wife. And was evermore condemned to remember her unfaithfulness."

She trembled. "You speak in riddles to confuse me. Release me."

He did not release her but strengthened his hold, pressing his free hand to her back as he pulled her to him.

"The Romans came and stole his kingdom from him. For years he waited to once more gain what had been taken from him."

"Your stories are folly. Let go of me, Eadric."

He looked down at his wife, and spied her fear. "For centuries, he carried with him the memory of his queen's betrayal. The memory of his brother's infidelity. The memory of his own humiliation. For centuries he carried the desire to have what he had lost. From one life to the next, he waited, and learned from his mistakes, and plotted."

"You think now that Edmund is dead, you will take his place? Husband to a princess does not make a man a king. No matter what stories you make up."

Women. Creatures of pleasure. And cruelty.

Such a pity. Little separated queens from whores between the bedclothes. Edith might have loved him otherwise. She might have made him forget.

Instead, she served as constant reminder of the politics of passion.

Eadric allowed a smile to play across his mouth. "Kings die too soon. I am fortunate I hold no such claim to crown or country. Look around you, sister to Edmund. You live in luxury and have no worry of treason, as your brother did, or his father before him."

"I was my kingdom's sacrifice."

There was that passionate anger that made his body

harden to lust. She would have ruled a land.

"I forgive you your rage, wife. I, like you, am bereft at our king's passing. How horrible it is to lose a loved one. Would you seek solace from your husband, Edith, for the mournful pain which consumes you?"

Her face flushed at his innuendo. Embarrassment turned to ire.

Her voice hissed against his cheek. "It is hatred, not heartache, which consumes me. Hatred of the monster I call husband."

"Would you rather I end your suffering now? Tonight? Imagine what loyalty you would prove if you gave your life to be reunited once more with your family."

"I hate you."

"Your passion is flattering," he teased as he stole a kiss from her. "More important than your passion, my dear, is your fealty. Are you loyal to me?"

****

The dank cold of winter clung to the walls, making the small chamber colder than it should have been had the fire still burned in the grate. Wynne stretched her limbs even before she opened her eyes, and met the warmth of the body next to hers. She moved closer to the only apparent source of heat in the room.

Khyryn's hand found hers. "Did you rest well?"

"Too well. The fire has gone out." She snuggled tightly against his body.

He rolled over and draped an arm and leg over her. Where his skin brushed her gown the warmth poured into her flesh. "Then you will have to warm yourself another way."

"And what of you? You and Daniel were up late."

"We have much in common."

She snorted. "Like what? Your love of wine?"

He stared into her eyes for a moment, making her very self-conscious.

"Daniel was not always a soldier for God. When he was young, he fought for kings."

"The monk was a mercenary?"

A smile lit Khyryn's eyes at her reasoning. "Not a mercenary, but definitely a soldier who saw battle. He left the army and cloistered himself when he was still dark-haired and fit to husband a wife."

"Why did he become a monk?"

"War does much to turn a man to madness. The Vikings have a word for it. They say a man possessed of a bloodlust loses control of his soul, and becomes—"

"A berserker. A creature so consumed with bloodlust he is unable to stop until everything in its path is vanquished."

"Aye. How do you know this?"

"In my time, women are educated. I've read about them. Their legend survived the centuries to be told in books. There are even TV shows and movies about them."

"What is *tvshos? Movees?"*

Wynn giggled and draped her arm over her head, and stretched her body, before answering. "You know the visions that Elleran sees? Well, in the time I came from, we can sit for hours and watch pictures like that."

"Visions?"

"Not quite. Like the stories people tell. We have storytellers too. But our storytellers can make their tales come to life, sort of, on flat surfaces like, umm…like magical tablets, so we can see the vision of the story."

"Not just the wizened ones see visions?"

"Nope. Everyone does. And sometimes the stories are of things as they happen."

"It is a great magic that all people have the gift of vision."

"Well, not everyone's vision is good. And most of it has nothing to do with truth."

"Do you miss it?

"Television? Yes. I could kill for a bit of news, or a good documentary." She giggled again. "I used to love the historical docudramas—the shows that talked about life in the Middle Ages."

This earned her a blank stare from Khyryn.

"Middle Ages is where we are now. This is *Middle Ages.*"

"Ah." Khyryn nodded. A silence grew between them for a moment. He reached out and laid his hand across her belly, massaging the mound that grew round. "Do you wish you could go back to that time?"

Wynne asked herself that question every day.

"You know, at first I didn't believe in any of this. Then I was pissed off—furious at what you had done. For one hundred and forty two days I have asked myself that same question. Every day the answer is different. Some days I miss everything about it. The food—the food is wonderful in the future. The seasonings, the variety—oh the decadence of flavors and...chocolate. Ooh, wait until you taste chocolate. It's better than sex.

One of his eyebrows nearly kissed his hairline.

"I missed baths, until we came here. Thank Heavens the Romans did invade or I wouldn't be nearly as comfortable as we are here. But then I think about how simple it is. You know, after my parents died, I missed them so much I didn't do anything other than work, so I wouldn't have to think about how much I missed them."

"You have not answered my question, Gwynndolwyn."

"It would have been so easy if I could hate you." She moved her hand to brush his cheek, tracing the outline of his mouth with her thumb. "So much easier if you hadn't made love to me. Hadn't saved those boys. And Bog..."

Wynn trailed her hand along his arm, coming to rest upon his hand where it laid on her abdomen. "Damn—"

"Shh. Quiet your curses. You'll pass them on to the babes."

"Today, Khyryn of Powys, I do not wish to go back to my own time." She squeezed his hand. "Tomorrow, I might change my mind."

She grinned at him and moved his hand in a circular motion across her belly until one of the babes kicked. When it did, she tugged his hand higher until it found her breast. "Gently," she whispered. "I'm tender."

Khyryn draped a leg over her thighs as he teased the nipple. "You are as ripe as a plum, ready to burst."

Hormones raged. Her breast swelled enthusiastically to his words and actions.

"Speak the truth, woman. Does Morpheus visit your bed to ravish you in your sleep? A Seer, after all, would entertain no less than a god."

Khyryn bent his head and suckled gently the untended breast through the cloth of her shift. When a moan escaped her lips, he captured both the sound and softness with his skilled mouth, making her brain spin.

She reveled in the kiss as his hand grazed her body, skimming material and flesh until it found the soft damp patch between her thighs.

Wynn moved against his hand anxiously, devouring his kiss. Against her thigh, his body hardened. A human furnace.

Much better than chocolate.

****

Cnut held out his arm and waited for the hawk to clutch the leather gauntlet he wore."

My Liege—"

He turned in his saddle to see the messenger riding toward him, the horse's hooves trampling the ground furiously.

Reigning his mount, the messenger pulled a missive from a pouch and held it out for Cnut to claim. The dark wax seal bore Edmund's mark.

Cnut broke the seal and read the black letters scrawled across the parchment.

The king is dead.

Edmund dead. By secret truce, his lands came now to Cnut.

The Seer had spoken truthfully.

Cnut now ruled. King of Angles and Saxons.

Chapter Thirty-One

Winchester, Summer 1017

Cnut motioned to the servant, and two goblets were filled. Pleased with his negotiation and with the sight before him he smiled. "We have a deal then?"

The demure woman who sat opposite England's new king bowed her head in consent, and returned his smile conspiratorially. "A woman usually prefers some measure of her future husband's endearment."

A marriage pact to forge an alliance. Norman and Danish. Their common ground...England.

"You will shortly have a crown, and court for your pleasure. What token would you have of mine?"

"Do you harbor any affection for me, sire, or am I merely convenient to your cause? After all, my sons could easily claim right to the throne. They are as entitled as are you."

Cnut drank from one of the goblets, as he assessed the woman who played at politics. Long had he admired her physical beauty when she had attended his father's court.

Fire in her eyes belied the truth of her passions. Aethelred had taken her too young as consort, barely more than a girl in his bed. Too young to serve as stepmother to Edmund. Too soon a widowed queen.

Too young to be without a husband in her bed, or a

master to her house.

He motioned to the servant who set the ewer on the table and exited. Alone. Finally.

He pushed back his chair and moved around the table to stand behind her chair. The cloth that draped her braid fell away from her hair, revealing an expanse of white flesh that blushed even as he watched her.

He slid his hands down the fabric of her sleeves, and wrapped his hands over hers as he bent his head to her ear. "A man lusts most for that which he cannot have. Long have I found your face fair, and wondered what pleasures awaited the king whose bed you graced."

Emma's hands coiled beneath his. He held her tight and continued. "I have claimed a kingdom for mine own. And so I take a queen, if it is your pleasure. Tell me, Emma, what would you have me give you?" His mouth trickled from her ear down her neck.

As her body tensed and her breath caught in her throat, so did his groin stiffen from desire. Finally, she inhaled deeply, and relaxed her body, yielding to the movement of his mouth upon her flesh. She withdrew one hand from his grasp, to snake her fingers across his jaw. She turned her head ever so slightly toward his so that her lips brushed his.

He released his hold and she moved to stand before him, matching his forwardness.

Norman consort. Mother of princes. A woman not afraid of her own sexual appetites. No gentle virgin.

Emma reached for his hand and drew it to her breast. She stepped into his embrace and dipped her free hand beneath the folds of his tunic. As he brought his mouth to hers she stroked him teasingly and answered. "Give me sons."

He offered her a wicked laugh. As clever and comely as any Danish princess.

An alliance indeed.

****

A season of bountiful yield.

Eadric ignored the girl in his bed, and continued to count the gold in the bags that littered his table. Danes and Dane geld.

Edmund's father had been right in one thing. Once the Dane geld was met the first time, the Danes had secured a hold on England that squeezed every drop of worth from the purse. And every coin counted gave him more wealth and more power.

Long live the king. Let Cnut take the crown. Gold, silver, and land made a much more valuable laurel.

Eadric Streona studied the ciphers of the sheriff's latest raid. North Umbria held vast wealth over many of the other regions. Between those and his holdings in Mercia, he had more wealth than any free man in England. Alderman to two, no...three kings, and still *he* sat in power, a bag of gold in one hand, and a fist full of ambition in the other.

He skimmed through the marks, watchful for any unusual notations. A moment of weakness in his collectors could mean tax not paid. Loyalty to one's king by tariff, and dutiful tithing went hand in hand.

A curious listing from Tewkesbury caught his eye. Monks had a talent for cyphers and for script. No doubt prayer and poverty left much time for hands to learn the skill of scribes. The pen strokes he studied now, however, were not the marks of a schooled monk. This hand he recognized well.

Penned by Khyryn.

Druid turned monk?

Praying for penance in an attempt to rid himself of guilt.

What would be more interesting than seeing Khyryn kneeling in supplication to King Cnut? Thus, subject to the alderman's justice.

"After the celebration of His Majesty's marriage to the Lady Emma, perhaps I should pay a visit to Tewkesbury. After having been gifted lands that stretch as far as the monastery, surely it would be in the King's best interest to ensure his taxes have been properly assessed."

He could take Edith. How would she fare, meeting her stepmother once more at court and bowing in obedience to her?

Edith would endear herself unto the court, as she had been trained to do. And Cnut would praise him for having married one so dutiful and loyal to the throne. *And I will be admired for Edith's ability to hide her hatred of the queen consort.*

Emma, a clever woman, had done very well for herself. One king's widow. Another king's consort. She would no doubt be the undoing of Cnut.

Women frequently were.

****

Tewkesbury, Autumn 1017

Cnut had found her. Had found them.

The dark script spilled across the vellum, straying from the cerise puddle of wax that sealed the missive in Cnut's hand.

Now, as king, he knew she had spoken of his future.

Her fingers trembled so that her arm ached. Again, for the umpteenth time, she set down on the table. The dark wood made the waxen seal shimmer even more in the waning light of the chamber.

One year separated Wynne from her past, or more precisely, her future. For a year she had lived among these people in an ancient time.

And thrived.

Curses be damned. She smiled at the irony of the thought.

For the first time in months, a nausea of panic welled inside her, threatening her like a tidal wave. She wanted to be far away from here.

Away from danger.

Cnut meant Eadric Streona. Streona meant danger.

A soft cry beckoned her to where two tiny alabaster infants lay, huddled together on a soft pallet of woven wool, stuffed with the soft wooly hair from the sheep. A thumb found the listless mouth and the babe quieted.

Derris and Hannah. Twins.

The moon had climbed high in the night sky when the Earth and Heavens tolled her time. Elleran and a woman from the village had delivered the twins. One the namesake of her uncle, and the reason she was here; the other for the girl whose life had been sacrificed for Khyryn's.

She had spent a year living in the sanctuary of the monastic village—a lavish lifestyle by comparison to other options. Gardening, and cooking, and working damn hard to make sure neither she, nor her babies, died.

All that work and safety could be wiped away once she opened that note.

"What does he want?"

Khyryn could enter a room silently, a skill that came in handy when dealing with infants.

She looked up at him as he untangled himself from his cloak and belt. Tall, broad shouldered, every bit the man she had swooned for on stage a year—and a century ago.

"I don't know."

"What does it say?"

"I did not open it."

Khyryn glanced at the letter, then at her. "Ignoring it will not make it vanish." He crossed to the table and took up the letter. Wynne noticed he, too, held it gingerly, stroking the seal with his thumb, hesitating to open Pandora's box.

"How did you know?"

"Brother Daniel caught me as I returned. He said a messenger delivered a letter and that the seal appeared to be a royal one. He said you had not been seen since."

"What should I have done? Danced around the yard singing, 'The king sent me a love note'? You know as well as I that Cnut wants a prophet's blessing."

A not so polite grin graced Khyryn's mouth and he countered, "Neither of us can know until we read it."

Gently he slipped his thumb between the folds of the letter until the seal gave way and the missive opened.

Wynne was sure she spied a grisly curl of smoke drift from within.

Khyryn read the contents silently.

"Well? What does it say?"

He finished reading, and glanced up at her. "Just as you thought, the king has sent you a love letter."

"What?" Wynne snatched at the note, and Khyryn's expression dissolved in a wicked grin.

"I see the way of it now," he teased. "You, Seer, are infatuated with the great Cnut. That is why you foretold his success so he might send you tomes of his affection and gratitude?"

Wynne threw a nasty glare at him then turned her attention to the note in her hand. "It says nothing of the sort."

"You are wrong, Seer. He says right there we are called to attend him—"

"As he feasts for the Winter Solstice. This is not a love note at all."

"Aye. It is. He has taken a new wife. He will feast, and he seeks to find you at his table to show her off…to you."

"Well, *we* will decline. We have the perfect excuse. Two babies, only half a year old are not traveling across this country just so he can show off his new queen."

Khyryn pulled her into his arms and squeezed her tightly. He smelled of sweat and dust, and horses. His mouth seized hers firmly, possessively, until she replied in kind.

Lifting his head from hers, he answered, "We will travel to the celebration."

"We can't. Derris and Hannah—"

"We will travel with our own entourage. You see much, Golden One. In this, however, know that Cnut's invitation should not be ignored. If he has sent a messenger two days' ride to find you to call you to him, there is more than a pheasant at hand. He seeks his prophet."

"That's ridiculous, Khyryn. I am no prophet. You

know that."

"Cnut does not. He knows you foresaw his victory. Now, he calls you to him, again. Failure to meet his invitation will anger him. You know what is to come. You offer prophecy. Therefore you offer great counsel."

"But that's ludicrous."

"Aye. That is the way of kings."

****

Winchester, November, 1017

Autumn spiraled quickly toward winter now. Samhain had passed and the solstice soon would bring yule celebrations and Christ mass.

"Is it very different from the world you know?"

Khyryn's voice was soft against her ear. He stood behind her with his arms holding her as if to keep her from falling away from the wall...to keep her from falling into the future and away from him.

She let him. "It is nothing now. However, it will be great in the future. Towering structures that seem to touch the clouds fill all the marshland and fields on either side of the river. A great abbey will one day stand at Westminster. And several palaces will surround Londinium."

Wynne whispered her memories of the city yet to be, lest someone hear their conversation. "More people than you have seen in all your lives on battlefields will move through these towns. They will ride in huge tunnels beneath the earth, from town to the other. Here, will stand a great church of stone and mortar. "

Now, only a simple structure, suitable for a king. No cathedral yet. Even the walls were different from the ones she had passed through so often in the future.

"You liked it?"

"Yes. Very much. I see it all with different eyes, though. I know the ruins that will be, and the future that exists. Being here, now...is humbling."

The houses that lined the land now were little more than huts strung together with wooden planks.

"One day the bridge Cnut felled in Londinium will be a center for commerce. Houses and businesses will fill it to excess. It will burn and be rebuilt. There will be a great fortress and keep where future kings will live and die, built of mortar and stone, and beefeaters will live here, to guard the king."

Khyryn's snorted. "And what are beefeaters?"

Wynn had to smile. The name sounded ridiculous the first time she heard it as well. "A special guard chosen to protect the Tower. Legend holds they were so special they were fed beef to boost their strength and voracity. They also have spectacularly colorful uniforms."

His second snort confirmed her suspicions.

"You don't believe me."

"Men do not dress to please women."

"They will. And if you snort once more, I'll wait until you are asleep and put a ring through your nose, pig."

"Swine do not wear—"

Wynne laughed outright at him. Happily. She inhaled deeply to bite back the lump that swelled in her throat. "I love you, Khyryn of Powys."

"As I love you."

"I never had a true love, there, you know. I never could say those words to anyone."

As if he had been holding his breath, Wynne felt

him sigh against her hair.

"Thank you," she said.

"For what?"

"For giving me back my memory and with it, someone to love."

He turned her around to face him and pressed his hand to her spine as he bent his head to her lips. Wynne met his kiss with a voracity that would have been deemed sinful had they been spied by anyone.

"Ahem—" Someone hailed them.

Gluttonous.

Khyryn turned to see who intruded, and Wynne spied one of the king's pages, nervously swaying side to side.

"What is it?" Kyryn's greeting betrayed his aggravation at having been denied the pleasure of his wife's lust.

"Pardon, sir. King and court assemble before the sun is high to receive the blessing of the Archbishop. The King's marriage to the Lady Emma, and their gift to the Archbishop, will be celebrated at the feast. King Cnut commands you both join him."

Khyryn found humor in the boy's demeanor. He had memorized the exact words spoken to him and then spit them out at the two strange guests who stole a passionate moment upon a king's wall.

Khyryn nodded to the page who then fled like a quail from the field. No doubt he would blush later when he told his friends around the night fire what he had witnessed.

When the boy was out of earshot she said, "We may have scarred him for life."

"I doubt so," he teased. "Boys have a keen sense of

which stable stalls to hide in to catch a glimpse of men and women together. However, he probably is taken aback that we are brazen enough to try it here at the very walls of the keep in the morning light."

In demonstration of such immodest intent, he grabbed her again, this time sliding his hand over the plump mound of her backside as me moved her toward the cold stone barrier. How round her breast and hips had become in motherhood. Touched by the goddess a thousand years ago, now she bloomed full in her womanhood.

His hand sent the message to his cock and he immediately found it difficult to quell the overwhelming need to claim her body.

"Khyryn—"

"Come." He tugged her behind him as he bounded down the steps and along the pathway toward their chamber. Modest as it might be, he needed some privacy if he hoped to find relief.

They crossed the threshold together, and nearly bumped into Gilda, the young woman who accompanied them to attend the babes.

"Out—"

"Sir?"

"Out." He spared no words of explanation to the girl.

"Gilda," Gwynndolwyn said, "We need a few minutes privacy. Perhaps fetch some bread and—"

"Out!"

The woman jumped at this last shout and scurried from the room like a hare from a fox.

"Khyryn, that was unneces—"

He stopped his wife's protest, taking full advantage

of her open mouth, claiming it with his own, raking his tongue over hers to steal her breath as he consumed her.

Her hands clutched at his tunic, as he pulled her to the pallet and slid the fabric of her gown up past her hips. He broke their embrace momentarily to shed his own tunic and leggings. The release of the cloth only served to excite him more.

His voice caught in his throat so he could not even whisper her name. His hands grazed the flesh of her thighs, and she arched her back as she wrapped her legs around his hips and pulled him ever closer.

He shoved the fabric of her gown and undershift up over her head and sank into the heat of her body. Gathering one supple breast in his mouth, he teased the nipple and a muffled moan escaped her.

Her flesh burned as much as his did with lust.

Khyryn released her breast and sought her mouth again. He brushed a hand over the soft mound of curls of her sex and found her ready. Her hips moved and she thrust against his hand bucking harder with each movement.

He thrust into her, burying his swollen shaft to its hilt. He met her frantic rhythm moving in and out, accelerating as his blood boiled in his veins and in his cock, until finally he exploded into her.

Fire and ice. No time, no space. No sound or light. Just the ecstasy of the release. Of the coupling. Two as one.

Again and again, her body clenched until they both were spent. His muscles quivered and he collapsed atop her, smothering her with tiny licks, gathering the beads of perspiration glistening on her skin.

Later he would give thanks to the Christian God

and to the Heavens that had first given her life a millennium ago. Now, he let the cool morning air temper the heat still roiling in his spine as he stayed inside her. His cock flickered teasingly and she giggled, then hugged him tighter.

One of the twins sighed contentedly from the corner.

"Bog is right to call you a witch. Wicked are you in bed, like a succubus, to tempt a man to madness. I could barely keep myself from taking you atop that wall, woman."

"Me? You are the berserker, throwing Gilda out and barely bringing me to lie down before you're naked and thrusting like a crazed rutting animal."

"A crazed rutting hart, is it? A stag claiming his doe?"

She grinned at him, her eyes wide with feigned surprise. "I wonder. Do all the men of this century bed women in this manner?"

He sobered and lowered his head toward hers. "That is no concern of yours. Is it?"

Her grin turned soft and tantalizing. In spite of his reproach, his groin stiffened inside her. She gathered her arms around his neck. "Only one man holds claim to my body, or my heart, Khyryn of Powys. And I would follow him to the ends of the earth."

Joined as one. She pulled him to her and kissed him gently.

He lifted his head and asked, "Even if it meant traveling through time?"

Chapter Thirty-Two

Winchester, 1017

Time stood still.

Wynne wiggled on tiptoe trying to see over the head of the rather round man who blocked her view of the dais. Some moments in time rushed too quickly. Others hung suspended, dangling for an eternity. Wynne considered Einstein's theory of relativity. If she were standing still, who was rushed at the speed of light?

.Winchester. No grand church, yet. However, the fortress built to house a king and court was magnificent by the day's standards. Evergreen draped the doorways in honor of the new season marked. Old and new. Pagan and priest.

Wynne's stomach grumbled petulantly. Her head pounded with a sinister protest to the fast imposed until after the mass. That, combined with the scents of wood, incense, and smelly revelers who filled the Hall made her head swim.

A horn heralded Cnut's entrance, as did the drumbeat that followed. Autumn exploded in one final, resplendent burst, with colors cast to honor both harvest and hearth. As if Cnut himself had ordered it, the trees littered the sky with confetti of gold and red and purple.

Wynne rubbed her temple to fend the dull ache in

her head.

Someone hoisted a banner with Cnut's crest, and the Dane ascended to his place before the court. With him, came the Archbishop, and another priest, as well as a woman not much older than she, herself.

Emma, Queen consort.

Small, fragile in appearance, she held no radiant beauty but exuded a grace that made even Wynne take notice. The woman stood before the crowd, with her head bowed before her audience, awaiting God's blessing.

The priest spoke in Latin, common to all in monastic life. Wynne watched as the Archbishop whispered to Cnut and to Emma and they sank to their knees before him.

From behind the round man, she could see no more of the ceremony but could hear the drone of the priest reciting the words she guessed were the same as those spoken in every such ceremony in her own time.

Though both had entered into the marriage contract in the summer's heat, this celebration acknowledged publicly their union.

"Sanctified by God's law, so shall you be received as husband and wife."

An echo of approval rose in a wave of "huzzah", as the audience offered their approval.

"As token of our fellowship to Christ," Cnut replied, "we gift this stone. May God desire, we will build a Church to honor his glory." Cnut's words electrified the crowd. The Norse warrior, bowing before the Christian God, and proclaiming his faith? It wielded great power among the audience.

A country divided by war, united in courtly fashion

by a Christian sacrament would be a country much more willing to support a new king. Especially when the new wife had been a queen to a previous king.

Wynne found it suspicious Cnut would marry the woman who had already borne sons to Edmund's father. Still, she knew enough about women's roles in medieval politics to suspect Emma probably had little choice in the matter.

The mass ended. Cnut and Emma welcomed their audience and ordered the throng to adjourn to the palace for the feast. Cnut, glimpsing Wynne, bade her come forward. She tugged Khyryn's sleeve and pulled him along as she moved toward the dais.

"Our Golden One is found and returned to us," said Cnut. He eyed Khyryn suspiciously for a moment. "And it would appear she is well cared for by her— protector."

Khryn bowed. Wynne followed his lead in this and curtsied low before the ruler.

"I trust you are well, Seer." Cnut grasped Emma's elbow and helped her descend the dais, as Wynne and Khyryn rose. "Emma, I should like you to meet our Seer. The Golden one has gift of prophecy from the heavens. She did foretell my victory at Ashingdon. A great asset to a king's court, do you not agree?"

A flicker of wariness flashed in the queen consort's eyes as she nodded at Wynne.

"Your majesty finds too much favor in my gifts. I know only that which has been shown to me."

"And what of our union? Will Emma give me fine strong sons to lead a kingdom when I am too old to do so?"

History books had not been kind to Emma,

branding her opportunistic and self- centered. Her sons, Edward and Harthacnut, would both wear the crown one day.

"As the Church has blessed your union, so shall the heavens bless you with fine, strong children."

Wynne could feel Emma's scrutiny as solidly as if the woman had raked her fingernails across her cheek.

Emma's retort was cold. "Golden One? No Christian name have I heard."

"Gwynndolwyn. I am Gwynndolwyn."

"Ah." The woman cocked an eyebrow. "And what of my children?"

Wynne took the opportunity to press her luck. "Your sons will find great success in the king's wake."

"You see, Emma, she said sons," he whispered. "A man's future is in the bedcovers, is it not, Khyryn of Powys."

"What of you, Gwynndolwyn?" the queen consort asked. "Have the Heavens blessed you with children?"

"Twins, your majesty. Born in the spring." As she answered, a familiar swelling in her breast warned her the two would soon be hungry.

Cnut's face broke into a grin. He nodded at Khyryn. "Twins! Khyryn of Powys, you are more than protector to our Seer, then. A man who can plant twins in a woman is given strength in more than his arm." He clapped Khyryn on the shoulder. "No doubt you have need of much of my wine, sir, to keep you bold enough to hold a woman who would bear you twins and leave them to attend a king's nuptials. But first we shall feast."

Cnut gathered his new wife and moved through the room, leaving Wynne and Khyryn to find their own table.

Wynne's skin tingled as if bugs had crawled across her shoulders. "Khyryn, I want to check on the—"

"My stepmother takes husbands as some men take wine. A new vintage to each sup."

Wynne turned to find a woman standing on the far side of Khyryn, speaking with some familiarity. As demure as Emma, but with dark hair and eyes. Much more Angle than Norman, she held herself tall and proud. Her words revealed as much as her expression hid of her opinion of Cnut's new wife.

"It appears you survived your ordeal at Uffyngdon after all, sir. Do you attend the king?"

"Not so much to the king, as the king's prophet."

Her posture wilted a bit, and she lowered her voice. "And what of the stable boys? Do they live?

"They are well taken care of, m'lady." Khyryn turned Wynne. "Lady Edith, I present Gwynndolwyn, a servant to His Majesty, and wife to mine own keeping."

Wynne bowed before the woman who spoke familiarly to Khyryn.

"Gwynndolwyn," he continued. "This is Lady Edith, step daughter to the queen consort, and wife to Cnut's most trusted alderman, Eadric Streona."

****

Eadric watched from an alcove, as the throng milled toward the plank wood tables set for the celebration. A tiresome gathering. Normans were scarce today. A few nobles, friends to Edith's father Edmund, attended the celebration. Better friend than foe. Emma's sons had fled England after their father's demise. Today certainly did not invite their favor. Shunned by their mother and by so many nobles who had supported their father, Emma's children sat in exile, awaiting another turn at the scraps of rule.

Pagans and Christians. Each feeding body and spirit with trivial ceremony.

Eadric surveyed the room seeking a companion for conversation. A few priests, another alderman, sundry landowners...no one to whom he owed anything other than contempt. His wife did catch a few glances and nods as she moved through the Hall. Perhaps he would grace her with his company.

His gaze fell upon the woman who had just risen to meet his wife's attention. And to the man beside her.

A ghost.

I watched her die.

Yet Gwynndolwyn stood halfway across the room talking to Edith as a flesh and blood creature—not the spectre he knew she must be.

Confusion and rage battled in his brain as he looked at the woman whose golden hair peeked from beneath her veil. By some magic of the old hag's, here she stood, flaunting her very existence, standing with the one man he wanted dead more than any other. Khyryn.

He watched as Gwynndolwyn's cheeks paled and she grasped Khyryn's arm. So, introductions had been made. Good. That meant she was no trick upon his mind. Flesh and blood. Mortal.

Astonishment yielded to appreciation for this amazing opportunity. Cnut's Seer, here at court, confined within Cnut's walls. Amid a hundred guests, anyone of whom could be named her murderer.

Including the man at her side.

Eadric retreated into the shadows. Though

possessed of a revelry, he had no appetite for feasting. Not yet. He had work to do.

****

"I'm leaving. Now." Wynne nearly spat the words at Khyryn. Her head throbbed.

"We must not leave now. "'Twould draw suspicion. Remember discretion?"

She gripped Khyryn's arm so tightly, she feared she would rip the fabric and claw through to his skin. He refused to listen to her. Her birthmark burned, as if she had been stung.

Her trencher lay untouched. Khyryn on the other hand had eaten everything put in front of him. For half the afternoon, she had endured the worst musical accompaniment, ill-cooked food, watered down wine, and the stench of the man sitting across from her while Eadric hovered nearby. She was certain of it.

"I'll show you discreet—" she whispered. She took up the goblet, drank half the contents, and then coughed so hard the spray covered the man across from her in a dark shower of fermented grapes.

Drunk from nerves, she spat, "My apologies, sir. My stomach will not find rest this day." She fanned herself, pretended to belch, then covered her mouth with her hand, as if to hold something else in. She purposely widened her eyes until the man across from her pushed his own seat back from the table, in an epic display of panic.

"Waste not the king's good wine," Khyryn tempered. To the others at their table, "Travel has unnerved my wife since childbirth. She should lie down."

Wynne clambered as clumsily as humanly possible,

361

allowing Khyryn to wrap his arm around her waist and lead her from the Hall, through the portico, and into a corridor that led toward the private chambers.

Once certain they were alone, she tugged free of his hold and slowed her pace. "'Travel has unnerved my wife since childbirth'? What kind of crap is that? What happened to discretion?"

Khyryn's brow creased. "It is hiding with your caution nae doubt. If you hoped to escape unnoticed, spewing wine all over the Duke of Sussex is not the way to accomplish the task."

"Eadric is here. He thinks I am dead. Once he knows we are here, how long will it take him to find a way to kill us?" The cool air circled her ankles, like a cat at her feet, a sensation that only served to make her more nervous. "We have to leave now, this instant."

He swung around in front of her, and she slammed against him. She tried to step around him, and he snared her in his arms.

She stomped his foot to make him move...unsuccessfully. "What is wrong with you, Khyryn? Don't you understand how dangerous it is to be here? "

"Gwynndolwyn, stay your steps for a moment and think about this. If we ride through those gates now, during the feast, we will be noticed. What is there to keep Eadric from having us followed and attacked along the road?"

"So you would just wait here for him to murder us in our beds? He is an advisor to Cnut."

"As are you, my love."

She stared at him. "Eadric has an army. We do not."

"Today, he has an army that revels in Cnut's nuptial celebration. They stand down this day. Everyone stands down this day. We are protected by Cnut. You are his Golden One, his Seer. No one would threaten you here. All is well. Set aside your fears."

"Have you forgotten what he is capable of?" A flash of that night at Uffyngdon burned her memory, and she shuddered.

He held her at arm's length. His words rasped with bridled tension. "I can forget nothing. That has been the problem for more than a thousand years. And that is why I cannot allow you to be unwary in your actions." For the first time in nearly a year, anguish pinched Khyryn's expression. "I will not lose you again. Elleran, for all her faults, advised you to trust me."

"I do, but—"

"The soul that holds this man was once my brother. I know his mind better than anyone else could."

Wynne splayed her hands across his chest. Beneath his tunic, his heart beat strong, and a bit faster even than it had a few hours ago. He did worry.

Fear constricted her throat. Her chest ached from the memory of her last meeting with the man who harbored the soul of a murderer.

"How does she do it?"

"Who?"

"His wife. Edith. How does she survive?"

"She is a king's daughter. Her entire life she has lived in battle of one sort or another. I suspect she spends as little time in his presence as she can."

"I would kill him."

"Alone, without a kinsman to give her aid or sanctuary, she would have nothing. At least her status affords her the comfort of a roof and servants to shield her from his attention. While he plots, she manages an estate that would rival the king's."

The thought of Eadric's hands upon her body made Wynne nauseous. "Still, I would kill him. Or myself."

"By tomorrow morning, Cnut's guests will be free to depart. If we wait until there are others traveling westward away from London, then we should be able to disappear inconspicuously. Eadric will be waiting for us to steal away like thieves."

Her breasts were heavy with milk. "I need to nurse. If I cannot leave, then I will keep to our chamber, and stay invisible to everyone."

Khyryn pressed his lips to her forehead. How warm and simple. And comforting.

"I do trust you, you know."

He held her tighter. "I am glad to hear you say it."

"I just don't trust the rest of them."

"A wise woman, are you."

Wrapped arm in arm, they made their way along the covered walkway toward the wooden structure which housed the guests. "It won't always look like this.

A noise near one of the archways ahead cut short Khyryn's retort. One of the guards had found a willing companion to help assuage his boredom.

Wynne pulled Khyryn into an adjacent portico, and placed a finger across his lips to silence him. He grabbed her to him and held her tight as they tried not to giggle at the promiscuous diversion next door.

The soft moans and grunts from the neighboring alcove crescendoed, then faded to hush rustling of wool and leather. As if they had only passed in the hallway, the two set to separate directions, back to their tasks. As soon as they had departed, Wynne followed Khyryn back into the corridor.

Recalling her own stolen morning passion, Wynne teased, "That'll stop once they are married."

They zigzagged their way through the myriad of huts that made up the guests quarters. Similar to the Viking longhouses, these were strung together to accommodate families or groups of people. The lack of individual chambers suddenly taunted Wynne. They only had a few people with them—Gilda to help with the twins, and a groom for the horses. However, now, she longed for privacy. Her breasts ached. Hannah and Derris must be fussing by now.

They rounded the corner, their own lodge in sight. Wynne cocked an ear, waiting for the familiar cry of one or both.

Silence.

Even as she neared the hut, her steps slowed, each footfall mired in fear. "Khyryn?"

Before she could mouth the words, he bounded toward the door that jutted crookedly outward.

Silence.

Wynne's limbs ignored her command. Her step faltered. She tried to move to follow Khyryn, only to find her feet firmly rooted, the earth holding her in place.

Silence.

The brightness of the afternoon faded. She stood, immobilized by fear and realization. The roar of the blood rushing through her veins deafened her to the sounds of the yard. To the sounds of her babies crying. They must be crying.

Why couldn't she hear them?

Air scorched her lungs. Her breasts swelled impatiently against the fabric of her shift. The heaviness in her limbs dragged her to her knees.

Color faded to grey, as Khyryn's figure shadowed the doorway, his face dark with rage. Inconsolable. Silent. Rage.

No.

Wynne called, but no sound left her lips.

Tears spilled down her cheeks, burning her face.

Not twenty feet from where she sank to the ground, her husband, her lover, the father of her children stood, emptyhanded, in the doorway of their quarters, his hands bathed in something dark and viscous.

No.

The roar and pounding of her heart ebbed, replaced by something more horrific.

Khyryn's feral howl.

Chapter Thirty-Three

Hannah and Derris…vanished.

Only Gilda's battered bloodied body remained in the chamber. Khyryn stood in the doorway, channeling the rage that threatened to ignite the very air around him. Gilda had given her life to protect the twins.

His children.

He knew Eadric—Uddryd—had done this, and lurked somewhere, unseen, enjoying this moment of vengeance. Yet Khyryn could not contain the primal cry that rose from his lungs at the thought of his babes, of Gwynndolwyn's babes, at the mercy of such a monster.

Gwynndolwyn sat crumpled, staring in disbelief as he tried to give voice to the horror of their abduction.

I will kill him.

Rage battled reason battled for power of his thoughts.

He hasn't killed them yet. Hannah and Derris are bait.

He leapt from the step, shouting for help, and gathered Gwynndolwyn into his arms. "They are safe. I know it. I feel it."

A sob escaped her as she clawed at his chest.

"Shh. Stop it. That is what he wants—"

"I warned you! I begged you to listen to me—"

"Gwynndolwyn, you have to—"

"I trusted you—"

She became an animal trapped, feral, and dangerous. Venom tinged her words as panic poisoned her and she beat at him, kicking to escape his embrace as she made for the door.

Khryryn wrenched her by the arm, and knocked her down in an attempt to keep her from the scene.

Let Eadric watch.

He knelt over his wife, and once more gathered her to him. "Shh. The twins are not within. Theirs is not the blood upon my hands. Shh. Gwynndolwyn. Listen to me!"

Rage burned in every muscle, readying him to move, to jump, to hunt.

Gwynndolwyn's screams waned to moans. But she heard him. "He took them. Where are my babies?"

"Shh. We will find them. Think, now. This is exactly what Eadric wants. Remember, I am more familiar with him than anyone can be. He wants us at our weakest. He desires our pain. He would use them as the bait to destroy us."

From his embrace, she shrieked her alarm. "Find him! Somebody! Find him! He has my babies!"

Nearly everyone remained in the great Hall. A handful of sentries emerged, to answer their call. Khyryn looked up to find several servants staring, as he stood hunched over his wife, the blood that had been on his hands, now smeared on his wife as well.

"Get off your asses and help us! Our servant is dead and our children are missing!"

Whether his voice or his words spurred them, the crowd, which had now grown to nearly two dozen, scurried into action. Two guards ran for the hut where the door still tilted open. Two other women moved cautiously toward Khyryn and Gwynndolwyn.

"Help me get her someplace warm. Before shock takes her completely."

"Come with me, then," the older one said. "Mistress would want te 'elp. Come, missus."

Khyryn scooped Gwynndolwyn from the ground, as the old woman waddled off toward the northernmost corner, prattling at the younger one. "Go te the stable and get Samuel. Tell 'im there's been a terrible accident an' te bring horse blankets an' some o' the strong drink tha' he an' his men 'ave been guzzlin'."

The faster she talked, the quicker she waddled, until she landed in front of another hut. "Then, quick as a cricket, get te the Hall, and sen' a message to Mistress. Hurry, child."

Through the layers of fabric, Khyryn knew Gwynndolwyn's skin had gone cold. Her threats and shouts had faded as quickly as they flared.

"I will kill him," she whispered.

"Shh. I told you to trust me, and I meant it. I'll see to it."

"I mean it, Khyryn. I will cut his throat."

He hugged her tighter. "You won't have the chance."

He crossed the threshold and set her down, just inside the longhouse, warmed by the hearth fire. "My thanks to you for your help," he said. His own limbs trembled as if he were a lamb.

"Doona fash. We'll set it right, my Bevvy and me. We're a team we are."

She spared a glance for Khyryn. The blood on him and on Gwynndolwyn hinted at something hideous, but she dared not ask the question. "Look a' you," she said, focussing on him, instead of their condition. "You're as shaky as missus. Come on, missus. Let's get you warm. You, too, sir."

"I am fine. See to her."

"D'you 'ave need t'talk te the sentries, then?"

"No!" Shivering, eyes clouded with worry, his wife straightened and shook the woman off. "Khyryn! Do not go out that door without me."

"I must talk to the sentries. They must know what I can tell them of it. Someone must have seen something."

"Not without me."

"You cannot go into that chamber—"

"Why not? You did. He stole our children. We need evidence—"

Khyryn's mouth went dry. "No. Stay here. I will not leave you behind. I promise. But I will not let you go in there. Let Cnut's guards handle this."

The vision of Gilda, her body broken, sprawled in a heap where the babies' pallet lay rose in his mind. Instead of cherubs beneath her, Khyryn had found a pool of blood. Her throat had been slashed so she could not scream.

Gilda's blood for their lives.

Damn Cnut. He had insisted everyone put down their weapons during the feast, save for a dagger with which to eat. Khyryn had left his sword in that room. Along with Hannah and Derris. And Gilda.

"I must get my sword. I shall return. Stay here with—" He had no idea the woman's name. "Forgive me—"

The woman nodded to him. "I am called Narda. I

serve Dolwyffa, niece to Emma. My Bevvy'll send word to my mistress, and she to her aunt."

"Your kindness is great, Narda." As graciously as he could, he bowed to the woman, then turned to leave.

Gwynndolwyn crossed the room and clutched his sleeve. "He stole our children. If the blood is not theirs, then he murdered an innocent woman. A human who did nothing to reap his vengeance."

Khyryn's anger welled once more at her words.

"You said it yourself, Khyryn. He wants us to cower, to be broken. Well, I'll not give him that. I'll not give him anything other than his own balls to choke on."

Tears glittered in her eyes as she stared up at him. He clasped her face in his hands, and brushed away one tear that slithered across her cheek. "We will find them. Alive. I promise you."

Khyryn returned to his own quarters. The few guards had grown to a milling crowd, as word spread throughout the camp. As he stepped to the door, a guard blocked his way, sword drawn.

"That's him that called for help," another sentry said. The guard stepped aside.

Inside, several men worked at wrapping the dead woman's body, so she could be carried from the room. The acrid, sweet scent of blood and death hovered in the room like a spectre.

"Who would commit such a foul deed within the king's walls on such a feast day?" asked one of the men.

"He has taken my children," Khyryn answered. "I must get them back."

"Who would do this?"

Khyryn chose his words cleverly. To accuse Eadric outright might do more harm. "No doubt an agent for someone working against Cnut. They waited until Cnut and his court were blissfully engaged in revelry, then struck. Look at how the woman was killed. Not stabbed, or bludgeoned. The murderer slit her throat so she could not cry out."

"Alert the King," said the sentry in charge, to the guard at the door. "Be discreet. If killers are within the gates, we do not want to create a panic."

Khyryn crossed to where he had hidden his sword, beneath his pallet.

Gone.

"I need my sword."

The sentry stared blankly at him.

"You have taken my sword, and I want back."

The sentry's wide, blank stare told Khyryn the truth of things. The sword had been removed before Cnut's men entered.

Damn Eadric. "Give me your sword, then, or one of your men's. Have them check every chamber, every crevice of this place. Those children must be found, lest they meet the same fate as Gilda."

The sentry held tight his sheathed sword. His eyes clouded with skepticism.

"I will need a sword, if I am to aid the king, man!"

The sentry's glare narrowed. "What of the King?"

"A killer or traitor in our midst obviously does not wish to be revealed."

Confusion replaced skepticism. Good.

"Cnut is in danger. How best to keep him off his guard, than to steal that which would disable his greatest weapon."

More confusion as the sentry looked around the room. Clearly the sentry had no idea whose chamber had hosted the murder. "The stolen twins belong to the Golden One. Cnut's Seer."

As if the world had suddenly stopped, a hush consumed the chamber. Pallor and recognition washed over the sentry's face. They might not know Khyryn, but everyone within these walls knew of Cnut's prophet. She had foreseen his victory at Ashingdon. She spoke the future.

Good.

"Who—who would dare—"

"Someone who knows how dangerous the truth can be. Now, if you value your position and Cnut...Give. Me. A. Sword."

****

The cold stench of fear tickled Edith's nose. She looked up and spied her cousin, Dolwyffa talking to a maid. The servant's animated gestures and wary glance suggested something troublesome.

Where is Eadric?

Edith had discovered long ago, whenever she sensed danger, her husband was party to it. She scanned the room, searching for him in the crowd.

Once more the hair on the back of her neck stood on end. She had not seen him all day. Whatever wickedness he perpetrated must be great if it propelled Dolwyffa's maid to the Hall to interrupt the revelry.

As Edith suspected, her young cousin's posture changed. Her face frowned in concern. The young woman grasped the maid by the shoulders, spoke quietly to her, and then sent the young woman out of the Hall. Once the girl had departed, Dolwyffa turned her attention to Emma.

What on earth could be so demanding that she would impose upon the King and the Queen consort?

Edith made an excuse to leave her table. Carefully, she wove through the gathering, moving toward her cousin. Damp fear encroached with each step.

Curse him. What had Eadric done now?

For an instant, Edith wondered at Emma's choice to marry Cnut. *Women seldom choose their future. Rather, we escape the fear of no future whatsoever.*

As much as she disliked her father's second wife, now consort to Cnut, Edith had to acknowledge the woman chose her future. Every step of the way.

A strong ruler needs a strong wife.

From the look on Emma's face, that task had just been met.

Edith met Dolwyffa as she departed Emma's table. "What is it, cousin? What has happened?"

Dolwyffa's face had gone completely ashen. "It is Cnut's Seer."

Gwynndolwyn. "What of her?"

"She is with Narda now. There has been a murder."

"A murder?" Edith's pulse quickened. She glanced to Emma and Cnut. Cnut's face changed from a healthy pink glow to red, then purple at his wife's words.

"Did Bevvy say who the dead man is?"

"Dead man?"

"Yes. Who was murdered?"

"Aye, a murder, but not a man."

Edith's heart dropped to her stomach. Not a man. "Then who, cousin?"

"Bevvy did not say. But the children have gone missing."

"Children? What children? Whose?"

"The Seer's. Not yet weaned. Twins."

The threat rang in her ears. Khyryn, protector to the Seer, children...gone...

Eadric had taken the children. Why, she could guess. Her husband did not enjoy losing, ever. Khyryn of Powys had escaped him once. She knew he had not forgotten. Whatever existed between the two men, her husband's anger still fed upon it.

He would have made a formidable king. She shuddered at the thought.

Edith turned on her heel and headed for the door. She had to find those children.

Feasts and kings be damned. Eadric had to be stopped.

****

Eadric Streona tossed the stone and moved the playing piece to win the game. Again. Gareth sighed in defeat. "That is another game I have won. Gareth, fortune does seem to sit upon my shoulder, and not yours, this day."

"As it should, sire."

Outside the counting house, in the camp, the sounds of chaos chimed as word of a grisly murder filtered through the court.

The guard cast a glance toward the door. "Should we not join them?"

"They will come to us. And find us engrossed in our game. Oblivious to the horrors of the day. Set up the game again. Perhaps, you will win this time."

Gareth did as ordered. They had just begun play when Cnut's soldiers entered.

"Pardon, Alderman. There has been a murder." The

man who spoke was tall and dark haired, and nervous.

"A murder? At Solstice? How dreadful. I pray it is no member of our court? The King—is he?" Eadric allowed shock and concern to play in his voice.

"Safe, for now," the soldier said, as he continued to glance around the small room. "Have you heard or seen anything suspicious?"

"I wish I had. As you can see, we have been busy with gaming. Gareth, you have not heard anything, have you?"

Gareth shook his head.

"Do you require another man? Gareth could—"

"No, sir. I will not keep you from your game."

Eadric smiled and nodded. Alert us if we can be of aid."

The soldier closed the door as he exited.

This game he played very well.

By nightfall, the entire court would mourn the Seer's lost twins. "How sad that Cnut's prophet should suffer the loss of her servant, and her babes. Her desolation must be great."

Gareth concentrated on the game. "What of her protector?"

"Khyryn is nearly as skilled at such games as I am. Once he realizes the infants are not here, they will find the guard who saw three men riding out on their own, to the north. No doubt, he will follow their trail. How tragic if he should be killed."

"And the children?"

"Their mother must be bereft. Often, babes do not see their first year marked before death claims them. Sickness, starvation, animal attacks. The threats are too numerous to fathom."

He studied his guardsman for a moment. The man showed no emotion. No nervousness, no repulsion, no fear. A year ago, Gareth would have squirmed at such callousness. Much had changed in a year's time. Eadric had forged a soldier with the makings of a general from the oaf who had groveled at his boots so short a time ago.

Perhaps when the time came, he would let Gareth join in the fun.

"The move is yours, sire."

"Indeed, it is."

Chapter Thirty-Four

"Gwynndolwyn," Cnut called, as she took up her horse's reins.

She turned to find the king bounding toward her, a throng of revelers struggling to keep up.

"My liege, I pray you forgive—" Her voice faltered.

He waved a hand in the air, dismissing her attempt. "I have heard. You and Khyryn take my men with you to aid your search."

Wynne bristled. For all she knew, one or more of his men might be responsible for aiding Eadric. "Grateful as we are for the offer, we can do this better without—"

Khyryn interrupted her. "One of your sentries saw three men ride out this afternoon. If we are quick, we might track them."

Emma had caught up to her husband. Concern and understanding marked her expression. She reached out to touch Wynne. "A mother protects fiercely. Much more so than a soldier. Heed my lord husband, however. Take two of his men, in case you have need of protection. For your children's sake."

Several men stood ready. Wynne nodded to Khryrn who chose two from their ranks.

"I would speak to Khyryn before you depart," Cnut said.

Emma reached for Wynne's hand and slipped something into her palm. Wynne looked down at the offering in her hand. A small, polished metal cross, encircled with a braid of gold and bronze. Gold. A golden cross. Small enough to be hidden beneath a gown, or a veil.

A token—not of faith—but of love.

Once a lover's token. Now given in faith.

"They are in God's hands. So be it with you. May our Lord and your husband see you safely to your babes."

A queen recognizes a kindred spirit.

The words whispered in her head.

There, in the courtyard, surrounded by a crowd, Wynne suddenly knew more about Cnut's queen than anyone ever would. Queen to more than one king, Emma had lived a life of duty. Not of passion. She had seen horrors to match Wynne's. Perhaps more. This golden token of love—perhaps the only true passion she had known—served as talisman to her unwavering strength. Strength she now gifted to a stranger.

Wynne clasped the queen's hand and brushed her lips reverently across her fingers in acknowledgement of the queen's blessing.

Lowering her voice to a whisper she warned, "Take care, my queen, that you and the king do not turn a blind eye to the viper within your own walls. Beware Eadric Streona."

Recognition flashed in the queen's eyes. Emma needed no warning. She knew the threat Eadric posed to all in this court.

Wynne tugged at the reins and withdrew to meet Khyryn and Marroc, and the two other riders. At her approach, Cnut and Khyryn broke their conversation.

As she and Khyryn rode through the gates, Wynne refused to look back.

No more looking back.

****

Khyryn crawled toward the hill fort. One of the two guards who accompanied them slunk close behind. Gwynndolwyn and the second guard remained close to the tree line, lest someone see them approaching. Should he fail, at least she might escape.

In his lifetimes, he had been druid, warrior, and monk. Those jobs had not prepared him for husband and father. Fighting as a soldier only endangered oneself. This battle threatened others.

Their ride had been quiet, and urgent. Gwynndolwyn for her part spared no words for the guards, so worried was she that they might be spies for Eadric.

Khyryn and Cnut had apprised both men of the situation before they left Winchester. Above all, they were to find the twins, and protect Cnut's Seer.

They had tracked a team of riders to a hill fort, north of Winchester. Naturally, Eadric had chosen a remote location to draw them. Atop the hill sat three huts, only one of which glowed in the afternoon's dusk. If they were still alive, the twins must be there.

When the guard had drawn even, Khyryn pointed out the illuminated hut. "Eadric most likely has them there."

"Eadric? Earl of Mercia?"

Khyryn did not look at the man but kept his gaze on the fort. "Aye."

"He took your children? And killed the woman?"

"He did."

"How do you know?"

"I have seen his work before. It is like a hare's tracks. Once seen, not forgotten."

"Why would he strike out against the nurse?"

"Not the nurse. The Seer."

"I do not understand. She is but a woman. She can do him no harm."

"Eadric fears this woman. Although he has Cnut's ear, so has she. When she speaks, it is of things yet to come. Would you not fear her prophecies if you had as much to lose as he?"

The guard considered Khyryn's words for a moment then nodded.

"Streona stood against Edmund to take Cnut's side. He has paid homage to many kings. Have you ever known the alderman to leave anything to chance?"

The guard sighed. Whether he knew it or not, the man had just revealed much of himself. He knew exactly the kind of person Alderman Eadric Streona, Earl of Mercia was.

Khyryn shuddered. *Concentrate.* "Find the twins. Leave Streona to me. I will scale the hill from the backside. Wait until you hear the owl's call then move toward the hut. I will meet you from the other side so we might catch him if he tries to escape. Be silent as the fog."

The guard nodded, and Khyryn moved, half crawling, half running toward the far side of the hill. In the distance, from the knoll, he could hear the soft woofle and snort of horses in yard. Steep though it was, the summer earth had long dried, so his feet did not sink into mud, or slide down the terrain. No crop rows, no plough tools. No one had used this fort for a residence for years. Above the trees, the moon rose boldly, almost full. She greeted the waning sun, and waited her turn with the earth.

He reached level ground once more, and saw the movement of the guard from across the yard and waved to him. They both moved toward the largest of the huts that stood behind two smaller ones. Three horses stood between the southwest hut and the larger one. Even from a distance, Khyryn could see dark spots on one of the horses' flanks. Large dark marks. Hand prints, smeared against the pale brown coat of the creature.

Bloodstains.

Two against three.

Khyryn motioned to the guard again. Signaling his sword, Khyryn instructed the guard to advance and distract the abductors, so he might rescue the twins.

The man nodded and unsheathed his sword. Khyryn, sword in hand, gave a nod and the two charged through the leather flap into the firelight.

Three men lay near the fire pit.

Asleep.

None budged as the guard charged the chamber. Nor did they bolt when Khyryn advanced.

Dead?

Drugged.

Khyryn found a drinking horn with some mead still pooled within. He dipped his finger in the liquid and sniffed it, careful to keep any from touching his lips.

He detected a scent of stick wort. He replaced the horn. He and the guard gingerly stepped around the three soldiers as they searched for signs of the other two riders.

In the shadows sat a basket layered with wool and linen. The unmistakable odor of an infant child wafted as he edged closer.

Empty.

Who would have drugged Streona's men and taken the infants?

More importantly, where were the babes now?

****

Daylight ebbed, the sun inching farther from sight as it sank behind the horizon. Soon, night would blanket the world.

There is no rest without my children.

Wynne had retreated into the comfort of the forest to wait. The guard Khyryn left behind, preferred to linger at the woodland's edge, as did Marroc, who tended their horses.

Goosebumps rose on her arms, and a shiver spidered down her spine.

A rustling in the bushes made Wynne freeze. Footsteps crackled against the dried leaves. Wynne reached into her boot for her *s'gian dhu*. Whatever lurked behind her, watching her, advancing, was no fox, this time.

As silently as she could, Wynne straightened and turned to face her attacker.

Branches in the overgrowth twitched and parted as her stalker stepped forward.

Aberswythe.

She embraced the man who once had been her father. "He has taken the twins."

Aberswythe's eyes saddened with acknowledgement. "You must return to your own time, for our own protection.

"You cannot be serious. I am not leaving my children behind to return to—"

"Elleran and I have the incantation that will send you to your own time, once more," he whispered.

"No. My place is here. Now. You cannot—"

"You belong to the future, my dear. That same destiny which brought you to us, reminds us all, with this most recent injustice your time is best served elsewhere."

"Not without my children. Not without Khyryn."

As if Aberswythe had been waiting for this, he smiled at her. "As it should be. All will be well. It is in the stones."

"What is in the stones?"

"Follow your heart's desire to the dragon's hill. There will you find your way home, child."

Wynne heard the guard call out to her. She turned to stop him from advancing. "I am here. Halt. Come no closer. I am—I will come to you momentarily. I have need of privacy."

The guard stayed where he was. A nervous cough told her he understood. Once certain he would not pursue her, Wynne turned back to Aberswythe.

Gone.

A ghost? A vision? A hallucination?

They must go with you. As surely as if he stood before her, Wynne heard his voice in the cold night air.

****

Khyryn and the guard shimmied down the hill, bounding for the woods.

Before they had made it to the tree line, Wynne emerged, astride her horse. Young Marroc held forth the reins to the other both men as they approached.

"They are gone," Khyryn said.

"Dragon's hill," she said.

"What of it?"

"That is where they are."

Though her hood draped her head, her features shone luminescent in the moon's light. Her face had lost the flush of anger and cold that had colored her cheeks as they rode. She was calm. Reserved. Haunted.

"Our heart's desire will be met there, and we will find our way home."

These words were not hers. A chill skittered across his shoulders. "Gwynndolwyn, tell me—"

She met her husband's gaze. No tears or smile. Only stoic determination.

As if in a trance, she coaxed him. "Come, druid son."

Aberswythe. She had seen Aberswythe. "How? Where?" Khyryn searched the darkened woods, looking for a glimpse of the pale robes or beard of his mentor and friend. No sound or sight did he glean.

"Ride," she commanded.

Khyryn and the other two men set heel to horse and followed as she rode away from the woods, and into the moonlight.

Chapter Thirty-Five

"Where is your mistress?" Eadric demanded.

The maid cowered at his words.

"Please, sir, I—I do not know. She has not slept in her bed, and did not call for me in the night—"

"Did not sleep in her bed?" He moved closer to the woman. "Tell me, does my wife often find comfort in another's bed?"

The girl did not meet his gaze. A look of confusion crossed her face.

"Where does she sleep if not in her own bed, woman?"

This time the maid flinched at his tone and shook her head. Nowhere, sir. She does not...that is, I do not know where Lady Edith is—"

He wrapped his hand around the maid's throat and gently pulled her to a stand. "If you did, would you tell me?"

She did not attempt to remove his hand. Fear, palpable, and sweet, trembled on the girl's lips. "Yes, sir."

"Tell me, then, where might she go to find solace of thought?"

"Streona—"

Cnut's voice caught Eadric by surprise.

Eadric released the woman who immediately fell to the floor in a grovel at the upstart king's presence.

"My Liege." Eadric bent low into a reverent bow, as he turned to greet the king.

"I hear your wife is unwell."

"I fear for her wellbeing, Highness. She is not in her chamber, as you can see."

Cnut glanced around the small room, then back to his alderman. "I am surprised her maid remains. My sentry tells me Edith rode with an escort before first light headed for Uffyngdon. I am surprised you did not ride with her."

Departed? Eadric concealed his surprise. "I-I am headed there now, by your leave, sire. I had some business to finish this morning. Tell me, what news of the murdered woman and of the missing children?"

Cnut grimaced. "Bad business. The woman was murdered and the two infants taken to frighten the Seer. She and her escort departed yester eve in search of the babes."

"Who would perpetrate such a heinous crime, here within your very walls?"

"Someone who wishes to threaten me, perhaps."

"How so?"

"If the Golden One is taken away from court, then I cannot seek her advice. See how clever someone is?"

Eadric kept his back straight and stalled an urge to smile.

"Luckily, I am well surrounded by sound advisors, such as yourself, who bring me loyalty as well as sound counsel."

"Thank you, sire."

"Yesterday must have weighed heavy on your wife's mind."

"Yesterday?"

"She has buried two kings. Now she watches her stepmother build a new kingdom with another, not of her family. No doubt it wearied her mind and heart. Delay not your departure to join her. She is no doubt distressed at the grief the abduction has caused."

Cnut turned his attention to the maid. He bade her rise from the floor.

Eadric watched with subtle amusement as the Danish king assessed her as he might a bit of livestock, before saying, "Send the girl to my chambers. Emma might have need of her assistance." He cupped her chin in his hand, as he winked at Eadric. "If not, then I can find sport to keep you busy." He dismissed her then beckoned Eadric, once more.

"Sire?" Eadric smiled at his liege.

"I shall see you to your horse. Do not worry about your belongings. Leave them here. No doubt you will return in a fortnight for the Christ mass."

His hands were tied. He could fathom no believable argument not to ride off in search of his wife.

"By my belongings, do you include my wife's maid?"

Cnut laughed out loud. "Not so fair of face, but the wench has firm breasts and can fair sit a man. I shall personally see her. She will be well tended until your return."

Eadric smiled. He would soon be reunited with his wife. Before he dealt with her disloyalty, he would make sure she suffered the humiliation of surrendering her maid to the barbaric appetites of the Dane.

****

Emma looked up from her prayer. Dolwyffa sat

engrossed in needlework. Morning had broken with winter's cold. The sky, so bright yesterday, now paled. Clouds hovered close to the ground, threatening snow, or at least, rain.

Cnut had confined all women to their quarters. Since word of Gwynndolwyn's servant's death, no woman dared to be alone.

A knock upon the door, brought them all to wary attention. Emma quietly moved toward the sound. She untied the rope that gave her some small sense of privacy and security. In her free hand, she held a dagger freed from her belt. When she opened the door, a scared and frantic young woman clumsily stumbled into the room.

Tara, Edith's maid, immediately broke into tears at the site of her queen.

"Shh, Tara, all is right, child."

"Mistress," the girl choked. "Mistress is gone. An' he asked me, but I did not know what to say. I was so afraid—"

"Who asked?"

"Himself. Master Streona."

The older woman beckoned the maid to her so she could soothe the servant girl. "Did he harm you?"

Tara pressed her hand to her own throat, yet shook her head. "He meant to. Then the king came and bade me come to you," she said to Emma.

"I told him to do what he must to make sure you did not fall into Eadric's hands."

Emma noted the blush on Tara's cheeks when she whispered, "He said he would find sport for me, which frightened me nearly as much as Master Streona."

Emma laughed outright. He is a fiendish man, our

king, is he not?"

The queen consort hugged Tara conspiratorially. "You must tell our king, when you see him, he is no match for the women of Britain. Our fierceness would wilt his ardor."

Dolwyffa laughed at her aunt. "No doubt, he will beg for mercy from us all."

The girl relaxed a bit at Emma's humor. Dolwyffa offered the girl a cup of mead warmed over the fire, to soothe the chattering teeth that marked the servant's anxiety.

"Fear not, young one. Your mistress is well enough. She is to Uffyngdon. She asked that you remain with us for a time. Once arrangements are made, you will join her."

Though Edith bore little love for Emma, the two held each other in some respect. When her stepdaughter had come to her yester eve, and voiced her fears, Emma had agreed to help her. To help them all.

A loud pounding on the door caused everyone to jump. Before anyone could move, the wood swung open, and Cnut stepped into the room. He tried to look ferocious and grim and ever much the great conqueror. However, merriment danced in his eyes and played upon his features.

"He is gone to Uffyngdon. I played well my deceit to make him think his wife had left in the night."

"Many thanks, sire." Emma moved to her husband and placed a kiss upon his cheek.

In answer, he grabbed his wife fiercely and took a proper kiss as payment for his success.

When he released his hold, Emma nodded to Tara. "You did scare the girl."

His smile broadened. "As it should be, wife. Keep your women well hid from Cnut's ravishing forces." He laughed at his own enthusiasm. "Take heed, maid, if I had no such fine woman in my bed as this one, I might find warmth elsewhere. But not this day."

Tara blushed so furiously, Emma feared the girl would faint. She elbowed her husband, who moved away from her and took a seat by the fire.

"You have made arrangements, then?"

Cnut's expression sobered at her question. He cast a warning glance at the young maid, and at his wife's niece.

"I sent word to the Archbishop of York. She will be taken care of. He will see her safe to sanctuary."

"And the other one? When you spoke to him, he agreed?"

"How could he not. He is as much a soldier as many I have led. He will not fail them. Or us. Soon, Eadric Streona will no longer pose a threat to this court. Or any other. Khyryn of Powys will see to that."

Emma smiled at her husband.

Vengeance? No. Justice.

By Christ Mass Eadric Streona, acquisitor, traitor, and murderer, would be dead.

****

Eadric kicked the table so hard it flew across the room and splintered against the wall.

Gone.

His soldiers drunk, the infants nowhere to be found, Khyryn and Cnut's Golden One—all gone. And all he had, were three bodies, examples of failure, snoring heavily. They certainly had served no such fine service to their master.

"Where are they?" he shouted. He kicked one of the unconscious guards, hoping to wake the man, to no avail. The man did not even react to Eadric's boot.

Two soldiers searched the adjacent buildings, and returned empty handed.

He had had them. He had watched them ride from Winchester, following the tracks of his men. He had planned it perfectly. Away from the village, he could exact his revenge upon them both.

A perfect plan. The parents pleading to spare their children's lives. Even he could not have created such a perfect setting for such a moment of vindication. For once, everything Khyryn held dear would have been ripped from him, as he, himself, had experienced so often.

He retrieved one of the drinking horns. Mead. How much mead had they consumed that they would oblivious to the world? Oblivious to him?

Eadric ran his finger around the edge of the horn, and gathered a few drops of the honey elixir that had so undone his men. He touched his tongue to his fingers. Honey, fermented, with something else. Slightly bitter. And familiar.

Edith.

He stepped out into the cool autumn air and listened for the sounds of the night. As he thought. Three horses. Which meant she had been quick about her work.

A clever woman after all, his wife. Edith had outdone him this time. He had not seen her depart Cnut's court. Nor had he suspected she even knew of this place. Apparently, she too, had her spies.

If her potion had drugged the guards, then she now

had the babes. With any luck, Khyryn and Gwynndolwyn, would ride toward Uffyngdon, in search of the infants.

And in search of me.

A wry smile tugged at his cheek. In another time and place, he could so value such a woman.

"Gareth!"

"Sir?"

Have your men take the three to the river and throw them in. Their carelessness makes them a liability. Make sure no one will be able to interrogate them further. When you are done, meet me at Uffyngdon.

"Will you not return to Cnut's court?"

"My place is at Uffyngdon." He sneered at his guardsman. "A husband's duty is to see his ill wife well-tended. Is it not?"

Gareth kicked at the embers in the round sunken hearth. "What of the camp?"

"We wouldn't want to waste a perfectly good fire, would we? Once you have disposed of the bodies, tell your men to rest. The fewer witnesses, the better. Give orders they are to kill anyone who shows up. You, however, I may have need of."

Gareth bowed in acquiescence, then set about calling his men to gather the sleeping guards.

Twice thwarted. No. Thrice. Three times he had been denied the pleasure of Khyryn's and Gwynndolwyn's pain. By ritual, he should thus be charmed to success, when next they met.

He reached into the secret slit in his tunic. There, close to his body, he found the small oblong stone he kept hidden. Lost, once, in battle, so many lifetimes ago, he had kept it upon his body ever since it came again into his keeping.

A gift of dryad and wyce, delivered by a spectre in the night. A gift of memory in keeping. And by so, he had enjoyed immortality of sorts. Soon vengeance would be his reward. A breeze had rushed through the trees one Beltane, carrying the hushed whisper of the strange shadowed figure who had set the stone upon the ground before him whispering, "This is your salvation. Keep it close, that you may know your enemies."

Eadric had always known his enemies.

He kicked his horse and started trotting down the hill. Elleran he had dealt with. That serpent lay beneath a rock. Edmund and Aethelred, cut down like weeds. He would soon enough have revenge against Khyryn and Gwynndolwyn.

All things came to him. Eventually.

As he rode back to Uffyngdon, Eadric considered his wife. So clever to have figured out his plan. So clever to have made for Uffyngdon. What better place to mete justice?

What proper reward for an alderman's wife who acted against her husband?

He grinned to himself as he rode for home. And all that   awaited   him.

Chapter Thirty-Six

Familiarity cloaked Wynne as they rode towards the gates of Uffyngdon. This time, she knew the evil that dwelled behind those walls. This time the only way out alive was at Eadric Streona's expense.

She had vowed she would kill him, and she meant it.

The guards and Marroc worked to keep up. Lighter and more anxious than they, she had ridden close to the horse's back, allowing the animal to sail fast as the wind.

They were no more than half a day's ride from Streona and the babes.

Once she had her twins and she held Eadric Streona's life, and that damned stone in her hands, they would all know an end to the curse Elleran set upon them ten centuries ago.

Khyryn met her gait, and grabbed the reins, slowing her horse. She struggled to pull free from his hand.

"Have you lost all reason? You cannot ride up to the gates like this. His men will have you dead before you cross the bridge.

"They are in there. I know it. Let me go."

"All the more reason to use caution."

"How will we get in if we do not force our way in?"

"Marroc."

"What about Marroc?" She stopped trying to grab her reins and let Khyryn lead the horses.

"Marroc served as stable boy at Uffyngdon until we took him to Teweksbury. He can get us in."

"Eadric will be waiting for us."

"He waits for us anyway. That is why he took the twins. Remember?"

The guard who had scaled the hill fort with Khyryn pulled up beside them. "You do not need the lad to open the gates. He would best be left outside, a messenger to Cnut if need arises."

Both stared at him.

"What plan have you?" Khyryn asked.

"No plan. Only royal edict and law. All must admit Cnut's guards or face penalty of treason. Even an alderman."

A short time later, Uffyngdon's gates opened to admit a party of four riders into Streona's stronghold.

Wynne's flesh prickled with each hoof fall upon the ground. Weather had little to do with the atmosphere here. A few people mulled about, tending to chores. For the most part, however, the courtyard stood unattended. Only three guards stood watch at the gate, which pleased Khyryn as much as it pleased her.

"Do you have your blade?" Khyryn whispered softly to her, and she nodded. Beneath her cloak she found the dagger she had slipped into her belt. Her other, smaller blade was tucked in her boot, as usual.

They dismounted, cautiously.

"Cnut sends us to speak with Alderman Streona," one of guards said.

"Then he has sent you to chase a snipe," the

groomsman teased. "Alderman Streona is not here. He waits upon the king in Winchester. Iddn tha' right?" the groomsman asked another man near the stables.

"Not here?"

"Aye. But mistress is. Rode in late last night, she did."

"Mistress is ill," the other man offered. "Said she is to her bed, should anyone come."

"Warm your bodies by the fire. I will let her know that you bring a message from the king."

"You say she is ill," Wynne said. "Perhaps I can serve her. I have knowledge of herbs. Take me to her that I might offer her comfort."

The two men conferred, and agreed. The younger man from the stables limped as he struggled toward what Wynne trusted were Edith's chambers.

Khyryn stopped her. "It could be a trap. Go to the main hall and wait. I'll bring Edith to you. You will be safer with Cnut's guards. "

Wynne allowed the guards to lead her toward the main building. She gripped the hilt of her dagger as she moved farther away from Khyryn.

The groomsman ushered Khyryn toward Edith's chambers, as the other man lead the rest of them to the main hall. Once at the door, she did not dare enter by herself.

Unlike the simple, newer structures at Winchester, Uffyngdon's buildings were more permanent. The rafters overhead were solid, the thatch above her, thick. At the far end, a great fire burned, its fury crackling as it beckoned her to its warmth. This room had been designed for comfort.

The two soldiers took up seats on a bench, leaving

Wynne standing in the center of the room. A movement in the corner caught her eye, as two cloaked figures, one behind the other stood facing Wynne. A hand moved to lift the hood, from the closest wearer.

Edith looked at Wynne with wide eyes. She pressed a finger to her lips imploring Wynne to silence.

Wynne raised her hand and brandished the small blade, so Eadric's wife bore no misconceptions about her ability to defend herself.

Edith smiled, sadly at her, as she opened her cloak and revealed a linen sling, snuggly cradling an infant against her body.

Derris.

Wynne choked back a squeal of disbelief. The second figure moved from behind Edith.

As her mistress had done, the servant lifted her cloak and revealed a similar sling. One tiny arm stretched into the cool air.

Hannah.

Wynne stumbled toward the women, collapsing into a bow of gratitude and silent weeping, as both women knelt before her so she might better see the flushed, alive faces of her twins.

The two guards shifted behind her and stood at the ready.

In a voice as quiet as a breeze, Edith spoke. "No mother should be so soon separated from her child. As soon as I heard, I sought to thwart his plan. Eadric did not see me depart court. He does not know I found your children. By now, however, he has discovered his guards drugged and his quarry stolen."

Edith now looked to the guards. "Go and fetch the babes' father."

Wynne fought back tears to ask, "How? Why?"

"My husband forgets women can be clever, too. Especially one who has lived so long in the shadow of his evil. His men were easily coerced to let the maid serve as wet nurse when the babes cried from hunger. I drugged the guards, and we fled. Take your babes, before we are found out, and flee as far from here as you can. Do not let your rage trap you here. He will kill us all with no remorse."

Hannah sighed against the wet nurse as the woman jostled the babe and removed the sling from her shoulder. Wynne untied her cloak as the woman gently handed her the bundle and slid the knotted fabric over her head. Wynne slid her arm through the sling so that Hannah curled, hammocked beneath her breast.

Without pausing, Edith did the same, carefully positioning Derris to rest beneath Wynne's other arm. Criss-crossed slings cradled a babe beneath each of Wynne's arms. Protected as robins beneath a mother's wing.

Edith stroked Derris's head then pulled the linen to protect him from the cool air.

Wynne grabbed her hand and squeezed it tightly. "Why would you risk your life to do this?"

Edith stared at her for a long, silent moment. "God has seen fit to give me no children, so the evil of my husband is not perpetuated upon the world. What legacy I would have, I must make. As he would take life, so I would preserve it."

Alive and safe. And delivered from an angel.

Edith lifted her gaze to meet Wynne's. A sad smile graced the woman's lips. "He is a good man, your Khyryn of Powys. Love him well. Heed my warning.

Flee before my husband and his men return to Uffyngdon ."

Derris wriggled beneath her, and Wynne felt the milk surge in her breasts. Hungry or not, soon she would have to take them to suckle just to relieve the pain.

Wynne looked down at the babes in her arms. She heard the door open once more to admit Khyryn. As she stroked Hannah's brow, something whooshed past her head. A soft thud behind her was met by a gasp. Wynne looked up to see Edith, who had stepped forward, sink to her knees. From her shoulder protruded a long shaft.

An arrow.

Stunned, Edith grasped at the shaft as it pierced her chest. A gurgling sound of pain bubbled from her throat as she struggled to stay upright.

Wynne screamed and scrambled to her feet, babes in arms, as she tried to flee. "Khyryn!"

A gloved hand clamped down over her face, and a second hand found her throat and squeezed hard enough to choke her.

Wynne's vision clouded then cleared as she fought against her attacker. To her right lay the sprawling lifeless figure of the wet nurse. To her left, collapsed, yet alive, lay the tormented figure of Lady Edith, an arrow between her chest and shoulder.

Before her, a satisfied grin upon his face, stood Eadric Streona.

Grabbing Edith by the hair, he yanked her to her knees again, closed his mouth over hers, and wrenched a kiss from her. "I had heard you were ill, wife. And now I find it is true. You are wounded most foully." He twisted the shaft and she howled in pain. "Pray it is not a mortal wound, my love. I would dislike being made a widower so young."

He let go his hold, and Edith fell to the floor.

Wynne's captor loosened his hold, slightly, so she could breathe. Still, her feet barely touched the floor. Across her chest, lay Derris and Hannah.

Eadric took a step toward her and brushed a finger across Hannah's head. Wynne wriggled to push his hand away, and he chuckled at the futile gesture.

Another noise from the entrance brought Eadric around. He dropped the bow he held and unsheathed his sword.

Wynne fought to scream against the hand and arm that held her mouth and threatened her airway.

Khyryn's footfall hastened then stopped as he moved into the light from the hearth.

"At last," Eadric said as he stood over Edith's stricken form. "A family reunion."

****

Khyryn stood frozen to the spot. As it did on the battlefield, time slowed. He heard the echo of his steps as he entered the Hall, even though his steps had stopped.

Eadric stood, not twenty feet from him, sword raised in defiance. At his feet lay Edith's body. Behind Streona stood his wife, his soul mate, holding their abducted twins as she struggled at the hands of one of Eadric's men.

"Let her go, "Khyryn called out.

Streona laughed, but did not move, nor did he instruct his man to do so.

"That is not the way this game is played. Surely, you know that.

"Gareth, sit her down so she might tend to her whelps. After all, she must surely want to feed them a last meal before they depart."

In her lap, one of the twins fussed, and Khyryn's gut clenched.

"Uddryd," Khyryn shouted. "Your quarrel is with me. As it has always been. Let her go."

Something quite like a hiss escaped Eadric's lips.

"Uddryd is a name I gave up long ago. I found it unlucky."

The baby cried out, and Khyryn flinched.

"Such a sad sound. A babe's hungry wail." Eadric's sword never wavered, but he stepped closer to Wynne. "What would you forfeit, Khyryn to save one child's life?"

The guard roughly dragged her to the chair nearest the fire and slammed her body against the wood. Though he removed the hand from her mouth, he kept one securely at her throat.

Red-rimmed eyes met Khyryn's as she gasped, drinking in air.

Would you give up your sword?"

Eadric's eyes flashed. "Drop your sword, Khyryn, and slide it over to me. One child's life depends on it."

As Eadric ordered, Khyryn let fall his sword, which he kicked across the room toward the hearth.

"Good." Eadric retrieved the sword and tossed it into the corner. "A Cymry weapon, that—" He motioned to the bow. "I daresay it will be the undoing of the English one day. It did fell the two you brought with you." He grinned. "The man who trained me to use it was quite proficient. Quite good, for hunting. As old as the ancient Greeks, so some would have us believe.

Wonderful hunters, the Cymry."

Wynne wimpered. Khyryn looked at her and found she had closed her eyes.

Eadric brushed a hand across her forehead. "Open your eyes, Gwynndolwyn. I want you to savor every moment of our time together. All of us."

She obeyed his command and opened her eyes. Khyryn dared another step toward her.

"Stay where you are, Khyryn. It is not your turn."

Eadric shifted his glance to Gwynndolwyn, and the bundles that rested in her lap. "You have not nursed for two days. You must be in great pain."

She did not answer him.

"Gareth," he commanded, "Use your dagger to open her gown so she can more easily take them to tit."

"No," Khyryn shouted.

"Take care, Gareth, not to harm her. Gwynndolwyn, be very careful not to move. We wouldn't want any unfortunate accidents, would we?"

Gareth moved his hand from her neck, withdrew a small blade from his belt, and did as Eadric had ordered. Deftly, he seized a clump of wool and linen in his hand and sliced through the fabric, exposing an ample amount of flesh as he let the fabric fall.

Her breasts heaved, damp beneath the cloth, and swollen to bursting. Both twins stirred.

Gwynndolwyn brushed the tears from her eyes as she gathered one to her breast, cooing softly to the other.

Khyryn stared at the man who had slain kings, and children, and who now threatened everything he held precious. "What evil has grown inside of you these lifetimes that you would do this? In another time, they might have been your own flesh."

"But they weren't. Were they? How many lifetimes have I awakened, with the memory of the two of you haunting me. Her deceitful body writhing beneath yours, even as she prepared to wed me. To make a fool of me."

"That was never her intention. That is why I went to Elleran in the first place—"

"Hag. You went to the hag for a gift. A potion. Poison perhaps. To kill a king. Instead she cursed you. And gifted me. With the memory so I would know you each time I met you. So I could defend myself against your treacheries."

"The only treachery was yours."

"Mine? Because I sliced the wickedness from her belly, even as the Romans marched toward our village?"

"Uddryd."

"She was mine, Khyryn. Mine by birthright. Mine by arrangement. Firstborn takes the kingdom, and the firstborn girl of his parents' choosing. Our parents chose her for me. Not you."

"She could not help her feelings, Uddryd—"

"Eadric! Uddryd is long dead. He died a slave to Caesar's army!"

Gwynndolwyn moved, and Gareth clamped a hand upon her shoulder. She cried out in pain.

Khyryn lunged. Eadric's sword swept up and clipped his ear.

"Not yet."

Khyryn faltered and fell back, moving away from the blade. His hand strayed to his ear, and blood dripped onto his fingers.

"What would you do to save both your children, Khyryn? Would you sacrifice your own life? Would you sacrifice your wife's? How far are you willing to go to save all three?"

"What guarantee do I have you won't kill them anyway."

Eadric edged toward Khyryn. With each step, the sword moved closer to him.

"Ah. My oath is as good as was hers when we wed. How is that? But I can make you a deal, a bargain between two old souls that once shared a brotherly love, so to speak. If you grovel sufficiently, I will spare the whelps the agony of a prolonged death. They will not suffer at my hands. Or at Gareth's. How is that? Would that ease your conscience...brother?"

He spat the endearment as he thrust the sword tip at Khyryn.

"You have done me one great favor, Khyryn. Really. If not for you, I doubt I would have ever found my true calling. You see, Aethelred and Edmund, and now Cnut, all find favor with a man so filled with enmity he kills with no remorse. That talent has made me the wealthiest man in Britain. More powerful than any king. "

Eadric stepped to where Gwynndolwyn sat. She had taken the second babe to nurse, now.

He wrapped his hand in her hair and tugged her head back slightly. "I thought you dead after our last meeting. How thrilled I am we can continue the game we started when last you visited."

She shuddered against him, and tried to pull away.

"Gareth, tie Khyryn soundly, then loop a noose around his neck so we can string him from the rafters. I think his last moments should be watching the Golden One's final gift to Cnut's most trusted advisor." He bent his head, and laved his tongue against her neck and up her cheek. "Hmm. Succulent fear. If you play along, perhaps I will not kill your children in front of you."

Wynne's hand shot up and clipped Eadric in the face. He let go of her hair, and slapped her across the face.

As Gareth stepped toward Khyryn, Edith struck out and clutched his ankle, causing him to trip. In mid fall, his dagger clattered to the floor. In an instant, Khyryn lunged for the blade, and grasped it as he rolled beneath the tumbling guard. Khyryn heard Gareth's head crack against the table as he fell.

Eadric spun around.

Khyryn followed through the roll and sprang up to meet Eadric, dagger thrusting up, tearing through wool and skin as it ripped through his abdomen, and sank beneath his rib cage.

Once more, time twisted in that mystical fashion. Khyryn heard his own breath, ragged and fast. He heard Gwynndolwyn cry out.

Blood spurted from Eadric's body and from his mouth as he fell against the blade, eyes bulging in disbelief. One hand dug at Khyryn's fist while the other reached for his throat. Khyryn twisted the blade, pulled it out, then thrust it in a second time, higher.

Metal struck bone, grating. Eadric's mouth fell open in a silent yell as he sank against Khyryn.

Only the cadence of his own heartbeat sounded as he shoved Eadric Streona away from him, crashing to the floor, his head bouncing against the hard earthen hearth.

As he landed, something tumbled from his tunic, and rolled across the floor to rest at Gwynndolwyn's feet.

A runestone.

Chapter Thirty-Seven

Uffyngdon

Gwynndolwyn pressed the golden cross into Edith's palm and closed her slender fingers over the trinket.

"May this aid you on your journey as it did me," she whispered as she bent to grace the pale cheek with a kiss. "Keep it close to your heart. When you see the Archbishop of York, show him the cross. He will know from whom it came."

Weary eyes, glistening with unshed tears, stared up at Gwynndolwyn. She had forced the arrow through the woman's shoulder, and had saved her life. Though her breathing had strengthened in the last few days, Edith would heal slowly.

"I owe you much, Golden One." Edith spared a glance for Khyryn and smiled at him. "Khyryn of Powys, keep careful watch over your prophet, and the babes she tends so carefully. I would see them grow as strong and full of goodness as their parents." She struggled for breath, and he bowed to kiss her hand.

Still clinging to Gwynndolwyn's hand she added, "If we should not meet in this lifetime, may we meet in another."

Two weeks had passed since Eadric had struck her. Christ Mass upon them, Cnut had sent an entourage of guards and servants to move her to the monastery at Whitby.

Khyryn cradled Derris on his hip and gently pulled his wife from Edith's bed.

"We must away. Come."

Without a word of argument, Gwynndolwyn nodded and gathered up Hannah.

A fortnight had passed since the nightmare ended.

One guard had died by Eadric's hand. The other survived, barely—thanks to Marroc and the sentries. Neither Gareth, nor the wet nurse survived.

Cnut had called for Eadric's head on a spike. Khyryn had delivered it.

They stepped out into the cold sunshine, and he and the babe both breathed the brisk, fresh air into their lungs. He tugged the infant's cowl over his head to keep him warm.

"Look," he said.

By the open gate, stood a familiar figure, bundled in a blue cloak. Staff in hand, he kicked at a small leather sack with the children who had gathered for an amusement. They giggled at his attempt to keep the small round sack from tumbling upon the ground.

"It is time," she said.

"For what?"

"Time to go where we belong."

The hair bristled on his neck. He had fought her on this each time she mentioned it.

Aberswythe smiled at them as they wandered through the gates.

"I am surprised to see you here to greet us." Khyryn lied, and knew the old man recognized it as such.

"How could I not come to see you off?"

"I have told her there is no safe way to do this. She would risk our children's lives—your grandchildren's lives—for this foolery."

"No folly, Khyryn. She speaks the truth."

Khyryn could not catch the words before they tumbled from his lips. "Whose truth?"

Gwynndolwyn smirked and kept on walking. They had no need for horses this day. Not for this journey.

"It is dangerous."

"No more than any other day, husband."

He would talk her out of it still. "You said you are happy here."

"My happiness has nothing to do with where I am. Only with the company I keep. I choose you. And Derris. And Hannah."

"Then we choose here."

Aberswythe and Gwynndolwyn both stopped, nearly causing him to collide into them.

She looked at the man who had been her father. And Khyryn's mentor. Impatience pursed her mouth into a frown. "Tell him. Once and for all. From your mouth. He refuses to believe me."

"Khyryn, you must go back."

"Why?"

"This is not her time." He laid his hands upon two small rounded heads the wriggled against their parents. "Nor theirs."

"That is not for you to say."

"No. The stones speak the truth of it. The prophecy says they will grow to their own destiny, in their own time. You must take them through the stones so they find their own calling, their own fate."

"I am not of their time."

"Nor is Gwynndolwyn of yours. You must travel with them to see them safely through the portal."

Gwynndolwyn began to walk. "And once there?"

"You know," Gwynndolwyn snapped. "I don't remember you whining so much when you dragged me though before."

"That was different."

"Really? How so?"

"I had to bring you here."

"Why?" she queried. A smile slithered across her face and her eyes glittered with victory. "Why, Khyryn? Why did you have to bring me through the stones?"

"Because..." He looked at Aberswythe for some support and found only the knowing smile. "Because the stones told him it must be so."

"Aha." Come on then, druid son."

"But what about the others. What of Bog and the boys?"

Aberswythe nodded. "They are in Daniel's care."

"What about Cnut. He will need an advisor."

"Fear not, husband. He no longer needs a Seer. He has a queen. I have seen her work. She will be advisor enough for him. Besides, I have seen the future. He does all right."

Aberswythe chortled this time.

Khyryn shot him a scowl.

Gwynndolwyn touched his arm. "I have thought it through. There is a wonderful place in Wales—Cymru to you—"

"I have a home in Cymru. Let us go there, now—"

"Your house is a ruin in the future. But Castell Henlys thrives. We can find work there. It is a living museum. You will love it. And wait until I teach you to drive. You can ride a horse well enough, but a roundabout in rush hour traffic… there is a true test of a man's mettle."

"I refuse."

"Then you risk our not making it through."

Fury and frustration pent up for days exploded in a rant as he slurred blasphemies at the both of them. When words failed him, he gave to shouts inaudible sounds, all meant to refute their plan.

Finally, Gwynndolwyn handed Hannah to Aberswythe, who already held Derris a safe distance from his wrath, and stepped in his path.

He longed to throttle her to make her see sense.

Instead, she wrapped her arms around his neck and locked her mouth over his.

Deep and forceful, she sucked the anger from him, enchanting him to witlessness. His body responded and he wrapped his arms around her. Her hand snaked its way up his thigh to find the painful truth between his legs. "That, husband," she whispered, "is the best reason I can give you, to shut up, and do what is right."

She sighed against him and he felt her heart beat in time with his own. "One thousand years is enough heartache, Khyryn. Do not let your fear restrain you. Aberswythe and Elleran crafted the incantation to send us home. Together. No more battlefields. No more curses."

He clung to her and drank in the sound of her voice, her scent, her reason.

"It is time to go home, husband."

****

Evening came early.

The moon rose quickly. Slender in the sky. The fire blazed high against the backdrop of the chalk dragon. Eternally chiseled from the earth, the creature waited, promising safe passage.

Aberswythe and Khyryn had set the stones and prepared the bowls and herbs while Wynne tended the twins. Eight months if they passed safely tonight. Their first teeth were cutting through, and they fussed at the soreness in their gums. Wynne fussed at the soreness in her breasts. "Baby food. And diapers," she said aloud.

In another three months they would be walking. Then talking.

Khyryn knelt beside her, in the firelight. "All is set."

As cold as the day had been, tonight her skin flushed warm.

They had built the circle around the mounded dirt where she had dug this afternoon. Beneath the earth she had placed a handful of the coins Edith and Cnut had each gifted them. A dowry of sorts. And nestled amid the treasure, the runestone taken from the excavation site. Once stolen. Soon returned. The rest, she had left in Aberswythe's care. Old druid hermits had little use for coin, but the reward would serve Daniel well, and would buy wine for Aberswythe on cold days should he wander from his cave.

She let her gown pool around her feet as she hugged the twins to her, each suckling gently in slumber. Khyryn pulled his tunic over his head and joined them. Folding her and their children in his embrace, he began to recite the words that would carry them forward.

"Whiter than snow be truth,

Sharp as sword, keen sight—
Undone the curse of long tooth
By fire, by wind and by night.
Ailim, beithe, luis,
give strength of triune to bear
Where one for two
Now two for four,
Through ancient stones of weir,
Let water cast upon the earth
As man onto the air,
These souls with *ceo druidecta*
with Rowan fruit to keep one safe
Through time, with fate and justice rare,
For truth's desire be sated there."

Wynne stepped closer to him, and wrapped her leg around his calf. This time she joined the chant. "Whiter than snow be truth…"

Her head began to throb as they finished together. "…For truth's desire be sated there."

"Whiter than snow be truth." She held her eyes shut, and spoke the words louder, echoing Khyryn's a third time, "Sharp as sword, keen sight—Undone the curse of long tooth—"

The ground trembled under foot, and Wynne's equilibrium faltered. She lost her balance, and Khyryn held her tightly. "*Ailim, beithe, luis*, give strength of *triune* to bear—"

The words slurred in her mouth, and she struggled, as if drunk. Her tongue could not form the sounds. "Through time, with fate, and justice rare…For truth's desire be sated there."

Darkness exploded into white light, brilliant and engulfing. Drowning in the brightness, she heard a baby's cry.

Too bright. No up. No down. Only...

Nothingness.

****

Rain splattered against the thatch before Wynne's brain found wakefulness.

Thank goodness, the roof had been patched. The only qualified thatcher in the county stayed busily employed during the warm months. He'd barely finished before the autumn rains set in.

Wynne rolled over and looked at the display on the wall. Seven-thirty.

Damn. They'd be late if they weren't in the car in forty minutes.

"Up!" she shouted. "Derris. Hannah. Get up. We're late."

She jumped out of bed, and made a mad dash for the shower. "Brush your teeth," she yelled at the twins as she turned the hot water faucet to warm. "And don't forget socks. I want no blisters tonight."

The running water and the deluge outside drowned out their replies. Speed shower. Soap under the arms, in the most important spots, a quick rinse, and—done.

She stepped onto the towel rug and brushed the bath towel over her body as she reached for her own toothbrush.

"Twenty minutes—"

"They are dressed—with socks—and are eating eggs with their toast."

Khyryn's arm slid beneath the towel as he pressed his mouth to her still wet neck. "You are the only late sleeper this morning, wife."

He set the steaming hot cup of coffee next to the

sink, and used his free hand to dab her body with the towel.

"Thank goodness for coffee. And hot water. And a husband who is handy in the kitchen. Other places, too."

His hair hung loose at his collar, and his shirtsleeves were rolled up to his elbow.

"Eighteen minutes," she teased as she leaned back against him.

"Not nearly enough time to dry you properly. You will have to drive with the car top down."

"Not likely. It's raining."

He nibbled her ear and grinned at her in the mirror. "Well, then, perhaps we should call it off and go back to bed."

"Not on your life. Or mine. Move. I have to get dressed."

Nineteen minutes later, she locked the door, climbed behind the driver's seat, and turned the key. Forty minutes later, she screeched to a halt in her favorite spot, and dispatched each of her charges.

She had conjured a miracle within the wood. She held their son and daughter—their legacy—safe within her keeping. From the coins she sold, she had taken over the faire and expanded it to a year-round venue.

Vendors' tents stood outside the wooden gates, selling seasonal wares. Autumn colors and silk foliage draped the gates and walls in the distance, inviting the crowds toward the opening performance.

One of the guards called to the doorkeeper to open the large side gate to admit them, not that it was necessary. She had a key.

As they wandered through the grounds, Khryryn

scanned the collection of merchants gathered in the courtyard. He nudged her and pointed.

In the distance, she saw a shimmer of white.

Aberswythe. Returned from his sojourn.

Good. Every Samhain festival needed a druid.

She knelt and drew Hannah and Derris close. "Look there. Do you see him?"

They nodded. "Yes," Hannah answered.

"Go on, then. Go get him. He'll be wanting to see you."

She popped them both gently on their bottoms, and the two first graders took off in a full sprint, calling out, "Grandpapa!"

She stood and immediately found the warmth of her husband's arms around her. "Do you think he has brought any others with him?"

"I never know what to expect." Khyryn's lips brushed the top of her head, sending a shiver of desire and emotion through her body. "Are you ready?"

"Always," she whispered, as she tugged her bodice into place. She reached out to him and wrapped her palm around his neck, then drew him to her, and kissed him lightly on the lips. "Show time."

To the gatekeeper, she shouted, "Geoffrey, throw open the gates. Let the faire games begin!"